KENTUCKY!

The twentieth exciting tale in the
WAGONS WEST series—a race against time to stop
another American tragedy, as the forces of law and
order ride out to stop a treacherous plot and insure
that justice rules this magnificent young land.

WAGONS WEST

KENTUCKY!

Ingenuity was the trait they made an American watchword . . . men and women of irresistible ambitions and desires who dared to reach for the limitless sky

TOBY HOLT—
His Wisconsin lumber empire shaken by economic upheaval, he strikes out once more in his nation's service—his mission to protect the President with his daring and perhaps his life.

LT. HENRY BLAKE—
Playing the role of a foolish American bewitched by a sensual German baroness, he is really a spy in terrible jeopardy and a man in danger of forever losing his heart.

BARONESS GISELA VON KIRCHBERG—
A voluptuous beauty of power and wealth, she is ruthless in business, cunning in her desires, and helpless to control her passion for the young Lt. Blake.

ORVILLE BEASLEY—
A brilliant, but demented psychopath, he has amassed great riches through murder, and now is plotting vengeance against all his enemies—Toby Holt, Marjorie White and President Ulysses S. Grant.

MARJORIE WHITE—
One of America's most talented photographers, she has accidently taken a picture of an assassin and now she is being stalked by a deadly man.

HERMANN BLUECHER—
The secretive head of German military intelligence, he has a gluttonous appetite for the forbidden and a lust for hunting down a young American spy.

CINDY HOLT—
Toby's impetuous sister, her pain at losing Henry Blake has driven her into a hasty marriage, but her heart is tormented by the lover she can't forget.

TIMMY HOLT—
Toby's daredevil son, his imagination is captured by the dream of a flying machine, but the thrill of a moment may lead to a misadventure no one will ever forget.

DIETER SCHUMANN—
An empire-builder who traded his fortune for a love money can't buy, he now has the chance to amass new millions . . . but their price may be the betrayal of a friend.

ALEXANDRA WOODLING—
The fiery-tempered Kentucky beauty, her tomboy ways and rebellious spirit seem to bedazzle a Toby Holt who has sworn that love is like trouble, foolish to go looking for, but dangerous to ignore.

Wagons West
INDEPENDENCE!—Volume I
NEBRASKA!—Volume II
WYOMING!—Volume III
OREGON!—Volume IV
TEXAS!—Volume V
CALIFORNIA!—Volume VI
COLORADO!—Volume VII
NEVADA!—Volume VIII
WASHINGTON!—Volume IX
MONTANA!—Volume X
DAKOTA!—Volume XI
UTAH!—Volume XII
IDAHO!—Volume XIII
MISSOURI!—Volume XIV
MISSISSIPPI!—Volume XV
LOUISIANA!—Volume XVI
TENNESSEE!—Volume XVII
ILLINOIS!—Volume XVIII
WISCONSIN!—Volume XIX
KENTUCKY!—Volume XX
ARIZONA!—Volume XXI
NEW MEXICO!—Volume XXII
OKLAHOMA!—Volume XXIII
CELEBRATION!—Volume XXIV

The Holts: An American Dynasty
OREGON LEGACY—Volume One
OKLAHOMA PRIDE—Volume Two
CAROLINA COURAGE—Volume Three
CALIFORNIA GLORY—Volume Four
HAWAII HERITAGE—Volume Five
SIERRA TRIUMPH—Volume Six
YUKON JUSTICE—Volume Seven
PACIFIC DESTINY—Volume Eight

*Wagons West * The Frontier Trilogy*
WESTWARD!—Volume One
EXPEDITION!—Volume Two
OUTPOST!—Volume Three

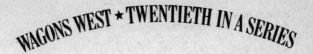

KENTUCKY!

DANA FULLER ROSS

BCI Producers of **The Memoirs of H.H. Lomax,**
The First Americans, and **The White Indian.**

Book Creations Inc., Canaan, NY • *Lyle Kenyon Engel, Founder*

BANTAM BOOKS
NEW YORK • TORONTO • LONDON • SYDNEY • AUCKLAND

KENTUCKY!

A Bantam Domain Book / published by arrangement with
Book Creations, Inc.

PUBLISHING HISTORY

Bantam edition published November 1987
Bantam reissue / June 1994

DOMAIN and the portrayal of a boxed "d" are trademarks of
Bantam Books, a division of Bantam Doubleday Dell Publishing
Group, Inc.

Produced by Book Creations, Inc.
Lyle Kenyon Engel, Founder

ISBN 0-553-80020-5

Published simultaneously in the United States and Canada

Bantam Books are published by Bantam Books, a division of
Bantam Doubleday Dell Publishing Group, Inc. Its trademark,
consisting of the words "Bantam Books" and the portrayal of a
rooster, is Registered in U.S. Patent and Trademark Office and in
other countries. Marca Registrada. Bantam Books, 1540 Broad-
way, New York, New York 10036.

PRINTED IN THE UNITED STATES OF AMERICA

OPM   0 9 8 7 6 5

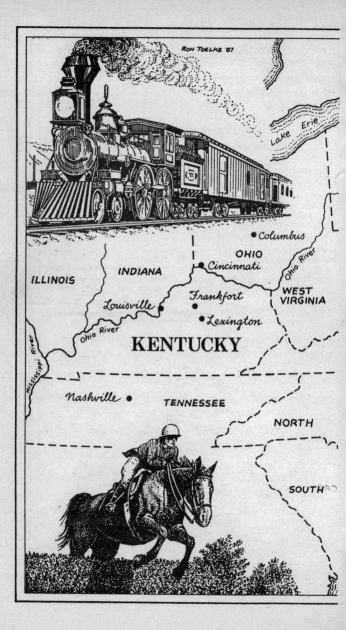

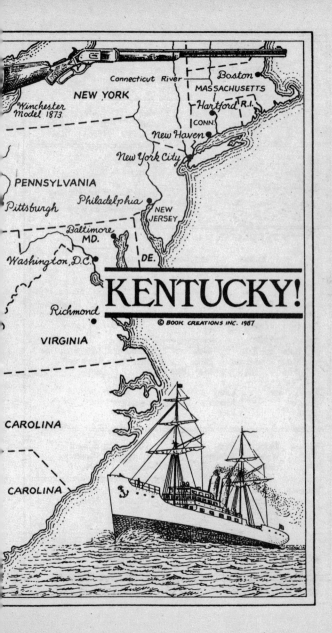

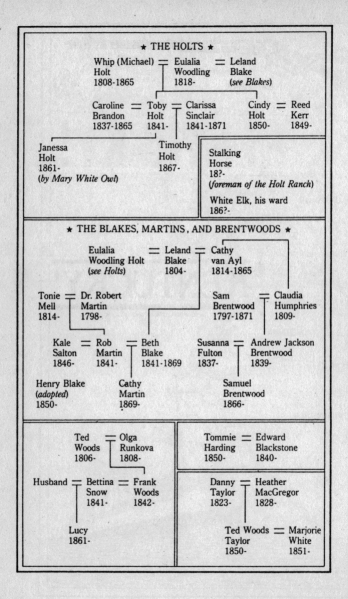

★ THE HOLTS ★

Whip (Michael) = Eulalia = Leland
Holt   Woodling   Blake
1808-1865   1818-   (see Blakes)

Caroline = Toby = Clarissa   Cindy = Reed
Brandon   Holt   Sinclair   Holt   Kerr
1837-1865 1841- 1841-1871   1850-   1849-

Janessa   Timothy
Holt   Holt
1861-   1867-
(by Mary White Owl)

Stalking
Horse
18?-
(foreman of the Holt Ranch)

White Elk, his ward
186?-

★ THE BLAKES, MARTINS, AND BRENTWOODS ★

Eulalia   = Leland = Cathy
Woodling Holt   Blake   van Ayl
(see Holts)   1804-   1814-1865

Tonie = Dr. Robert   Sam   = Claudia
Mell   Martin   Brentwood   Humphries
1814-   1798-   1797-1871   1809-

Kale = Rob = Beth   Susanna = Andrew Jackson
Salton Martin Blake   Fulton   Brentwood
1846-   1841- 1841-1869 1837-   1839-

Henry Blake   Cathy   Samuel
(adopted)   Martin   Brentwood
1850-   1869-   1866-

Ted = Olga   Tommie = Edward
Woods Runkova   Harding   Blackstone
1806- 1808-   1850-   1840-

Husband = Bettina = Frank   Danny = Heather
          Snow   Woods   Taylor   MacGregor
          1841-   1842-   1823-   1828-

Lucy   Ted Woods = Marjorie
1861-   Taylor   White
                            1850-   1851-

KENTUCKY!

I

The instant that James Gifford stepped into the ram-shackle, abandoned warehouse near the Louisville docks, strong hands suddenly gripped him. Materializing out of the darkness, four large men seized his limbs and pinned his arms behind his back.

With a sinking feeling in the pit of his stomach, Gifford knew that at some point he had made a mistake. More than a serious mistake, it had been fatal.

A match flared, illuminating a fifth man, whom Gifford knew as Howard Cummings. The four men gripping his arms and legs were thugs from the waterfront taverns, brutal and stupid. Cummings was a smaller man with a dour face and eyes that gleamed with sly, calculating intelligence. His gaze also reflected a fanatical, single-minded dedication to a purpose, an obsession that possessed his very soul.

Cummings lit a lantern and held it up to Gifford's face. The four thugs, reeking of cheap whiskey, were silent as they kept up their viselike grip. Cummings was also silent, his eyes deadly as he glared at Gifford. A long, tense moment passed, the quiet punctuated by the sound of a riverboat horn at the docks on the Ohio River.

Gifford broke the silence. "What's wrong, Cummings?"

1

he asked. "You told me to meet you here to talk about the plan. I've done exactly what you said."

"You've done more than I said," Cummings replied in a soft, deadly hiss, his thin lips twisted in a sardonic smile. "You sent a telegram to someone today, didn't you?"

Chilling fear gripped Gifford as he realized that his first reaction had been correct: He had made a fatal mistake. Quickly he tried to think of an innocent explanation for the telegram. "You told me I would have to go to Connecticut," he said. "I sent a telegram to my relatives to let them know I'd be gone for a few months."

Laughing harshly, Cummings took a piece of paper from his pocket and unfolded it. "So you have relatives in Washington?" he jeered. "You didn't tell me about them. And you certainly didn't tell me that the deputy director of the Secret Service is a relative of yours."

Glancing at the paper, Gifford realized that Cummings must have bribed someone in the telegraph office and got a copy of the telegram. The fear that was racing through him faded, his professional training taking over. Years before, he had resigned himself to the fact that the time might come when he would have to die in fulfilling his duty, which was the protection of the President of the United States. Now that time was here.

"You won't succeed," Gifford said. "You failed in Frankfort, and you'll fail in Connecticut."

Cummings sneered. "The only thing I intended to do in Frankfort was to make him worry," he said. "To keep him from sleeping good at night. The people I hired got out of hand, but that won't happen again. Connecticut is where I've planned all along to kill him, and everything will go according to my plan."

"But why?" Gifford asked. "What happened to you isn't the President's fault, and killing him won't make you wealthy again."

"It *is* his fault!" Cummings snarled. "He was the one

who signed the law that stopped silver coinage and made silver worth no more than iron. If killing him won't make my silver mine worth what it used to be, then I'll kill the next president, too, if he doesn't heed my warning. And the one who takes *his* place, if necessary. Sooner or later I'll get what I want."

"No, you won't," Gifford said. "You'll get what you deserve, which is a prison cell for even attempting to do what you're doing. But you'll never succeed in killing him."

"Oh, I'll kill him," Cummings said, nodding to one of the men holding Gifford. "But you won't be alive to see it."

One of the four thugs pulled out a knife, and its keen blade gleamed in the dim light. Gifford struggled, trying to twist away and avoid it. But the men gripped him even more tightly. Searing pain suddenly enveloped his throat, the knife slashing across it.

His strength ebbed rapidly, and he slumped to the floor as the men released him. Cummings gave a harsh laugh, the sound seeming to come from a long distance away through the numb sensation gripping Gifford. Tossing a coin on the floor, Cummings walked to the door, followed by the other men. Gifford knew that the coin was a silver dollar.

His consciousness fading rapidly and darkness closing in around him, Gifford slid a hand across the floor. He knew of only one clue that he could leave behind—a name. His fingers wet with his own blood, he struggled to lift his hand to the wall to write the name.

Toby Holt, in his office at the North Chicago Lumber Company, was reading a letter and a legal document from the other two major stockholders in the firm, Edward Blackstone and Rob Martin.

With the Panic of 1873 in full force, the market for

lumber had diminished to virtually nothing, and the company was operating at a loss. Three weeks before, Toby had written to Edward and Rob, asking them if they could advance enough money for operating expenses until the crisis passed. The letter and the document were their reply.

In essence, the letter said that the two men were no longer able to invest additional sums in the company, but that since Toby had continued to do so, the enclosed legal document assigned to him their interest in the firm.

Now, with the exception of the ten percent that belonged to Frank Woods, Toby owned the entire company. However, as Edward wryly remarked in the letter, it appeared that he owned nothing more than ninety percent of a doomed proposition. The firm seemed destined to share the fate of the thousands of other companies that had gone bankrupt since the financial crisis struck.

The murmur of activity in the front room carried into Toby's office as he glanced back over the letter and grimly contemplated the situation. Harold Phinney, the office manager, and the rest of the staff were maintaining their routine of duties against the day when they would be out of work like millions of others. The foreman, James Henshaw, and the workmen were doing the same outside.

A sense of responsibility toward those people was the only thing that kept Toby at his desk. Over six feet tall, he was lean and sinewy, with bold, tanned features reflecting that he was a man of action. Much of his life had been spent in the service of his nation, on assignments ranging from surveying routes for railroads to the governorship of Idaho Territory. By temperament, Toby preferred a life of outdoor activity to the day-to-day concerns of running a business, but he was determined to keep the workers at the lumber company employed for as long as possible.

Toby heard the front door open and a man come in. As the man spoke with Harold Phinney, Toby recognized the voice and quickly got up from his desk and stepped to the door. As he had thought, it was Thomas Haines, whom he had met several years before in Washington, while on an assignment for the government. A large, heavyset man, Haines was the deputy director of the Secret Service.

Haines smiled warmly, shaking hands with Toby. "It's good to see you again, Toby," he said. "I heard that you had a lumber company here, and I decided to take advantage of the opportunity to come and see you."

Toby knew Haines would not go out of his way merely to pay a social visit, and after exchanging a few pleasant words, he led the man outside, where they would be able to talk without being overheard.

The lumberyard was noisy and bustling, the air rich with the scent of lumber from the tall stacks of boards and beams lining the fence. At the saw house in the center of the yard, smoke billowed up from the flue over the steam engine that provided the cutting power, and the saws whined through wood as the workmen fed in fresh logs.

Walking across the yard with Haines, Toby told him about the poor prospects of the company. "It's good that you came to see me now," he said. "In a few weeks I probably won't be here."

"Things are that bad?" Haines asked sympathetically.

Toby nodded and explained that he had already reduced all wages, including those paid to the men at the logging camp up the lake in Wisconsin, and had cut other expenses to a minimum. However, so little lumber was being sold that the company was still operating at a loss.

"But I'm certainly not the only one in this situation," Toby continued. "I have a friend, a former competitor named Dieter Schumann, who lives in Milwaukee. He was once a very wealthy man, but he lost everything and is now working on the docks."

"Yes, many people are in the same boat now," Haines

mused. "What are your plans for the immediate future, Toby?"

"I intend to return home to Oregon, at least for a time," Toby replied. "My sister, Cindy, will be getting married in three weeks, and I want to be there. Cindy's been looking after my children ever since my wife died, and I'll have to make arrangements for them."

"I heard that you had lost Clarissa," Haines said, "and I'm truly sorry. But that was quite a while ago, wasn't it? You're a young man yet, and you can always get married again. It would be best for the children."

Toby shrugged. "My children aren't the easiest in the world to deal with, and I'd have to find a mighty patient woman. In any case, Tom, I'm not planning on getting married again for a good while—if ever."

"A lot of people who get married weren't planning on it," Haines replied with a smile. He put an arm around Toby's shoulder and walked with him toward the pier where the steam launch tied up between trips to the logging camp. When they were well out of earshot of the men in the yard, Haines broached the subject he had come to talk about.

Two weeks before, he told Toby, the President had visited Frankfort, Kentucky, and while he was there a demonstration occurred. That in itself was not unusual, especially since the demonstrators had been protesting the government's demonetization of silver, an extremely unpopular policy.

"But the crowd turned suddenly violent," Haines said, "and we had to hurry the President away. The Frankfort police broke up the protesters and made several arrests."

"That does sound troubling," Toby commented.

Haines went on to explain that no further incidents had marred the President's visit to Kentucky and that those arrested had been charged merely with disturbing the peace. However, when there was even a hint of a threat against the President, a full investigation was always made. Haines had assigned an undercover agent named James Gifford to check into the matter.

Several days after arriving in Kentucky, Gifford had sent Haines a telegram from Louisville, stating that he had discovered a plot to kill the President. Haines had immediately dispatched a full undercover team and sent a reply to Gifford, giving him instructions to meet the other agents. Gifford, however, had failed to show up at the rendezvous. He had been found in an abandoned warehouse in Louisville, his throat cut.

"Before Jim died," Haines said, "he managed to write something on the wall in his own blood. It was a name—Talcott. It obviously meant something to him, but it doesn't to us. None of those arrested in Frankfort was named Talcott. We keep our own files on people who might be a threat to the President, and I had them gone through thoroughly to see if there was any mention of the name. There wasn't."

"Were there any other clues?" Toby asked.

"Yes. Oddly enough, there was a silver dollar on the floor beside Jim's body," Haines replied. "Considering the subject of the demonstration, someone might be telling us that the motivation behind the plot against the President is the demonetization of silver. There are thousands of people who own silver stocks and shares in silver mines that were made worthless when silver coinage was stopped. I had a couple of men work with officials at the stock exchange to review all of the names, but there was no Talcott."

"Have your men found any other leads in Louisville?" Toby asked.

Haines shook his head and told Toby that a Secret Service team, assisted by the Louisville police, was investigating, but with no success so far. Another Secret Service team was working with the Frankfort police, who routinely made tintypes of everyone arrested. The tintypes of the men taken to the station after the demonstration had been examined, but although several of the protesters had proved to be petty criminals, no suspects had emerged. The investigation in both cities was continuing.

"I don't have a lot of hope they'll find anything," Haines continued. "I believe the main problem facing us now is that those who killed Jim and who are plotting to kill the President might know or might be able to find out who the Secret Service agents are, even those who are acting under cover. Many of the silver mine owners were extremely wealthy people before silver coinage was stopped. If some of them are involved, they could have contacts in Washington."

"Yes, that would be a serious problem," Toby agreed. "They'd be able to anticipate every move you make."

"That's true, and it brings me to why I came to see you," Haines said. "You've performed many public services, Toby, but you have no links at all with the Secret Service. No one can connect you with us, so I decided to ask you if you would investigate this plot against the President. I realize that this would be a hardship on you, particularly at this time, but would you consider it?"

"Of course," Toby replied quickly. "My first duty is to my nation. I'm ready to begin immediately."

Haines nodded and smiled warmly. "I knew I could depend on you, Toby, and I'm very grateful. Of course you will be adequately compensated for your time—"

Toby started to object, saying that he wasn't interested in being paid, but Haines was adamant. "In any case," Haines continued, changing the subject, "it would be better for us if you didn't begin right away. For all I know, I could have been followed here by someone involved in the plot. If that did happen and you set off tomorrow for Kentucky, they'd know what you're doing. Besides, the President is in no immediate danger."

"Are you certain about that?" Toby asked.

"Yes, absolutely," Haines replied. "He's remaining close to the White House, and he's under constant guard. It would be better for you to make whatever arrangements you can regarding your business here, and to attend your sister's wedding in Oregon. Then, if I *was* followed here, my visit with you would appear to be nothing more than a social call on an old friend."

"Yes, that's true," Toby agreed. "All right. I won't begin on the investigation until after the wedding. That's three weeks away."

"That will be soon enough," Haines said. "In the meantime, I'll make arrangements for you to have a temporary appointment as a United States marshal."

After discussing a few more details, Toby and Haines walked across the lumberyard toward the gate, where Haines's carriage was waiting. At the gate, Haines gripped his friend's hand. "The nation has depended on you many times before, Toby," he said, "but never in a matter more vital than this. I have every confidence that you'll come through for us."

"I'll do my best, Tom," Toby replied. "I promise you that."

When the carriage had gone, Toby walked back into the lumberyard, thinking about the unexpected turn his life had taken. Along with his concern for the President and his satisfaction at having the opportunity to serve his country, he felt a sense of regret about the lumber company. When he had founded the company, he had intended it to provide financial security for his children as they grew into adulthood. Now he would not even be able to oversee its demise.

He also knew that its demise would come quickly now. The foreman, James Henshaw, was a good yard supervisor, but he was only a supervisor, not a business manager. Similarly, Frank Woods was expert at handling lumberjacks and running a logging camp, but he would be lost trying to manage the entire company. Once Toby himself left, he reflected, the company could fold within a matter of days.

As he mulled over this grim prospect, a possible solution to the problem suddenly occurred to him. While it appeared that nothing would ultimately save the company, there might be one person who could keep it afloat and the workers employed for as long as he himself could. The more Toby thought about it, the better he liked the idea. He decided to act on it immediately.

On the same afternoon that Thomas Haines talked with Toby Holt, the man whom James Gifford had known as Howard Cummings arrived by train in a small city in Connecticut. Located in the rolling hills northeast of Hartford, the city was named Talcott.

The man, whose real name was Orville Beasley, left the train station and walked toward the center of town. Talcott was set on a slope, and many of its streets provided a panoramic view of the surrounding countryside. The buildings were decorated with red, white, and blue bunting in observation of a year-long centennial that would culminate in a gala celebration in September, on the one hundredth anniversary of the date of the city's incorporation.

However, Beasley was not interested in the scenery, and the decorations interested him even less, because patriotism was a feeling he had never experienced. During the Civil War, he had fled to Nevada to avoid being drafted. Once there, he had found that working as a shill in a gambling hall was far more lucrative than his former activities as a swindler in cities along the East Coast.

Although the hardships of prospecting had discouraged him from attempting it himself, he had always envied those who discovered riches on their claims. Consequently he had invested small amounts in the development of several claims, one of which had struck it rich, making him the part owner of a silver mine. After becoming the sole owner through the simple means of killing his partner, he had grown independently wealthy.

For a time he had lived in luxury, with money for the best clothes, the finest food and liquor, and the most expensive women. Then, after the Panic, his good fortune had ended abruptly with the demonetization of silver. The once-precious metal had dropped to a small fraction of its former value, and he had become obsessed with seeking revenge and forcing the government to resume silver coinage.

Talcott was a county seat, with a courthouse facing a park situated in the center of the city. Businesses lined the streets around the park, their windows decorated with flags and bunting. Reaching the courthouse, Beasley checked his watch, then crossed to the park and waited impatiently in front of a large statue for a man who was supposed to meet him.

The sidewalks all around bustled with activity, but the park itself was almost deserted on the sunny weekday afternoon. Preoccupied, Beasley paid no attention to a woman a dozen or so yards away. When he finally glanced at her, she was picking up a large camera on a tripod and carrying it away.

Looking at the camera, Beasley stiffened. He realized that the woman had photographed the statue, and him along with it.

In the disorder that had occurred in Frankfort, he had been among those who had been arrested. He had been released after convincing the police he was only an innocent bystander, but he had been photographed at the station.

Frankfort, Kentucky, was a long distance away, and it was extremely unlikely that any connection would be made between the tintype of him at the police station there and the photograph that the woman had just made. But even that remote chance was too much of a risk.

Fuming, Beasley briefly considered following the woman and breaking the photographic plate. But she was already crossing the street, where there were too many witnesses, and in the next moment the man who was supposed to meet him finally showed up. A short, sallow-faced, small-time criminal named Ira Farley, he had furtive, diffident mannerisms. Grinning as he approached, he held out his hand to Beasley, only to recoil at the man's furious glare.

"You were supposed to meet me here at three o'clock!" Beasley snarled. "You're thirty minutes late!"

"I—I'm sorry, Mr. Beasley," Farley stammered, "I'm truly sorry. But you told me to always be certain that no one is following me, and I didn't allow myself enough time to get here by a roundabout way. I could've met you at the train station, and I would have been there when you—"

"I didn't want you to meet me at the train station!" Beasley snapped. "I wanted you to meet me here, and I told you to be here at three o'clock. I don't want excuses, Farley. You're being paid well to follow orders, so do it! Have you inquired about renting the office I want?"

Grinning again, Farley nodded rapidly. "I did better than that, Mr. Beasley. I rented it, and it's all ready for you."

"You rented it?" Beasley growled skeptically.

"I certainly did," Farley replied with self-satisfaction. He turned toward a street at the side of the park and started to lift a hand. "It's the very office you said you—"

"Don't point at it, idiot!" Beasley barked. He glanced around to see if anyone was watching them. "There was a law firm in that office," he said. "How did you get them out?"

"I told you that I can get things done, Mr. Beasley,"

Farley said defensively. "It took me about three weeks, but I did it. Every couple of nights after they locked up, I went upstairs and dropped a big rat through the window over the door. They finally gave up and moved, and the day after they left I rented the office." He took a key out of his pocket. "Here's the key. The office is yours for as long as you want it."

Mollified, Beasley took the key. "So you used rats to get rid of them, eh? I'm not surprised they moved."

Farley gleefully went into detail on how and where he had obtained the rats, then, out of curiosity, began to ask Beasley why he had wanted that particular office.

With a sharp retort Beasley cut off the question, saying it was none of Farley's concern. Among the men Beasley had hired, several knew isolated bits and pieces of information about what he was doing, but no one knew the whole plan. And his reason for wanting the office was at the very heart of his plan.

In September, on the day of the gala centennial celebration, he knew that the park would be the focus of activities. There would be speeches by officials, who on such occasions always stood on a podium on the courthouse steps. The steps were less than a hundred yards from the office window, which was one of the only ones with a view unobstructed by the large elms lining the square. And the back entrance to the office building was in an alleyway that gave easy access to a quiet street leading directly out of the city.

On the day of the centennial celebration, one of the speakers would be Representative John Stevens, whose congressional district included the city of Talcott. Beasley was certain that the congressman wouldn't miss the occasion for anything, especially since the man's reelection prospects were only fair at best.

He also knew that Stevens, a former army officer who had served under the President during the war, was one of Grant's best friends and most ardent supporters in Congress. Stevens sponsored legislation that the President wanted and fought legislation that the President opposed.

The incident in Frankfort, Beasley knew, had alarmed the Secret Service—the presence of an undercover agent proved that. But several months would pass quietly before the Talcott celebration, months during which the President would begin chafing at the restrictions imposed on his movements by the Secret Service. On the day of the centennial celebration, with Stevens's reelection in question, the President would almost surely be present to garner support and votes for his friend.

Grant himself, Beasley gloated, was probably yet unaware that he would be visiting Talcott. But through studying the President's closest associates, his past schedule, and the kind of affairs he invariably attended, Beasley had finally found the perfect place sufficiently in advance to prepare a flawless plan. No one else would even suspect that this was where he would strike.

However, Beasley reminded himself, many things still remained to be done. Although the distance from the window to the courthouse steps was an easy rifle shot, he wanted to leave nothing to chance. He intended to make an accurate estimate of the distance and elevation, then find a similar place to practice with a rifle. He had to buy horses, and there were other details.

There was also the photograph that the woman in the park had made of him. "Are there many photographists here?" he asked, turning to Farley.

Farley looked surprised at the question, then shrugged. "I've noticed four or five studios," he replied, "but there may be more. Do you want to have a likeness made?"

"No, I don't!" Beasley snapped. "While I was waiting here for you, a woman made a photograph of that statue. I believe I was in it too, and I don't want anyone to have a likeness of me. Do you know of a lady photographist here?"

Farley shook his head. "She could have been just a woman who's interested in photography as a hobby—there are plenty of them about."

"I don't think so." Beasley frowned. "The camera looked expensive, and she didn't act like a hobbyist. We'll have to make some quiet inquiries at the studios here and find out who she is. One way or another, I must get that photographic plate and destroy it."

Farley grinned as a thought occurred to him. "There's a centennial information office just down the street, and the old ladies who take turns working there know all about everyone in town. They could probably tell us if a lady photographist has a studio here."

Beasley pondered the suggestion a moment, then nodded and told Farley to lead the way. They walked out of the park and down a street to a small storefront office that was cluttered with racks of books and pamphlets concerning the history of the city. They went inside, and an elderly woman seated behind a desk greeted them graciously.

Beasley told her about the woman he had seen in the park. "She left before I had an opportunity to speak with her," he said. "But I noticed that she appeared to be making some very interesting photographs, and I'd like to ask her about buying copies of them. Do you know of a lady photographist in the city?"

The woman shook her head. "No, there isn't one, as far as I know, young man, so I'm afraid I can't help you. . . ." Her puzzled expression suddenly changed. "Oh, I believe I may know the lady you saw. Was she somewhat attractive, in her twenties, and wearing a dark dress, cape, and hat?"

"Yes, that's right," Beasley replied.

"That was Marjorie White," the woman pronounced with authority. "Although, if you ask me, it should be Marjorie Taylor. You see, she's married to a man named

Taylor, but she still uses her maiden name professionally. I don't approve of the practice, but it *is* a well-known name. She's the one who made the famous slides of the Great Chicago Fire. She came in here yesterday to get information about the city."

The name meant nothing to Beasley, and the fire had failed to stir even his passing interest. "Then she doesn't have a studio here?" he asked.

The woman shook her head. "No, she's from Boston."

"Boston?" Beasley echoed, puzzled. "Why would she come here to make photographs?"

"Because of the centennial celebration," the woman replied, somewhat offended. "Mrs. White travels from place to place, taking photographs, and I believe she is finished here and intends to leave today." She glanced at the clock on the wall. "In fact, she's probably on the train that's departing at this very moment. But if it's of any help to you, young man, her business partner, a man named Hemmings, lives in Boston. He's also a photographist, and he helps her develop her pictures."

Beasley frowned as he listened. The problems involved in obtaining and destroying the photographic plate were rapidly becoming more complicated. "Is she returning directly to Boston, then?"

The woman's puzzled look returned. "I'm sorry, but I'm not sure. She mentioned something about Boston, but I'm not certain if she intends to go back there immediately." Again she brightened. "However, if you wish to buy copies of the photographs she made here, you'll be able to do that very easily. You see, they're to be turned into stereopticon slides and sold through the Acme Stereopticon Company in Baltimore."

It took a few seconds for Beasley to absorb the full implications of what the woman had said, and then only through a supreme effort of will did he conceal his reaction. The photograph of the statue and him was going to be made into a stereopticon slide that would be sold across the country! "You're certain that the same thing will be done with all the photographs she made here?" he asked.

"Yes, I'm positive," the woman replied cheerfully. "And I'm looking forward to when they'll be listed in the catalog so I can order them myself. I have copies of all of her other slides, and Mrs. White autographed the boxes for me."

Beasley mumbled a thanks for the information, then turned and left the office, Farley close on his heels.

When they were back on the street, Farley hesitantly started to ask Beasley what he intended to do next. Beasley wheeled on him furiously, snarling at him to be silent. He struggled to clear his mind of the panic swelling within him so that he could analyze the situation and decide upon a course of action.

Before, it had seemed improbable that a connection would be made between the tintype in the police station at Frankfort and the photograph that the woman had made. But once the stereopticon slides flooded the country, it was improbable that a connection would *not* be made. Any policeman who had seen him in Frankfort and who saw the Connecticut slide would probably remember him.

That would not reveal the full extent of his plan, but the connection between his presence in Frankfort and in Talcott might make somebody curious. And after Grant and Stevens were killed, there would be an exhaustive investigation, which would almost certainly identify him as a suspect and make him a wanted man.

He had many things to do before his plan was complete. But now all of them had to wait while he went to Boston to find and destroy that photographic plate. And if Marjorie White, the man named Hemmings, or anyone else got in his way, he would kill them.

II

In Boston, Clayton Hemmings, Marjorie White's business partner, sat at his desk in despair and aimlessly leafed through a new catalog from the Acme Stereopticon Company.

The fact that all of the prices in the catalog had been reduced—which would in turn reduce the amount that he and Marjorie received from the sales of their slides—was almost a moot point. The sales of the slides had plummeted, because few people had the money to buy them.

Marjorie was living on the savings that she had accumulated while the slides of the Great Chicago Fire had been bringing in thousands of dollars. And he and his family were living on money that he had been borrowing from Marjorie at regular intervals.

With painful, bitter amusement, Clayton recalled his conversations with Marjorie about her share of the money when it had been pouring in. He had jokingly accused her of being childish and simplistic in her method of handling money—which was to store stacks of gold coins in a bank safety deposit box.

He had explained how he was multiplying his own money by investing it in stocks and bonds. Marjorie had stubbornly refused to heed his advice, insisting on having her share of the profits in gold coins so she could continue stacking them away. But now she had money, and he was penniless.

However, he reflected in an agony of shame, not all of her money had been stored away. A few months before, several large checks from the catalog company had arrived at the same time as a prospectus on an issue of railroad stock. He had meant to use her share of the checks for only a short time, certain that she would never find out what he had done. But the railroad stock, like the other stocks and bonds he owned, had suddenly become worthless.

He had never been able to summon the courage to tell her about it, but he knew that she would eventually find out. Marjorie trusted him implicitly, but her attitude toward the stereopticon company went to the opposite pole—a total distrust. During her brief stays in Boston, she occasionally asked to see the account books in order to examine them diligently, searching for evidence of chicanery on the part of the company.

Clayton had never been able to commit the outright theft of altering the account books, and he did not intend to do so. During the past months, Marjorie had had other things on her mind each time she had been in Boston, but sooner or later she would again ask to see the books. Then she would discover what he had done.

What made the situation even worse was that he had taken the money from the one person who had done the most for him and for his family. Years ago, after the darkroom explosion and fire that had crippled him and turned the left side of his face into a mass of scar tissue, everything had seemed lost. Unable to bear the morbidly curious stares and shocked glances when he walked down the street, he had become a recluse, and his family, who meant more to him than his own life, had sunk into the depths of poverty.

Then he had met Marjorie. The most talented photographist he had ever worked with, she had endured grueling hardships during the first years of their partnership. Sleeping on train station benches and going without meals, she had traveled from place to place to make plates for stereopticon slides, shipping them back to him to be developed.

The trickle of money from the company that distributed the slides had turned into a modest income for both of them, and then, when fate placed Marjorie at the scene of the Great Chicago Fire, that income had increased tenfold.

Through Marjorie, his family had been rescued from poverty and his life had become bearable once again. And in return for all she had done for him, he had borrowed part of her money and lost it in an investment scheme! Clayton knew that she would probably forgive him when she found out, but he also knew that he would never be able to forgive himself. And he would never be able to face her and his wife when they found out what he had done.

Hearing his wife coming along the hall toward his office at the rear of the house, Clayton averted his face. Never able to forget his disfigurement, he could not endure the direct gaze of even the woman he loved.

The door opened and Clara came in with a tray neatly laid out with his lunch—a sandwich and a glass of water.

A tall, attractive woman who confronted adversity with an unflinching, cheerful attitude, Clara smiled as she put the tray on his desk. "It's a beautiful day outside today, Clay," she commented. "The weather this spring has been the most pleasant that I can remember."

Clayton glanced at her from the corner of his eye and nodded. "Yes, the weather has been very pleasant."

"The children have certainly been enjoying it," Clara said, smiling. "While they were getting ready for school this morning, Fred told me that it would be much better if classes were held at night. He said that would leave the day free for playing, and he wouldn't have to go to bed on time! I suppose he thinks he can do without sleep."

"He apparently does," Clayton agreed, forcing a smile. "Fred is forever coming up with ideas as useful as that one."

"Yes, that's our little Freddy," Clara said, laughing. "Well, I'd better get busy and prepare lunch for the children." As she started to turn to the door, she hesitated, her smile fading. "Please try not to worry about things so much, Clay. Brooding only makes them seem that much worse, you know."

Clayton nodded. "Yes, I know."

"You have the time now to read and do the other things you enjoy, and you should take advantage of it. When the sales of the slides pick up, which is certain to happen, you'll wish that you had the leisure you have now. We've been through hard times before, and this will pass just like the others did."

"Yes, that's right, Clara."

Clara searched for something else to say, her blue eyes clouded with concern as she looked at her husband. Then, unable to think of anything more, she smiled again and turned to the door.

After she left, Clayton looked at the thin sandwich on the tray and wondered if she and the children would have as much for their lunch. Clara was hoarding pennies as carefully as she had during the lean years after his accident. But this time those pennies were borrowed from Marjorie, from whom he had stolen thousands of dollars.

Any time now, Marjorie would be returning from Connecticut. Then she intended to take a vacation and go to Oregon to see her husband and attend the wedding of a friend's sister. Clayton was positive that she would ask to see the account books before she left.

He closed the slide catalog. During the past weeks,

he had concluded that he was nothing more than a burden to his wife and Marjorie. Clara was an attractive, competent woman who could easily find a husband more deserving of her. And Marjorie did most of the work, yet received only half of the income from their partnership.

Opening a desk drawer, Clayton took out a letter he had written several days before. It explained about the money he had taken and why it would be far better for everyone if he were simply not present. Not mentioned in the letter was his yearning, frantic eagerness to escape from all of the problems and the crushing despair that had been increasing daily.

It was time, he reflected sadly, to stop hesitating and to act.

He put the letter on his desk, then picked up the glass of water from the tray and stepped out into the hall. Adjacent to his office was the darkroom where he developed and printed slides. He went in, closed the door behind him, and put the water on the workbench. Then he stepped to the cabinet where chemicals were stored.

He reached up to the top shelf and took down a jar of developer for wet collodion plates. Although the crystalline powder was a highly effective developer, it was so dangerous that it was rarely used. With a skull and crossbones on the label, the jar contained potassium cyanide.

Working rapidly to avoid having second thoughts, Clayton opened the jar and spooned an ounce of the chemical into the glass of water. He picked up the glass and drank the solution quickly, fighting the automatic impulse to choke on the acridly bitter taste.

Excruciating pains began in his stomach almost immediately, followed by shortness of breath. Clayton lay down on the floor and steeled himself against the pain, waiting for unconsciousness.

In Germany, Henry Blake and Richard Koehler were

returning from a morning of hunting in the hills surrounding Grevenhof, the estate of the Baroness Gisela von Kirchberg. As they walked, they discussed the upcoming wedding of Henry's former fiancée, Cindy Holt, to his old West Point classmate, Reed Kerr.

It had been a pleasant outing for the two friends, the weather fair and the game plentiful. Always an affable man, Richard was even more relaxed and informal when he exchanged his uniform of a captain of Prussian dragoons for hunting garb. He had known Henry for more than two years, ever since Henry had been attached as a U.S. Army observer to Richard's unit during the Franco-Prussian War. Henry was now posted as a military observer at the Mauser Arms Works factory in Frankfurt-am-Main.

Sunshine dappled the forest trail, and a dozen yards behind the two men the gamekeeper followed quietly, his canvas bags filled with hare, snipe, and pheasant.

As the discussion of the wedding continued, Henry wondered aloud why he had been sent an announcement and invitation. Under the circumstances, he said, it seemed somewhat strange. The most reasonable explanation was that it was simply to inform him of the wedding. After all, even though he had alienated the family when he had broken the engagement, he was still Cindy's stepbrother by adoption.

Richard agreed. "Yes, since you are a member of the family," he offered, "it was certainly correct to send you an invitation. I'm sure it was not sent out of spite. Cindy is not at all a spiteful woman."

Henry nodded, noting Richard's favorable remark about Cindy. Richard, it seemed, went out of his way these days to compliment Cindy.

So far their conversation had been in English, with Richard occasionally hesitating over a construction or searching for a word. Now, however, he changed to his native language. "Since you will be returning soon to the United

States, Heinrich," he said, "it might heal feelings between you and your family if you went to Oregon to attend the wedding."

Henry replied in flawless German. "No, I won't have time, Richard. The weapons procurement detachment I am to organize will be in Connecticut, on the East Coast, and when I'm done there I'll be returning directly to my observer post here. Besides, I wouldn't enjoy attending the wedding, and the others wouldn't enjoy my being there. It will take many years for my family to forgive me for breaking the engagement, if they ever do. No, I'll simply send a present, along with my best wishes."

"That is probably a wise course," Richard agreed. He talked for a while about his own fiancée, Ulrica Fremmel, then unexpectedly told Henry that he had something to confess. When he had returned to Germany from his visit to the United States the previous year, he explained, he had written to Cindy and hinted strongly for an invitation to return to Portland to see her.

Henry was taken aback, never having suspected Richard's romantic interest in Cindy. Upon reflection, however, he decided that it was less than surprising, since Cindy was a beautiful, charming woman. "Well, that's hardly a matter to confess to me, Richard."

"Yes, it is, Heinrich," Richard said firmly. "You see, I wrote the letter while you and Cindy were still engaged. That was a dishonorable act toward a fellow officer and a friend."

Henry shook his head. "I must disagree. Perhaps it wasn't the best form, but it wasn't dishonorable. You knew I was involved with Gisela, and that makes a difference."

"That is what I tried to tell myself," Richard said ruefully. "In any case, I offer my apologies. But I cannot say that I regret what I did."

The two men fell silent for a few minutes, until they came in sight of Grevenhof. Richard took out his watch.

"It appears that I will have time to catch the afternoon train from the village. If I hurry—"

"No, don't leave this afternoon," Henry interrupted. "Stay until tomorrow morning, and we'll have another evening to talk."

"I wish I could," Richard replied, "but I really must return to my post."

Henry knew it was useless to argue. He was well aware that there was another reason why Richard wanted to leave that afternoon: Gisela. She was Richard's aunt, and the two of them never got along well when they were together for more than a few hours.

Gisela could be domineering, but it seemed to Henry that Richard was often tactless with her. At dinner the previous evening, for example, he had remarked that she appeared to be gaining weight, which he should have known would enrage her. Defensive over the fact that she was older than Henry, Gisela was very sensitive about her appearance.

The two men crossed the landscaped grounds at the rear of Grevenhof. Situated on a wide plateau overlooking the Main River and the village of Grevenburg, the palatial mansion dominated the landscape. On a height above stood the weathered ruins of Castle Greven, and in the distance rose the spires of the ancient city of Mainz, at the junction of the Main and the Rhine rivers.

As Richard hurried upstairs to pack his bag and change, Henry told the butler to order the carriage. Richard reappeared a short while later, wearing his bright dragoon uniform and carrying his plumed helmet.

While a servant carried the bags out to the carriage, Henry and Richard walked to the west wing, which was occupied by Gisela's business offices. The two men passed through a large room where clerks and accountants worked at tables set in neat rows, to a smaller anteroom with only a pair of desks.

At one of the desks sat Helmut Brunner, Gisela's senior business adviser, and at the other sat her legal adviser, who was also her father and Richard's grandfather, Emil Koehler. A mild, amiable man with white, thinning hair, he bore no resemblance to Gisela, particularly in disposition. Rather, his square, lined face strongly reflected Richard's bold, handsome features.

The two men stood up and exchanged pleasantries with Henry and Richard, and the elder Koehler expressed regret that Richard was leaving. His grandson, he knew, would probably not visit again while Henry was gone.

Pleading lateness, Richard excused himself and went to the door to his aunt's office, paused to straighten his uniform tunic, then knocked and entered. Henry followed him in.

It was an immense room, the largest in the wing, with tall, narrow windows and a mural in pastel shades on the lofty ceiling. The vast expanse of space, plus the fact that the room was virtually empty, created an austere, intimidating atmosphere. The gleaming floor led back to the only furniture—the desk where Gisela sat at the far end of the room.

Richard's spurs jangled loudly in the silence as he and Henry crossed the room. Gisela looked up from a sheaf of papers. With that one glance, Henry felt the force of her compelling, charismatic personality. She took off her pince-nez spectacles and stood up as they approached.

Always eager to extend a warm welcome to Henry's friends, she smiled as Richard bowed respectfully. But it was evident that she was still annoyed over the remark of the previous evening about her weight, for her smile had a frosty edge. Henry thought her extremely beautiful no matter what her mood.

In darker moments Gisela complained about finding gray hairs at her temples, but her luxuriously thick, long hair, which she wore swept up, was a gleaming black that made the deep blue of her eyes even more striking. Her characteristically Teutonic face combined a dramatic delicacy of features with a forbidding aspect that reflected the ruthless side of her nature. As she looked at Henry, however, her eyes became soft with her complete, unqualified devotion to him.

"I see that you are in uniform, Richard," Gisela remarked. "Must you leave us so soon?"

"Regretfully, I must, Baroness," Richard replied. "I have enjoyed my visit, but I must return to my duties."

"Of course, your duties," Gisela echoed with understanding.

"Thank you very much for your hospitality, Baroness, and for making my visit an enjoyable one."

"It was my pleasure."

They exchanged a few more words, Richard bowed again over Gisela's hand, and then he and Henry turned to leave. Gisela went back to her papers.

Henry saw Richard out to the carriage. The exchange between nephew and aunt, more cordial than some of their conversations, had still contained an undertone of hostility, which bothered Henry. He mentioned this to his friend before they parted.

Richard laughed heartily. "Heinrich, you have brought us together," he replied, "and that alone is an accomplishment. Before we knew you, the baroness and I rarely spoke to each other."

Henry had to be content with that, and the two of them shook hands. Richard stepped into the carriage and signaled to the driver.

Gisela had ended her workday and was waiting for Henry after he went upstairs and changed for dinner. She was wearing a silk dressing gown and soft slippers, and Henry joined her on the couch in the sitting room between their apartments. As he poured glasses of the wine that had been set out for them, Gisela asked if he and Richard had enjoyed their hunt.

As they talked, they were also communicating at another level. The top of Gisela's gown fell open to reveal
her large, high breasts, but it was more a blunt offer than
coy invitation, for she had a lusty aggressiveness in everything she did. Sitting close to him, a hand on his thigh,
she gazed at Henry as they sipped their wine and talked.

The subject changed to his upcoming trip and what
he needed to do before he left. When Henry mentioned
the wedding present for Cindy and Reed, Gisela smiled
and shook her head. "I sent them a present a few days
after you received the announcement," she said. "And I
enclosed your card with it, of course."

Henry looked annoyed. "Gisela, to me that is the
same as accepting money from you, which you know I
won't do."

Gisela reached up and caressed his face. "Will you
deny me the pleasure of doing small things for you, loved
one? It was only a small thing, and I enjoyed doing it.
Now, please stop frowning at me."

Henry sighed and looked away. "You should have at
least mentioned it to me before you sent it. What was it,
anyway?"

"I apologize for not mentioning it to you," Gisela
said, and sipped her wine. "I sent a set of china."

"What kind of china?"

"A small set," Gisela replied, eager to dismiss the
subject. "It will be useful, and I am sure they will like it."

Henry took a drink of wine, reflecting that the china
would undoubtedly be a more than adequate present; the
so-called pocket money Gisela had put in his baggage
when he had gone to the United States the previous year
had amounted to more than five times his annual army
salary. "Thank you for sending it, but in the future please
tell me before you do things like that."

"You are more than welcome, and I will," Gisela said.
"For example, I will now tell you that the director of the

Berlin Trust Company in Hartford, Connecticut, is one of my financial agents in America. I have written to him and instructed him to assist you in any matter, whether financial or personal."

"I won't need anything, Gisela."

"No one can see into the future, loved one. The Berlin Trust Company is also establishing a branch of Blake Enterprises, Limited, of England in the United States. You may be asked to sign some documents, in your capacity as a principal of the company."

Henry nodded. He unquestioningly trusted Gisela's business judgment, and he had little objection to being used as a figurehead in a number of her complex, widespread affairs. "Very well. Are you certain you won't be able to come to the United States while I'm there? You'd enjoy it."

Gisela sighed wistfully. "I truly wish I could, but it will be impossible. When you return, though, I will give you memories of lovemaking that you will cherish into your old age. Your friend Randolph Churchill is there now, isn't he? You'll be able to visit and talk with him."

"Yes, if he's not too busy courting Jennie Jerome," Henry said. "But his companionship, as much as I enjoy it, is a poor substitute for yours. I'll also worry constantly about your illness. You'll write to me often and let me know how you feel, won't you?"

"Of course," Gisela replied, laughing. "But you have no need to worry about my illness, loved one. I have felt perfectly well for months."

Her light dismissal of the subject was worrisome to Henry, because her illness was a serious matter. The attacks of nausea and stomach pain she suffered at intervals, the doctor had said, were symptoms of a condition known as perityphlitic abscess, for which there was no cure.

Henry thought again about her unusual acceptance of

their coming separation. She had denied it when he had asked her about it weeks before, and now he brought up the subject once more: "Gisela, do you wish to be by yourself for a few months?"

Her eyes wide, Gisela stared at him in astonishment. "Do you mean am I pleased that we will be apart?" she demanded. "Of course not! Have you become insane?"

"I hope not," he said. "Perhaps I'm mistaken, but it appears to me that you're not altogether displeased."

"You are terribly mistaken!" Gisela almost shouted, hurt and angry. "Shall I tear at my hair and scream while I run up and down the stairs? That is what I feel like doing! How could you say such a thing to me?"

Henry put their wineglasses on the table in front of the couch, then took Gisela into his arms and pulled her to him. He kissed her for a long time. "I'm sorry," he said.

The resentment slowly faded from her eyes, and she put her hands on his shoulders and stretched up to kiss him again. She was soft and perfumed in his arms, and her warm, sweet mouth lightly brushing his cheeks and lips awakened a stirring within him that he could not easily resist.

"We could have our dinner brought up here," she whispered against his lips. She nestled closer, smiling as another thought occurred to her. "We could have dinner in bed and eat while we make love. We've never done that."

"No, we haven't," Henry chuckled. "It could be messy, though."

"Not if we eat slowly," Gisela whispered, her lips tugging at his. "We could feed each other and eat slowly, and also make love very slowly."

"We may get gravy on the bedsheets."

"They can be washed," Gisela replied softly. "Or you could force me to eat it off the bedsheets. If you tied my hands behind my back with the drape cords, I would be helpless and compelled to do as you command."

Henry broke into laughter, but Gisela pulled herself higher against him, her lips against his ear as she continued whispering, her suggestions for their dinner and lovemaking becoming more bizarre. Then they both began laughing, holding each other and kissing.

Soon their laughter faded, their kisses and the touch of their bodies becoming more insistent. At last Henry gathered her up in his arms and carried her into her bedroom. As he undressed, Gisela slipped out of her robe and lay naked on the silk sheets, waiting and watching, a vision of beauty. Her lovely face was framed by her long, thick hair tumbled on the pillow, and her soft skin was milky white in the dim light.

Gisela lifted her arms as he came to her. They touched and met, their bodies joining in the way that was so familiar to them, yet always different. Gisela's sighs of desire and the impatient lift of her soft, warm body against his had the extra measure of urgency that Henry had noted in her lovemaking of the past days.

Later, when she lay quiet in his arms, Henry reflected that her fierce grasping for total fulfillment confirmed her anxiety about their approaching separation. Yet at the same time, he knew there was something more. His years with Gisela had been turbulent, and they had changed him, transformed his very being, making him almost part of her. He knew that she loved him; yet he was also sure that, for some reason, she viewed their coming separation with a ready acceptance. That was uncharacteristic of her, and totally perplexing to him.

In an opulent mansion in the wealthy Kurstenhaus district of Berlin, Karl Schneider was having dinner with the head of internal security of German military intelligence, Hermann Bluecher.

Schneider, an agent assigned by Bluecher to surveillance over Henry Blake, had come to Berlin to report on the American lieutenant's impending journey to the United States. But that subject and all others had been put aside during dinner, because Bluecher did not converse while eating.

Servants silently moved about the luxurious dining room as a large music box at one side played softly. The long, gleaming table was filled with dishes, the main course capon roasted in butter. The food was too rich for Schneider, and while eating a small portion he had watched Bleucher devour three bowls of truffle soup, two whole capons, a platter of spicy dressing, and several bowls of vegetables. Now he was masticating his way through a chocolate cake.

Of medium height but weighing well over three hundred pounds, the spymaster sat at the head of the table in a large, strong chair that had been specially built to hold his bulk. Gravy from the chicken still glistened on the rolling mounds of double chins under his round, puffy face as he methodically forked chunks of cake into his mouth. He sighed and murmured in gluttonous satisfaction as he chewed, intestinal rumblings in his mountainous belly climaxing in occasional cavernous belches.

When the meal was finished, a servant stepped to Schneider's side with a finger bowl. A servant beside Bluecher held a basin of hot water and a towel, with which the fat man washed gravy off his face and chins. Then the servant produced a whisk broom and brushed a blizzard of crumbs off Bluecher's bulging stomach as the man ponderously heaved himself out of his chair.

"And so," Bluecher wheezed, his voice surprisingly high-pitched and soft, "did you enjoy your dinner, my friend?"

"It was delicious, sir," Schneider replied, rising and bowing. "It is also a great honor to be your guest."

"No, I am honored to have your company for dinner, my friend. Come, let us go into the library and sit in comfort while we talk."

Schneider silently bowed again and followed as Bluecher waddled out of the room, down a dark hallway, and through another door. The library was large and crowded with books, but its most striking feature was not the bookshelves themselves, but the pilasters between them, each of which contained a niche displaying a life-size statue of a nude woman. The statues were startlingly realistic, expertly painted in skin tones and complete with wigs and body hair. The plush, oversize chair in front of the cold fireplace was upholstered in soft, costly chamois that was formed into a pattern that Schneider could have sworn resembled a mass of women's breasts. As Bluecher lowered himself into this strange seat, he waved his guest to a straight chair on the other side of the fireplace.

A servant poured glasses of brandy, then held out a box from which Bluecher and Schneider selected cigars. While waiting for the servant to finish and leave, Bluecher gazed up at a painting of a nude over the fireplace, his pudgy fingers moving over the padded mounds on the arm of his chair.

Schneider glanced curiously around the library, having heard that it housed the largest collection of pornography in Europe. The setting certainly appeared appropriate, but Schneider was not fooled. There was more here than pornography, and Bluecher was certainly more than the congenial, overweight decadent he appeared to be.

Behind his host's mild exterior, Schneider knew, was a savagely ruthless nature and a subtle, brilliant mind that had been honed to a fine edge by the best universities in Europe. The authority of his government post was only a token of the formidable power he actually wielded. That power was exercised through a hidden web of agents that reached out from Berlin, and most of whom were unknown to even the other heads of German intelligence.

A complex, many-faceted man, Bluecher was a master in the intricate plot and counterplot of intelligence. The one completely straightforward and unvarying side of his nature was his fierce nationalism. In that respect he was entirely predictable, always striving for what was best for Germany. However, his view of what was best for Germany did not always coincide with that held by Chancellor Bismarck and the rest of the government.

"And so," Bluecher said, as the door closed behind the servant, "the American is returning to the United States."

Schneider nodded and began relating what he had found out during the past few days. Lieutenant Blake, he explained, would be sailing the following week from Bremerhaven to New York, then proceeding to the state of Connecticut, where he would be setting up a new system of military weapons procurement for his government.

"Which is his ostensible purpose for being at Mauser Arms Works," Bluecher commented matter-of-factly. "His returning home for that reason is wise, because it will keep the stupid politicians and other fools in our government pacified. In the meantime, the American will continue to steal our secrets. What day will he leave?"

Schneider avoided the flinty eyes peering out at him from the rolls of fat. "I am not certain about the precise date, sir. As you ordered, I have sacrificed learning some things in order to avoid any risk of detection. If the Baroness von Kirchberg found out that her lover was under surveillance . . ."

The sentence was left unfinished; the baroness's volatile temper and the influence she commanded in government circles were well known. "Yes, she would be troublesome," Bluecher commented, puffing on his cigar. "Politicians are the poodles of the rich and titled, and they must come to heel when ordered. They must also truckle to other nations, as well as please the ignorant masses. So it is left up to us to serve the best interests of the nation. Who has been helping you?"

"Weiditz, sir. He has proved a very capable agent."

"Is he also a courageous agent?"

"Yes, sir. Weiditz will undertake any risk, as long as he is certain his family will be cared for, should he be imprisoned or killed. But all of your agents are certain of that, of course."

Bluecher nodded. The agreement was a firm bond holding his agents loyally to him, as though to a father. Unknown to most of them, however, was that the more comely family members of deceased agents were sometimes called upon to serve Bluecher's sexual appetites. But in all instances, the families of his employees who met with unfortunate circumstances were provided with every necessity and at least modest comfort.

"Is he skilled with firearms?"

"Yes, sir. Weiditz is an expert with both rifles and pistols."

Silence fell, Bluecher stroking his bulging chins with his puffy fingers as he looked away and pondered. The last question had been revealing, and Schneider already knew what he would be ordered to do. The only points to be resolved were when and how it must be done.

In the past, Bluecher had ordered agents to kill those whom he considered threats to Germany. And in his view, a foreign military officer who had gained access to a German armaments factory was certainly a distinct threat.

Schneider knew that Lieutenant Henry Blake was a doomed man.

III

The preparations for the wedding of Cindy Holt and Reed Kerr had been dominating the conversation and activities at the Holt ranch, but to Timmy Holt a related matter was of much more importance.

Riding home in the wagon in which Calvin Rogers took him to and from school each day, Timmy pondered the subject. He had viewed the wedding preparations with something between equanimity and indifference until a few days before, when he had suddenly realized that his aunt not only would be acquiring a husband, but would also be *living* with him—and not at the ranch. Since then, the subject had become a desperate worry for him.

His world had always been safe, organized, and comfortable. But the very foundation of that world, his aunt, would soon be leaving, dropping everything into a turmoil with her departure. The near future was a dark unknown that troubled him deeply.

Timmy looked up at the man beside him on the seat. Calvin Rogers, a hot-air balloonist, had been seriously injured in a failed ascent at the county fair the previous year. Thin, pale, and scarred from that accident, as well as from previous ones, he still had difficulty getting about, and while he had been recuperating at the ranch, he had become Timmy's constant companion. More patient and

skillful than other adults in helping Timmy with his school-
work, he also shared the boy's fascination with kites, rockets, gliders, steam locomotives, balloons—in general,
anything that could be made to move over the earth or fly
into the air.

Unlike other adults, Calvin also never tired of an-
swering questions or of discussing subjects that interested
Timmy. Timmy had talked with him once before about the
worrisome matter related to the wedding, and now he
brought it up again.

"When Aunt Cindy leaves," Timmy said, "maybe my
dad will get you to look after me and Janessa. Or maybe
Stalking Horse."

Calvin pursed his lips and slowly shook his head.
"No, I don't believe he'll want either me or Stalking
Horse to look after you and your sister, Timmy. I believe
he'll want a lady to do it."

"What lady?"

"I don't know, Timmy. We'll have to wait and see
what happens."

Timmy frowned and looked away. In spite of all Calvin's other sterling qualities, he remained an adult. His
reply was the same exasperating answer Timmy had heard
over and over from adults.

"Lieutenant Reed lives at the fort," Timmy pointed
out, trying a different approach, "and Aunt Cindy lives at
the ranch. Why can't they just keep on living where they
are after they're married?"

Calvin shook his head firmly. "No, they can't do that,
Timmy. Miss Cindy will move to the fort."

"Why?"

"Because married people always live together, if they
can."

"Why?"

Calvin hesitated, stroking his chin. "Just because they
do, Timmy," he replied. "Just because."

The reply was another standard answer from adults, indicating an end to any further discussion of the point in question, and Timmy fell morosely silent. They were approaching the ranch house, and when Calvin pulled the wagon to a halt near the front porch, Timmy gathered up his books and climbed down. As he went up the steps and inside, he heard women's voices coming from a bedroom. The seamstress was at the house again for his aunt to try on her wedding dress. As the screen door slammed behind him, his sister Janessa came out of the bedroom.

In every respect that made an iota of difference to Timmy, Janessa was an adult, with merely a somewhat smaller stature than other adults. Although she was only twelve years old, she looked, talked, and acted precisely like his aunt. Now she smiled and kissed his forehead, pointed toward the kitchen, and said exactly what his aunt said each time he came into the house:

"Stop slamming the screen door, Timmy."

They went into the kitchen, where Timmy started to sit down at the table, until Janessa stabbed a finger toward the sink. He pulled a chair up so that he could reach the pump handle, and obediently washed his hands as Janessa took a cake from the food safe and cut him a piece. As he sat back down and began eating, Janessa poured him a glass of milk and put it in front of him, telling him the same things that his aunt always did, and in the same resigned, mildly admonishing tone:

"Eat with your fork, Timmy, not your hands. . . . No, don't lick your fingers. . . . Excuse yourself when you belch."

As he continued eating, Janessa went to the cabinet and did the one thing that clearly set her apart from his aunt: She took out the store-bought cigarettes she kept there and lit one. She puffed on it, watching him eat.

It occurred to Timmy that she might be a source of information on the problem that was troubling him. "Janessa,

KENTUCKY!

39

who's going to look after us when Aunt Cindy leaves?" he asked.

"I don't know," she replied. "We'll just have to wait and see what happens."

Her answer was what Timmy had expected, but her tone was troubled, and she frowned momentarily while replying. Timmy realized that her situation was the same as his, and she, too, might be worried. "Have you asked Aunt Cindy?" he tried.

Janessa shook her head. "No, of course not. She has too much on her mind to worry about small details."

"*Small details?* What's going to happen to us isn't a small detail. When I finish my cake, I'll go ask her."

Janessa looked at him narrowly. "You leave her alone," she said. "When Dad gets here, we'll find out what he intends to do. That will be soon enough for us."

It would not, Timmy reflected, be soon enough. His world was threatened with disruption, and even an hour was too long for him to wait before finding out what would happen. Remaining silent as Janessa began tidying things, he decided to go to his aunt and ask her about it.

When he finished his cake, Janessa was standing at the sink, with her back to him. Sliding down from his chair and tiptoeing toward the hall, Timmy was absolutely silent. But like his aunt, Janessa appeared to have the uncanny ability to read his mind. Suddenly she turned, crossed the kitchen with long steps, and reached toward him.

Quickly he forgot his intention to talk with his aunt, his only thought now to avoid that hand reaching for him. But if anything, Janessa moved even faster than his aunt, who could reach out with blinding speed. Timmy dodged, ducked, and twisted away, all to no avail. He was suddenly motionless, his ear clamped between Janessa's thumb and forefinger with a firm pressure that made any movement excruciatingly painful.

With his head cocked to one side to relieve the pressure on his ear, Timmy lifted to his toes and took short steps as Janessa led him toward the back door. Pushing it open, she released his ear. "If you pester Cindy, I'll take a switch to you," she warned. "Now go out and play—and you'd better be good."

Rubbing his ear as he retreated outside, Timmy immediately dismissed the incident as yet another unsuccessful challenge of authority. Calvin, who had finished unharnessing the horse and had put it in the corral, was leaning on his cane and limping heavily as he walked across the yard. Seeing Timmy, he pointed to the shed where their kites and other projects were kept, and Timmy grinned and ran to join him.

The entire quality and scope, if not the nature, of Timmy's hobbies had changed since Calvin had recovered sufficiently to help him with them. They were now more work than play—even if Timmy did enjoy the work—and were organized into a logical process of experimentation and learning. No longer did Timmy merely build kites and try to fly them. Now he had to learn why he built them in a given shape, and why they reacted in the way they did. Also, the range of Timmy's interests had widened to include astronomy, and rough sketches that he had made of celestial maps were on the wall inside the shed. Also hanging on the wall were several pulleys and wooden gears. Calvin, an engineer by education, was teaching him the rudiments of gear ratios and the principles of block-and-tackle assemblies.

The latest project Calvin had been helping him with was a large glider. It was some four feet long, had a wingspan of almost five feet, and was made of newspaper glued over a framework of thin strips of ash. Modeled on designs developed by European experimenters, it was launched with a catapult consisting of a large rubber band mounted on a wooden board.

Timmy slung the catapult over his shoulder and carried the glider balanced on his head as the two of them headed toward the near pasture. Calvin had left his cane behind and taken up a pair of crutches for the longer walk.

This particular glider had already been modified and partially rebuilt several times, Calvin allowing Timmy to try out his ideas and make mistakes. Timmy's final mistake had been one of ambition, when he had made a stronger catapult to launch the glider higher. The catapult had collapsed the fragile ash frame, so the boy had gone back to the smaller catapult after he and Calvin had repaired the glider.

When they reached one of the higher elevations in the rolling pasture, Calvin eased down to a sitting position. Timmy began launching the glider, racing down the hill after it, and running back up to launch it again. An occasional gust of wind lifted the small craft higher and into a longer glide, causing Timmy to whoop gleefully. Calvin smiled as he watched.

Finally breathless from running up and down the hill, Timmy sat down beside Calvin to rest. The paper skin of the glider had been torn in several places during the landings, and Calvin took out a small bag of flour, a water bottle, and squares of newspaper to patch the holes. As they mixed flour glue and repaired the damage, Timmy wistfully commented that he wished they could build a glider he could fly in himself.

Smiling, Calvin touched the deep scar on Timmy's forehead, the result of a serious injury when the boy had tried to fly with a glider of his own design before Calvin had come to the ranch. "You wouldn't want to hurt yourself like that again, would you, Timmy?"

Timmy shook his head. "No, but that happened because I didn't know what I was doing. What about that man in England you read to me about, who built a glider twenty years ago, and a man flew on it. If he could do it, we can."

"Sir George Cayley," Calvin said. "Yes, that's right, Timmy. But there are a couple of points mentioned in the book that you're overlooking. The first is that Cayley's coachman flew on that glider, not Cayley, and that should tell you something. The second is that Cayley was a wealthy man. It cost a lot of money to build that glider—money we don't have. In fact, money for anything is in pretty short supply now."

The fact that money was scarce had had little direct effect upon Timmy, but he knew that his aunt was more careful about purchases, and very few horses were being sold from the ranch. "Well, could we build a larger model than this one?"

"No, I don't think so," Calvin replied patiently; it was not the first time the boy had made the suggestion. "Larger expanses of newspaper glued to a frame with flour paste would be too fragile. This one wouldn't get nearly as many holes in it if it was smaller."

"We could use feed bags for fabric and sew it to the frame."

Calvin laughed and shook his head. "Then it would be so heavy that no catapult could launch it. No, we'd better stay with this size and just experiment with design. Here, you can start flying it again."

Timmy picked up the glider, still not satisfied that it would be impossible to build a larger model. Along with his precocious mechanical ability, he had the tenacious mind of a Holt and refused to accept that anything he wanted to do was impossible. Thinking about the problems involved, he launched the glider and ran after it.

As he was coming back up the hill after launching the glider several more times, an idea occurred to him. Panting, he hurried over to Calvin. "Calvin, would a Hale rocket push a glider into the air?" he asked.

Calvin hesitated. The suggestion was a complete departure from the usual avenue of experimentation. "I don't know, Timmy," he said after giving it some thought. "Where would you get a Hale rocket?"

"From Fort Vancouver. When the rocket companies go to the artillery range to practice, the general tells Aunt Cindy about it so I can go watch. I've heard the soldiers talk about Hale rockets, and I know all about them. When they've been in storage a long time, they might not work right, so they're destroyed. The soldiers take out the exploding part, which they call a—" The boy paused, searching for a word.

"Warhead," Calvin offered.

"That's it," Timmy said. "The warhead. The soldiers take out the warheads, then sometimes they practice with the parts that fly. Or sometimes they just burn them up. But after the warheads are taken out, they store the rockets in a building at the artillery range."

"I don't think we could go out there," Calvin said.

"Sure we could!" Timmy replied excitedly. "A road leads right out to the building, and no one ever uses it unless they're practicing on the artillery range. We could take the wagon and get some rockets, then build a big glider and cover the frame with feed bags. We could build a glider ten times the size of this one!"

Calvin laughed heartily, shaking his head. "No, we'd better leave the Hale rockets alone, Timmy," he said. "There are plenty of experiments we can try with a glider the size we have."

Disappointed, the boy turned away. He put the glider on the catapult and launched it again, then raced down the hill after it. Watching him, Calvin thought about the novel suggestion the boy had made. It would, he reflected, be a very interesting experiment.

When Marjorie White arrived at the Hemmings home

in Boston, what had been a routine return from a routine trip became an emotional turmoil.

Clara Hemmings, her eyes red and swollen from weeping, met her at the door and fell into her arms, clinging and sobbing. Marjorie led her into the parlor and sat down on the couch with her, asking what was wrong.

It took several minutes for Marjorie to piece together what had happened. Clara was almost incoherent as she clutched a handkerchief to her face and sobbed; but at length she indicated the funeral home business card on the table, then fumbled in her apron pocket and took out a letter, which she pushed into Marjorie's hand. It was from Clayton and explained everything.

As Marjorie scanned the lines of Clayton's neat handwriting, her initial shock changed to grief. What hurt her most of all was the apology about the money. The money he had borrowed meant next to nothing to her, and it seemed almost inconceivable that Clayton had allowed it to assume such importance in his mind.

Tears filled her eyes and began spilling over as Marjorie finished reading the letter. Then, to make matters worse, Clara began apologizing, too. "I'm sorry that he took that money, Marjorie," she said, wiping at her eyes with her handkerchief. "Somehow or other I'll pay back every cent of it, regardless of how much—"

"Clara, forget about the money," Marjorie interrupted almost sharply. "It means nothing whatsoever to me, so please don't ever mention it again."

Nodding and sobbing, Clara fell silent. Marjorie struggled to control her own tears, forcing herself to think about Clara's situation. Clayton had left no money and had no insurance, so the woman and her children would be destitute within a matter of days, unless some arrangements were made for them.

As she pondered the problem, Marjorie knew that she also had to make arrangements for herself. Even thinking about it now was distasteful, but her work had to go on. Someone who was sufficiently skilled had to be found to take Clayton's place, because she could not do everything herself.

"Clara," she said, "I believe it would be better for you and the children to leave the city, to go someplace where expenses will be less. If you agree, you should start thinking about where you would like to go."

"I don't know where to go or what to do," Clara replied tearfully. "You decide, and I'll do whatever you say."

The responsibility for the family would be a heavy burden, Marjorie reflected, but someone had to shoulder it. Certainly Clara was in no condition to make important decisions; and Marjorie knew the woman had no close relatives.

"Very well, Clara," she said. "First, you must get some rest while I see to things. Have the children eaten?"

"There's food in the kitchen, but I don't think they've eaten much. They're all worried about what's going to happen, especially little Clay."

Marjorie stood up and helped Clara from the couch. "You lie down and get some rest, and I'll talk to the children. Don't worry about anything, Clara; I'll take care of it."

Her tone, conveying confidence that Marjorie did not feel, satisfied Clara. She tearfully expressed her gratitude as Marjorie led her along the hall to her bedroom.

Dealing with the children was easier. Clayton was a handsome boy of fourteen who bore a close resemblance to his father. He and his younger brother and sister were more frightened than grief-stricken, and Marjorie talked to them to reassure them. After they all had eaten, Marjorie had Clayton fetch a carriage for her, then left the younger children in his charge, saying she would be back in a few hours.

Outside, she handed the driver the funeral home business card.

"Sullivan Funeral Home—yes, I know where that is," the man said. "I heard about poor Mr. Hemmings from the boy, ma'am, and I'm truly sorry. But if you'll allow me to say, that Sullivan's a hard one to deal with."

"Thank you, but so am I," Marjorie replied.

The driver raised an eyebrow, then climbed up to the box and set off downtown. When the carriage stopped in front of the funeral home, Marjorie asked the driver a few pointed questions about Sullivan's reputation, then told the man to wait for her, since she would be only a few minutes.

Sullivan was a small man with a shrewish face and shifty eyes. Unctuous and professionally solemn at first, he became less civil when Marjorie made a point of explaining that the family was well respected in the city but had limited financial means.

"Maybe I'd better talk with the widow instead of you," he said. "I'm sure she'll want everything done with proper dignity and respect."

"No more than I do. But like most of the people with whom you deal, Mr. Sullivan, she is in no state to exercise judgment. I am, so let's settle and be done with it. How much?"

"Well, the service will include the casket, flowers, interment at the churchyard down the street, and the pallbearers, unless you supply your own. It'll be done right, but you're not going to pinch pennies, are you?"

"No more than you grasp for them. How much?"

Sullivan's eyes moved toward Marjorie's and then darted away. "I can do it for fifty dollars," he said.

"That's absurd. What is the cost of each part of the service?"

"It's an all or nothing price—that's the only way I do business," he replied stubbornly. His gaze slid toward

Marjorie again. "I haven't said anything to the minister down the street about how the deceased died. He might have second thoughts about having a suicide buried in his churchyard."

Marjorie reddened. "And I've said nothing to the many friends that the family and I have here. I'm a photographist, and Mr. Hemmings was one of the best-known photographists in the city. We have friends on the staff of every newspaper and in every police precinct here, and they would be glad to help me if I asked them. For example, how would you like an inquiry into how much jewelry you've been selling to pawnshops?" Marjorie had picked up this last piece of information from the carriage driver.

Sullivan stiffened with outrage. "Are you accusing me of stealing jewelry from bodies and selling it?" he squawked. "I'll not stand here and listen to any such—"

"I'm accusing you of nothing!" Marjorie snapped back. "I'm responding to a threat with a threat, and one that you'd better heed. You've robbed bereaved widows and orphans for so long that you've forgotten how to deal with anyone else. But if you start making trouble with me, I'll step on you like a cockroach! Now quote me a reasonable price."

Trembling and breathing heavily, Sullivan looked away. "Forty dollars," he said curtly.

"Twenty," Marjorie countered.

"No, I can't do it for that," Sullivan growled. "The doctor sent for me, and I came and got the deceased in good faith. You'd better get somebody else, because twenty dollars won't cover my expenses or my—"

"You wanted the job, and you've got it. I'll pay you thirty dollars, and that's all. And if I see a single flower that's wilted from being used for another funeral, you'll wish you'd never heard of me."

"I wish that already," Sullivan grumbled. "Everything will be done right, but I want the money in advance."

Marjorie paid him, making sure she got a receipt, then left, walking back out to the carriage.

Her next stop, only a few blocks away, was very familiar to her. The Whitmore Photography Studio was where she had first begun learning her profession years before. Jason Whitmore, the owner, had since followed her progress and successes with fatherly interest.

A tall, white-haired man of sixty, Whitmore greeted her warmly. He had been well acquainted with Clayton Hemmings and expressed astonishment and dismay when Marjorie told him the news. They went into the back office and sat down, and Marjorie related the entire story.

"This is bad news, very bad indeed," he said when she had finished. "What will Clara do?"

"She's leaving everything to me, and I'm at a complete loss. I feel that she and the children should move to a rural area, though, where things aren't as expensive."

"Yes, that's a good idea," Jason agreed. "I'll ask around and see if I can find you a place. In the meantime, I'll be more than glad to help, with money or in any other way that I can."

"I wouldn't ask for money, Jason. But if you could either sell or rent their house, with the furniture perhaps, that would be a big help."

"I'll be glad to, Marjorie. It's difficult to sell a house for a reasonable price nowadays, but renting a furnished house will be easy. It'll give Clara some income, at least."

"Yes, that's true," Marjorie said, standing up. "I appreciate your help, Jason, and I'll notify you when the house will be empty. And please let me know if you hear of a place available outside the city."

Marjorie knew that her biggest remaining problem was to find a new home for Clara and the children, but even as she was walking back out to the carriage, a possible solution suddenly occurred to her. It was so obvious that she wondered how she had avoided thinking of it immediately.

With that problem resolved in her mind, Marjorie quickly took care of her remaining business. She stopped next at a telegraph office, where she wrote two telegrams. The first was to Claude Leggett, a friend who owned a photography studio in Chicago. She stated that Clayton Hemmings had died, and asked Claude if he would take over the developing of her stereopticon plates and slides. She requested him to reply immediately by telegram.

The second telegram was to the man whom she knew she could depend upon most for help: Toby Holt. He had many resources at his disposal, and, if nothing else, Clara and the children could stay in a cabin at his logging camp until better arrangements could be made for them. The telegram briefly described the circumstances and asked for his help, then stated that she was bringing Clara and the children to Chicago.

Before, it had appeared to Marjorie that moving Clara and her children out of the city would take weeks, even months, but now everything was falling rapidly into place, and they could leave as soon as their belongings were packed and shipped. The carriage driver even recommended a reasonable shipping firm, owned by his cousin, and after a brief stop there, Marjorie returned to the Hemmings home.

Clara's eyes were still red and swollen from weeping when she met Marjorie at the front door, but she was rested, her hair was neat, and she had changed into a clean dress.

"I'm certainly grateful for everything you've done," she said when Marjorie finished explaining the arrangements she had made. "I don't know what I'd have done if you hadn't been here. And if you think that we should go to Chicago, then that's what we'll do."

After they discussed what had to be readied for the shippers, Clara called the children, and they all set to work. Marjorie organized the equipment and supplies in the office and the darkroom. Nearly every object reminded her of Clayton, which made her sorrow and sense of loss more keen.

The next day was pleasant and sunny, a sharp contrast to Marjorie's mood and to Clara's dark mourning clothes. The funeral service was modest but appropriate, not reflecting any lingering resentment that Sullivan might have felt. Afterward, Marjorie talked with Jason Whitmore for a few minutes and told him about the arrangements she had made, and he agreed to take her and the family to the railroad station later in the day.

The men from the removals and shipping firm arrived at the house in the early afternoon. While they were crating the various belongings and carrying the crates out to the dray, a messenger boy arrived with a telegram for Marjorie. From Claude Leggett, it was an emphatically affirmative reply to the telegram she had sent to him.

The afternoon passed, but no reply came from Toby Holt. Knowing that he spent part of his time at his logging camp up the lake from Chicago, Marjorie assumed he was there, so she was not overly concerned. She realized that she was, in a way, thrusting onto another a responsibility she herself had assumed, but out of everyone she had ever met, Toby Holt was the only person she could do that to and not feel guilty.

As the workers carried out the last of the crates, Jason Whitmore arrived in a carriage. Marjorie gave him the keys to the house, and he helped carry out the hand baggage, including Marjorie's equipment cases. As the carriage moved away, Clara and the children looked back down the street tearfully, but Marjorie was confident she was doing the right thing.

She was married to Ted Taylor and loved him deeply,

but when she needed advice or assistance, her mind automatically turned to Toby Holt. The archetypal American, he was as strong and enduring as the towering mountains of the country that he loved so much. Marjorie knew that as soon as she reached him, Clara and her children would be secure.

In Milwaukee, Toby Holt was waiting to sit down to dinner with Dieter Schumann and his family. He was in the kitchen of a small, three-room house in a district of modest homes, an entirely different setting from where he had last dined with the Schumanns. The family had then lived in a huge brick mansion in the wealthiest section of Milwaukee.

Keenly aware of the straitened financial circumstances of his hosts, Toby regretted that he had arrived late in the day and had been prevailed upon to stay for dinner. "I should have visited either earlier or later," he said. "I don't like being an uninvited guest for dinner."

"It's impossible for you to be an uninvited guest here," Dieter replied emphatically. "You have a standing invitation."

"We have plenty of food," Abigail Schumann assured him, "and we're more than pleased to have you for dinner, Toby."

Toby smiled, thinking about the contrast from the first time he had met Dieter, a heavyset man in his late forties. They had been enemies then, Dieter a hardened businessman without principles or scruples, with personal gain his only purpose in life. He had since changed, becoming devoted to his family and making new friends, yet some things about him remained the same. With his strong chin always in a firm line and his burly shoulders hunched forward, he was an aggressive, forceful man, a natural leader.

Abigail, a vivacious, attractive woman of twenty-five,

was obviously happy in her new circumstances. When Toby had first met her, she had excelled in the role of model wife, managing her large household efficiently; but now she was more in her element, closer to her modest upbringing. Her hands were red from hard work, yet she had an air of cheerful contentment as she quieted her two small sons and bustled about the kitchen.

As Toby sat down at the table, he noticed for the first time the large pans on the stove, indicating there was indeed more than ample food. Dieter, grimy from his day on the docks, went to the sink and washed as Abigail dished up the food. When they were all seated, they bowed their heads as Dieter said a blessing, and then Abigail began passing dishes around.

The dinner was one of the most enjoyable Toby had eaten in months. A smoked, sugar-cured pork roast was accompanied by green peas flavored with pan drippings, plus fried potatoes with bits of onion in them. There was also light, crusty homemade bread, and large glasses of spiced cider.

As they ate, Dieter got around to explaining the abundance of food on the table. "The advantage of being a day laborer," he said, "is that I can work when I wish. It doesn't pay much, but I'm known as a good worker, so I have a job whenever I go to the docks. But I don't go there every day, because Abigail and I take the children out into the country at least once a week."

Abigail smiled. "I prepare a lunch, and we take a horsecar as far as the line goes to the edge of the city. Then we hike along the country roads for miles. It makes a lovely outing, and the children enjoy it as much as Dieter and I do."

"I'm sure it does make a pleasant outing," Toby commented. "Well worth missing a day's wages at the docks."

Dieter smiled, exchanging a glance with Abigail. "In fact, Toby, I make more on such a day than I do in any day on the docks," he said. "Last week, for example, I met a farmer whose windmill pump had stopped working, and he didn't know how to repair it. The leather gaskets in the pump head had rotted away, so I made new ones out of an old pair of boots he had. In return, he gave us all the food we could carry."

"We were hours getting home that day," Abigail said, laughing merrily. "Dieter carried a smoked pork hindquarter and a huge bag of potatoes. I carried potatoes and eggs, and the boys carried baskets of onions and carrots. But we finally made it home."

Dieter went on to explain that it had not been an unusual incident. While farmers needed hired help as much as ever, none of them had the money to pay for it. By working for a few hours at a farm and taking his pay in produce, Dieter had been obtaining enough food in one day to last his family for a week or longer.

"That's the American way," Toby commented. "Americans have always been quick to adapt to circumstances and use whatever is at hand."

"Exactly," Dieter agreed. "And the nation will pull through this economic crisis and be stronger than ever. But in the meantime, there have been some dislocations and breakdowns in the economy. For example, railroads and drayage firms have gone bankrupt, and as a result farmers have barns and smokehouses bulging with food, while food prices are rising in the cities because enough isn't reaching them."

"Yes, and the fact that the government stopped silver coinage has made the situation worse," Toby said. "I realize it was stopped to prevent foreign speculation in silver here, and I'm sure it did that, but it's had bad effects as well. There's a shortage of cash money."

Dieter commented in agreement, then asked Toby about his lumber company. Toby described the poor financial state of the lumber mill in Chicago and the logging camp in Wisconsin.

"The entire lumber industry is in the same condition or worse," Toby said, "as I'm sure you know."

They had finished eating, and Abigail was clearing the table. She put the dishes in the sink and poured coffee for everyone, then sat back down. Dieter took out a corncob pipe and filled it while talking to Toby. "We enjoy having you visit us, Toby," he said, "but unless I'm greatly mistaken, this is something more than just a social visit."

"It is," Toby replied. "I've kept my company going so the workers will have jobs, but now I've been asked to perform a task for the government, one that I can't discuss. You know the lumber and logging business, Dieter, and I'd like to hire you to run my company. You'd be able to keep it going as long as I could, or longer."

Dieter lit his pipe and puffed on it, thinking. He glanced at Abigail. "Would you mind moving to Chicago?" he asked.

"No, not if that's what we need to do," she replied promptly. "Work doesn't come to anyone, so we must go to it."

Toby shook his head doubtfully. "I'm not at all certain the job will last long enough for you to move your family, Dieter."

"Let me worry about that," Dieter said with a smile. "I believe I can make it last longer than you think. What kind of terms would I have?"

"Name the terms you want."

"Absolute control to run the company as I see fit, and ten percent of the net profits. Also, I want to know where you are at all times in the event I need to contact you."

Toby frowned. "I must not have made the financial condition of the company quite clear," he said. "You would have absolute control, because I'd expect to have the same myself. And it would be no trouble keeping you informed of where I am for the next few months. But as far as the net profits go, there simply aren't any. You'd be working for ten percent of nothing."

"Not for very long," Dieter replied. "I think I know of a way to change that. Abigail and I have seen scores of farms lately, and the one thing they all need is lumber. They all have barns, silos, or houses that are falling apart. How many yard hands do you have?"

"Twenty-two."

Nodding in satisfaction, Dieter began explaining his idea, which was to return to the ancient system of barter. He planned to send a man out to surrounding farms to take orders for lumber and bargain with the farmers for their produce; drays filled with lumber would follow, and they would return with loads of produce.

"I'd start paying the workers part of their wages in produce," Dieter said, "which would reduce company expenses and cash outlay. The workers would end up with much more food than that part of their wages would buy, since food prices are very high in Chicago."

"You'd still have tons of produce left," Toby said.

"Yes, that's right," Dieter agreed. "Enough to more than pay the remainder of the company expenses, even if it were sold at very low prices. Abigail's parents are grocers, but they're having to close their store because of the trouble they have obtaining goods. They would probably be willing to come to Chicago and take over the sales of the produce."

"Far more than willing," Abigail added. "Mom and Dad would be delighted to have an opportunity like that."

Toby hesitated, thinking about the management problems involved in what Dieter had described. They would be a nightmare, because relative values would have to be worked out for various kinds of lumber and produce. The drays would have to be scheduled efficiently, and many other problems would have to be resolved.

However, he reflected, Dieter was a resourceful, experienced manager. If anyone could do it, he could. "I'm willing to try it if you are," Toby said. "Things couldn't be any worse than they are now."

Dieter put out his hand. "Here's hoping that they'll soon be much better. You've just hired a manager for your company, Toby."

The two men shook hands, sealing the agreement. Toby took out his watch and looked at it. "If I hurry, I can catch the next train north," he said.

After he had thanked Abigail for the delicious meal and said good-bye to her and the children, Toby walked with Dieter to the train station, and the two of them discussed the details of their arrangement. Dieter, happy to take on a new challenge, wanted to commence work as soon as possible, and to begin by moving his family and belongings to Chicago. Toby agreed to dispatch one of the company drays for that purpose when he returned to Chicago.

Toby also brought up a guideline that Dieter had to observe in managing the company, a standard he insisted could not be compromised. Although Dieter had now changed, his past business practices had been unprincipled, and Toby would not have his company associated with activities that were illegal or unethical even in appearance. Dieter replied that he understood and would conduct the company business accordingly.

It was dark by the time Toby boarded his train at the almost-deserted depot near the Milwaukee docks. The train was a short one, only four cars, and many of the seats were empty. During the past months, Toby had seen ample evidence of the financial crisis. But as the train raced northward through the night, for the first time in months Toby had reason to be hopeful about his personal affairs. It appeared just barely possible that Dieter would be able to keep the lumber company afloat until the financial crisis ended.

The small town of Wedowee was quiet and deserted when the train pulled in. Toby walked along the dark main street toward the livery stable, where a horse from the logging camp was boarded. A sleepy stable boy saddled the animal, and Toby mounted it and rode out of town along the moonlit road.

When he finally reached the logging camp, hours later, it was long past midnight. Moonlight illuminated a large garden where the lumberjacks now spent part of their time growing food to reduce the need to buy and ship in supplies, and hogs stirred in a pen near the corral. Toby unsaddled the horse and put it in the corral, then crossed the clearing to the cabin he used when visiting the camp.

Paper rustled in the darkness as Toby opened the door. Striking a match, he saw that two messages and a telegram were pinned to the screen door. He took them down, went inside, and lit a lamp.

One of the messages was a note from Albert Crowell, the owner of the steam launch that towed timber from the logging camp to the lumberyard in Chicago. It said that he had arrived several hours before, bringing the attached message and telegram from the Chicago office. The launch was docked at the pier below the logging camp, and Toby could return on it to Chicago the next day, if he chose.

The second message was from Claude Leggett, who owned a photography studio in Chicago. It stated that Marjorie White had cabled ahead to notify them she would arrive in Chicago two days later—all of which made little sense to Toby until he opened the telegram and read it.

From Marjorie, the telegram informed him that her business partner, Clayton Hemmings, had suddenly died, and she was bringing Clara Hemmings and her three children to Chicago. It ended with a request for his assistance in arranging accommodations and a means of support for them.

Surprised at the abrupt news, but pleased to be able to help Marjorie, Toby thought about what he could do for the Hemmings woman and her children. He looked again at the date of the telegram and of the message from Claude. Marjorie had already left Boston en route to Chicago, so there was no point in sending a reply to the telegram.

Orville Beasley had also found out that Marjorie and the Hemmings family had left Boston.

Taking a hired carriage to the address where the Hemmings family had lived, Beasley had intended to reconnoiter the house and return after dark, armed and ready to do whatever was necessary to destroy the photographic plate of himself. But as he approached the address, he saw a loaded wagon on the street, a family apparently moving into the house.

Beasley called to the driver to stop, then dismounted from the carriage. A man, a woman, and four children were carrying belongings from the wagon into the house. Beasley lifted his hat to the woman and nodded to the man.

"Good day," he said. "I'm a friend of the Hemmings family, and I intended to call on them. Have they moved?"

The man turned to the woman. "Is that the name of the people who lived here?" he asked.

"Yes, that's it," the woman replied. "Hemmings, and a woman named White. She must have been either a relative or a boarder."

"Yep, they've moved all right," the man said, turning back to Beasley. "They left only a day or two ago. You just missed them."

Beasley silently cursed his bad luck. "I didn't know they were moving," he said with great self-control, "and I don't want to lose contact with them. Could you tell me where they've gone?"

The man and the woman exchanged a blank look. "I haven't the faintest idea," the man said. "We rented the house from a fellow named Whitmore, a photographist who owns a studio down on Marlow Street. Maybe he knows."

Still concealing his annoyance, Beasley thanked the couple, returned to the carriage, and directed the driver to take him to the Whitmore photography studio.

As the carriage moved back toward the center of the city, Beasley fumed in silence. In addition to enduring the delay and the complications of finding and destroying the photographic plate, he was drawing unwanted attention to himself by making inquiries.

In all likelihood, the man named Whitmore was acquainted with Marjorie White and the Hemmings family, so Beasley would not be able to masquerade as a friend of the family. He would have to use a story that was closer to the truth, which would be dangerous.

At the photography studio, Beasley asked the woman behind the counter if he could speak to the owner, and she disappeared through a curtained doorway. A minute later, a sharp-eyed older man emerged, smelling of chemicals and wiping his hands on a towel. "I'm Jason Whitmore," he said. "You wanted to talk with me?"

"Yes, I believe you know Marjorie White," Beasley said. "I met her a few days ago and arranged to buy some photographs from her. She told me that she stayed with the Hemmings family when she was here, but I find they have moved. Could you give me her present address?"

Jason Whitmore pursed his lips, folded the towel, and put it on the counter. "You must be from Connecticut," he said.

The remark made Beasley uneasy, revealing that the

man already knew too much. "Why do you say that?" he replied.

"Because that's the last place Marjorie went to take photographs. What kind of photographs did she agree to sell you?"

The man's eyes were wary, suggesting that Beasley had said something wrong. Beasley tried to brush it off. "Photographs of some interesting scenes," he replied casually. "I offered to pay her well, and I assumed it was an ordinary thing for her to do. She is a professional photographist, isn't she?"

"Yes, she is," Whitmore said. "In fact, she's the best professional photographist I've ever known. But she usually does only stereopticon slides. In order to make an ordinary photograph, she would have to use an entirely different kind of photographic plate." He reached behind the counter and produced a writing pad and pencil. "However, you can leave your name and address, and I'll see that Marjorie gets it."

Realizing that he had indeed said something wrong through his ignorance about photography, Beasley made one last try. "It would save time and trouble if you would give me her address," he said.

"No, I can't do that," Whitmore replied firmly.

The man's wariness had turned into suspicion, and Beasley, to avoid any more trouble, tried to look unconcerned as he picked up the pencil to write a fictitious name and address. With his mind more on the man watching him than on what he was doing, Beasley began writing the name he had used in Kentucky—Howard Cummings.

As he realized his mistake, he paused for a split second. There was a possibility that someone might make a connection between what had happened in Kentucky and a name written on a piece of paper in a Boston photography studio, but it was extremely remote. On the other hand, it would make Whitmore very suspicious indeed to change the name.

Beasley finished writing the name and added a fictitious address. He thanked Whitmore, who nodded curtly in reply, and then went back out to his carriage.

As the carriage drove him to his hotel, Beasley was furious. It was absolutely imperative for him to destroy the photographic plate before stereopticon slides from it were sold across the country. But now his means of finding the plate had been firmly blocked.

At the hotel, Beasley went to his room. He opened a bottle of whiskey and poured himself a drink, then sat down and pondered what to do next. For a moment he contemplated breaking into the Whitmore studio at night and searching for the address, but he dismissed the idea as too risky with too little chance of success.

Then he recalled that the woman at the centennial information office in Talcott had mentioned the name of the company that sold the slides Marjorie White made. It was the Acme Stereopticon Company in Baltimore. Surely they would have her new address, or would have it shortly, and a clerk could be bribed to give it to him.

Beasley took his suitcase out of the closet and began throwing clothes into it. Before, he pondered grimly, he would have killed Marjorie White and others out of necessity if they interfered with his plan. But now it would be a pleasure to kill them.

IV

Toby Holt was awakened by the cheerful chattering of birds in the forest and the bright early morning sunshine streaming through his cabin window. As he was shaving, the fresh breeze stirred the curtains, carrying with it a tangy odor of woodsmoke from the kitchen stove in the Woods house nearby. Moments later, the smell blended with the appetizing scents of coffee boiling and bacon frying. Toby finished shaving and dressing and went outside.

An ax was chopping into wood behind the house, creating echoes that rippled through the forest clearing. Toby walked around the house. Frank Woods, huge and burly in his checked wool shirt and denim trousers, was effortlessly splitting thick chunks of firewood on the chopping block with single blows of a heavy felling ax.

Glimpsing Toby, he stopped and smiled. "Good morning, Toby," he said. "Did you get the messages and telegrams on your door?"

"Yes, thanks, Frank. Can I help you there?"

"No, I was just cutting some stove wood for Bettina." He stuck the ax into the chopping block and gathered up the wood he had split. "Let's go in and have breakfast."

In the kitchen, Bettina Woods, tall, shapely, and attractive, was turning strips of bacon in a pan on the stove. Lucy, her daughter, a small, quiet girl of twelve, was setting the table. Bettina greeted Toby warmly, and Lucy shyly smiled at him as Frank stepped to the stove and dumped the wood into a box beside it.

Bettina brought a fire-blackened coffeepot to the table as Toby and Frank sat down. After taking a sip of the rich, delicious coffee, Toby began telling Bettina and Frank about the results of his trip to Milwaukee.

While the three of them had been close friends for years, something more than simple friendship was in Bettina and Frank's attitude toward Toby. Two years before, he had arrived with the steam launch and rescued them only minutes before they would have perished in a raging forest fire, which had been ignited by airborne embers from the Great Chicago Fire far to the south. Since then, they had regarded him as someone more than special in their lives.

Yet today there was also a forced cheerfulness in their manner. The two had invested money, hopes, and years of their lives in the lumber company, and its failure would be a severe blow to them. The signs of their scrimping and saving to avoid this outcome had beome increasingly evident. Their clothes were worn and patched, and plans they had made to send Lucy to a special boarding school in Chicago had been canceled. The girl had developed a stutter in recent years, and Toby was aware that Frank and Bettina were greatly concerned about her. And now he himself was leaving, which they regarded as the death knell of the company.

In describing the results of his trip to Milwaukee, Toby deferred mentioning Dieter's idea for keeping the company in operation, because he did not want to build his friends' hopes too high. After all, Dieter's idea was risky, with only a modest chance of success.

"So Schumann has agreed to take the job as company manager," Frank commented when Toby finished talking.

Toby nodded. "There's no doubt in my mind he'll do a good job—better than I could."

Both Bettina and Frank shook their heads in disagreement. "No one could do better than you, Toby," Bettina said, taking a pan of biscuits out of the oven. "Frank and I know you have to leave, because your duty to the nation comes first, as it should. But when you leave, the best man for the job is leaving."

"I appreciate your sentiments," Toby said, "but the truth is Dieter Schumann is a better business manager than I am. He has a particular cast of mind for it that I don't have, and it made him a millionaire before he lost all of his money in stocks and bonds."

"That wasn't the only thing that made him a millionaire," Frank muttered darkly. "He didn't cut corners so much as he just chopped them off. I'll accept him as manager because you want me to, Toby, but you're the only one who could get me to do it."

"I feel the same," Bettina said, putting the biscuits on the table. "I can't forget how we first came to know of him."

"That's all in the past," Toby replied. "Believe me, he's a changed man. He's as good a man as you would want to meet."

Bettina pursed her lips, reserving judgment, and Frank's expression revealed the same attitude. Toby knew it was useless to argue.

The food was delicious, the thick rashers of bacon fried so that they were crunchy outside and tender on the inside. A large platter of fried eggs was flanked by another piled high with crisp patties made from leftover mashed potatoes. The steaming hot biscuits had been made with buttermilk, giving them a tangy flavor, and there were jars of wild honey and homemade jams and jellies.

As they ate, Toby told Frank and Bettina about the

telegram from Marjorie White. "I haven't given much thought yet as to what to do about the lady and her children," he said. "There are a few possibilities, though, and I'm sure I can work out something once I talk with her."

"If her husband has just died," Bettina commented, "she probably isn't in a state of mind to think about what she wants to do. But with Cindy getting married, you'll need someone to look after your children and your household at the ranch, won't you?"

"Yes, that's a possibility," Toby agreed. "But I'll have to get to know her first. Dealing with Janessa and Timmy isn't always easy."

Frank brought up another subject. "Albert told me last night that he was going to wait to see if you wanted to return to Chicago with him."

"I'd like to return today," Toby said. "But I want to go to Ursula Guthrie's brewery this morning and buy some of Maida's beer."

Frank smiled, knowing that Ursula and Fred Guthrie could use the business. Ursula and her temperamental daughter, Maida Oberg, who was the master brewer, had recently immigrated from Germany and set up a brewery not too far from the logging camp. But like most businesses of late, it had been hit hard by the economic depression. "All right, I'll tell Albert that you'll be ready to go back around noon or so," Frank said. "What kind of terms did you work out with Schumann, by the way?"

Toby had finished eating, and he sat back. He could see no way to avoid mentioning Dieter's plans. He began cautiously: "I don't want you to start getting your hopes up too much," he said, "but Dieter believes he can put the company back on its feet. So instead of a salary, he asked for—and I agreed to give him—ten percent of the profits."

Frank and Bettina exchanged a glance, then looked at Toby with quickened interest as he explained what Dieter planned to do. "I don't know whether it will work or not," Toby said as he finished. "I foresee many problems, but maybe he can deal with them. Also, he may come up with other ideas as time goes along. We'll just have to see what happens."

"He won't need any other ideas!" Frank exclaimed triumphantly, slapping a hand down on the table. "I believe that'll save the company!"

"I do as well," Bettina said, not as loudly, but she was no less enthusiastic. "With all the produce he will have, selling it will occupy several people; but he'll probably work out a way to do that."

Toby nodded, worried that Frank and Bettina were too excited. "He's already done that, Bettina. His in-laws are grocers, and he intends to bring them to Chicago and set them up to sell the produce. But as I said, I don't want you to be too hopeful. Dieter isn't a magician."

"No, but you yourself said he's the best manager you've ever known," Frank pointed out. "He's shown that in how soon he came up with this idea—and I don't think anyone could have come up with a better one."

"Well, we'll see," Toby said with measured restraint.

But Frank was still excited. "Toby, I can understand your attitude and why you want to be cautious. But all that aside, what is your honest opinion of Schumann's chances of keeping the company going?"

"I'm reserving judgment," Toby said. "And I'm glad that I'm not taking on the job that Dieter is, because it's the kind that will keep a man from sleeping nights and put him in an early grave." He pushed his chair back and stood up. "I'd better be on my way to the brewery. Bettina, the breakfast was a treat. With your cooking, Frank would be as fat as a butterball if he didn't have such a contrary nature."

Bettina and Frank laughed heartily, their earlier gloom dispelled, and even the normally subdued Lucy looked cheerful. She and Bettina began clearing off the table as Frank and Toby went outside.

The two men crossed the clearing to the corral. As they harnessed a team of horses to the wagon, Frank commented on Toby's purpose in going to the brewery.

"It might seem foolish to many people to take beer all the way from Wisconsin to Oregon," he said. "But to anyone who's ever tasted Maida's beer, it wouldn't seem a bit foolish."

Toby smiled. "It'll be more than worth the trouble of getting it there. As soon as people taste it, I'm sure it'll be the favorite drink at the wedding reception."

Frank became thoughtful. "Too bad Bettina and I can't be there. It's been a long time since we've seen our family and our old friends. Didn't you say that Andy Brentwood might be there? Where's he stationed now?"

"He's been serving as General Crook's commander of cavalry in the Arizona Territory," Toby replied. "Yes, he may be at the wedding, and I hope he brings Susanna with him. And Ted and Marjorie plan to be there." He gathered up the reins and climbed into the wagon. "I'll be back as soon as I can, Frank."

As he drove away, Toby was vaguely troubled. Despite his warning about becoming too optimistic, Frank and Bettina had become exuberant over the possibility that the company would stay in business. That was understandable, but Toby hoped their excitement was not destined to turn to disappointment.

After riding through the sleepy town of Colmer and many miles over the forest road without meeting a soul, Toby reached the turnoff to the brewery. Once a faint trail through the trees, the uphill track had been made as wide as the main road by logging-camp wagons coming to pick up beer. But now weeds were once again sprouting, the forest closing in.

Halfway up the hill, the track opened onto a clearing that covered several acres. The first time Toby had been here only a barn had stood in the clearing. Now there was a sprawling two-story house, which had been begun and completed despite the financial panic. In addition to Fred and Ursula Guthrie and her daughter Maida Oberg, Paddy Rafferty—the brewery's cooper, carpenter, and jack-of-all-trades—lived in the house, together with Paddy's wife, Colleen, and their three children.

The barn, converted into an immense stone building, now housed the brewery. At the foot of the hill beyond, an expanse of slope had been cut away and faced with stone, with a single door giving entrance to a huge cavern where the casks of beer were stored. A few yards from the cavern entrance was a pond fed by wooden troughs leading from a spring higher up the hill. The spring was the reason the brewery was located miles from any market, for it provided the pure artesian water that Maida Oberg demanded in making her beer.

The Raffertys and the Guthries were all working in the large vegetable garden set back from the house, and they waved and called out happily as Toby drove up. Fred Guthrie, almost as tall and as muscular as Frank Woods, limped along on his wooden leg, a few steps behind the buxom, maturely attractive Ursula. Paddy Rafferty, a wide, habitual smile on his face, was as good-naturedly garrulous as his pretty wife was demure, and they and their children all had red hair, sparkling blue eyes, and rosy cheeks.

Toby exchanged warm greetings but regretfully shook his head at their invitation to stay for lunch. "I'd enjoy nothing better, but the steam launch is waiting for me," he explained. "I came to buy three casks of beer to take to my sister's wedding in Oregon."

"We're not short of beer," Fred volunteered wryly. "We'll be glad to sell three casks, and we'd be gladder still to sell three hundred."

The others laughed, but in their laughter was the same undertone of anxiety that Toby had earlier detected in Frank and Bettina. In this clearing was their happy world, and it was threatened. "Sure and it's been weeks since you visited us, Toby," Paddy commented in his thick brogue. "You won't let it be that long again, will you?"

"I'm afraid I may have to," Toby replied. "After I go to Oregon, I'll be traveling for several months on some work I've been asked to do for the government. But if I have an opportunity to visit, I'll certainly take advantage of it."

"Well, we won't keep you if you must be going," Ursula said. "Fred, I will make certain he gets three of the casks that Maida said is choice beer."

Fred nodded, and he and the others said good-bye to Toby, then went back to the vegetable garden. Toby led the team as he and Ursula walked toward the brewery. The stonework, only a few months old, already had a patina of moss on the north side. Ursula explained that Maida had been cultivating the moss, because its wild yeast spores added some subtle ingredient to her beer.

Ursula led Toby inside to see Maida. The vast building was dim and cool, and for a former barn it was spotlessly clean. Giant tuns stood in straight rows on the stone floor, and the air was thick with the fumes of fermenting beer. In a corner, test tubes, hydrometers, and various glassware and instruments were stacked in racks and on workbenches. It looked like, and in fact was, a laboratory.

Maida Oberg sat at one of the workbenches. Bottles and glasses of beer were lined up in front of her, and she was writing with an old-fashioned quill in one of the thick ledgers in which she kept records of each tun of beer as it matured. Pretty and slender, with delicate white skin, large dark eyes, and thick black hair, she had a detached air about her.

Her response to Toby's greeting was an absent nod. Pointing to a bottle on the bench, Ursula asked something in German and received another silent nod in reply. Ursula filled a glass from the bottle and handed it to Toby.

He took a drink, then smiled. "It's delicious, as always," he said. "I never liked beer until I tasted Maida's."

"Maida says that I always serve it too cold," Ursula commented. "She says it should be only slightly cool, as that is."

"The taste is richer," Toby agreed. "Still, on a warm day there's nothing like a glass of this beer when it's good and cold." He took another drink, then glanced around. "As thick as the fumes are in here, I don't see how Maida stays sober enough to work."

"She is accustomed to it," Ursula replied. "Her father began training her as soon as she could walk, and she was only five when he started taking her to the brewery with him. For a time he had to carry her home each night, because she would be as drunk as a lord."

Although Toby thought it unhealthful for anyone to have led such a narrowly restricted life from early childhood, Maida, as far as he could tell, was perfectly content. Certainly a stranger would never suspect that the skill and knowledge of generations of master brewers should reside in her slender frame.

Toby and Ursula went back out into the sunshine, and he led the team to the storage cavern. Ursula opened the heavy door, lit a lantern, and Toby followed her inside.

The vast cavern, as far as Toby could see in the dim light, was filled with long rows of casks on wooden racks that reached up to the ceiling. Ursula indicated a row halfway back, and Toby hoisted a heavy cask to his shoulder and carried it out to the wagon.

After he had loaded the three casks onto the wagon, he paid Ursula, and she thanked him. "You're more than welcome," Toby said, putting his wallet away. "I only wish that I could buy more. Are you selling many casks now?"

"No, very few," she replied. "However, Paddy has stopped accepting wages, and our only expense is supplies for Maida. I still have some money saved from when the sales were good, and it will last for a few more months. By then, perhaps the sales will increase."

Toby nodded toward the brewery and the house. "It would have been prudent to wait instead of getting all this work done," he said.

"Yes, you are right," Ursula agreed ruefully. "But Maida wanted her brewery and her cellar immediately, so we had to do it. And when we moved out of the barn, we had to have a house, of course."

Toby could easily understand the situation. Between the mother and the daughter, Maida clearly was the leader, the heart of the business; yet she neither knew nor cared about outside circumstances. "I must be honest," he said. "I don't think things will change anytime soon. Have you thought about what you'll do in that event?"

Ursula sighed deeply. "John Kirchner, the dealer in Milwaukee who sells us Maida's supplies, is a wealthy man. He has made a standing offer to buy the brewery at a more than reasonable price. We will be able to remain here, but we will be his employees. If I must, I will sell to him, because Maida must continue making beer. She has nothing else."

"Well, perhaps it won't come to that," Toby said.

"Perhaps not," Ursula replied quietly, looking around. "This is my dream, Toby, all I have ever wanted. But if I must sell it, I will have had my dream for a time. Most people never have that much." The tall, buxom woman smiled serenely, but in her blue eyes were tears. Like most immigrants, she was willing to toil endlessly for what she wanted, but she had been caught up in circumstances beyond her control.

Toby, not knowing what to say, started to make his farewells, but Ursula, her control crumbling, broke into sobs. Toby put his arms around her and comforted her, and after a while she smiled at him and blinked back tears. When he was sure she was all right, he stepped into the wagon. He turned back and waved as he drove off down the hill.

Frank Woods was waiting for him back at the logging camp. With little visible effort, the burly man gathered up two of the bulky casks, one under each arm, while Toby hoisted the third onto his own shoulder, and the two of them set off down the zigzag path to the pier. Frank informed Toby that his baggage had already been loaded onto the launch.

Smoke rose from the stack of the broad, stubby vessel, and a cable from its stern was attached to a raft of ten huge logs floating outside the holding basin. The launch's crew were sitting on deck behind the wheelhouse. Captain Albert Crowell was a portly man of fifty, and the deckhand was a gangling youth named Turner. The engineer, Jimson, was an unshaven, wiry veteran sailor who was prone to argue with the captain.

The three stepped to the rail to help with the heavy casks. "I appreciate your waiting for me, Albert," Toby said as he stepped on board.

Albert replied affably, helping him put down his cask. "It's never any trouble to wait for you, Toby."

Jimson grunted sourly as he and Turner took one of the casks from Frank. "It ain't no trouble for you," he grumbled. "But if the boiler blows a rivet from setting here at the pier with a full head of steam, you ain't the one who's got to fix it."

"The boiler isn't about to blow a rivet, Jimson," the captain replied patiently. "But if you weren't complaining about that, you'd find some other reason to clap your jawbone."

"That's true, I guess," Jimson agreed gloomily. "So many repairs on this launch of yours have been put off during the past months that I see something that needs fixing everywhere I look."

"There's nothing wrong with this launch that a little scraping and hammering won't fix," the captain snapped, becoming annoyed. "If I listened to you, I'd replace every fitting as soon as it got tarnished. Now close your mouth and get that beer into the wheelhouse."

Jimson muttered as he and a grinning Turner obeyed orders. After the casks had been stowed away, Jimson descended through a deck hatch to the engine room. Turner cast off the mooring lines, and the launch moved slowly away from the pier, the captain sitting on his seat in the wheelhouse while keeping his eye on the tow line and occasionally glancing ahead.

When they were well out into the lake, Jimson came back on deck and stood with Turner at the wheelhouse door to listen as Toby and the captain talked. With little work of late for steam vessels on the lake, the anticipated failure of the lumber company was a very real threat to all of them. Frank had already told them about Dieter Schumann's plan, and Toby explained it again, warning them not to be too optimistic.

In Jimson's case, at least, the warning was not necessary. "Well," he commented when Toby finished, "it looks like we'll be climbing out of thornbushes and jumping into a briar patch."

"If somebody gave you a bag of gold, Jimson," the captain replied, "you'd complain about how heavy it was."

"I would if I saw pig iron under gold paint," Jimson countered. "But I guess we're so bad off now that nothing could be no worser."

The captain shook his head, dismissing Jimson's reservations, and asked Toby for more details of what Dieter intended to do. Toby gave them what information he could, and then the conversation turned to other subjects, filling the hours of the long, slow voyage down the lake to Chicago.

It was late at night when the lights of the vast city came into view. The launch eased up to the lumberyard pier, and while Toby helped the crew unhook the logs and carry the casks of beer to the shed, the yard's night watchman saddled a horse for him.

Before leaving, Toby reined up at the gate and looked around in the moonlight. The protection of the President, an infinitely more vital matter than the continued existence of the company, lay ahead of him. Yet the company and its workers were still important to him, and control over their fate was being passed to another. Resigning himself to the situation, Toby rode on through the gate and along the street toward his boardinghouse.

There was much to do at the lumberyard the next morning, and the hours passed quickly for Toby. After making arrangements to join Claude Leggett at the railroad station to meet Marjorie's train, he called the yard workers together and broke the news to them of his own imminent departure and the provisions he had made for Dieter Schumann to assume management of the company. He briefly described Dieter's plans and, as he had done before, cautioned against overoptimism, but the workers seemed eager to try anything that might keep the company going. A dray was dispatched to Milwaukee to help Dieter with the move, and by then it was well past noon and time for Toby to meet Marjorie's train.

At the station, Toby found Claude Leggett waiting on the platform, and they stood talking until the train pulled in. Toby glanced back and forth along the platform and finally saw Marjorie coming down the steps at the end of a car. As always when traveling, she had her equipment cases with her.

Marjorie spotted Toby, and putting down her cases, she smiled radiantly and waved. The chubby Claude puffed and trotted to keep up with Toby as he strode toward Marjorie.

She put her arms around Toby and embraced him warmly, then stepped back, smiling up at him. "Toby, you never change."

"Neither do you, Marjorie," he chuckled, picking up her heavy cases for her. During the Chicago fire, Toby had risked his life to save Marjorie's equipment cases from the blaze—an act that had forever endeared him to the young woman.

Marjorie greeted Claude, shaking hands with him, then turned to the woman and the three children with her and introduced them to the men.

Clara Hemmings wore mourning clothes, and the filmy black veil over her face partially obscured her features. Despite the lines of fatigue and sorrow on her face, however, she was a very attractive woman. Toby greeted her kindly and spoke reassuringly to the children.

While two porters stacked the baggage on handcarts and Claude spoke to Clara Hemmings, Toby quietly asked Marjorie how her partner had died. Marjorie didn't answer immediately. "It was the most dreadful thing imaginable, Toby. Could we wait until later to talk about it?"

"Yes, of course," Toby replied.

"I know our coming here was abrupt, to say the least. But I didn't know what to do, and having you to turn to was a godsend."

Toby shrugged off her thanks. The porters followed them outside to a carriage, and Toby gave the driver the address of his boardinghouse, where he had arranged for extra rooms. During the drive, as Toby talked with Clara, he thought more seriously of hiring her as a housekeeper and to care for his children. His first impression of her was very favorable, and the conduct of her children revealed that she was loving but strict with them.

However, he reflected, he would have to know more about her, because dealing with his children would not be easy for most women. Janessa, with her serious, independent nature, responded to persuasion but rebelled against direction, and she needed tolerant understanding more than guidance. Timmy, of course, had a sunny disposition and was no trouble at all to get along with, but nothing was more difficult than controlling the imaginative, strong-willed, and somewhat wild boy. Toby knew that whoever took Cindy's place would have her work cut out for her.

Having talked Calvin Rogers into bringing the wagon across the Columbia River on the ferry, Timmy Holt pointed as they drove up the slope away from the dock. "Head toward those tall trees behind the houses, Calvin," he said. "There's a road there that goes around the fort to the artillery range."

"Okay, Timmy," Calvin replied, humoring the boy. "But we're just going to take a quick look, because your aunt doesn't know where you are. She'll get worried if we're not home soon."

"She knows I'm with you," Timmy said confidently. "Besides, we can catch the next ferry back, and nobody will know the difference."

Calvin was not so sure they would not be missed, and he snapped the reins, urging the horse into a faster walk. They passed through the small town that had grown up near the fort, skirted the row of houses for senior officers where General Blake and Timmy's grandmother Eulalia lived, then approached the trees Timmy had pointed to.

An old logging road turned off through the trees, and Calvin followed it at Timmy's direction, the wagon wheels bouncing over ruts under the high weeds. The dense forest closed in on both sides, and after several minutes Calvin started to express doubts about continuing on along the road. Just then the trees opened out ahead, and the way was blocked by a gate.

The gate was strong but old and weathered, and a large board in the center of it looked suspiciously like a No Trespassing sign from which the paint had peeled. As the boy scrambled down from the wagon to open the gate, Calvin shook his head doubtfully. "I don't know if we should go through that gate, Timmy," he said.

"It'll be all right," Timmy replied. "People go through it all the time to get cattle and horses that stray across the fence."

The boy opened the gate, closed it behind the wagon after Calvin had driven through, then climbed back up to the seat. In the field before them, the rutted track joined a smooth, well-traveled road that led from the fort back into the vast military reservation. Turning onto the road, Calvin had an increasing feeling that he was where he was not supposed to be.

"I think we'd better go back now, Timmy," he said. "If we don't, we'll probably get run out of here presently."

"No, no one is here," the boy replied, pointing. "See that tall pole over there? When the range is being used, a red flag is run up it. And we're almost there. We just have to go over that ridge ahead."

When they reached the top of the low ridge, Timmy pointed to a line of widely spaced embankments in the distance, explaining that they were cannon positions. Off to one side were several small sheds with a distinctly military appearance. They were set in a rigidly straight line, and the area around them was conspicuously neat.

Pointing to a large, fire-blackened pit, Timmy explained that it was where the propulsion units of Hale rockets were destroyed when they became too old to be reliable. "The soldiers use a few of them for practice, but most of them are burned," he said. "They're chained down and broken open with an ax, but Sergeant Thompson told me that one got loose about a year ago and flew over to that hill there."

Calvin looked at the new growth on the hill, the telltale sign of a recent forest fire. "That must be three or four miles from here," he commented.

"Yes, it's a long way," Timmy agreed. "If part of it hadn't been broken open with an ax, it would have probably gone a lot farther. The soldiers had to go over there and put out the fire." He pointed to the sheds. "The second one is where they keep the old rockets that are ready to burn."

Calvin's growing apprehension was overcome by a sense of relief when he saw that the sheds were all securely locked with heavy padlocks. "Well, we've seen everything," he said. "We'd better go now."

The boy leaped down from the wagon and ran to the second shed. Kneeling beside it, he felt under a corner with his hand. Then he stood up, grinning triumphantly and lifting a key. "The soldiers keep this one here in case they forget to bring the one at the fort," he said. "Come on, let's take a look."

After glancing around guiltily, Calvin picked up his cane and slowly climbed down from the wagon. The boy opened the door and went inside, and Calvin followed him in.

A score or more of Hale rocket propulsion units were stacked on one side of the small building, the warheads removed from them. Looking like polished logs, they were some eight inches in diameter and six feet long, made of thick cardboard coated with layers of varnish.

Timmy grinned gleefully, pointing. "They're just going to be burned, Calvin," he whispered excitedly. "We could take some of them and see if they will push a big glider into the air, and no one would know."

While Calvin disliked disappointing the boy, he felt extremely uneasy about taking any of the propulsion units. Rockets could be dangerous, particularly those that were already considered unreliable.

Calvin bit his lip and shook his head, his eyes glued to the propulsion units. "I don't know, Timmy," he murmured doubtfully. "I don't know."

V

"Clara is very grateful that you hired her as your house-keeper," Marjorie said, as she sat facing Toby on the train pulling out of Chicago. Clara and the children were all sitting together in seats diagonally across the aisle. "And the boys especially are thrilled over the prospect of living on a ranch in Oregon."

"I was fortunate in hiring someone as qualified as she is," Toby replied. "If it weren't for her and Dieter Schumann, I'd be in serious trouble right now."

As she moved her equipment cases so they would take up less space between the seats, Marjorie commented about her impression of Dieter Schumann. "There's no question in my mind that you hired the right man to manage your company," she said. "I've never met anyone who inspired more confidence in his ability as a business-man."

"Yes, he's the right man for the job," Toby agreed. "I have full confidence in him, yet right up until we boarded the train, I still felt there might be things about the company that I had forgotten to tell him."

Marjorie laughed. "I felt the same way about Claude, and in fact there is one thing that slipped my mind in the rush of these past days. I still have the photographic plates

80

in my cases that I used in Connecticut, and I should have left them with Claude for him to develop."

"Can't you mail them back to him?" Toby asked.

"It wouldn't be worth the trouble and cost," Marjorie said. "In any event, it will be weeks before he sends any slides to the company in Baltimore, and I'll return here well before then. And if I have time, I might just develop them at a studio in Portland."

Toby nodded and looked out the window. Marjorie was about to tell him of her visit to Talcott, Connecticut, and the centennial celebration there, but she changed her mind, seeing that he was lost in thought.

Actually, Toby was thinking about the upcoming wedding between his sister and Reed Kerr. While he was certain it would be a happy occasion, one aspect of it still worried him. Ever since he had first heard about the wedding plans, he had wondered if Cindy was rushing into a marriage to escape the emotional turmoil of her broken engagement with Henry Blake.

Toby had still not gotten over his resentment at how his sister had been treated. Henry had been his close friend for many years but had as good as betrayed their friendship in the way he had dealt with Cindy.

Henry Blake, Toby reflected, had always been the right man for Cindy, or at least he had thought so. Their love had seemed indestructible, their personalities a perfect match. But Henry was now virtually lost to the family, pursuing his own life far away from those who had loved him.

In the luxurious private rail car with the Kirchberg arms on its sides, Henry Blake was arriving in the port city of Bremerhaven. When the train stopped, he put on his cap and stepped toward the door.

The private car was at the end of a passenger train, and through the lace curtains over the windows Henry could see that the platform was crowded with people leaving the train. As they did at every stop, people were walking toward the large, gleaming private car for a closer look.

The servant who had attended to Henry during the journey from Grevenburg was busy with the baggage at the end of the car. As Henry opened the door, the man spoke to him. "Sir, shall I have all your baggage sent straight to the ship, or do you want part of it sent to the hotel where you will be staying tonight?"

Henry had started down the steps to the platform, but he turned and went back into the car to decide what to do with his baggage.

That single step saved his life, taking him out of the path of a bullet that was sent speeding on its deadly mission at the same instant. The edge of the thick, polished hardwood door a foot away suddenly exploded into splinters, and the thunderous report of a rifle resounded through the train station.

The people on the platform froze, their expressions reflecting shock and terror. The servant, his face blanched, looked at Henry in consternation. Henry stepped farther back from the doorway, and at the same instant the rifle roared again, the bullet clipping the top edge of the door and slamming into the carpeted floor where Henry had been standing.

As the echoes of the shots reverberated under the lofty ceiling, there was an eerie stillness on the platform; then a surge of movement passed through the crowd, and the scene turned into pandemonium. People fell and were trampled underfoot by others scrambling back into the train cars or racing toward the station doors in a bedlam of panic-stricken screams and shouts. Henry stepped to a cabinet and opened it to take out the pistol that was kept in the private car.

The servant, speechless for a moment, finally found

his voice. "Sir, is someone shooting at us?" he asked. "Who could it be?"

"Someone is apparently shooting at *me*," Henry replied. He took out the pistol and closed the cabinet door. "I have no idea who it is."

As he turned away from the cabinet, another rifle shot rang out over the uproar on the platform. A window not far from the servant collapsed into shards of glass, and the bullet slammed into the floor, the servant flinching and looking at the broken pane in terror.

"Get to the center of the car and lie under the table," Henry directed.

The man scrambled to the floor as Henry stepped toward the door, checking the cylinder in the revolver to make certain the weapon was loaded. He looked at the bullet holes in the floor. The bullets had come from a sharp, high angle, the assailant apparently firing through a roof window above the platform, or possibly from the steel girders that supported the high ceiling.

Henry estimated that the doors at each end of the car, as well as those opening onto the platform, were probably in the line of fire, for the bullets had come from almost directly overhead. He turned and stepped to the door on the opposite side of the car. Slowly opening it a crack, he peered out.

Several feet below was the sooty gravel between the track on which the train stood and a parallel track. Beyond was another platform, now empty except for three porters crouching behind a baggage cart and peering fearfully up at the girders.

The commotion on the platform beside the train had died away, and a steely quiet had settled. Opening the door wider, Henry leaned out and quickly ducked back inside. The quiet was shattered by the roar of another rifle shot, a geyser of gravel and dust leaping up below the door as the bullet struck.

Henry closed the door and stepped away from it. Knowing that he was trapped inside the car, he seethed with frustration. As he stood there, he heard the sharp crack of a pistol on the platform beside the train. He crossed the car and looked out a window.

A policeman, running along the platform, was firing his pistol up at the man, who must have been visible in the girders. The rifle thundered once again. The policeman jerked and stumbled as the bullet struck him. His pistol fell from his hand, and he collapsed onto the platform.

Henry, rage swelling within him, watched as the policeman lay there, wounded and in pain. Taking off his cap and tunic, he walked back to the open door and looked out. The nearest shelter was a baggage cart beside the freight office door. The cart was some fifty feet from the train, across an open expanse of platform. A dash there approached being suicidal, Henry knew, but he had to do something. He put the pistol under his belt and poised himself to run out the door.

At the same moment he heard the rumble of a train approaching. He stepped back to the door on the other side of the car, opened it a crack, and looked out. A passenger train was pulling in on the adjacent track, drawing up to the platform opposite.

The engine was venting steam, as they always did when slowing, and the thick white cloud around the locomotive offered a means of concealment for Henry to slip out of the car as the train passed. But such a move might be as dangerous as running across the platform.

The luxurious private car had been built to maximum allowable width, and there were never more than bare inches of clearance between it and structures alongside the track. Henry was well aware he could easily be crushed as the approaching locomotive passed.

If he opened the door wide enough to slip out, he reflected, the man in the girders would know what he intended to do. Instead, he stepped to a window and pulled it open. The train, its hiss of steam and rumble of wheels growing louder, came into view.

As the steam billowing ahead of the engine swirled around and into the private car, Henry began climbing out the window. The locomotive's fireman was leaning from the off-side window, and his eyes widened with alarm as he glimpsed Henry through the steam. He blew the whistle on the engine in warning, a shattering blast of sound.

The whistle drew the attention of the man in the girders. He must have spotted Henry through the steam, for a second later the rifle fired again. Evidently the steam spoiled his aim, however, and the bullet slammed into the car a foot from the window as Henry slid on out and hung from the sill for an instant.

The rifle fired once more, the bullet ripping into metal only inches from Henry, and then the steam eddying around him was dense. Through it, the engine was a huge, dark mass looming over him and drawing closer, looking certain to crush him against the side of the car. He dropped to the gravel between the tracks, somehow keeping his footing and flattening himself against the car.

The noise from the engine became deafening, and the edge of the cowcatcher brushed his trousers as it swept past; then the huge wheels and drive shaft rumbled by, scant inches from him. The engine passed, and the steam began thinning as the coal car approached. Henry cautiously dropped to his knees, then ducked and rolled under the private car.

Its brakes squealing, the adjacent train stopped as Henry crawled forward along the ties under the car. Passengers stepped off the train in a hubbub of voices and footsteps. Then pistols began firing at the far end of the station; policemen apparently were shooting from cover at the man in the girders. The rifle thundered, returning the fire.

Bullets ricocheted through the station, and over the roar of the gunfire, screams again arose as people on the platform scurried for cover. The policemen were too far from the man in the girders for their pistols to be effective, and the gunfire died away. The noise from the platform also faded, quiet settling in the station once again as Henry reached the front of the private car.

Lying on his back under the end of the car, Henry took the pistol from his belt and cocked it. He stuck his head out and looked up past the coupling at the girders. The light was dim near the high ceiling, but he immediately spotted the man, who was sitting at a junction of thick girders directly above the platform.

The man, also seeing Henry, shouldered his rifle. Henry lifted the pistol and snapped off a shot. The bullet missed the man, but it hit the girder under him and made him flinch, spoiling his aim. The return shot tore into the front of the private car.

As the man quickly worked the bolt on the rifle, Henry cocked the pistol, took careful aim, and gently squeezed the trigger. The man was aiming the rifle as the bullet struck him.

The rifle sagged and fired. The bullet ripped into the platform, and the weapon slipped from the man's hands. It tumbled downward as the man slowly toppled from the girders and plummeted. The rifle hit the platform with a clatter, sliding across it, and a second later the body struck nearby with a dull thud.

The wounded policeman being his first concern, Henry leaped up onto the platform and hurried to the man. The officer, his face pale and twisted in pain, was gripping his blood-soaked thigh. "Thank you, sir," he said. "He might have shot me again."

A tall, burly police sergeant arrived at a run and

leaned over the wounded policeman. "It is not a fatal wound, Kurt," he comforted the man. "A doctor will be here in a few minutes." He turned to Henry. "I am Sergeant Gretz, sir. We are very grateful to you for shooting the man before he killed someone."

"I am pleased I could be of service," Henry replied in German, shaking hands with the man. "But after all, he was shooting at me. I am Lieutenant Henry Blake of the United States Army."

"You are an American?" the policeman exclaimed in surprise. Henry was bareheaded and in his shirtsleeves, and without his uniform to give him away, his Prussian accent passed as genuine. The sergeant shook his head in amazement. "Your German is as perfect as your marksmanship with a pistol, sir. Come, let us look at the dead man to see if you know who he was and why he was trying to kill you."

The stationmaster and a number of policemen had gathered around the sprawled body. "This man was inquiring about the Kirchberg private car, Sergeant Gretz," the stationmaster said. "He was asking what time it would arrive."

Henry looked at the body, that of a man of average size and build, about forty years old, and dressed in workman's clothing. "I've never seen him before, Sergeant," he said. "I have no idea why he was trying to kill me."

Gretz frowned, then bent over the body and searched the pockets. They were empty except for extra rifle bullets. The sergeant straightened up. "He must have been an anarchist," he said.

"Yes, the dirty swine," the stationmaster agreed. "They have been causing trouble in the city recently."

"Indeed they have," Gretz said. "The attack must not have been against you personally, Lieutenant Blake, but only because you were in the Kirchberg private car, which to them represents wealth and authority. Somehow or other, this fellow must have found out that it was arriving here today, and he decided to attack it. That seems to me a logical explanation for what happened."

Henry glanced at the dead man's rifle as a policeman carried it away. It was new, a military model Mauser. He turned back to the police sergeant and nodded noncommittally. "Perhaps so, Sergeant."

"I'm sure that's what happened," Gretz said confidently. "Would you come to the police station and make a written statement, sir?"

"I'll be pleased to cooperate in any way I can. However, I do have accommodations on a steamer that departs tomorrow."

"Do not worry—the entire matter will be finished within the hour. I have a carriage at the front of the station, and the driver will take you wherever you wish to go as soon as we have your statement."

As Henry walked back to the private car to get his cap and tunic, he glanced up at the girders. It appeared that the trouble anarchists had been creating in the city had made the police sergeant too ready to attribute everything to them. While it would be comforting to believe that his assailant had merely been an anarchist, it left too much unexplained.

The man had known that the private car would arrive, which suggested an organized network to transmit information. Anarchists were violent extremists whose main weakness was lack of organization. They also thrived on publicity, and an anarchist would be more likely to scatter leaflets while shooting than to have nothing in his pockets.

That left the identity of the man and the reason for the attack unanswered questions, and extremely disquieting ones at that. Only a single fact about the incident was completely clear to Henry: The attack had come within a hairbreadth of succeeding, and only remarkably good luck had intervened between him and certain death.

* * *

Standing beside the entrance to the train station waiting room, Karl Schneider watched as Henry Blake left with the policemen. As soon as they were out of sight, he went into the waiting room and crossed to the telegraph company counter.

Schneider wrote out a telegram to an address in Berlin. The message was an innocuous one. It concerned the arrival of a relative to attend the funeral of a friend, and its meaning would be clear to Hermann Bluecher: The attack had failed, and Weiditz was dead.

After paying for the telegram, Schneider left the station and walked the short distance to the cheap hotel where he and Weiditz had been staying. As he gathered up Weiditz's belongings, he felt no sense of loss or remorse about the man. In his profession, such feelings were a dangerous weakness.

Instead, he was relieved that he did not have to report the failure to Bluecher in person, and he was bewildered that the attack had failed. Weiditz, of course, might well have been killed or imprisoned in any case, the plan sacrificing an agent in favor of certainty of success. But somehow the American had escaped unscathed.

Schneider put Weiditz's belongings in a garbage bin behind the hotel, then returned to his own room. Reasonably certain of what he would be ordered to do next, he made sure he would be ready to proceed. In his baggage was a passport and other papers that identified him as a Swiss businessman named Otto Brunfels. He checked the papers, then carefully went through his belongings and examined each article to ensure that nothing would contradict his assumed identity.

Exactly five hours after he had sent the telegram, Schneider returned to the train station. A message was waiting for him at the telegraph company counter. It consisted of a single sentence, wishing him a safe and

successful journey. Schneider went out to the street, where
carriages for hire were parked, and instructed a driver to
take him to the offices of the Hamburg Line.

At the steamship line office, the clerk recommended
a berth on a smaller and more economical vessel, but
Schneider insisted on the *Loewengau*, the ship on which
Henry Blake would be traveling. The clerk pored over
passenger lists and finally found a vacant bunk, in a steer-
age cabin that Schneider could share with three other
men. Schneider paid for the ticket, then returned to his
hotel.

In his room, he put a valise on the bed and removed
everything from it. Then he released the latches on the
false bottom and lifted it out. Under it, held firmly in
place by straps, were two pistols and four knives. He
selected a knife and took a whetstone from another bag,
then sat down and began sharpening the hard steel edge.

No surgeon's scalpel received more care than the
knives in the suitcase, and the blade was already as keen
as a razor. But the sensuous whisper of the stone against
the gleaming steel touched something deep within Schneider, satisfying a gnawing hunger and preparing him men-
tally for what he intended to do.

A knife, his weapon of choice, was the weapon with
which he had never failed. With a swift, unexpected attack
and a quick thrust to the heart, it was impossible to fail.
This time, he reflected as he gently stroked the blade with
the whetstone, the American would not escape.

VI

The following evening, a murmur of conversation and the muted clatter of dishware were a soft background noise as Henry ate dinner in the main dining room of the luxury steamer *Loewengau*. The incident at the train station, which he had consciously dismissed, was pushed even farther from his thoughts by his relaxed surroundings.

The vast dining room was sumptuously furnished, with crystal chandeliers, thick carpeting, and elegantly set tables. Silver and china emblazoned with the crest of the Hamburg Line gleamed on spotless linen, and the stewards moving silently about and serving the meal wore tunics and gloves that were snowy white against the teak and rosewood paneling. Diamonds sparkled at every table, with the diners all in formal attire.

Henry, as one of the passengers with luxury stateroom accommodations, was seated at the captain's table. A woman of about sixty was beside him. Candidly straightforward in the manner of many older people, she wore with aplomb a plain, knitted shawl that clashed with her costly gown and jewelry. It was for the chill at sea, she explained to the others at the table.

Henry had already learned that she was the Countess Lautzenberg, a distant relative of the deceased prince consort of Britain, and was en route to the court in London. Having heard of Henry, she was curious about him. "And so," she commented, holding her lorgnette by its bejeweled handle and peering at him through it, "you are the Baroness von Kirchberg's young American friend. How did you meet her?"

"We met in France, during the siege of Paris," Henry replied. "Her nephew, Captain Richard Koehler, is a friend of mine. The baroness visited him while he was with the army in France, and he introduced us."

"How very interesting," the woman said. "And so, you are returning to America now. Will you come back to Germany and to the baroness soon?"

Henry said that he would, after he had finished his business in the United States. As the dowager countess turned to address someone on the other side of the table, Henry glanced around the dining room. Since he had come on board, he had seen no one he knew among the passengers, but now, as he looked across the room, he spotted a man to whom he had been introduced the previous year.

Middle-aged and with thin, pale features and an aloof bearing, he was one Englishman Henry would never forget. His icy blue eyes met Henry's, and he lifted his wineglass and nodded. Henry lifted his own glass, responding in kind to the greeting.

The countess, observing the gesture, looked at Henry curiously. "Have you seen someone you know, Lieutenant Blake?" she asked.

"Yes, a man I met in London last year," Henry replied. "He is Sir Charles Willoughby of the British Foreign Office."

Lifting her lorgnette, the woman craned her neck and peered across the room, then nodded indifferently. As he and the countess continued chatting, Henry reflected that Willoughby was an official of the Foreign Office in name

only. More accurately, he was a member of the British
secret intelligence service.

The previous year, when Henry had traveled to England with Gisela, he had, at the request of his own State
Department, visited the British military college at Sandhurst
to quietly investigate rumors about a foreign officer there.

The mysterious officer had turned out to be none
other than Alphonse Ferdinand, the sixteen-year-old son
and heir of the recently deposed Queen Isabella II of
Spain, a country now torn by civil war. Through a fortunate set of circumstances, Henry's timely presence had
foiled a plot on the boy's life, and subsequent events had
made clear that Great Britain was secretly planning to
install the exiled Alphonse on the Spanish throne. By
thwarting the assassination attempt, Henry had earned the
gratitude of the British government, but he had also at-
tracted the attention of their secret intelligence service,
and Willoughby had paid him an official call in London to
tell him as much.

Henry noticed that Willoughby was talking to a somewhat younger companion, who appeared to share his reti-
cent mannerisms. The two exchanged only occasional
remarks, both of them silent more than they talked. Finishing dinner at the same time, they left the dining room
together.

When he had finished dinner, Henry excused himself
and went outside. Like most of the other men leaving the
room, he walked along the deck to the ship's saloon to
have a cigar and brandy. The spacious saloon had the
atmosphere of a gentleman's club, with leather couches
and chairs.

Willoughby, seated beside the man who had been
with him in the dining room, beckoned Henry. Their
meeting the year before had ended on a cordial note, and
the Englishman was amiable as he stood and greeted
Henry and introduced his companion. "A countryman of

yours, Lieutenant Blake," he said. "Allow me to introduce you to Clifford Anderson of your State Department. Clifford, this is Lieutenant Henry Blake, of whom I have spoken."

The man, who seemed as reserved as Willoughby, had a fixed, unsettling gaze. Yet he seemed friendly enough as he shook Henry's hand.

"I've been looking forward to meeting you," Anderson said. "Sir Charles has spoken very highly of you."

"I'm pleased to meet you, sir," Henry replied. "Are you traveling to the United States or returning to the embassy in London? I assume you're stationed there."

Anderson hesitated, glanced at the men seated nearby, then replied in a softer tone. "I'm en route to London, but I'm not assigned to a specific embassy."

Henry, made a bit uneasy by the man's strange gaze, voiced regret that he would not have the pleasure of Anderson's company for the entire voyage, and then the subject was dropped. But the man's hesitation and indirect reply had been revealing. Although the United States lacked a foreign intelligence service as such, Anderson's duties were evidently of the same general nature as Willoughby's.

A steward approached, asking if the three men wanted to order drinks, and Willoughby shook his head. "Nothing for me, thank you," he said. "Clifford, let's go to my cabin. I have cigars and brandy there, and it's more private. You'll join us, won't you, Henry?"

Henry, surprised to be addressed by his first name, nodded and followed the men out of the saloon. Only a few people were strolling the dark decks, and Willoughby and Anderson were both silent as they led Henry into a passageway and along it to Willoughby's stateroom.

Inside the well-furnished cabin, the Englishman produced cigars and brandy and directed Henry and Anderson to have seats. As soon as Anderson sat down, he excused himself and, to Henry's astonishment, removed a glass eye and put it into his waistcoat pocket, then put on an eyepatch. "More comfortable this way," he explained with a smile.

Willoughby lit their cigars, then took a seat. "This is much better than the saloon, isn't it?" he commented. "It isn't as luxurious as Henry's accommodations, I daresay, but then I don't have his influence among the Germans."

"Who does?" Anderson said dryly. "It's remarkable how you managed to get access to Mauser Arms Works, Henry."

Willoughby puffed on his cigar, his cold blue eyes reflective. "Henry has a talent for gaining entree into such situations, Clifford, which has brought him extraordinary successes." He smiled thinly. "Situations of both an official and a personal nature, I might add. Speaking of your personal situation, Henry, I trust the baroness is well?"

"Yes, she is," Henry replied. "Although she might become a little upset when she finds out what happened to me yesterday. It was a situation I would rather have avoided." He briefly described the incident at the train station. "The police sergeant was convinced that the man was an anarchist," he concluded, "but I'm not so certain."

The two men were silent for a long moment. Finally Willoughby spoke. "I agree it's unlikely that the man was an anarchist. Are you on cordial terms with the military officers at Mauser?"

"Yes, the best of terms with all of them," Henry replied. "I've detected no hostility in anyone. Of course I could be mistaken."

"Some professions can be hazardous," Anderson commented frankly, pointing to his eyepatch. "Their perils can be unexpected and can come from unexpected sources. In your case, Henry, another possibility arises when you consider that the baroness must have enemies. Could one of them have been behind the attack?"

"I don't think so," Henry replied. "If that had been the case, the attack would probably have come in Frankfurt, and a weapon that is commonly available to civilians would have been used. The gunman had a military model Mauser, a new one. In fact, it was identical to those that the Spanish agents used at Sandhurst last year. That may mean nothing, or it could be significant."

"Significant in what way?" Willoughby asked.

"You'll recall that I saw the Spanish agents on the train when I went to Sandhurst. Two of them were disposed of later, but there was a third one. He was never caught, and it has occurred to me that he has ample reason to feel some hostility toward me."

Willoughby looked skeptical. "It's a possibility, of course."

Henry shrugged. "As you can see," he said, "I've been weighing even the most remote possibilities, trying to find some logical reason for that attack. And I've found none."

"Well," Willoughby said, "if you ever discover who it was, I shall be delighted to assist you in any way I can in dealing with him. Until then, please be very cautious."

"You can be certain of that," Henry said with a smile. "By the way, how is our friend at Sandhurst?"

"He is well," Willoughby replied. "In fact, Clifford and I will probably visit him soon, and we'll tell him that you were asking about him. And we'll convey to him your best wishes, of course. May I ask the purpose of your trip to the United States?"

Henry explained that he was going to Connecticut to establish a weapons procurement detachment and would probably return to Germany within the year.

"At least," Anderson said, "if the Germans ever begin having second thoughts about your being at Mauser, you can point to this as a valid result of your work there. And

I'm sure you'll enjoy being back in the States for a few months."

"I certainly will," Henry replied. "Though I won't have time for many social activities."

"I understand your friend Lord Randolph Churchill is in New York," Willoughby put in.

"Yes, and I hope to see him," Henry said. "His last letter mentioned that he'd be visiting his fiancée's family for some time."

The conversation continued, turning to European politics and other subjects, and it was late at night when Anderson and Henry finally returned to their cabins.

The next day, it became apparent to Henry that he had formed the beginnings of a firm friendship with the two men and that they enjoyed his companionship as much as he did theirs. They sought him out, coming to his cabin for him, and he spent most of the day walking on deck with them and talking. That evening, after dinner, Henry again accompanied them to Willoughby's cabin.

As it had done the night before, the conversation turned to politics. The absolute degree to which the two men trusted Henry became evident when they began talking about Alphonse Ferdinand's prospects for becoming king of Spain. Apparently his support in his own country was growing, the people becoming ever more weary of the civil war there. Willoughby went as far as to suggest that the plan to place him on the throne would be carried out within a year.

"And if and when he does take the throne," Willoughby commented to Anderson, the Englishman's pale blue eyes glinting with amusement, "our young Henry will have a strong ally in an exceedingly high place. During the short time Henry was at Sandhurst, our friend there became very fond of him. Isn't that so, Henry?"

"Yes, I suppose it is," Henry said, but his smile faded as he recalled the young Spaniard's isolation at the foreign military college. "I'm very fond of him as well, and to tell the truth, I feel sorry for the lad. He has people all around him, but no friends. I realize that I can't simply post a letter to him through the mails, but I would like to write to him. I'm certain he'd like to hear from me."

Willoughby hesitated at the unstated suggestion. "Yes, he would enjoy receiving it," he replied at last. "Very well, give me the letter before we dock at Southampton in the morning, and I'll see that it's delivered."

"I could go to my cabin and write it now," Henry said, smiling and rising. "I'd be back in less than an hour."

"Good, then," Willoughby said. "We'll be expecting you."

The quiet of late evening was beginning to settle over the ship as Henry went back along the passageway to the deck, then up a ladderway to the next deck, where his stateroom was located. He went inside, lighted a lamp, and sat down at the desk.

Henry shared with Alphonse an interest in firearms—in fact, they had met on a firing range—and he had intended to write only a short letter, most of it about recent developments in weapons. However, his fondness for the young Spaniard made the sentences flow easily from his pen, and he filled page after page.

More than an hour had passed by the time he finished the letter, put it in his pocket, and headed back to Willoughby's room. Most of the passengers had gone to their cabins for the night, and the deck was dark and deserted, with only a few small lanterns glowing dimly along the bulkheads. The rail was only faintly visible between the shadows cast by the enormous lifeboats, and the darkness made the vast sea beyond feel closer. Henry headed for the illuminated ladderway, passing a lifeboat that was a mass of thick shadows.

The attack was so sudden and unexpected that it almost succeeded. There was a sound of movement, and

Henry turned his head toward the lifeboat and saw polished steel flash in the light. By instinct he turned aside, and the razor-sharp knife, instead of plunging into the left side of his chest, stabbed into his left shoulder.

With pain lancing down his arm, Henry grasped the attacker's wrist. The man was Henry's size, about six feet tall and some two hundred pounds. He had the initiative, and he was determined. The knife pulled out of Henry's shoulder, the man jerking it free to stab again.

Gripping the wrist with both hands, Henry teetered for a second on the bare edge of being killed. Then, without conscious thought, he began using the Indian techniques of hand-to-hand combat that he had learned as a boy on the western plains. Still holding the man's wrist, he backed quickly away to pull his opponent off balance. The man fell into the trap, stumbling forward, yet still tried to twist his arm free and stab again even as he fought to regain his balance.

The steel gleamed within an inch of his chest as Henry let go with his good hand and hit the man in the face, lifting his knee at the same time. The man avoided the full force of the punch, but the Indian two-point attack was unexpected. Henry's knee slammed solidly into the man's groin, drawing a gasp of pain.

Now the arm with the knife was not as difficult to hold back, and starting to take control of the struggle, Henry swung his right fist into his foe's stomach. The blow landed solidly, but the man was desperate, and he heaved himself at Henry with frantic, renewed determination.

Henry backed away once more, again pulling his attacker off balance. As the man stumbled forward, Henry sidestepped deftly and shoved him to one side. At the same time, he put a foot between the man's feet and tripped him. As the man began falling, Henry leaped onto him. They both crashed to the deck, Henry on top and driving a knee into the pit of his opponent's stomach.

Breath burst from the man's lungs as his head hit the deck with a solid thud, and Henry pounded a fist into the unguarded face. He gripped the man's right forearm with both hands, turning the knife toward him. Then he threw his weight against the knife and drove it into the man's chest.

Every muscle in the body under him tensed in a convulsive tremor, then went limp. Gasping for breath, and with throbbing pain enveloping his shoulder, Henry climbed to his feet. He pressed his tunic and shirt against his wound as he glanced around, thinking about what to do. Nothing moved on the dark deck, no one else having observed the fight.

The thought of going for the captain of the ship and reporting the incident occurred to Henry, but he immediately dismissed it, thinking about the sergeant at the railroad station. He bent over the body, feeling in the pockets.

A passport and wallet were inside the coat. Henry put them in his pocket, then dragged the body to the rail. Favoring his left shoulder, he lifted the body and heaved it overboard.

A second or two later, he heard a splash. Holding his wounded shoulder, he peered down at the deck in the dim light. He could see no blood, and if there were any telltale stains, he knew they would be washed away by the sailors who scrubbed the decks before dawn each morning. He walked toward the ladderway.

Outside the dim passageway leading to Willoughby's cabin, Henry first looked to make certain that no one was anywhere in sight; then he walked quickly down the corridor. The Englishman's thin, pale face reflected no reaction when the door was opened to Henry's knock, but he quickly pulled Henry inside and glanced out into the passageway before closing and locking the door.

Anderson immediately stood up and led Henry to the lavatory. He began helping Henry take off his tunic and shirt, while Willoughby poured a large glass of brandy and took a clean towel from a drawer. Stepping into the lavatory, the Englishman handed Henry the glass and quickly tore the towel into strips.

Willoughby inspected the deep cut on Henry's shoulder, then had him sit down while he poured some of the brandy over the wound to cleanse it. "I'm sure it's very painful," he said as he began applying the bandages, "but it's a clean flesh wound. It should heal without difficulty. I know a discreet doctor in Southampton, if you would like him to look at it."

Henry shook his head and took a deep drink of the brandy to help fight the pain. Then, while Anderson sponged the blood off him with a washcloth and Willoughby finished the bandaging, he told them what had happened. They both agreed that he had been right to dispose of the body quietly, and even appeared bemused that he would have considered doing anything else.

"No, the last thing we need is outsiders prowling about in our affairs," Willoughby said, tying a last knot on the bandage. "There, that should do, Henry. Now you can sit in a proper chair and have another drink."

Henry gathered up his tunic and shirt and followed the two men back into the cabin. He took out the passport and wallet and handed them, along with the letter for Alphonse, to Willoughby. Then, his glass refilled with brandy, he sat down and sipped it as Anderson and Willoughby examined the passport and the contents of the wallet.

"Otto Brunfels," Willoughby mused, thumbing through the passport. "A Swiss. Does that mean anything to you, Henry?"

"No, nothing," Henry replied. "But I believe I can assume that the attack tonight and the one at the train station were connected."

"Yes, little doubt about that," Willoughby said, and Anderson nodded in agreement. "This time, however, we at least have a passport and wallet. Henry, I would like to keep these and give them to a specialist in documents employed by my organization. If he can find out anything useful, I shall pass it along to you."

Henry readily agreed with the suggestion. He and the two men continued talking for a few minutes, then he finished his brandy, put on his tunic, and left, refusing Anderson's offer to escort him to his cabin. As he walked along the dim passageways and decks, he looked at the areas of dark shadow more carefully than ever before.

Although he was weary and weak from loss of blood, Henry slept poorly. The pain in his shoulder made him wakeful, and during the dark, early hours of the morning, the motion of the ship changed as they approached Spithead and entered the lee of the Isle of Wight. When dawn broke, tugs were nudging the *Loewengau* up to a pier among the crowded Southampton docks.

Others began stirring on the ship, and Henry got out of bed. The sharp pain in his shoulder was even worse than the night before, making it difficult for him to wash and shave. He put the bloodstained tunic and shirt where the room steward would not see them until he had an opportunity to throw them overboard, then took out a new uniform and dressed himself with some difficulty.

Passengers were beginning to disembark when he left his stateroom. He met Willoughby and Anderson on the deck where the fight had taken place. It was still damp from being scrubbed, and there was no sign of blood. Willoughby commented on the fact in satisfaction, and the three of them went down to the gangplank on a lower deck.

"I'll notify you if the documents reveal anything," Willoughby said, shaking hands in farewell. "The most important thing, though, is for you to be very watchful, particularly when you're alone."

Anderson also shook his hand. "The pleasure was all mine, Henry," he said, his expression uncharacteristically warm. "I'm sure we'll meet again soon. In the meantime, as Sir Charles said, please be cautious."

Henry watched the two men join the passengers filing down the gangplank, then disappear into the crowd on the pier. He went back up the ladderways and along the passage to his stateroom.

Through the morning, muffled sounds of activity on deck carried into the stateroom as cargo was loaded and passengers going to New York came aboard. Henry had the steward bring him lunch, and afterward he fell asleep. He was awakened in early afternoon by a knock on the door.

To his surprise, it turned out to be an attorney whom he had met in London the previous year. A dapper, white-haired man by the name of James Hollingsworth, he was one of Gisela's business agents in England.

The man handed Henry a telegram in explanation of his visit. From Gisela, it was a peremptory command for Hollingsworth to travel to Southampton and meet the *Loewengau,* personally seek out Henry aboard the ship, and immediately send her a telegram reporting on his physical well-being.

The reason behind the errand was a mystery to Hollingsworth, until Henry told him what had happened in the train station at Bremerhaven. "The police determined that the man was an anarchist," Henry concluded. "Still, I can't understand why Gisela sent you this telegram. Surely the servant in the private car must have told her I was uninjured."

"It would appear," Hollingsworth said with dry amusement, "that the baroness wanted a second opinion."

"So it would," Henry agreed. "I'm sorry you had to

make such a long trip for so little purpose. Will you come
in and have a drink?"

"I would be delighted to, but I'd better leave it for
another time," Hollingsworth replied. "The crew is almost
ready to haul in the gangplank, so I must leave." He
hesitated, looking at Henry more closely. "You seem a bit
pale, I must say. Are you sure you're quite well?"

"I'd feel much better," Henry temporized, "if I hadn't
been so free with the brandy last evening."

Hollingsworth chuckled. "Anyway, it was a pleasure
seeing you again, Lieutenant Blake. Good-bye."

"The pleasure was mine, Mr. Hollingsworth."

Henry closed the door, sighed in relief, and stepped
back to the bed. He sat down and looked fondly at the
photograph of Gisela he had put on the night table.

Gisela never smiled when she had her likeness made,
and the face in the photograph was the one she turned to
the world rather than to him. But even unsmiling, she was
bewitchingly beautiful. Only days had passed since Henry
had left Grevenhof, but already he felt lonely for her. The
months ahead promised to be long and dreary.

The ship moved away from the pier, and Henry realized it would soon be dinnertime. Knowing he would be
missed if he failed to appear at the captain's table, he got
up from the bed and began dressing in his formal uniform.

As he moved about, the pain in his shoulder became
intense once more. But it was minor compared to the
turmoil of thoughts it evoked. He now knew for certain
that someone was determined to kill him. And he did not
know when or how the next attack would occur.

VII

Orville Beasley's horse cantered along a rutted road through rolling Maryland farmland, the taller buildings of Baltimore barely visible through the heat haze that blurred the horizon behind him.

Two weeks before, while awaiting developments at the Acme Stereopticon Company in the city, he had begun searching the surrounding countryside for a location that fit his requirements. He had soon found a suitable place, and each day since then he had been leaving his hotel early in the morning, a rifle case under his arm, and hiring a horse to ride out of town.

With the black case now resting across the saddle in front of him, Beasley continued on the highway until he reached an overgrown side road that disappeared into a clump of scrub-covered hills.

The soil here was rocky and unsuitable for farming, and the only visible use that had ever been made of the hills was an excavation for a quarry. Even that limited use had apparently proved uneconomical, for the quarry had been abandoned years before. But this barren, isolated place was perfect for Beasley's purpose.

A half hour before, Beasley had passed a large field planted in watermelons. The melons had not been ripe, but he had dismounted and chosen two, each about the size of a man's head, and put them in his saddlebags.

Now, after dismounting near the base of the deserted quarry, he took out the watermelons, put them aside, and then took out two sheets of paper. Using twigs he picked up from the ground, he pinned the sheets to the quarry wall in a place where the dirt was churned up from being struck by bullets during the past days.

After remounting his horse, Beasley rode out of the quarry and up to the overlooking bluffs. He dismounted at a place that he had estimated was the same distance and elevation from the sheets of paper as the office window in Talcott was from the courthouse steps.

Beasley took the rifle out of the case and opened a box of ammunition, reviewing in his mind what he would do in the office on the day that he finally took his revenge. On the floor beside the window he would place a message, weighted down with a silver dollar, warning those in authority to reinstate silver coinage or he would strike again. In the alley behind the building, Farley would be waiting with horses, providing a quick and easy escape in the midst of the confusion.

After loading the rifle, Beasley began shooting at the sheets of paper. He fired several rounds at one, then stepped to the side of the cloud of gunpowder smoke to fire at the other sheet. Then he commenced firing at the two targets in rapid sequence. While he had never been an expert with a rifle, the past days of practice had vastly improved his marksmanship, and nearly every bullet struck one of the sheets of paper.

He had used up several boxes of ammunition in the past days, yet the practice had not become boring to Beasley. Each time he lifted the rifle, he envisioned a large, noisy crowd below. When he aimed the rifle, he saw Representative John Stevens and President Grant over the sights. His lips twisted into a taut, gleeful smile as he fired.

After a while, the sheets of paper pulled free of the twigs and slid to the ground. Beasley mounted his horse and rode back down to the quarry. He had brought the melons to test an idea he had heard about years before. Anything that would make his vengeance and warning more dramatic was worth trying.

Beasley scooped out two small depressions where the sheets of paper had been and wedged the melons into them. Then he rode back up to the edge of the bluff. Using a different box of ammunition, he reloaded the rifle.

The bullets were identical to the others except in one detail. Years before, Beasley had heard that boring a hole in the tip of a bullet would cause it to mushroom upon impact, thus making it far more deadly. Using a sharp nail, he had bored a hole in the tip of each bullet.

Beasley fired at one melon, then stepped to one side of the cloud of gunpowder smoke and fired at the other one. He fanned the smoke away and looked in perplexity. The melons seemed to have completely disappeared. He mounted his horse and rode back down to the quarry.

As he entered the quarry, he saw tiny bits of melon rind around the depressions. Realizing what had happened, he burst into laughter. The melons had apparently exploded when the bullets struck them, the firm, green pulp turning into a thin, glistening smear of color that dampened the soil around the depressions.

Beasley continued laughing, thinking about what the bullets would do to the two men's heads. Even more amusing to him was the terror that the sight would create among the crowd. Immensely satisfied with the results of his target practice that day, he rode out of the quarry and back along the road.

Beasley was still in a buoyant mood as he reentered the city. After returning the horse to the livery stable, he walked back to his hotel. Occasionally he laughed to himself in satisfaction, drawing curious stares from passersby.

Another cause for satisfaction awaited Beasley an hour later. The Acme Stereopticon Company was located a few blocks from his hotel, and after he had put his rifle away in his room, he waited in his accustomed place for the exodus from the building at the end of the day.

As the workers began filing out, Beasley saw the one for whom he was waiting, a young clerk who worked in the mailroom. Every other evening, the man had merely glanced at him and shook his head as he passed. But this time he beckoned surreptitiously, and Beasley followed at a discreet distance.

The clerk stopped and waited in a doorway along the street. When Beasley stepped into the doorway, the man took out a folded sheet of paper. "This is a letter from Marjorie White that arrived in the mail today," he said, glancing around nervously. "After the sales manager read it, I got it back and made a copy of it for the office files."

Beasley took the letter. "Are you sure she has sent nothing else?" he asked.

"I'm positive," the man replied. "We won't get any more slides from her until the sales manager writes and asks for them, and he hasn't written to her. The only other thing we'll get from her are proofs of slides. The sales manager will look at them and pick out a set, then he'll write to her and let her know which ones he wants to list in the catalog."

Beasley nodded and slipped the man a ten-dollar gold piece. "If you receive any of those proofs from her, I want them. I want them, and I don't want anyone else to see them."

"All right—but that'll cause questions," the man muttered, glancing around again. "So it'll cost you more."

"I'll pay more. You just make certain that I get them and that no one else sees them."

The man nodded, then stepped out of the doorway and walked away down the street. Beasley unfolded the letter from Marjorie White and read it. Addressed to the sales manager of the company, it informed him that her business partner had died. A man named Claude Leggett would now be developing her slides, and his address in Chicago was given.

At the end of the letter, there was a reference to slides of the centennial celebration in Talcott. Within the next few weeks, it said, the plates would be developed and proofs sent to the company for a set of slides to be selected from them.

Folding the letter and putting it in his pocket, Beasley thought about what to do. The mailroom clerk would intercept the proofs, which would prevent the distribution of the slides across the country. However, as a safety measure, prudence dictated that the photographic plate made of him in Talcott be destroyed.

Now that he knew where the plate was, he would go to Chicago and destroy it. But there was no need for haste, because weeks would pass before it would be even a remote threat. For now, he decided with a smile, he would stay in Baltimore and continue his target practice at the quarry, using melons and bullets with holes bored in their tips. He had enjoyed that immensely.

The wound on Henry Blake's shoulder had virtually healed by the time he disembarked in New York. Although the physical scar it left was negligible, Henry now had an increased sense of caution that would remain with him for the rest of his life.

In the waiting room of the train station in New York, he sat on a bench that was against the wall. Every so often he unobtrusively scanned the people moving about near him, watching for eyes that were either looking at him or carefully avoiding contact with his own.

When he walked to his train, he automatically avoided passing too close to places where someone might be waiting in hiding for him. And once on the train, he chose a seat at the end of a car, with his back to a wall. By the time he sat down, he had glanced at each person in the car and noted anyone who appeared in the least suspicious. At dinnertime he tipped the steward to seat him at the end of the dining car.

It was early evening when the train arrived in Washington. Despite the financial crisis, the continuing activities of government made the city appear much the same as before, the train station crowded with military personnel and government employees. Now uneasy in large crowds, Henry quickly left the station and went to a hotel.

The next morning, he walked along the bustling streets to the War Department, which was housed in a large building a few blocks from the White House. Henry went straight to the office occupied by his project officer, John Simpson, the deputy undersecretary of war for ordnance.

Simpson was a tall, energetic man in his early forties. After greeting Henry warmly, he took him along a corridor to the office of his own superior, Charles Rollins, the undersecretary of war for matériel. Rollins, a dapper older man with white hair and a mustache, immediately put his other work aside and told the two men to pull up chairs and sit down.

When asked routinely about his voyage, Henry astonished the two men by describing the attempts to kill him in Bremerhaven and on the ship. The formerly cheerful atmosphere in the office abruptly faded, and Simpson and Rollins frowned in concern as they listened.

"And you have no idea of why it happened?" Rollins asked when Henry finished. "Or who instigated it?"

"No, sir," Henry replied. "The man on the ship had documents in his pockets, and I gave them to a friend in the British Foreign Office who promised to have them examined by an expert. I hope that wasn't out of line. In any case, I doubt that they'll reveal anything concrete about who was involved."

"Perhaps it was German military intelligence," Simpson suggested. "They could be worried about your presence at Mauser."

Henry shook his head firmly. "If they wanted me out of there, they would have acted through official channels first, and long ago. And even if they tried to and failed, I would have heard about it through friends."

"I must say," Rollins observed with a touch of dry humor, "you seem to have become very well entrenched over there. I'll have to be careful I don't lose you to the State Department." He sighed. "But the worst thing, of course, would be for you to fall victim to an assassin's bullet or knife."

"Given the fate of your two assailants," Simpson commented, "whoever was behind the attacks must realize he's up against an exceptional adversary. Perhaps that will give him reason to reconsider what he's doing. Fortunately, you're back in your own country now, so you should be safer."

"I certainly hope so," Henry said. "But that won't stop me from trying to grow eyes in the back of my head."

Rollins smiled, but his own eyes still mirrored his concern. After promising to look into the matter as far as diplomatic discretion allowed, he concluded, "Please do be careful, Lieutenant. And in the meantime, of course, if there's any way at all in which we can help, you need only ask." Picking up a page of notes from his desk, he began to talk about the new arms procurement detachment.

"As I recall," he said, looking at Henry, "establishing this detachment was your idea, so it's only fair and logical that you're the one to carry it out. But we've gone ahead and laid the groundwork for you. If I'm not mistaken, the detachment personnel are already in place in Connecticut, aren't they, John?"

"Yes, sir," Simpson replied. "Everything is ready for Lieutenant Blake to take command."

"Good," Rollins said. "Lieutenant, I don't want to rush you on this project, because it is vitally important. Take whatever time you need to organize everything properly." He paused, looking questioningly at Henry. "I realize arrangements have already been made for you to return to the Mauser factory in Germany, and we certainly consider it worthwhile to have you there, but if you think your life may be in danger—"

Henry shook his head. "Sir, I see no reason why I can't finish up what I have to do here in six months or so, and then I'll be more than happy to return to Germany, if that's where my government needs me."

Rollins smiled in satisfaction as he stood up, ending the meeting. "Excellent. Six months sounds good to me, and I'm sure it will to the secretary. And if you need any personal leave, we'll arrange it. In the meantime, as I said, if there's any way we can help you with any problems that arise, please let us know."

Henry thanked Rollins, shook hands with him, and then he and Simpson left the office. They still had many details to discuss, and after taking lunch in Simpson's office, they resumed work.

The key to Henry's plan of the previous year was that most small-arms factories under contract to the government were located in Connecticut, making that state the logical place for a detachment of specialists who would inspect shipments before they were sent to the field. Taking papers out of a folder and handing them to Henry, Simpson explained that an office building had been rented in Hartford, the state capital. A staff of six civilian specialists, five soldiers, and a second lieutenant had been selected and assigned to the detachment.

"They appear to be a good group of personnel," Henry commented, scrutinizing the list Simpson handed him. "Are any arms shipments due out soon from the factories?"

"No, so you should have ample opportunity to get yourself organized." He handed another folder to Henry. "There's one other thing I'd like you to attend to, if you would. Winchester Repeating Arms Company of New Haven has designed a new carbine and will soon have it in production. They've recommended it for the cavalry, so I'd like you to go to the factory, test it, and write a report on it. That folder contains all the correspondence pertaining to it, and I'll let you know when the factory begins production."

They talked a while longer, and it was agreed that Simpson would send a telegram to notify the detachment's second-in-command that Henry would be arriving within the next day or two. When everything was settled, Henry shook hands with Simpson, gathered up his folders, and left.

As he walked back to his hotel, Henry thought about Secretary Rollins's offer to arrange leave for him. Although going to Cindy's wedding was out of the question, he wished that he could find a way to bridge the chasm of misunderstanding between the Holts, the Blakes, and himself. He feared that in breaking his engagement with Cindy, he had alienated them all forever.

Henry especially longed to heal the rift between Toby Holt and himself. The man had been a major force in his life, and they had shared many experiences. But after their last meeting in Chicago the previous year, contact between them had been broken.

Feeling lonely and friendless in his own country, Henry stopped at the registration desk in the hotel lobby and asked the clerk for a telegram form and pen and paper. He sat down at a table and wrote out a telegram to Gisela, informing her that he had arrived safely and giving

her the address of his office in Connecticut. Then he
wrote a short letter to Randolph Churchill in New York,
informing him that he would be in the United States for
the next few months. Leaving the telegram and the letter
with the desk clerk to dispatch, Henry went to his room
and packed his bags.

Henry's train departed Washington before dawn the
following morning and made excellent time up the coast.
There was a slight delay in New York City, and he had to
change trains at New Haven, but he still arrived in Hartford before the end of the work day.

To Henry's surprise, his second-in-command was waiting on the platform. A well-built lieutenant in his early
twenties, the man approached with a briskly energetic
stride as Henry stepped off the train. "Lieutenant Blake?"
he said, saluting. "I'm Walter Stafford, sir, and I'm pleased
to meet you." Stafford had a marked southern drawl, and
Henry recalled from the personnel roster that he was from
South Carolina, a graduate of the Citadel.

"I'm pleased to meet you, Walter," Henry replied,
returning the salute and shaking hands. "I appreciate your
coming to the station."

"I have a carriage waiting, sir, and a man will pick up
your baggage. I trust you had a comfortable journey?"

Henry talked with Stafford as they walked into the
station, and it became immediately apparent to him that
Stafford was a disciplined, dedicated officer, as well as a
true southern gentleman, who must have felt somewhat
out of place in Connecticut.

"I'll certainly do my best here, sir," Stafford said,
"but I was hoping to be assigned to the cavalry. I understand you're assigned to the Mauser factory in Germany.
How did you obtain that plum?"

"The opportunity became available while I was a military observer with the German Army in France."

Noting that the reply imparted very little information, Stafford did not pursue the subject. In front of the station, they boarded the waiting carriage, and as they drove off, Stafford told Henry about the arrangements that had been made for quartering the men. The unmarried soldiers lived in a boardinghouse near the detachment's headquarters, and Stafford himself had rented an apartment in a private home and had made provision for Henry to do the same. After describing the apartment, he said that the arrangements made with the landlord were contingent upon Henry's approval.

"I'm sure I'll be completely satisfied with it," Henry said.

Stafford was somewhat taken aback by Henry's terse replies, and silence fell in the carriage. A few minutes later they arrived at their destination, a large, comfortable home in one of the best residential areas of the city. The only drawback about the apartment, which Stafford had not mentioned, was the woman of the house, Mrs. Curtis. A domineering widow, she clearly resented the economic necessity of taking in a lodger, especially a soldier.

To the young southerner's bemusement, however, the woman's suspicious manner changed before his eyes into eagerness for Henry Blake to accept the apartment. She became almost gushing in the face of the man's urbane, reserved attitude.

When all the arrangements had been settled, Stafford helped Henry carry his bags to his rooms. The young lieutenant noticed that the first thing Henry did was open one of his bags and take out two photographs of a woman.

The pictures, identical except for size, were in ornate gold frames, and Henry put the small one on the bedside table and the large one on the desk in the sitting room. Stafford reflected that although the woman in the pictures was strikingly beautiful, she was unsmiling and looked hard and formidable.

"She is very attractive, sir," he commented. "May I ask her name?"

"Gisela von Kirchberg."

Again, the reply was cordial enough but did not encourage further questions. Stafford dropped the subject, and he and Henry left the apartment and walked at a brisk pace along the wide, tree-lined streets to the detachment's office near the center of the city. Apparently Lieutenant Blake intended to set to work before he had even unpacked, Stafford reflected. Certainly the next few months promised to be busy ones.

On the fifth day after Henry had come to Hartford, two personal letters arrived for him in the mail. One was postmarked London, the other New York.

Opening the letter from London first, Henry found a brief, unsigned note that was obviously from Willoughby, along with an enclosed letter from Alphonse Ferdinand. The note stated that the items Henry had wanted examined were excellent forgeries and that a mutual friend, who would arrive in the United States within a few weeks, would supply more information.

Reflecting that the mutual friend could only be Anderson, Henry opened the letter from Ferdinand. He smiled fondly as he read it. Much of it consisted of repeated thanks for Henry's letter, and there was a page about Ferdinand's improving marksmanship with rifles and pistols.

Next he opened the letter from New York, which was from Randolph Churchill, and he smiled again as he read. Churchill and his fiancée had decided to be married six weeks later in a ceremony at the British consulate in the city. Enclosed with the letter was a wedding invitation. Henry opened the appointment calendar on his desk and marked the date.

The letter for which he was waiting with greatest

anticipation, however, was delivered some three weeks later by Stafford. As the lieutenant handed over the large, heavy envelope, Henry saw the colorful Kirchberg arms embossed on the reverse side. "It's from Germany, sir," Stafford said. "It must be from your lady friend."

Henry smiled. "Yes, it's from her. Thank you very much, Walter."

"You're quite welcome, sir," Stafford said. "I couldn't help but notice the crest on the envelope. Does your lady friend happen to live in a titled household?"

"She is the Baroness von Kirchberg."

The expression of polite inquiry on Stafford's face changed to surprise, and he was speechless for a moment. "Yes, I see," he finally said, and left Henry alone.

Eagerly he opened the envelope and took out the letter. It was very long, some twenty pages filled with the small, even lines of backward-slanted German script in which Gisela always wrote. Smiling and shaking his head in disbelief, Henry looked at the thick stack of pages, then settled himself comfortably in his chair and began reading.

The first part of the letter concerned the incident in Bremerhaven and her distress until she received a telegram from Hollingsworth. There was reference to a complaint she had sent to the minister of justice in Berlin, and Henry chuckled as he read the sentence. Knowing Gisela's tendency for understatement, he was certain that the "complaint" had been more of a harshly threatening protest.

Pages were filled with expressions of love and devotion, with other matters that she considered insignificant scattered among them. She had shipped to him his favorite chair from their sitting room; she had bought him a chinoiserie liquor cabinet and shipped it to him, along with cases of liquor and wine, tins of sweetmeats, and other delicacies.

Reaching the last pages, Henry read more slowly.

When he had finally finished, he sighed in regret. But he also felt less lonely for Gisela, for the letter gave him a sense of contact with her across the miles. He took out pen and paper to write a reply.

He wrote slowly, pausing occasionally to form a ponderous German grammatical construction in his mind. But things to write about kept occurring to him, another thought springing to mind as he completed each sentence. When he had finished, he was surprised to see that hours had passed and that his reply was nearly as long as the letter he had received from Gisela.

VIII

Much had changed since Toby had last seen Portland, but he had little time to look around at the sights as his family and friends greeted him at the packet pier.

The train ride from Chicago to San Francisco had been uneventful—although to the Hemmings children it had been a source of endless fascination—and the Pacific Ocean had been seasonably calm, allowing the coastal steam packet to make good time. Marjorie had been delighted to see her husband, Ted Taylor, awaiting them on the pier, and Toby's sister and children had been there as well, accompanied by Stalking Horse, the foreman of his ranch.

Now, as they all rode out of the city in two wagons, Toby driving the lead wagon with Cindy sitting next to him and Ted and Marjorie in the back, he was pleased to hear the voices of the Hemmings children and Timmy raised in friendly laughter in the other wagon.

"So what do you think of Clara?" Toby asked his sister.

"My first impression was very favorable," Cindy replied. "I believe she'll do fine as a housekeeper and in looking after the children. But she's attractive and still fairly young, and in time she might marry again."

Toby nodded and, glancing back again, reflected that

there were other reasons why Clara might not stay. Stalking Horse was restraining Timmy as the boy tried to climb down to the wagon tongue between the team to demonstrate to the Hemmings children how to walk along it while the wagon was in motion. Janessa had lit a cigarette, and as she puffed on it, Clara regarded her with a stunned expression.

"I understand Andy Brentwood intended to come here for the wedding, if he could," Toby said. "Have you heard from him?"

"Yes, he arrived three days ago," Cindy replied. "He's staying in the bachelor officer quarters over at the fort. He visited the ranch and said he was looking forward to seeing you. Reed brought a lawyer over with some papers for me to read, and Colonel Brentwood came with them."

"Lawyer and papers?" Toby questioned. "To get married?"

Cindy laughed. "The estate Reed's parents left him when they died is in a trust that he receives when he gets married. Quite a large sum is involved, but he never said a word to me about it until he showed up with that lawyer. That's just like him, though. He's never wanted to be anything except a soldier."

Toby nodded, deciding that the present moment was as good as any to broach the delicate subject of his sister's short engagement. "Things developed very suddenly between you two, didn't they?" he commented. "Day after tomorrow, you'll be a married woman. Are you having any second thoughts?"

"Of course not," Cindy replied.

Her answer, Toby noted, was too quick. It sounded almost defensive, which troubled him. Even more worrisome, he could see in her eyes and in the firm line of her chin the stubbornness of a Holt who had decided upon a course of action and was determined to follow it.

"I love you, Cindy," he said quietly. "Your happiness

means a great deal to me, and I hope you're doing what
you really want to do."

"I am, Toby."

Her tone indicated that the subject was not open to
discussion, and in any event, Toby reflected, there was
nothing he could do about it. He smiled at her, and the
hint of friction that had arisen between them faded as they
began talking about other things.

The snowcap on Mount Hood gleamed in the distance
as they reached the ranch. The large, rambling house, a
brick-and-clapboard structure that had expanded around
the original log cabin Whip Holt had built, was far more
than simply home to Toby. It represented something that
was stable and enduring, his point of reference in the
world.

Everyone gathered in the kitchen, where Cindy had
left a big pot of stew in the oven. As the women set the
table and dished up the food, Toby was pleased to see that
Clara was adjusting rapidly. It appeared she had already
discovered that the secret to harmony with Janessa was to
leave her alone; and she seemed as capable as anyone of
controlling Timmy.

The table was crowded, but the food was plentiful
and delicious. After dinner, Toby went out to talk to the
ranch hands and was introduced to Calvin Rogers. Then,
after fetching Cindy's wedding gift—a set of silverware he
had bought in Chicago—he saddled a horse and rode back
through the gathering dusk to the city. He boarded the
Fort Vancouver ferry, and once across the river, he rode
past the town and the fort to the quarters for married
senior officers.

His stepfather and mother lived in a large, comfortable house at the end of the row. Toby knocked on the
door, and his mother opened it. At fifty-five, Eulalia Blake
had a striking, mature beauty that was enhanced by her

smile of delight when she saw Toby. As he embraced and kissed her, his stepfather came out of the parlor.

Nearing seventy, Major General Leland Blake was tall and white-haired. Even without his coat and collar, and with his suspenders slipped off his shoulders for comfort, he was still a commanding figure of a man. He smiled happily as he greeted his stepson.

"This is my wedding present for Cindy and Reed," Toby said as they all went inside.

Taking and opening the case of silverware, Eulalia gasped in pleasure. "It's beautiful, Toby!" she exclaimed. "My word, this must have cost you a pretty penny. I'll put it in the dining room right now with the rest of the presents."

Following his mother into the other room, Toby was impressed as he glanced around. Both Cindy and Reed had many friends, and their wedding presents covered the large dining table as well as the long buffet against the wall.

As Eulalia made room for the silverware, Toby looked more closely at the presents and the calling cards propped in front of them. Andrew Brentwood had brought a set of crystal glasses, and a silver coffee service had Lee and Eulalia Blake's card in front of it. But one present, on a separate table at the end of the buffet, almost dwarfed the rest combined.

It was a full china service for twelve—an array of plates, bowls, and cups of different sizes, together with accessory pieces. Toby stepped to the table and picked up a dish. It was thin, delicate porcelain, with an ornate floral pattern edged in gold leaf. The mark on the bottom of the dish was Meissen of Germany.

Instead of the usual card with the china, there was a European style *carte de visite*. Henry Blake's photograph was on it, with his rank in German and his first name in its Germanic form. Toby was speechless for a moment, amazed over the valuable set of china. It must have cost well over a thousand dollars—far more than Henry could afford on a first lieutenant's pay.

"Henry certainly was generous," Toby commented. "He must have spent a year's pay on this."

"It cost more than that," Eulalia said acidly. "He was undoubtedly trying to ease his guilty conscience." She sighed, her love of beautiful things overcoming her resentment. Picking up a dish, she smiled wistfully as she looked at it. "It's almost transparent, yet you'd be surprised how strong it is, Toby. Even the sharpest knife won't scratch the glaze on these plates." She put the dish back down, and Toby thought she looked sad as she turned away from the table.

In the parlor, Eulalia told Toby about the wedding plans. There were too many guests to have the wedding at the fort chapel and the reception at her home, so the ceremony would be at a church in Portland, and the reception would be in a tent at the fairgrounds. Andrew Brentwood and some soldiers from the fort would be putting up the tent the following morning.

"Maybe I'll have time to give them a hand," Toby said. "I'll stop at the fort and see Andy before I go back across the river."

Lee paused in filling his pipe. "You'll probably find him in the officers' mess, Toby. I meant to ask—how is your lumber business in Chicago faring?"

Toby shook his head ruefully. "Not so well right now, sir. But I'm afraid it's out of my hands. You see, I've been asked to perform a mission for the government—one that I can say very little about. In the meantime, I've had to hire a manager to run my company. It may go under, or it may not."

"We certainly hope it doesn't, Toby," Eulalia said. She purposely avoided the subject of his special mission. "Lee and I were talking the other night about what you might do concerning Janessa and Timmy after Cindy is married. If you wish, I'll look after them."

Toby thanked his mother, then explained that he had hired a woman to be housekeeper at the ranch. Eulalia nodded in approval.

"Well, I'm pleased that you found someone suitable," she said. "But what you really need to do is get married again. You need a wife, and those children need a mother."

"No, no," Toby chuckled. "The two things a man should never look for are trouble and a wife. If he finds either, he should deal with it then. But he should never go looking for them."

Eulalia frowned as Lee burst into hearty laughter. "You men," she said in resignation. Suddenly a thought occurred to her. "Toby, will what you're doing for the government occupy your time completely during the next few weeks?"

Toby shook his head. "I'll probably be involved in it for months, but it won't take every moment of my time. Why do you ask?"

"I received a letter from a distant cousin of mine." She stood up and went to a cabinet. "His name is Alex Woodling, and he owns a horse farm near Lexington, Kentucky." She opened a drawer, took out a letter, and handed it to Toby. "His farm isn't doing well, and he asked for advice on selling horses to the cavalry."

Toby opened the letter and read it. The writing style was that of an earlier generation, the sentences ponderous and old-fashioned, and most of the letter consisted of apologies for asking Eulalia's help. The sentiments were evocative of a sincere, courteous man, and Toby felt favorably inclined toward the writer, even though he had never heard of him before.

Lee Blake puffed on his pipe and didn't speak until Toby had finished reading. "The cavalry is buying very few horses now, Toby," he said. "However, Eulalia and I have discussed it, and the man is family. We're willing to make him a loan, if that will help, but this is a matter better dealt with in person. Would you be able to visit him and discuss it with him?"

"Yes, sir," Toby replied, folding and pocketing the letter. "In fact, I'd intended to go to Kentucky when I left here, so it'll be no trouble. But it may be a few weeks before I get to Lexington."

"That's quite all right," Eulalia said. "I'll write to him and let him know that you'll be visiting. If he'll accept a loan, we can have the money transferred to a bank in Lexington."

Toby nodded and stood up. "I'll let you know what he says. It's getting late, so I'd better be on my way." He shook hands with Lee, then followed his mother out.

At the door he kissed her good night, but he had one more thing to say before he left. "It seems to me, Mama, that Cindy decided very quickly to marry Reed. Too quickly, in fact. I tried to talk to her about it, but I couldn't get anywhere."

Eulalia frowned. "I tried to discuss it with her, too, but she didn't want to talk about it. She told me she had made up her mind, and that was the end of it. But she's an adult, after all, and no one else can or should try to make up her mind for her."

"Yes, that's true," Toby agreed. "Well, perhaps I'm looking for a problem where there isn't any. Good night, Mama."

"Good night, Toby."

Toby rode the short distance to the fort and across the quadrangle to the officers' mess. It was one of the original buildings of the fort, and its small windows glowed brightly in the darkness. Toby took off his hat and ducked his head as he went through the low doorway.

Furnished and paneled in solid oak, the room brought to mind a small, expensive restaurant, but the flags, sa-

bers, and battle honors on the walls lent a military atmosphere. The room was quiet and almost empty. Andrew
Brentwood, Reed Kerr, and two other officers were seated
at a corner table.

Exclaiming happily, Andrew stood up and stepped
toward Toby as he came in. Dark-haired and with strong,
chiseled features, Andy Brentwood, at only thirty-four
years of age, was one of the youngest colonels in the army.
He gripped Toby's hand. "So you're finally here, Toby,"
he said. "I've been looking forward to seeing you again."

"No more than I've been looking forward to seeing
you, Andy," Toby said. "How are Susanna and little Sam?"

"They're fine," Andrew replied. "Susanna wanted to
come here with me, but she's helping my mother with the
shipping business in Independence. Business is very poor,
and she couldn't leave."

"I can well understand," Toby said wryly. He turned
to Reed and shook hands with him. "Well, Reed, within a
couple of days I'll be greeting you as a relative, won't I?"

"Yes, sir," Reed said with a smile. "And that'll be the
happiest day of my life. You know Lieutenant Aberly and
Captain Thompson, don't you?"

Toby greeted the two officers, exchanged a few words
with them, then turned back to Andrew. "Andy, I just
dropped in to see you for a moment and have to be on my
way. But I understand you'll be at the fairgrounds tomorrow to put up the tent for the reception. I'll give you a
hand, if you don't mind, and we can talk then."

"I'll look forward to it, Toby."

As Toby rode out of the fort, he felt less uneasy about
Cindy's marriage. Reed Kerr was a forthright, honest man
with the bearing of a leader, a fine army officer. He had
many good qualities, and if Cindy loved him, nothing else
mattered.

Their engagement had been a short one, but that was
not so unusual. And as his mother had said, it was Cindy's

decision. As he rode down the hill toward the ferry slip, Toby dismissed his doubts about the approaching wedding.

The next morning began in a rush of activity at the Holt ranch. Breakfast was delicious if noisy in the crowded kitchen—thick slices of sugar-cured ham, eggs, hot biscuits, and strong coffee. Shortly after the meal, Ted and Marjorie left for town to find a photography studio where Marjorie could develop some photographic plates, and Calvin Rogers drove up in the wagon to take Timmy to school. Clara Hemmings led her children out to join them, intending to enroll all three before classes ended for the summer. Janessa, who customarily remained in town after school in order to study medicine and Latin with old Dr. Martin, went to saddle her mare to follow them.

Toby accompanied her to the corral. "I'll have to leave the day after the wedding," he said, tightening the saddle girth for her. "That won't give me as much time to spend with you as I'd like. In fact, no amount of time would be enough." He smiled as he helped Janessa up to the saddle. "But I'll make time, because I want to have some long talks with you."

"There *are* some things I need to discuss," Janessa said, gathering up her reins. She looked troubled and avoided Toby's gaze. "In fact, there's something I should probably mention to you right away, but I'm not sure if it wouldn't just be tattling."

Toby frowned. "If it's something you feel you should say, then you probably should, Janessa. Besides, I know you're not a tattler."

Janessa deliberated a moment, then spoke quietly. "Timmy's been acting like he's up to something, sneaking around. Usually I can tell what he's doing, but this time I haven't been able to. It's the same way he was acting before he hurt himself with that kite."

"That certainly isn't tattling," Toby said firmly. "I'm glad you told me, and I'll look into it."

Toby waved as his daughter rode away. Whatever Timmy was doing, he thought, it had to be something he was working on with Calvin Rogers. Toby wondered if the man could be a bad influence. The last thing Timmy needed was someone to help him get into dangerous situations, because the boy was all too capable of doing that by himself.

He dismissed the problem for the moment and went to talk to Stalking Horse about the business affairs of the ranch. After Calvin Rogers returned from town with the wagon and had dropped off Clara Hemmings at the house, Toby went to have a word with him.

As the thin, pale man descended with his cane from the wagon, Toby felt sorry for him. But his son's safety came first, and Toby was determined to get at the truth.

"Calvin, I'd like to talk with you about the things you and Timmy are working on," he said.

"Yes, sir, Mr. Holt," Calvin replied with a smile. "We keep them over here in this shed. I'll show you."

They walked to the shed, the man limping on his cane and describing what he and Timmy had been doing. It sounded innocent enough, and it looked perfectly safe when they went into the shed and Calvin began showing the various projects to Toby. For a moment, Toby even forgot the purpose of the interview, so surprised and pleased he was to discover that Timmy apparently had a grasp of scientific principles far in advance of his years.

"He's learned quite a bit about block and tackles," Calvin said, pointing to a set of pulleys hanging on the wall. "He also picked up the various applications of gear assemblies so fast that it amazed me. When he gets some grounding in mathematics, he'll be able to design them himself."

Toby shook his head in disbelief. "The boy has always

been interested in mechanical things, but I didn't realize he was this far along."

"He seems to have an innate ability in mechanics," Calvin said. "There's no telling what he'll be able to do once he has a few years of school behind him." He took down from the wall an assembly of newspaper glued over thin strips of wood. "But his main interest is in things that fly. He designed this glider himself."

Toby was abruptly reminded of his purpose in talking with the man. "And this is all you've been working on with Timmy?" he asked, glancing around.

Calvin hesitated. "Well, no, Mr. Holt. We're building a much larger glider in the woods up at the head of the creek. It's too large to carry back and forth, and we're going to try out a different means of propulsion on it. We've been working on it for a few weeks, and Timmy is very, very excited about it."

"He doesn't intend to try to fly on it himself, does he?" Toby asked. "I'm pleased that he has interests like this, but I don't want him getting hurt."

"Of course you don't," Calvin said quietly. "And you can be assured that I won't let him, Mr. Holt. And he won't be flying on anything. If I'd been here when he tried to fly with that kite, he wouldn't have tried it."

The man's voice rang with sincerity, and Toby could see that he was extremely fond of Timmy. Thinking for a moment, Toby concluded that Timmy had been viewing the project in the woods as a secret—which a boy naturally would—and had thereby stirred Janessa's suspicions. He nodded, satisfied. "I couldn't ask for any better assurance than that. Is there anything I could buy that would help Timmy in his interests?"

Calvin pondered for a moment. "Well, actually there is, Mr. Holt. A farmer along the road named Jake Willis has an old road locomotive that a relative gave him, and he's never had it in operating condition. He might sell it

for a few dollars. Even if it could never be repaired, I'm
sure Timmy would enjoy working on it."

"All right, I'll go talk to Jake about it. He's so tight-
fisted, though, that he makes the eagles on coins squeal."

Toby felt relieved having spoken to Calvin Rogers,
and later, on his way to Portland to help Andrew with the
reception tent, he stopped at the Willis farm and managed
to bargain the old man down to twelve dollars for what
Willis himself admitted was "the most expensive chicken
roost west of the Mississippi." Toby even got the man to
agree to haul the machine by oxen to the Holt ranch.

When Toby reached the Portland fairgrounds, a half
dozen soldiers were busy unloading wooden tables and
benches from a wagon. Nearby, other soldiers were spreading a huge tent on the ground and preparing to raise it.

Andrew Brentwood, in his shirtsleeves along with the
other soldiers, was helping with the tent. After waving a
greeting, Toby tethered his horse in the shade, took off his
coat, and walked over to help the soldiers positioning the
two long, heavy poles that supported the peak of the tent.
When they were in place, the other soldiers came over to
help, and with everyone gripping the guy ropes and pulling, the two poles rose into the air, the canvas fabric
draping down around them. The men then began pegging
down the ropes, and the tent quickly took shape.

Later, with the sides rolled up and the breeze sweep-
ing through the tent, Toby and Andrew sat at one of the
benches and talked. The other soldiers, their work finished, had departed, and Eulalia had not yet arrived to
take charge of the decorations.

"Reed is a fine officer," Andrew was saying, "and I'm
sure he and Cindy will be very happy. But to be truthful
about it, Toby, I can't help but regret that circumstances
came between Cindy and Henry Blake."

"Circumstances?" Toby questioned. "You can call it
that if you like, Andy, but Henry Blake made those cir-

cumstances himself. He became involved with that German woman, so it isn't as though some misfortune intervened. Henry did it himself."

Andrew frowned, taking out his pipe and tobacco pouch. As he began filling the pipe, he slowly shook his head. "I know that you and Henry were like brothers, so this is something that I can't let stand the way it is. But before I go on, I must ask you to treat what I tell you with utmost discretion. It shouldn't go beyond you and your parents."

"Yes, of course," Toby said, puzzled.

Andrew lit his pipe, then continued. "Henry discussed the situation with you in Chicago last year, didn't he? How much do you know about the woman he became involved with?"

"Not very much," Toby replied. "I know that she's German, but for some reason she was in France when Henry met her. He said that she owns a grocery business— and that's about all I know."

Andrew looked up in surprise. "Henry didn't make himself quite clear, I'm afraid. She had a foodstuffs wholesale firm at one time, but she expanded it into an immense fortune. The reason she was in France was to rush into Paris with tons of food the moment the German siege was lifted. The populace had been starving, of course, and she charged enough to carry off a good part of the gold in Paris by the time food began arriving from other places."

"You mean she charged starving people exorbitant prices for food?" Toby commented in disapproval. "To say the least, Andy, I don't admire the way she chose to make her money."

"Neither do I, but it tells you something about her. Certainly she's different from any woman I've ever met. In any event, Henry became involved with her because I ordered him to get to know her as well as he could."

It was Toby's turn to be surprised. Andy went on to

explain that the military observer detachment he had commanded in France, to which Henry had been assigned, had been gleaning very few facts of value before Henry met the woman. Then she had begun providing priceless information, and Henry's intelligence reports had been read with keen interest at the highest levels in Washington.

"And through her," Andrew continued, "Henry knew in advance when Paris would surrender. That information enabled Washington to take actions that will be of benefit to the country for years to come. It also got Henry promoted to first lieutenant, as you may recall."

"How did she get all this information, Andy?" Toby asked.

"Well, she's a baroness—the Baroness von Kirchberg— and she lived in the town where all the German generals were quartered." He nodded as Toby looked surprised again. "Henry didn't mention that? Well, that's characteristic of him. She's the same one who arranged for him to be posted at Mauser Arms Works, and through her he has social access to the highest political circles in Germany. He's undoubtedly been sending reports of incalculable value to Washington."

"I can see why all this must be treated with discretion," Toby commented, still frowning. "Something that puzzled me has also been explained. The wedding gift from Henry is far too expensive for a first lieutenant to afford."

"Yes, the baroness probably sent it," Andrew said. "She undoubtedly does things for him now and then, but at the same time I'm sure Henry has no interest at all in her money."

Toby had to agree. "I'm sure he wouldn't. Yet I have to wonder what does interest him in her. I don't think I could stay in the same room with a woman who charged starving people high prices for food."

Andrew puffed on his pipe and shrugged. "There's

more to her than that, Toby. She's remarkably beautiful, and she can be equally charming, when she chooses. What impressed me most when I met her was her intelligence, though. I've little doubt that if she was a man and interested in politics, she would be in Bismarck's chair at this very moment."

"Do you think she simply manipulated Henry, then?"

"Not to any great extent," Andrew replied, "because Henry has a sharp mind himself. No, what drew him to her, I believe, was the woman's sheer intensity of character. She adores Henry, and I don't think any man could resist her."

Hearing a carriage approaching, Toby turned. It was an army vehicle from the fort, and he could see his mother in the cab. "I certainly appreciate your telling me about this, Andy," he said as they stepped out of the tent. "Now I understand what happened."

"I felt that I had to explain Henry's side of it. I wish I could explain it to the general and your mother, but I've never mentioned it to them, of course."

"No, you couldn't. They'd get angry if you even brought up his name."

"That's what I thought. Maybe you could get them to listen, though. Just please remember what I said about discretion."

"Yes, I will. When I find the right moment, I'll talk to the general and explain it to him. But it would be pointless to tell Mama about it now. She simply has a closed mind on some things."

Andrew nodded in agreement, and the conversation ended as the carriage drew up and Toby stepped forward to open the door and help his mother down.

Eulalia had several boxes of bunting and colorful garlands with her, and in a matter of minutes she had Toby, Andrew, and even the carriage driver hard at work decorating the tent. Telling his mother about Henry, Toby decided, was the last thing he wanted to do.

When Toby returned alone to the ranch late in the afternoon, he found that the road locomotive had already been delivered. Timmy, home from school, raced around from behind the main barn to thank him for it.

Covered with rust from climbing around on the machine, the boy was exuberant. "I never dreamed I'd have my own road locomotive, Dad," he said in delight. "It's the best present you could ever get for me!"

"I'm glad you like it, Timmy," Toby chuckled. "Just be careful and don't hurt yourself—"

The boy was already running back to the barn. Toby finished unsaddling his horse, then joined Cindy, Clara, and Ted and Marjorie, who were seated around the lawn table in the shade, drinking lemonade. Janessa came out with a glass for him, then handed Marjorie a letter, telling her that it had been among the mail a ranch hand had just picked up at the post office.

"It's from Jason Whitmore, in Boston," Marjorie said, looking at the writing and opening the envelope. "If everyone will excuse me, I'll see what he has to say." She read the first page and smiled. "He's already rented your house, Clara, for the amount we suggested. As soon as you establish a bank account here, he'll start having the rental payments transferred to it."

Marjorie frowned, however, as she read on. Separating a smaller piece of paper enclosed with the letter, she glanced in puzzlement between it and the letter.

"Is something wrong?" Ted asked quietly.

Marjorie shook her head. "No, it's simply strange, Ted. A man named Howard Cummings asked for my address. Jason didn't like the way he acted, so he told him to write down his own address and said he would send it to me. This is it here."

"Why did he want your address?" Ted asked.

Marjorie shrugged. "Cummings told Jason that he met me in Connecticut and I agreed to sell him some photographs. But that simply isn't true. I didn't meet anyone there with that name."

Ted leaned over and took the piece of paper from Marjorie. "Did you have any arguments in Connecticut or do anything there to make someone mad at you?" he asked.

Cindy laughed and interjected a comment. "The man was only trying to get your address, Marjorie," she said, winking. "You should tell your friend Jason to send messages like that only when Ted isn't around."

All three women laughed, but Ted repeated his question: "Did you have any arguments there to do anything to make someone mad at you?"

Everyone sobered, including Marjorie. She thought for a moment, then shook her head. "No, nothing happened, Ted. This man Cummings must have confused me with someone else. I'm sure it's simply a mistake."

Clara and Cindy both agreed. Marjorie put the letter back into the envelope, dismissing it as she and the other two women began discussing the wedding.

Ted exchanged a glance with Toby. Toby saw that the young lawman's instincts had been alerted and that Ted did not think the incident had been a mistake or a coincidence. Neither did Toby.

IX

Standing in the position of best man, Toby observed that Cindy was nervous during the wedding ceremony— the first time he recalled ever seeing her nervous. Although he tried to dismiss the thought, he wondered if she was thinking about Henry Blake, as he was.

Reed Kerr was also nervous, his hand unsteady when Toby gave him the ring. But the two of them, Toby reflected, made an extremely handsome couple. Cindy was strikingly beautiful in her long white dress and train, and Reed was the epitome of a fine young officer in his dress uniform.

Cindy's stepfather, Leland Blake, was tall and stiffly straight in his major general's uniform. Janessa was the maid of honor, and Toby thought she looked charming in her frilly dress.

The church was crowded, but the only sound was the minister's voice. When the ceremony drew to an end, however, and Cindy and Reed kissed, the silence was broken as the guests began talking excitedly. Everyone stood up, and the young officers among the congregation crowded toward the altar to demand their kiss from Cindy.

Toby took Janessa aside. "Well, I suppose we might as well wait outside," he suggested. But Ted was already helping Marjorie to bring up her camera and equipment cases from a corner of the church, and Toby and Janessa were required to pose for pictures of the wedding party. Eulalia, wiping away tears, joined the group.

Later, as the wedding procession made its way toward the fairgrounds, people on the streets laughed and waved to the passing carriages. Toby waved back. "This is probably the largest wedding Portland has seen for quite a while," he commented to Janessa, who was sitting next to him.

"It's the biggest one I've ever seen," Janessa said. "It was a beautiful ceremony, but I still think the groom doesn't deserve the bride."

Toby smiled, reflecting that in Janessa's opinion no man deserved Cindy. The previous evening, he and Janessa had talked for a while, and for the first time he had realized the intensity of the emotional attachment between his sister and daughter. It was difficult to believe there had been friction between them when they had first met.

The procession reached the fairgrounds, and the regimental band inside the tent struck up the traditional wedding march. The vehicles pulled to a halt, and the guests flooded into the tent, applauding when the bride and groom followed.

The music changed to a waltz, and the guests stood back as Cindy and Reed took a turn around the dance floor. Soon others began choosing partners and joining them, and Toby danced with Janessa, Marjorie, Eulalia, and Cindy in turn. When he finally left the dance floor, Toby received many sidelong glances from young women who would have readily accepted an invitation to be his partner. Indeed, both Cindy and Marjorie had teased him that he was one of the most eligible bachelors at the gathering and clearly the focus of feminine attention. Since returning to Portland, however, Toby had not had many opportunities to talk with Janessa, which he enjoyed more than anything else, and he decided to get himself something to drink and seek her out.

Word had already spread among the guests about how delicious the Oberg Beer was, and Toby had to stand in line with the men to get a mug for himself. He found Janessa sitting alone at a table in a far corner of the tent, somewhat out of place in the gathering.

The subject she immediately brought up was unexpected, to say the least. "Dad, Dr. Martin told me that you know Dr. Wizneuski, who now spends part of his time as the director of the charity hospital in town. Dr. Martin has talked to him, and he's agreed to let me work with the two of them at the hospital. But Clara and Grandmother will probably object to it, unless they know I have your permission. Do I? And will you talk to them?"

Taking a sip of beer, Toby reflected that his mother would object very strongly for a variety of reasons, beginning with the fact that Janessa would be seeing people in a state of undress. He himself did not like the idea of her working at the hospital, since the patients there included seamen crippled by venereal disease, dockworkers injured in drunken brawls, and others of similar dissolute character.

Yet Toby had always been in favor of having Janessa study with the doctor; she already had been trained in herbal medicine by her late mother. Still, she was very young to be working at a charity hospital. "Janessa, you're only twelve years old," he said. "Wouldn't it be better to wait and get practical experience when you go to medical school?"

"It isn't really for practical experience, Dad," she replied. "The reason I want to do this is to watch Dr. Martin try out some new procedures in medicine."

"What sort of procedures?"

"Antisepsis, for example. Some doctors believe that using a solution of diluted carbolic on open wounds and amputations kills germs that cause infection and gangrene. It's been debated for years, and Dr. Martin has had good results with it. He wants to try it some more."

Recalling the times he had been in army hospitals during the Civil War, Toby reflected that more patients had died from infection than from wounds. "But some doctors don't believe it's effective?"

Janessa nodded. "They say that the discharge from wounds is normal and healthy, and they don't want to do anything to stop it. But Dr. Martin says there are other reasons they're afraid to try it. A doctor who uses a procedure that hasn't been proved over the years is at risk of being sued if the patient dies."

Toby nodded. "I understand. What do you think your mother would have thought about it?"

Janessa shrugged. "I don't know. Herbal healers just treat symptoms, Dr. Martin says. They don't deal with the nature of disease or with germ theory."

Toby took another sip of beer, still not quite used to his daughter's matter-of-fact conversational manner. He could just as well have been talking to an adult.

"It's been said," he offered, "that there's nothing more honorable than healing the ill, and the last thing I want to do is discourage you. However, I feel I have to consider your age, so I'll tell you what I'll do. If you'll agree to work only in the women's and children's ward, I'll tell your grandmother and Clara you have my permission—"

"Oh, thank you, Dad!" Janessa burst out, a rare, brilliant smile wreathing her face as she hugged him. "Thank you so much."

Amused by her quick agreement, Toby chuckled. "Is that a better deal than you were expecting, honey?"

"Yes, sir," Janessa replied candidly. "I thought you might say only the children's ward."

They both laughed heartily, and as the music continued booming, the young couples dancing and enjoying themselves, no one found more pleasure in the passing hours than Toby, who was content to sit and talk with Janessa.

Their conversation was interrupted when the band played a fanfare and Cindy stood on the bandstand to toss her bouquet. There was an outburst of merriment as a young woman caught it, and then Cindy and Reed left. The music and dancing quickly resumed.

An hour later, there was another interruption. Several guests who were standing outside the tent began shouting and pointing to the sky. Soon everyone was hurrying outside, gazing upward and exclaiming in astonishment. The excitement quickly spread to the street adjacent to the fairgrounds, where people were emerging from their houses and looking up at the sky.

Some of the people were speculating that the object was an extraordinarily strange bird, but at first glance Toby saw that it was manufactured. However, it was an amazing sight, defying the law of gravity and flying like a bird, except that its wings did not flap.

"What in the world do you think it is?" Janessa exclaimed.

"I don't know," Toby replied. "As far as I can recall, I've never heard or read of anything like that, Janessa."

"Whatever it is, it's pretty big."

Toby voiced his agreement. Although the object was high in the air, he could see that it was much larger than any bird. The wings looked to be at least fifteen feet from tip to tip. The slender body appeared about as long, and there was another, smaller set of wings at the rear. Most astonishingly, smoke trailed from under the wings as the object flew from south to north over the edge of the city. Already at an altitude of a thousand feet or more, it was gradually climbing higher.

Delighted and curious cries arose from the people watching. A social reporter from the newspaper was frantically sketching in his notebook.

By now the object was moving away from the fairgrounds, and some in the crowd began running after it. As

Toby gazed upward, he thought the shape of the flying object seemed strangely familiar. And the smoke flowing back from the wings was even more familiar. It looked exactly like the smoke trails from Hale rockets.

As he was watching, the smoke from the left wing thinned to a wisp and disappeared, and the object began turning in a wide circle and descending. "Dad, it's coming down!" Janessa exclaimed excitedly. "Where do you think it will fall?"

"It's hard to say," Toby replied. "It seems to be circling back. . . ."

As he spoke, the smoke from the right wing thinned to a trickle, and the object began spiraling downward more rapidly. The people around the tent spread out, trying to anticipate where the object would fall so they could examine it more closely. Toby took Janessa by the hand and began walking with her in the general direction the crowd was taking.

As the object descended, Toby saw that the smoke had indeed been coming from Hale rocket propulsion units, which were fastened under the wings. Sparks still trailed from the smoldering cardboard tubes. The entire construction looked primitive, with cloth covering a wooden frame, but it remained the most intriguing, ingenious thing Toby had ever seen.

A roar of cheers rang out as the object cleared a tall tree and skimmed lower in a wide circle. It glided over the tethered horses and vehicles, causing the animals to plunge and buck in fear. Moving at a high speed now, it circled over the tent and veered toward the street.

The people on the fairgrounds excitedly gave chase, while those in the street scattered and fled out of the object's path as it bore down on them. Toby, still holding Janessa's hand, was in the forefront of those racing toward the street. They watched as the flying object zoomed between a house belonging to Horace Biddle, a storekeeper in the city, and the adjacent house.

Abruptly it slammed into the top of the outhouse behind the Biddle home and crumpled to the ground. In a matter of seconds, the smoldering rocket tubes ignited the broken mass of fabric and wood, and as flames began to leap up, a collective groan of disappointment rose from the approaching crowd. The groans ceased, however, when a penetrating shriek of fright issued from inside the outhouse.

The wooden door flew open. Winifred Biddle, a heavy-set woman of fifty, ran out with her skirt hiked up as she tugged at her underwear. Stopping and turning, she looked back in astonishment at the flames beginning to envelop the outhouse. Then, suddenly becoming aware of the scores of people watching, she gaped at the crowd and froze.

For a moment Winifred was motionless, gripping the waistband of her underwear, with her skirt still up around her ample thighs. Her eyes were wide, but her brain still refused to believe that a flaming object had just fallen from the sky onto her outhouse and that her backyard was filled with an audience to observe her panic-stricken exit.

The crowd was also silent and motionless, sharing Winifred's astonishment. Then someone began laughing. The laughter immediately spread through the crowd, and Winifred, her face turning crimson with mortification, flipped down her skirt, raced to her back porch, and disappeared into the house as she shouted to one of her children to go get their father.

It was at that instant that Toby recalled where he had seen something similar to the object. But before he could say anything, Janessa spoke.

"Dad," she said, "Timmy and Calvin Rogers made that thing. That's why Timmy's been sneaking around lately."

Toby nodded, realizing that the glider Calvin had shown him was simply a smaller-scale replica of what he and Timmy had been building in the woods, minus the

Hale rockets. It was undeniably ingenious, but it had also resulted in someone's property being damaged.

People were pushing past him, gathering around the burning outhouse. Leading Janessa, Toby picked his way out of the crowd, intending to return to the ranch to fetch Timmy and Calvin and make them face Horace Biddle with what they had done. But he and Janessa were still walking back to the fairgrounds when they saw Calvin and Timmy themselves, driving quickly toward the city in the wagon. The Hemmings children were with them, along with several ranch hands who had not attended the wedding. All of them were laughing and talking excitedly.

"Say, Mr. Holt," one of the ranch hands called, "did you see that glider contraption? When it flew up out of the woods and over the ranch, we thought the world was coming to an end!"

"Yes, I saw it," Toby replied. "It landed on Horace Biddle's outhouse. No one was hurt, luckily, but it burned down the outhouse."

The laughter faded, and Timmy's wide grin changed into an expression of guilt. Calvin bowed his head contritely. "It was all my fault, Mr. Holt," he said. "I thought the glider would go a different way, where it wouldn't damage anything. After all you've done for me, I'm very sorry for having caused you this trouble."

"Well," Toby replied calmly, "we don't know yet what trouble has been caused. Horace Biddle is the one who'll have to decide that. If it's only money he wants to fix the outhouse, I'll take care of that. But we'll have to go and talk with him."

Calvin nodded regretfully and apologized again. Toby and Janessa hopped into the wagon and rode with them the short distance back to the Biddle house.

A large crowd of people were still in the Biddles' backyard. Horace Biddle had come home from his store and was talking to the newspaper reporter, speculating along with the other bystanders as to what had crashed into the outhouse.

Toby led Calvin and Timmy through the crowd and greeted Biddle, then stood aside as Calvin explained what had happened. Biddle and the others listened in silent amazement.

"They've come to apologize for what happened," Toby interrupted as people in the crowd started to shout questions. "And, of course, Mr. Biddle, we'll make whatever compensation you think is fair."

"Compensation?" the portly storekeeper said, clearly surprised. "Toby, I don't want any compensation, or any apologies, for that matter. That necessary house didn't cost me more than fifty cents' worth of crude lumber anyway." He shook his head, looking at the remains of the glider. "I still can't believe that contraption flew all the way from your ranch to here."

Calvin assured him that it had, and the newspaper reporter, who had been writing in his notebook as he listened, interjected a question: "Was this an original experiment, or has it been done by someone else?"

"As far as I know," Calvin replied proudly, "Timmy and I were the first to do it. I haven't read about anything similar, and I try to keep up with the latest experiments in flight."

"So do I," the reporter said eagerly, "and I haven't read about anything like this ever being done before. That glider will be of great interest throughout the country. What do you intend to undertake next?"

Leaning on his cane, Calvin hesitated and turned to Toby, who answered the question for him: "Calvin Rogers and Timmy Holt will be working on a road locomotive that was being used as a chicken roost," he said. "I doubt if it will ever run again, so it certainly won't fly."

Calvin laughed, nodding in agreement, and Biddle joined in the laughter spreading through the crowd.

Only Timmy remained silent, staring intently at the wreckage of all his hard work.

The city was still teeming with excitement over the glider when Toby rode to the docks at sunset to take the ferry to Fort Vancouver. People were laughing and relating their reactions to the sight, and Toby was approached several times on the street to be told it was a fascinating display, the most amazing thing anyone had ever seen.

The ferry itself was almost deserted, and the laughter and excitement of the day were left behind as he crossed the river. Toby felt a strange, lonely nostalgia. The wedding had been a happy event, but it had also marked a change in his own life, separating him from Cindy.

When he reached the other side of the river, he saw that his feelings were shared by another. A few hundred yards upriver from the ferry slip, he spotted Lee Blake sitting on his horse on a grassy knoll, the place where the the general went when he wanted to be by himself. Straight and tall in the saddle despite his years, he was staring out over the river.

Reluctant to intrude upon his stepfather's moment of solitude, Toby decided to ride to the house first, but Lee saw him and waved. A short while later Toby reined up and exchanged greetings with his stepfather.

"If you want to be alone, sir," Toby said, "I'll certainly understand. People need to be by themselves now and then."

Lee smiled and shook his head. "Eulalia is the one who needs to be alone, so I came here. She's feeling a bit sad, Toby, as mothers do when their daughters marry. However, I feel somewhat the same myself. When you get older, you'll find that certain milestones in life are a cause for reflection and sadness, even if the event is a happy one."

"Then I must be getting older, sir," Toby replied

with a smile. "The same thing was running through my mind as I crossed the river."

Lee smiled back. "Did you come over to talk with your mother about something?"

"Yes, but it can wait until tomorrow," Toby said. "Janessa will be working with Dr. Martin at the charity hospital, and I want Mama to know that she has my permission to do so."

Lee shook his head in wry amusement. "I'm glad I won't be the one to tell her that."

"There's also something I'd like to discuss with you, sir," Toby continued. "And you may have as hard a time understanding and accepting it as Mama will have with Janessa's working at the hospital. It concerns the reasons that Henry broke his engagement with Cindy."

The humor disappeared from Lee Blake's face. His aged, weathered features settled into the stony lines of the hurt and disappointment Henry had caused when he ended the engagement. "There's very little that's fit to say on that subject," Lee said quietly.

"I've found out some facts you aren't aware of, sir. I'd like for you to hear me out, at least."

"I'm listening," Lee replied curtly.

The sun was setting in a blaze of color as Toby began relating what Andrew Brentwood had told him. The scattered clouds, tinted a reddish gold, made shimmering reflections in the broad, rippling expanse of the river. As the sun sank lower, the reflections changed shade, darkened, and slowly disappeared.

When Toby had finished talking, the expression on Lee Blake's face had not altered, but his eyes had changed. The pain and disappointment in them had been replaced by tears that gleamed in the last light of day.

He was silent for a long moment; then he cleared his throat and nodded. "I appreciate your telling me about that, Toby."

"I thought it best, sir. While we might not like or agree with Henry's reasons for doing what he did, at least we know he had reasons for doing it. I don't think Mama could understand, but I can, and I knew that you would as well."

Lee sighed heavily and looked away. "I'm an old man, and my life has been an eventful one," he said. "But two days stand out above all others. One was when I married your mother, and the other was when I adopted Hank. I finally had a son, and no father has ever had more love or pride in a son. Then what he did came between us. . . ." His voice faded. He cleared his throat again and continued. "But you've given him back to me, Toby."

"When I've finished with what I've been asked to do for the government," Toby said, "I believe it would be a good idea for me to go and see Henry."

"Yes, it would," Lee agreed. "You've always been like a brother to him. In the meantime, I'll write a letter to the lad." He gathered up his reins and turned his horse. "Let's go to the officers' mess, and I'll buy you a drink."

The letter from his adoptive father was covered with forwarding instructions when it reached Henry Blake. Originally addressed to Germany, it had fortunately been intercepted in New York by an astute military postal clerk who must have known Henry was no longer in Germany. The man had readdressed the letter to the War Department in Washington, and it had subsequently been forwarded to Connecticut. An immense sense of relief and joy flooded through Henry as he read it; once more he was on at least cordial terms with the two most important men in his life, his father and Toby Holt.

The return address on the letter was his father's official address at the fort. What that implied was confirmed by a candid statement in the letter: Eulalia's attitude toward him would probably never change. Henry hesitated to write a reply—which a clerk at the fort might deliver directly to his father's quarters—because the last thing he wanted to do was to create friction between Lee and Eulalia.

An indirect but safer means of reply would be through Toby, and the letter had mentioned that Toby was planning to visit Henry sometime in the future. Henry immediately wrote a short letter to Toby, addressing it to his lumber company in Chicago. In it he described his pleasure upon receiving the letter from his father, and he informed Toby that he would be in Connecticut for the next few months.

That evening, while Henry was sitting in his apartment and reading the letter once again, there was a quiet knock on the door. He got up to answer it and was surprised to see Clifford Anderson waiting outside in the dim light.

The man's stony face relaxed in a warm smile as Henry shook his hand and ushered him in.

"Will you have a brandy, Clifford?" Henry asked after his guest was seated. "If you prefer it, I have a good cognac. Or would you like schnapps?"

"Brandy is fine," Anderson replied, taking out his glass eye and putting it in a waistcoat pocket. He slid his black patch on, and his single eye scanned Henry's expensive leather easy chair, the large, ornate liquor cabinet with well-stocked shelves, and the other elegant furnishings. "You believe in comfort—and not only on shipboard," he commented dryly.

"Gisela sent me most of these things," Henry said as he poured glasses of brandy. He put the glasses and a box of cigars on the table. "If you would like something to eat—"

"No, thank you," Anderson replied, after taking a sip of brandy. He put down the glass and took a cigar from the box. "I've been traveling for weeks, and most of all I wanted a good chair and a friendly face. Now I've found both, so I can be comfortable for a time."

Henry lighted Anderson's cigar, then his own. He asked about Sir Charles Willoughby, who Anderson said was fine, and then about their "friend" at Sandhurst, Alphonse Ferdinand.

"He's also well," Anderson replied. "In fact, he may have a change of status soon—within a matter of months. More and more key figures in Spain are secretly agreeing to support him."

"That's good to hear, and I'm sure the Spanish people will be happy to see an end to the fighting."

"Indeed," Anderson said. "By the way, how is your shoulder these days?"

"Like new," Henry said, smiling. "Sir Charles sent me a note concerning the documents I left with him on the ship. He said that they were excellent forgeries and that you would have more information on them."

"Yes, that's right. They were indistinguishable from authentic documents, with one exception. The Swiss government buys paper from a factory in France to print its official documents, and the ones you gave Sir Charles were printed on paper made in Germany."

A momentary silence fell, the information having raised a discomforting possibility. Henry toyed with his cigar and frowned. The facts about the documents indicated that a large organization with a full range of resources had been behind the attempts to kill him, and the only organization of that nature in Germany that Henry could think of was military intelligence.

"I had discounted the possibility that German military intelligence sent those men to kill me," Henry said. "In fact, I have more than once spoken to General Reinfeldt, who is the current head of intelligence, and I thought I was on good terms with him. Perhaps I'd better think again."

"No," Anderson said, shaking his head. "According to our information, Reinfeldt does not go around trying to kill people—especially not Americans in peacetime. It's totally unlike him. And Bismarck would not hear of it."

"Then where did the man get the documents, Clifford?"

"Sir Charles consulted with his colleagues in London, and the consensus among them is that there may be a rogue elephant in German intelligence. One name bandied about was that of Hermann Bluecher, who is in charge of internal security."

· Henry took a sip of brandy. "I've never even heard the name before. That surprises me, because I thought I at least knew the names of all the higher officials in German intelligence."

"I hadn't heard of him either until Sir Charles told me. Even the British know little about him, but they suspect a number of things. For example, there have been hints that he has a network of agents unknown even to the other officials in German intelligence and that he pursues private initiatives. Apparently he's quite wealthy and can do what he pleases."

"Did Sir Charles have any idea of why Bluecher would want to have me killed?"

"There are suggestions that he is an extreme nationalist. The other officials in German intelligence have turned a blind eye to your presence at Mauser, but Bluecher might not be so discriminating."

Henry nodded. "Can you tell me anything more about him? Or do you think Sir Charles knows more than he is at liberty to tell?"

"Oh, no. I'm sure he's being entirely straightforward," Anderson replied firmly. "Sir Charles views you as a valuable ally and doesn't want anything to happen to you. Beyond that, he simply likes you. Bluecher is in fact extremely secretive, even for a senior official in his profession. Sir Charles says he's a monstrously overweight man and rarely appears in public. And he must be very efficient in his duties, because he has held his post through several changes in the head of German intelligence. His only apparent weakness is a fondness for pleasures of the flesh—which he pursues, however, in ways that don't make him vulnerable. He's wealthy and well educated, and that's about all I can tell you. We don't even know where he lives. But even if you found him, you have nothing more than suspicions to confront him with. And of course you would make yourself an embarrassment to Washington."

Henry thought about the description Anderson had given. Such an enemy was indeed a serious threat.

The two men fell silent, and to break the tension Anderson got up to look at the photograph of Gisela on the desk. "I was misled about her by British understatement," he commented. "Sir Charles merely said that she was very attractive."

Henry laughed. "She certainly is that. Are you returning to Europe soon, Clifford? I assume you're here to report to the State Department on the developments concerning our friend at Sandhurst."

"Yes, I am," Clifford replied, taking out his watch and glancing at it. "In fact, I must be back in Washington tomorrow, so I'll have to leave soon to catch my train. Then I'll be returning to Europe. Before I leave, however, there's another matter I'd like to bring up, something that you may be able to help me with." Anderson began explaining about a former friend of his in the State Department named John Lawrence, who had died two years ago. The man's children, in their twenties, were named Valerie and John. Valerie was a well-known actress—Henry immediately recognized her name—and John, a journalist, was currently in prison in Germany.

During the Franco-Prussian War, Anderson continued, John had been caught going through German lines into Paris with information in his notebook about troop dispositions. If the information had been forwarded to a newspaper in the United States, as intended, it would have been nothing more than news. Under the circumstances, however, it had been vital intelligence, and John Lawrence had been arrested as a spy and taken to the military prison in Trier, where he had been ever since.

"Naturally the State Department has been trying to get him released," Anderson said. "The officials in Washington have been working through the ambassador there with as little fanfare as possible."

"That's well advised," Henry commented. "If we badgered the Germans into bringing him to trial, he'd probably be convicted and hanged. I mean no disrespect to your deceased friend, Clifford, but what his son did was very stupid."

"Of course it was," Anderson agreed. "But you know how journalists are. They don't believe that the rules other people must follow apply to them. Anyway, there's been no progress in getting him released, and it occurred to me that you might be able to use your influence. Perhaps it would help if you came to Washington and spoke to the German ambassador."

Henry took the last puffs on his cigar and put it down. "I'll do all I can, of course. Instead of the ambassador in Washington, though, I believe I'd have more success in working through the consul in New York. I met him in Berlin last year, and we're on cordial terms."

"That sounds more promising than anything yet," Anderson said. "Will you write to him, then?"

"Better yet, I'll see him in person," Henry replied. "I'm going to New York at the end of the week to attend Lord Randolph Churchill's wedding, so it won't even be out of my way."

"Excellent," Anderson said. "Valerie lives in New York, and as you might expect, she is extremely anxious about her brother. While you're there, do you think you could find time to visit her and tell her the results of your meeting with the consul?"

Henry said it would be no trouble at all, and Anderson took out a notebook and jotted her address on a page, which he tore out and put on the table. After he put his notebook away, he took off his eyepatch and restored his glass eye to its place. "It's almost time for my train, so I must run," he said.

As Henry went with him to the door, Anderson apologized for bringing nothing but bad news. "I realize that the information Sir Charles obtained about the men who attacked you is less than reassuring. However, it was his intention to make you cautious, not to reassure you."

"He's already succeeded," Henry said with a smile as they shook hands. "Nothing out of the ordinary has occurred since I've been here, but I am being careful."

"Please continue to do so, then. If Sir Charles and I get further information or opinions on what happened, we will write."

The two men said good-bye, and Anderson left. He disappeared quickly into the night, his soft footsteps fading into silence. Standing in the doorway and looking out into the darkness, Henry suddenly realized that he was silhouetted by the light behind him, making him an easy target. He stepped back and closed the door.

X

Randolph Churchill had made arrangements for his friends to stay at the Fairmount Club while in New York, and after Henry had been shown to a room on the third floor of the ornate iron-and-brick building, he went back outside and hired a carriage to take him to the German consulate.

The consulate, a fifteen-minute ride downtown, was housed in a large brownstone building set back from the street. The receptionist looked askance at Henry when he admitted he didn't have an appointment to see the consul, but she took his card and sent a clerk upstairs with it.

A few minutes later, the consul himself, a dapper little man of forty by the name of Erich Kreuger, hurried down the wide staircase. Seeing Henry, he waved and called out.

"Heinrich! It is so good to see a friend from Berlin! What are you doing in the United States?"

Henry smiled and offered his hand. "It's a pleasure to see you again, Erich. And why shouldn't I be in the United States? This is my native country, isn't it?"

Kreuger hesitated, then laughed heartily. "Of course it is," he replied. "But you speak and look so much like a Prussian that I must stop and think about it. Have you just arrived from Germany?"

"No, I've been here for a few months now. I'm organizing a procurement detachment in Connecticut, applying what I learned at Mauser Arms Works. I'll return to Germany within another three or four months."

"And without a doubt, the baroness is very lonely in your absence," Kreuger said with a wink. "I trust she is well?"

As they exchanged news, Kreuger led Henry up the staircase and along a hall to his office. After accepting a glass of cognac, Henry brought up the purpose of his visit. "My call isn't entirely social, I'm afraid," he said. "I've come to see if you can help me with a favor I'm trying to do for a friend." As he began explaining about John Lawrence, Kreuger's smile faded into a pained expression. By the time Henry had finished, the man was shaking his head doubtfully.

"This is a very difficult situation, Heinrich," he said. "Through his foolishness, this young Lawrence committed a serious offense."

"It was serious, and the man was stupid," Henry agreed. "However, he's now been in prison for two years. Perhaps that may be considered sufficient punishment for what he did."

Kreuger pondered a moment. "Well, even if he was spying for the French," he said philosophically, "he couldn't have done irreparable harm. We won the war, didn't we? I'll tell you what—I'll send a telegram to my brother Ernst in the War Office and ask him to look into the matter. Also, I have a friend on the Chancellor's staff who may be able to help, and I'll send him a telegram. And there are others who may be able to help. It will be two or three days before I receive replies, however. Will you be here that long?"

Henry nodded. "I'm here to attend a wedding this Sunday. If necessary, I'll stay an extra day or two. I have a room at the Fairmount Club."

"The Fairmount Club?" Kreuger echoed, impressed. "Very well—I will send a message to you there as soon as I hear something."

The two men talked a while longer, and it was late in the afternoon when Henry left the consulate. The street where Valerie Lawrence lived was only a few blocks away, near the theater district, and Henry walked the distance.

The address turned out to be a luxurious apartment building, and Miss Lawrence's rooms were on the second floor. A maid answered Henry's knock, opening the chained door a crack as she peered out at him.

"Miss Lawrence doesn't receive visitors at home," the woman said after Henry introduced himself. "Perhaps if you waited outside the stage door with the other men—" Her expression suddenly changed. "Blake, did you say? Henry Blake? Are you here about her brother?"

"Yes, that's right."

The chain rattled down, and the door opened. "Excuse me, sir, I didn't realize who you were. Miss Lawrence received a telegram from Washington about you, and she's been looking forward to seeing you. I'll tell her you're here."

Henry took in his surroundings as the maid disappeared through a drape-covered doorway. The decor seemed very bohemian to him, even for an actress's residence. The walls were filled with colorful murals in the French impressionist style, while the wood trim was covered with red silk chenille that matched the drape over the doorway.

A moment later, Henry learned that the maid had understated Valerie Lawrence's eagerness to see him. An exclamation came from another room, followed by hurried footsteps. The drape over the doorway was snatched aside, and a young woman in a dressing gown burst into the entry, her face more like an apparition's than a human being's.

Except for her large blue eyes, her features were

almost completely covered by a layer of thick white cream. Her hair was pushed up under a mobcap, and her mouth was a thin, barely perceptible line. Her dressing gown was draped around her well below her soft, shapely shoulders. Obviously she wore nothing under it, because her large breasts were almost completely exposed.

"Henry Blake?" she said, her eyes taking in his uniform. "The telegram I received didn't mention you were a *soldier*." She pronounced the word with evident distaste.

"Then we begin on an even basis," he replied. "I wasn't informed that you would be ready to go to a Halloween ball."

Valerie lifted a hand to her face, suddenly aware of her appearance. Henry's joking comment fell flat, however, and she pulled up her dressing gown. "I beg your pardon," she said. "I really don't see what an army lieutenant can do about a problem that the entire State Department hasn't been able to solve, but I'll send a message to the theater and tell the director to have my understudy do the first performance this evening—"

"No, please don't disrupt your schedule," Henry cut in. "I have very little to tell you thus far, and it will take only a few minutes."

Valerie hesitated. "Very well. We can talk while I finish getting ready. Come this way."

They went through the drape-covered doorway, and Henry saw that although it was late afternoon, the day was just beginning for Valerie Lawrence. Her coffee and toast awaited her on a neatly laid tray, but other than that, the room looked like a tornado had struck it, with clothes, newspapers, and other things flung about. Against one wall, a dressing table with a mirror was covered with a clutter of jars, cans, and boxes containing cosmetics. Valerie tossed things off a chair on the opposite side of the room so that Henry could sit down.

She offered him coffee or a drink, which he politely

declined. After searching through a jumble on the table, she produced a box of cork-tipped cigarettes and offered him one, which he also declined. She lit one for herself. "When I received the telegram," she said, "I made arrangements for passes to the theater. I also talked to an extra in the cast about providing entertainment. I'll introduce you to her at the theater this evening."

"I appreciate your thoughtfulness," Henry replied, "but I don't require companionship, and I have other matters to occupy me while I'm here."

After taking a few deep puffs, Valerie tossed her cigarette into an ashtray, picked up a towel, and began wiping the cream off her face. "She's young and quite attractive, if you're worried about that. And she'll be just as friendly as you want her to be, which should appeal to a soldier."

Henry's patience was beginning to wear thin. "Soldiers are precisely like other men, Miss Lawrence," he said. "Thank you again, but I don't need a companion. I've talked with the German consul, and he's agreed to make inquiries about your brother's release."

Valerie glanced at him and shrugged. "Who is the German consul here, and how do you happen to know him?"

"His name is Erich Kreuger, and I met him in Berlin."

"Well, how did you get to know Mr. Anderson?"

"I met him in Europe through a mutual acquaintance."

Valerie glanced at him in the mirror, then resumed wiping cream from her face. "You don't talk much about yourself, do you? Why does Mr. Anderson think you can do more than the State Department about getting John released?"

"I don't know what Mr. Anderson thinks, but the State Department has been working on the problem through official channels, and I'm proceeding on a personal basis with a man I know, which is sometimes more effective."

"I certainly hope it will be"—Valerie sighed theatrically—"and I do appreciate what you're doing for John. His being in that prison has been a torture for me, and I know it's been absolutely horrible for him." She refolded the towel and began wiping away the last traces of cream. "Does the consul think he'll be able to get John released?"

"He'll try, but it's a difficult situation, and you shouldn't get your hopes up too much. However, he does have very good connections in the German government, and I believe he can do as much as anyone could."

Valerie tossed down the towel and pulled off her mobcap. Her long, brown hair spilled down over her shoulders, and she picked up a brush and began brushing it. "I'm still curious about how you got involved in this," she said. "How did an army lieutenant come to be roaming around Europe and meeting consuls, State Department officials, and people like that?"

"I haven't been roaming around Europe," Henry replied. "A few German Army officers are stationed here, and a few Americans are stationed there. I happen to be one of them, and I meet a variety of people in my normal official and social activities."

"So you do have social activities?" Valerie remarked dryly. "I was beginning to wonder."

Henry smiled thinly. "Believe me, I don't suffer from a lack of companionship."

"I'll bet you don't," Valerie countered, looking at him in the mirror as she brushed her hair. "You are a very handsome man, Lieutenant Blake—the type of man people usually describe as mysterious and dangerous. So you're stationed in Germany? I don't believe I'd like that place."

"Why do you say that?"

"Because of the way they treated my brother. There was no reason at all for John to be locked up. Everyone knew he was a journalist. Germans must be either very stupid or very vindictive people."

"No, they're neither," Henry said. "And from my understanding of the situation, the field commander who decided your brother's case acted very leniently."

"*Leniently?*" Valerie exclaimed in sudden anger, wheeling on him. "What on earth would you have considered severe treatment?"

"For him to have been shot out of hand, which was entirely within the field commander's prerogative. Your brother was caught going through German lines with detailed information on troop dispositions. That made him a spy by definition, Miss Lawrence, and the fact that he was a journalist was completely irrelevant."

Valerie glared at him. "I see," she commented acidly, "that the freedom of the press means nothing to you."

"On the contrary," Henry replied evenly, "I stand ready to defend all of our freedoms with my life, as have many American soldiers before me. However, freedom of the press doesn't exempt newspapers and journalists from the laws, customs, and standards that apply to others. Especially in foreign countries."

"That," she said angrily, "is exactly the narrow-minded point of view I would expect from someone in the military."

"You have the right to express your opinion, of course," Henry said coldly, standing up. "Consul Kreuger is sending telegrams to Germany today, and he should have replies to them within the next two or three days. When he does, I'll let you know."

Valerie nodded grudgingly, then turned toward the mirror and began arranging her hair. "Very well. The maid will see you out."

"I'll see myself out. Good day, Miss Lawrence."

When he was back outside, Henry flagged down a carriage for hire to return to the Fairmount Club. One thing was certain: He was not looking forward to his next meeting with Valerie Lawrence. She obviously loved her brother and was deeply concerned about him, but that was the only agreeable trait Henry had detected in her.

The next day, Henry went to buy a wedding present for Churchill and Jennie Jerome. At the Cast Iron Palace, a grand emporium in the fashionable shopping district between Eighth and Twenty-third streets, he rode a steam elevator up to the floor where fine crystal, china, and silver were on display. The sales clerk who came to his assistance recommended the silver.

"We have many excellent values in fine silver, sir," he said. "All of the prices on our silver goods have been reduced."

"They have?"

"Yes, sir. The reduction in the value of the metal when silver coinage was stopped has now reached the retail level."

The clerk talked on, but Henry only half listened. His mind was on another matter entirely.

Several weeks before, the director of the Berlin Trust Company of Hartford, one of Gisela's American agents, had brought Henry a set of documents to sign as a principal of Blake Enterprises. The man had begun a long, involved explanation about the documents, until Henry had asked him to forgo it and simply signed. He had little interest in the matter, yet he had ascertained that the documents established a revolving cash account for the purpose of purchasing stocks and transferring them to Blake Enterprises. The stocks were being bought at deep discounts, and for a good reason. They were silver stocks, which by conventional wisdom were virtually worthless.

Tens of thousands of dollars were being transferred through foreign exchanges in Europe to the revolving account. In the past, Henry knew, some things had not always turned out as Gisela expected. She had made a few minor misjudgments. He wondered if she had finally made a serious mistake, spending tens of thousands on bales of worthless silver stocks.

Dismissing the uneasy thought, Henry chose a silver coffee service. He paid for it and had it gift wrapped, then left the emporium and walked uptown to the Jerome house in the fashionable residential district between Washington and Madison squares. After dropping off the present and paying his respects to Mrs. Jerome—who in the course of their conversation proudly informed him that one of her grandparents was an Iroquois Indian—he had lunch back at the Fairmount Club. Afterward, he strolled around the city to see the sights.

The bachelor party that evening was a sedate affair, most of the guests politicians and businessmen. During the meal, Henry was seated beside a man named Theodore Roosevelt, whom Churchill and Jennie had told him about. Roosevelt was fond of talking about his two sons, a namesake called Teddy and a younger boy named Elliott. Both boys were firearms enthusiasts, and the elder Roosevelt promised to introduce them to Henry at the wedding.

When the meal was finished, a succession of toasts to the future groom were made and drunk, and then the gathering broke up into smaller groups. Perhaps because of his encounter the previous day with Valerie Lawrence, Henry felt unsettled and lonely for Gisela, and as he was returning to his room, he decided to take a walk before going to bed.

The night air was pleasant, and he strolled along the streets at random, heading in the general direction of downtown. It was late at night, and the city was dark and quiet, only a few taverns and restaurants still open. The occasional vehicles that passed stirred echoes among the tall buildings, and most of the pedestrians were men, who laughed, talked, and sang drunkenly as they made their way home.

After a time, his wanderings led him into a poorer

section of the city, where the narrow streets were lined with noisy taverns, small, shabby shops, and dingy tenement buildings. Henry's thoughts were still of Gisela, but the part of his mind that remained aware of his surroundings never rested now, and when three men began following him at a distance of half a block, he was immediately alert.

Unlike others, the men were quiet, their footsteps soft. Henry passed a streetlight, then glanced back as he walked along the following dark stretch. The men stepped out into the street to avoid the light. Without looking back again, Henry kept walking and listened as the footsteps became louder.

He turned a corner and started down a cross street. The footsteps continued drawing closer. At the next streetlight Henry turned the corner again, then walked rapidly and quietly to a deep, dark doorway a few yards along the street. Waiting in the doorway, he watched the street.

A moment later, the three came around the corner, then stopped in confusion, looking down the street. Henry saw them clearly for the first time. Wearing grimy workmen's clothing, they were bearded and unkempt, and they fingered short, stout clubs as they murmured among themselves and glanced around.

The three were common thugs, so inept that Henry found them almost amusing in comparison to the professionals who had tried to kill him before. He stepped out of the doorway and stood before them. "You've been following me, and now you've caught up with me," he said. "So what do you want to do about it?"

The men exchanged glances and looked at Henry warily. Two of them tucked their clubs under their coats and turned to leave. The third one paused, until Henry started toward him.

"We wasn't following you," the man mumbled, backing away. "We ain't looking for no trouble with you."

Henry let him go, almost disappointed the man had not challenged him. The three were obviously looking for someone to rob, and Henry had half a mind to go after them.

When he continued walking, it did not occur to him that he was following the three men until he saw them silhouetted against a streetlight several blocks ahead. Out of curiosity and concern, he watched as a carriage passed them, the men and women inside it laughing and talking drunkenly. At the next block, where a few seedy-looking establishments were still open, the carriage pulled over to the opposite side of the street and stopped outside a tavern. The men and women got out.

In the light at the tavern entrance, Henry saw to his surprise that one of the women was Valerie Lawrence. The three thugs continued down the street toward the tavern, eyeing Valerie and the others. Henry walked faster, watching.

Valerie was with another woman and three men, but the men appeared to be the sort of foppish ne'er-do-wells who loitered around stage entrances and sought after actresses. Even if they had been sober, they would probably have been incapable of protecting the women against the three thugs.

Still laughing and talking noisily, Valerie and the others disappeared into the tavern. The three thugs stepped into a doorway a few yards from the carriage. Henry hung back, keeping to the shadows and weighing what to do.

Even if Valerie had been a complete stranger, he knew he would have been compelled to warn her and the others. But they were drunk, and he was in no mood to endure ridicule. At the same time, he had no intention of waiting until Valerie and the others decided to leave, then protecting them if the three thugs did attack.

A moment later, however, before they could have had even a single drink, Valerie and the others began filing back out to the street. Henry looked at them in surprise, then at the doorway where the three men had hidden. Sure enough, the three came out of the doorway, walking toward the two women and the men. Henry stepped off the curb and crossed the street with long strides.

As he had anticipated, the thugs began snatching at the women's jewelry and purses. Also as he had anticipated, the three men with the women recoiled from the threat of the clubs, as the women screamed and tried to protect their belongings. One of the thugs glimpsed Henry as he reached them.

The man, slow and awkward on his feet, swung his club. Henry dodged it easily and caught the man's arm, pulling him off balance. As the man stumbled, Henry twisted the arm up behind the man's back, then jerked it higher. The man screamed, and the club fell from his fingers as the other two dropped their loot and rushed Henry.

Grabbing the club, Henry shoved the man toward the first of the attackers. The two collided heavily, almost falling as Henry closed with the third man. Again Henry parried the first blow, then slapped his own club down across the man's knuckles. That drew a howl of pain, which was cut off as Henry punched the man solidly in the face, reeling him backward. The other attacker, losing heart, dropped his club and ran. His companions glanced once at Henry, then followed.

The incident, over nearly as quickly as it had begun, had more or less sobered Valerie and the others. Henry tossed the club away, retrieved the women's purses, and approached Valerie. "Are you all right?" he asked.

Valerie collected herself, replied with a nod, then began looking around at the pavement near her feet. She picked up a small brown paper package that she had apparently dropped during the scuffle. Strangely, she seemed more worried about it than about her purse or jewelry. She pocketed the package, then took her purse as Henry handed it to her. In a subdued voice she introduced him to the others.

Her resentment toward him was still evident, but the three male companions were loud and profuse in their thanks, while the other woman was both grateful and openly inviting.

Her name was Crystal DeVonne, and Henry gathered that she was also an actress. Her speech was somewhat slurred. "Will you be in the city for a few days, honey?" she asked as he handed her her purse. "I'll give you my address so you can pay me a call."

"I'll be here only a short time," Henry replied, then turned to Valerie. "Come on, I'll walk you home."

"Walk?" she exclaimed. "No, I don't need you to escort me, and I certainly don't intend to walk. It's miles from here!"

"What you do after you get home is your own concern," Henry said, "but I intend to see that you get there safely. The walk will be good for you and sober you up." He took her aside and said more quietly, "Now, Miss Lawrence, unless you want me to carry you over my shoulder, you'd better start walking."

Fuming with anger, Valerie glared at him, then looked to the others for support. The three men, wanting no trouble with Henry, decided to take an amused view of the situation. Crystal was of even less help. "You can walk *me* home, honey," she offered. "Or if you wish, you can just walk me down the street and into the alley."

The three men laughed, but the woman remained completely serious. Valerie, as angry at her friends as at Henry, turned and strode away. Henry caught up with her, and the two of them walked silently until the noise and light of the tavern were left behind.

"I have on slippers, not soldier's boots," Valerie grumbled. "The heels on them weren't made for walking very far."

"You'll manage."

They fell silent again. At a corner, Henry put his hand under Valerie's elbow to help her off the curb, and she angrily jerked away from him. Still not completely sober, she weaved on her feet until he took her arm and steadied her. She pulled away again.

"It amazes me," she said through clenched teeth, "how you can be so infuriating while you're doing something helpful. I would almost prefer to be robbed by those three than to have you around."

"That's what will happen next time. And there will be a next time, if you continue crawling through taverns in neighborhoods like this."

Valerie was silent for a moment. "I don't need you to tell me this isn't a safe place," she said at last. "We wouldn't have come here, but we couldn't find our usual dealer to buy a few pipes of gow."

All at once Henry understood why she had been in the tavern for only a brief time, as well as her concern over the package she had dropped. "That's opium you have there?" he exclaimed angrily, taking her arm and stopping her. He reached into her pocket for the package, then stepped to the curb and threw it into a gutter drain. "There's the best place for that."

Valerie was speechless for a moment. Then her voice echoed along the quiet street. "You idiot! What gives you the right to butt into my business and try to tell me what to do?"

Henry had expected such a reaction, but still he had to force himself to keep his temper. "I've seen opium dens in the West, and I've seen the miserable, pitiful wrecks that opium will make of even strong, healthy men. But you're the first woman I've ever met who's stupid enough to use it!"

Valerie muttered something under her breath, but she had no ready reply, and they resumed walking along the street. "That gow cost me twenty dollars," she grumbled.

"Better to throw the money away" was Henry's curt reply.

"You just don't understand," she said resentfully. "If you knew how hard I have to work, you'd see why I need something to help me get away from it now and then. In addition to regular evening performances, I have matinees three days a week. And on top of that, when a play is near the end of its run, I'm learning a new script and rehearsing a new play. It's been years since I've had a vacation or even a day off."

Henry shrugged. "There are millions of men and women who work just as hard."

"I don't even know why I bother talking to you."

Valerie was silent for several minutes as they walked along the deserted street. Then she spoke, her voice becoming louder with each word. "What I need," she said, "is a pair of slippers with low heels! And for you to leave me alone!" She turned to him, stretching up and shouting at the top of her voice. "To leave me alone! Just leave me alone!"

Her voice breaking with a sob, she stumbled. Henry took her arm and steadied her, but she jerked away again and continued walking. She said nothing, but her rapid breathing revealed that she was barely keeping herself from bursting into tears of anger and frustration. Henry knew that she was depressed and in pain, the effects of the alcohol she had drunk turning into a hangover, and she had begun limping.

When a carriage for hire came along the street, Henry called and waved to the driver. Valerie, instead of pulling away, leaned on him heavily as he helped her into the cab, and then she collapsed wearily on the seat. In front of her apartment, Henry asked the driver to wait. Taking

Valerie's arm, he helped her out of the carriage and up the stairs to her rooms.

She took out her key and unlocked the door, then glared up at him. "I appreciate what you're doing for my brother," she said coldly, "and I'm grateful that you drove away those robbers. Other than that, I detest you more than anyone I've ever met."

Henry touched his cap. "And a good evening to you as well, Miss Lawrence," he said, then turned and left.

The wedding the next day was at the British consulate, in the small private chapel, and Henry sat near the back. With the men in immaculate formal attire and the women arrayed in jewels and costly, stylish gowns, the guests provided a display of finery that made Henry's dress uniform seem plain by comparison.

The reception was held under bright awnings in the garden behind the Jerome mansion, with an orchestra providing music, and long tables filled with delicacies and wines. Henry danced with the bride, then with Mrs. Jerome, and later stood on the sidelines and talked with the men he had met at the bachelor party.

Theodore Roosevelt introduced his sons, Teddy and Elliott. Teddy's eyes looked odd behind his thick glasses, and he had the slow, controlled breathing of an asthmatic, but in all other respects he was a handsome, well-built youth of fifteen, and Henry was impressed by his exhaustive knowledge of firearms.

Soon after the bride and groom left, Henry returned to the Fairmount Club, where he hoped he would have a message from the German consul. He was eager to finish his business in New York and be done with the troublesome Valerie Lawrence.

But there were no messages, and it wasn't until the following day, when Henry was reading a newspaper in the club's library, that a steward handed him an envelope on a tray. It was a note from Erich Kreuger—a single sentence requesting Henry's presence at the consulate as soon as convenient.

Less than twenty minutes later, Henry was being escorted upstairs to the consul's office.

"You're very prompt, Heinrich," Kreuger said as they shook hands. "I have good news for you. John Lawrence will be released from prison within the next two weeks."

Henry had not expected such immediate results. "You mean everything has been arranged already? There's no possibility for a misunderstanding?"

Kreuger picked up a folder from his desk and handed it to Henry. It contained several telegrams that had arrived that morning, which together presented the sequence of events that had taken place in Germany. The military authorities had been persuaded to turn John Lawrence over to the Ministry of Justice, which in turn had been persuaded to express a lack of interest in prosecuting the case.

Henry returned the folder and thanked Kreuger for his help. "Even though I've never met Lawrence, I have a friend in the State Department who's very close to the family. And Lawrence's sister, Valerie, loves him very much. She'll be delighted at the news."

"Valerie Lawrence?" Kreuger said, lifting his eyebrows. "Are you referring to the famous actress?"

"Yes, she's Lawrence's sister."

"She is?" Kreuger looked flabbergasted. "My wife and I have gone three—no, four times to see the play she is presently starring in. Would it be possible for me to meet her, Heinrich? And perhaps you could make arrangements for my wife to meet her. She would be thrilled."

Henry hesitated only an instant. "I'm not on the best of terms with Miss Lawrence, but I'll be happy to go and tell her that you wish to see her. Then you can tell her the good news yourself."

The consul couldn't have been more pleased, and Henry went back downstairs and took a carriage the few blocks to Valerie's apartment hotel. As he looked at his watch, however, a potential problem occurred to him. It was shortly after noon, and Valerie was a very late riser.

He knocked on the apartment door several times before there was a response. Finally, the sleepy-eyed maid opened the door a crack. Apparently she slept late, too. "Miss Lawrence isn't awake yet, sir."

"The German consul wishes to talk with her about her brother," Henry said. "I'm sure that's something she'll want to be awakened for."

The maid unchained and opened the door, and Henry stepped inside. "It will take me a while to wake her up, sir," the maid said. "If she's awakened too quickly, she's out of sorts all day."

"I believe this instance qualifies as an exception," Henry said. He had no intention of waiting around in Valerie Lawrence's apartment, and when the maid was slow to respond, he took matters into his own hands. "Go make coffee, then, and I'll wake her for you."

The woman looked doubtful, but she obediently disappeared down the hall. Henry crossed the dressing room toward Valerie's bedroom door. The room was dark, the shades drawn, and he walked across newspapers and almost got his feet tangled in a gown and fell. He put the gown on a chair and went into the bedroom.

The bedroom was also dark, and Henry went to the window and opened the drapes, letting daylight in. Everything in the room was bright pink.

The light failed to disturb Valerie, who was sleeping soundly under covers that looked as though they had been thrown about all night. "Wake up, Valerie," Henry said, walking toward the bed.

Valerie stirred and mumbled something, then turned over and pulled the rumpled covers over her head.

"I said wake up," Henry repeated, but he still got no response. He took the edge of the covers to yank them off her. "It's your brother. We have to go to—"

His voice broke off, for he had pulled back the covers only to find that Valerie, an extremely shapely woman, slept entirely in the nude. He replaced the covers.

To his further surprise, she was now awake and didn't seem to object to his presence. "What do you have in mind to do?" she drawled lazily, gazing confusedly up at him.

"I have in mind taking you to see the German consul," he said. He turned and walked toward the door. "The maid is making coffee, so get up, please."

In much less time than Henry had expected, Valerie appeared in the parlor. She was wearing a striking, stylish green muslin dress. As she pinned on a matching hat, she spoke but avoided his gaze. "I'm almost afraid to ask," she said, "but is the news good or bad?"

Henry saw no reason to keep her in suspense. "The consul wants to see you in person," he said. "He and his wife are ardent admirers of yours, so he would hardly want to deliver bad news in person, would he?"

"So John is being released from prison!" she gasped. "When will he return home?"

"I'll leave that for the consul to tell you," Henry replied. "He's looking forward to breaking the news himself, so please act surprised."

Valerie nodded, dabbing at suddenly tear-filled eyes with a handkerchief. The maid had poured coffee, but Valerie ignored it. She quickly gathered up her cape, parasol, and reticule and followed Henry downstairs to the waiting carriage.

During the short ride to the consulate, Valerie was a different woman. Although she said little and avoided Henry's gaze, she was completely civil, and Henry assumed that her mind was occupied with thoughts of her brother.

At the consulate, word had spread that the famous Valerie Lawrence would be arriving, and most of the staff had found some excuse to be in the lobby. Donning her stage persona like the cape drawn carelessly about her shoulders, Valerie made a grand entrance on Henry's arm, her long parasol tapping the floor as she gazed haughtily at her admirers.

Henry escorted her upstairs and into the consul's office, where he introduced her to Kreuger. The little man bowed deeply over her hand.

When Kreuger told her that her brother would be released within two weeks, for an instant Henry saw the same woman she had been in the carriage. Tears of happiness came to her eyes, and her façade slipped away. Then she recovered herself and performed for the consul.

A hand on her heaving bosom, she swayed weakly and fluttered her eyelashes. Solicitously helping her to a chair, Kreuger bellowed to his secretary to bring smelling salts. The secretary rushed in with a small bottle, which Kreuger wafted under Valerie's nose. He hovered worriedly, chafing her hands and apologizing for not breaking the news to her more gently.

Recovering from her simulated fainting spell, Valerie expressed her gratitude in gushing, grandiloquent phrases. The consul, flushing with pleasure, responded modestly. "It was a privilege to be of service to you, Miss Lawrence," he said. "It is also an honor to do something for someone who has enriched people's lives as much as you have."

"You are far too kind, Herr Kreuger," Valerie replied, "and what you have done for my brother restores my heart to me. If there is anything I can do in return, of course, you need only ask."

Kreuger hesitated, then smiled meekly. "It would

please my wife greatly to meet you," he said. "The next
time we attend a performance of your play, would it be
possible for me to take her to your dressing room?"

"That would hardly be adequate thanks for what you've
done," Valerie said. "The one hundredth performance of
the play will be a week from next Saturday, and the
producer is giving a party for the cast afterward. I'll send
you box-seat tickets, and you and your wife will be my
guests at the party."

His eyes opening wide, Kreuger began stuttering his
thanks. Valerie dismissed the matter with a dramatic wave
of the hand. "It is I who thank you, Herr Kreuger. I will
look forward to seeing you and your wife a week from
Saturday."

Henry shook hands with an effusive Kreuger, then
escorted Valerie back downstairs.

In the carriage, Henry chuckled as Valerie relaxed
with a satisfied sigh. "If your performances on stage are as
good as that one," he said, "it's little wonder that you're a
famous actress."

For the first time that morning, Valerie looked straight
at him. "People expect it of me, and they're disappointed
when it isn't forthcoming." She paused a moment, then
went on. "Like last night. My performance at the theater
wasn't the best, but I managed to get through it, and
without any opium."

Henry noticed that her hands were shaking, and he
started to say something, but she interrupted.

"I owe you an apology, Lieutenant Blake. You were
right about the opium. I didn't think I would develop an
addiction to it, but I have. I've given it up now, and I
don't feel entirely well."

Henry didn't know what to reply. "Perhaps a doctor
could give you something that would help—"

"No, I don't need anything," she said firmly. "I've
decided to give it up, and I will. It's merely a matter of

waiting until the desire goes away, and I can deal with that." She sighed, looking out the window. "And you were right about other things as well."

Henry was both surprised and curious. He was seeing yet another part of Valerie Lawrence, and despite his reservations about her character, he realized that her success on stage was due to something more than her considerable beauty. Her face reflected intelligence and determination, and he guessed that she would be able to stop using opium, or do anything else she desired, once she set her mind to it.

He took her hand. "You're a very brave woman, Miss Lawrence, and I had the wrong opinion about you. Perhaps you and I could start over again and be friends."

"You have a friend for life in me," Valerie said, turning back toward him, her eyes once again filling with tears. "And I know that somewhere there is a very, very lucky woman. What is her name?"

Henry smiled. "I'm a lucky man, and her name is Gisela."

Valerie wiped away tears with a handkerchief. "That's a pretty name. It must be German. And you're not married?"

Henry shook his head.

Valerie had recovered her composure quickly. "That's very risqué, isn't it?" she teased him. "Perhaps there's some hope for you after all, Lieutenant Blake."

They both began laughing, and by the time they said good-bye at Valerie's apartment, they were indeed friends, and even promised to write to each other. As Henry made his way back downstairs, he marveled at Valerie's change of heart. He had never seen someone undergo a dramatic transformation so quickly, but then again, he reminded himself, Valerie was an actress and an entirely different breed of woman from what he was used to. Certainly she was nothing like Gisela.

As he drove back to the Fairmount Club, Henry was in a buoyant mood and felt almost reluctant to leave the city. The chain of events that had begun with Clifford Anderson's visit to Hartford had come to a successful conclusion for everyone involved—especially for John Lawrence—and as far as Henry himself was concerned, he could not have asked for a more satisfying or productive weekend.

XI

A few days after his return to Hartford, Henry took an early train to New Haven, where he was to test a new Winchester rifle that had just gone into production. A few minutes' brisk walk from the station brought him to the main factory of Winchester Arms, on the edge of the city's business district.

The factory was a large brick building, four stories tall and occupying an entire city block. The receptionist immediately escorted Henry to an office on the second floor.

"I've been looking forward to your visit, Lieutenant Blake," the production manager, a Mr. Hawkins, commented when they were seated. "The company has put considerable effort into this rifle, and we think it's a good one."

"As long as it's a Winchester, I know that it's a good weapon," Henry said. "Whether it's suitable for army use, though, is another matter. I understand it's a lever action carbine."

"That's right. It was designed as a saddle gun. Two of our engineers are at the testing range now with some samples. I'll take you out there later, if you'd like."

Henry agreed to the suggestion, and after he and Hawkins had reviewed the design specifications and production schedule for the rifle, Henry taking notes for his report, they drove a carriage out of the city to the company firing range.

At the firing positions, Hawkins introduced Henry to the two engineers who were testing the weapons, and Henry noticed that both men had an air of satisfied confidence. As Henry examined the rifles being tested, all three of the Winchester employees stood aside, silent except when asked a question. Some of the rifles had undergone endurance tests and were covered with rust, while others were battered from being hammered and thrown about. There was also a selection of rifles just off the production line, being checked as a routine quality control procedure.

The engineers and Hawkins smiled as Henry picked up one of the battered rifles to see if the action still worked smoothly, which it did. Henry put the rifle down and picked up one that was in good condition. As he shouldered it, getting the feel of the weapon, he understood the reason for the intense satisfaction he had detected in the three men. The Winchester Model 1873 was the most exceptional rifle he had ever seen.

While the company had an enviable reputation for producing fine weapons, this time it had outdone itself. The lever-action carbine, chambered in a hefty .44-40 that would stop a grizzly bear, was still a light, slender weapon. Its clean design and proportions also made it a pleasure to handle.

Taking bullets from a box on a bench, Henry loaded the rifle, then began firing at one of the targets. The stock rested snugly against his shoulder, and the forearm grip was in just the right place for a natural, easy stance and accurate aim. The positioning of the lever made reloading the chamber smooth and easy, and the shots blended together into a steady roar.

When Henry stopped firing, Hawkins and the two

engineers peered down the range. The bullet holes were grouped tightly in the center of the bull's eye.

"I've never seen shooting like that before!" one of the engineers said in awestruck tones, and the others echoed his opinion.

Henry put down the rifle and picked up one that was damaged. He loaded the weapon and began firing again, emptying the magazine. Although the stock was cracked and the magazine housing was dented, the rifle fired smoothly and was still accurate.

Again the three men commented on Henry's marksmanship, but he only nodded absently in acknowledgment, fascinated by the rifle. It was ironic, he reflected, that he had spent more than a year trying to learn the manufacturing secrets of Mauser, while in the meantime Winchester had designed a rifle that was far superior to the German weapon in many ways.

There was also something characteristically American about the Winchester. Slender, light, and graceful, it had been designed as a civilian saddle gun. Coincidentally, however, it also happened to be the finest cavalry rifle Henry had ever seen.

Henry was tempted to remain at the range longer for the sheer pleasure of firing the new Winchester, but he had all the information he needed to prepare his report, and the time for his train to leave was drawing near. He thanked the engineers, and then he and Hawkins returned to the factory.

Later, as Henry rode the train back to Hartford, he thought about his work at Mauser, to which he would soon be returning. He knew that his time there would not be wasted, especially since it afforded him the opportunity to ferret out information about new manufacturing processes that could be of great value to his country. But he also knew he could find out nothing there that would produce a better cavalry weapon than the new model Winchester.

He intended to make his report on the rifle as favorable as he could, because he wanted the cavalry armed with the best possible weapon as soon as time permitted.

It was late at night when he arrived back at his apartment. As he lit the lamp in his sitting room, he saw a letter on the desk and immediately recognized the handwriting on the envelope. It was from Toby Holt.

Henry opened the envelope and eagerly read the letter. It expressed satisfaction that the misunderstanding between them had been cleared up and said that Toby intended to visit him in Connecticut as soon as he could, but that he was currently tied up doing work for the government.

The letter was warm and friendly, and Henry smiled as he reread it. Then he turned the envelope to the light of the lamp and looked at the postmark. Whatever mission Toby was performing for the government, he mused, it had taken him to Louisville, Kentucky.

The name that James Gifford had scrawled on the wall of the abandoned warehouse in Louisville had faded to a faint brown mark, and Toby Holt looked at it in the dying afternoon light. During the weeks he had been in Kentucky, Toby had come to the warehouse several times with the police detective who had investigated Gifford's murder. They had searched for hours for any clues that might have been overlooked, but so far they had found nothing.

This time, too, the search was futile. The detective shook his head as he looked around. "I don't think we're going to find anything, Marshal Holt," he said.

The title referred to the United States marshal's badge on Toby's vest under his coat. He nodded and started walking back toward the carriage with the detective. During the past weeks, Toby had reviewed the voluminous reports made by the Louisville police and the Secret Service, who had interviewed people and canvassed the warehouse area for witnesses. The exhaustive investigation had revealed no hint of who had killed Gifford.

"I've done about all I can here," Toby said as they reached the carriage. "Tomorrow I'll take a train down to Frankfort. That's where those demonstrators who threatened the President were arrested, and the Secret Service spent longer there. Perhaps I'll find something in their reports."

"Let's hope so," the detective said, but in fact his voice reflected more hope than confidence that any new leads would develop. Even Toby felt unusually pessimistic. In addition to a lack of clues as to who had killed Gifford, the name that the man had written on the wall of the warehouse remained an enigma. Only one Talcott had been found in Louisville, but he was a small, meek man who worked at a bank and had no conceivable connection to the case.

Back in town, Toby was dropped off at his hotel. He started to go inside, then decided to check first to see if he had any mail. As Dieter Schumann had requested, Toby had been keeping him informed of his whereabouts, and Dieter had been forwarding mail to him. Toby walked the short distance to the post office, where the clerk handed him a large, thick envelope addressed to him in Dieter's handwriting.

Back at his hotel, Toby inspected the contents of the envelope in perplexity. A hastily written note from Dieter was attached to a mortgage deed for Toby to sign. The deed was a legal document in which Toby assumed responsibility for the outstanding debts of a bankrupt ironworks and pledged his lumber company as security for those debts.

The note began with a statement that the lumber company was not yet making a profit, but its financial condition was improving. That was followed by a cryptic sentence saying that the ironworks included a large warehouse of unsold iron goods, which Dieter wanted. The note ended with a request for Toby to sign the mortgage and return it as soon as possible.

With a lumber company near bankruptcy, Toby reflected, the last thing he needed was a bankrupt ironworks. Even if the works had still been in operation, he knew nothing at all about iron manufacturing or sales. However, he did know that iron goods were in even less demand than lumber. That made the question of why Dieter wanted the iron goods even more puzzling.

Carefully reading the deed, Toby saw that a bank in Chicago was the present unhappy holder of the mortgage on the ironworks. The value the bank placed on that particular holding was amply revealed by the fact that it would accept a near-bankrupt lumber company as full security for the ironworks and everything that went with it, including debts.

As he continued reading the mortgage, Toby frowned. He wondered if Dieter was up to some of his old tricks. For all the world, the transaction looked like an elaborate scheme to conceal the financial condition of the lumber company from some unwary soul. Toby wondered if the next letter he received from Dieter would be about someone who wanted to invest heavily in the lumber company.

Deciding he needed a fuller explanation before he signed anything, Toby resolved to write to Dieter the next day and ask him why he wanted the ironworks. With the thought of the mortgage still troubling him, he got ready to go downstairs for dinner.

The next morning, however, Toby changed his mind. To question Dieter's judgment, he decided, would violate the spirit of the agreement between them. He had to trust the man's word and accept on faith that Dieter had sound reasons for wanting the ironworks, even though the deal appeared illogical.

After leaving the hotel, Toby went to the post office and mailed the signed mortgage, with a note attached informing Dieter that he was going to Frankfort. A short time later, he was on a train heading eastward.

The valley of the Ohio River was quickly left behind, and soon the train was passing through the bluegrass country that extended across the center of Kentucky. Scattered among the large crop fields were lush pastures bounded by split-rail fences, with thoroughbred horses grazing peacefully.

Looking at the passing scenery, Toby thought about his plans to visit his mother's cousin, Alex Woodling. The man raised hunters—horses bred and trained to ride cross-country after hounds—rather than racing thoroughbreds. But both breeds were expensive luxuries for which there now was little demand, and Toby wondered if a modest loan would be enough to tide Woodling over the depression.

The train reached Frankfort in midafternoon. After checking into a hotel, Toby walked along the sleepy, tree-shaded streets to the city's police headquarters.

The chief of police was a heavyset, gray-haired man by the name of Bill Walters. He had been expecting Toby, whom he knew by reputation, and after describing the extent of the investigations by his officers and the Secret Service agents, he took Toby to a small room with a table nearly covered with papers and stacks of folders, including the arrest records of the demonstrators.

Toby shook his head and smiled wryly. "Looks like I have a lot of reading to do," he commented.

Walters opened one of the arrest records. "All of these men were booked and questioned," he explained. "Those who apparently weren't involved in the demonstration were released, but their records are here, too.

The ones booked were all drifters, and they were jailed for trial. A few days later, Agent Gifford showed up and checked in with us. The next thing we heard was that he had been found dead in Louisville."

"What do you think might have led him there?"

"It's hard to say, Marshal. One of those drifters might have told him something."

"Have you questioned any of them since Gifford's murder?"

The police chief shook his head. "No, they were only charged with disturbing the peace. By the time the investigations started, they had all served their time on the county farm or whatever and had apparently moved on. In any event, my men couldn't find any of them in the places where drifters usually stay here in the city."

Toby pondered the point for a moment. "That's reasonable enough, I suppose. Frankfort isn't the sort of place where drifters will stay for long, is it?"

"No, it isn't. And there's nothing that links those drifters with Gifford's death. In fact, considering that he wasn't robbed and that a dollar was left beside his body, there's every reason to believe they had nothing to do with it."

Toby had already come to the same conclusion. "I understand nothing turned up here on the name Talcott."

"No, nothing. A family with that name lived here years ago, but they moved out west."

"I see. Well, I'd better get to work on these files."

The police chief left, and Toby sat down and looked in resignation at the tall stacks of folders. Somewhere in the mass of reports, he knew, could be a significant fact that had been overlooked. Or there might be something that he could link with Louisville and that might lead to another clue. He picked up the top folder and began reading.

The remainder of the day passed, Toby barely making

a dent in the first stack of folders. The next day, after having breakfast at his hotel, he returned to the office and resumed going through the reports.

The arrest records also contained detailed likenesses of the demonstrators. Like many police departments, the one in Frankfort now routinely made tintypes of everyone arrested, and the likenesses were glued onto the records.

Still, the files revealed nothing to Toby. The men were of various ages and from various parts of the country, the only common link between them the fact that they were vagrants. The tintypes showed ragged, unshaven men, several of them appearing to be drunk.

The records on the bystanders who had been released after questioning were in a separate, thin folder. Toby started to look at them when a thought suddenly struck him. He stepped over to the chief's office.

"It just occurred to me," he said as Walters looked up from his desk, "I haven't seen in any of the reports what sentence the demonstrators received. Do you know what it was?"

The chief shook his head. "They were charged with disturbing the peace, so it was probably a week or so on the county farm. I'll send a clerk over to the courthouse to find out for certain, if you'd like."

Toby said it was a good idea, and as a clerk came in to take down the names on the arrest records, Toby turned back to the file on the bystanders.

One name in it—Howard Cummings—seemed vaguely familiar. Toby studied the tintype, which showed a man with a thin, sour-looking face. Unable to recall where he had heard the name, Toby put the file aside and began leafing through another.

An hour later, the police chief stepped into the doorway. He was holding the paper on which the clerk had taken down the names, and his stolid face reflected contained excitement. "The demonstrators," he said slowly, "were sentenced to a week on the county farm or a five-dollar fine. Each and every one of them paid the fine."

Toby sat back in his chair in surprise, immediately understanding the unspoken point: The demonstrators, presumably penniless vagrants, had all possessed enough money to pay the fine. "That's certainly something worth checking into, isn't it?" he commented.

"You're mighty right it is," Walters agreed. "We might finally have a lead to follow. I'll get out bulletins on these men right away, to every large city within a couple hundred miles of here."

Toby sat thinking after the chief left the room. Looking at the record on Cummings once more, he tried to recall where he had heard the name.

It was not until the following morning that he remembered. Howard Cummings was the name Marjorie White had mentioned when she had received a letter from a friend in Boston. He was the man who claimed to have met her in Connecticut—a meeting that Marjorie said had never occurred.

As he thought about it, Toby concluded that the most likely explanation was sheer coincidence, that two different men named Howard Cummings were involved. It was a common enough name, and any connection between a bystander at a demonstration in Kentucky and a man who claimed to have met Marjorie in Connecticut seemed too remote.

One fact continued to trouble Toby, however. The man had obviously known that Marjorie had been in Connecticut. Then he had traveled to Boston, trying to get her address. That had taken a lot of time and effort, and it suggested the man had strong reasons. However, while it seemed suspicious, it had nothing to do with the threat against the President.

When he returned to police headquarters, Toby discussed the coincidence with Chief Walters. The chief agreed that any connection with the case at hand seemed unlikely.

"I'll tell you, though," he added, "I've seen too many strange things happen to discount any possibility. It might be a good idea to keep that record on Cummings in a safe place so we'll have it ready at hand."

"Marjorie had an address written by the man who was trying to find her," Toby said. "I could write to her and see if she still has it."

"If she does, we could have it checked out. And we could compare the handwriting with the signature on the arrest record," the captain said. "It might prove well worth the trouble."

"I'll send her a telegram," Toby said. "In the meantime, I need to go to Lexington to talk with a relative who has a farm outside the city. It'll probably be a few days before you have any results on the bulletins or before I hear from Marjorie. She's a traveling photographist, but her partner will know where to find her."

"If anything comes up," the chief reassured him, "I can get in touch with you through the police department in Lexington. We're only twenty-five miles away."

The next morning, Toby took the train for Lexington. After checking in with the police chief there, he got directions to the Woodling horse farm, some ten miles outside of town. He checked his bags at the hotel, stopped at the post office to arrange to have his mail held for him, then rented a horse and set out on the main road south.

It was a sunny afternoon, and the ride was pleasant. He was now deep in the bluegrass region, and on either side of the road tree-lined avenues led back through lush pastures to farmhouses, barns, and an occasional graceful old antebellum mansion with a white-columned portico.

Several miles from the city, Toby turned as directed onto a side road bordered by tall hedges. At long intervals there were openings in the hedge, at lanes leading back into farms, giving him glimpses of farmhouses, crop fields, and stock grazing in pastures.

As he was riding along, Toby heard hoofbeats in a field to his left, behind the tall hedge. He listened to them absently, his mind on other things, until they suddenly became louder. It sounded as if a horse was galloping straight toward the other side of the hedge.

Toby waited for the hoofbeats to veer away, but they did not. Bewildered, he glanced up at the top of the hedge. An exceptionally strong, agile hunter might just be able to clear it, but such a blind jump would be extremely foolish under any circumstances. His bewilderment turned to alarm as he realized that the horse was indeed headed straight toward him. Toby leaned back on his reins, trying to stop his horse and turn it. The hoofbeats abruptly ceased, giving way to an ominous silence.

As his own horse slid to a stop, a huge black stallion soared across the hedge scant feet in front of him. Toby's disapproval over the rider's lack of judgment was abruptly overcome by an entirely different reaction. His life had been spent around horses, but he had never seen so brilliant a display of skill and daring.

It was a magnificent sight, a sleek, powerful horse and a supremely skilled rider throwing caution to the winds as they hurled themselves at the far edge of what horse and rider could do. The stallion was in perfect form, its forelegs folded and its muscular rear legs poised to catch its weight. The rider, a youth in tight white riding breeches and tall boots, with colorful jacket and cap, was leaning low over the horse's neck to give it its head for the jump.

Then, as Toby's horse shied back in fright, the stallion was startled and lost its balance. Instead of taking its weight on its powerful rear legs, the horse pitched forward and landed on its forelegs. It stumbled and almost fell, catapulting the youth off and into a roadside ditch. The

stallion quickly regained its footing and, apparently unhurt, trotted lightly away, its head high and its tail lashing.

The youth, also seeming to be unhurt, had landed
with an oath, his bottom stuck up in the air. Dismounting,
Toby tied his horse to the hedge and strode angrily toward
the boy. "Son, you need a good thrashing for being so
foolish!" he snapped. "You could have killed someone or
broken that horse's legs."

Reaching the ditch, Toby grasped the back of the
boy's belt to haul him to his feet. But something seemed
wrong, and even as he was bending over the youth, his
mind registered that the hips in the tight white trousers
were very gracefully curved indeed. As he tugged on the
belt and righted the youth, the cap fell off, revealing
unusually long hair. The hair, however, was too short for a
girl, and girls did not wear tight riding breeches.

But the curve of the snug-fitting jacket as the rider
turned to face Toby told another story. The youth was a
small, slender woman, about eighteen, with large hazel
eyes and an angelic face. Pushing back her tousled auburn
hair, she started to say something. Then she fell silent and
stared at him. He looked back at her in silence.

The seconds passed slowly as they stared at each
other, Toby experiencing a welter of reactions. The young
woman was hardly more than a child, and dressed like a
boy. Yet the silence between them rang with tension, the
atmosphere electric with their abrupt, overpowering attraction to each other.

While there had been several women in Toby's life,
the emotions seething within him were an utterly new
experience, as if he had fallen in love for the first time.
Some intangible quality about the woman captivated him
completely.

Common sense, however, told him that his feelings
were absurd. She was extremely attractive, admittedly,
but years too young for him, more of a gamine girl than an

adult. Still, her hazel eyes, mirroring his feelings, were like the glow of an inviting fire, mesmerizing him.

Finally taking control of himself, Toby picked up her cap and handed it to her. "I'm sorry I scolded you, young lady, but it was foolish of you to jump your horse over that hedge. . . . My name is Toby Holt."

The young woman had started to reply until he said his name. Her smile fading, she pulled her short hair back with one hand and put on her cap. "I would have been all right if you hadn't been in the way," she said.

Her voice, with its southern lilt, was like the chiming of silver bells to Toby. But her total lack of logic took him aback, leaving him speechless for a moment. "What do you mean?" he demanded, finding his voice. "Young lady, this is a public road!"

"What difference does that make?" she challenged. "I would have been all right if you hadn't been in the way."

Then he saw that she was teasing him, her eyes dancing with mischief. Something about her seemed familiar. The lines of her pretty mouth, chin, and nose were vaguely evocative of someone close to him, giving Toby a feeling of *déjà vu* that reached back to his childhood. But his intense reaction to her made it difficult for him to think clearly.

Suddenly he laughed and shook his head. "Young lady, your father needs to take you in hand."

She turned and walked to her horse. "He can't reach far enough or fast enough," she called back over her shoulder.

Toby smiled at her retort, suddenly feeling reluctant to have her leave. "Are you certain you aren't hurt?" he asked.

She waved a hand dismissively, vaulted lightly into her saddle, and pulled her cap down firmly on her head. The huge horse was prancing, impatient to be away. Gathering up the reins, the young woman leaned forward and nudged the stallion with her heels, and in an instant it broke into a headlong run.

As the stallion raced past, the young woman flashed a smile at Toby, and he felt himself smiling in return. Then dust kicked up by the pounding hooves swirled around him. The horse picked up speed, veered toward the right in response to a tug on the reins, and gathered itself and leaped soaring over the hedge.

The last Toby saw of the young woman was her shapely hips in the tight breeches. As the hoofbeats faded on the other side of the hedge, he stood there for a moment, bemused. He did not even know her name, he reflected— which was just as well. The last thing he needed was to become involved with a tomboy woman who was years too young for him.

At the same time, the exhilarating emotions he had felt moments ago still stirred within him. He mounted his horse and continued along the road, trying to dismiss the incident. But he was unable to force the young woman from his thoughts, for her sudden appearance had some-how changed even the day around him, making it brighter, more colorful, and alive.

Farther along the road, Toby came to another opening in the hedge, where the signpost read, *Fair Oaks, Alexander Woodling*. Toby turned his horse onto the tree-lined drive.

In the distance he saw a large, white-painted mansion fronted by a classical portico, with whitewashed barns set back to one side. Thirty to forty horses were scattered over the near pasture, all of them large, muscular hunters. It was a beautiful farm, Toby thought, but the buildings were in need of painting and repairs, and there were other signs of hard times.

Weeds were growing up through the cracks in the wide expanse of flagstone in front of the main entrance, and the tall, dust-coated windows were without curtains, making the house look deserted. A tall, burly man of about sixty, with white hair and a beard, stepped around the corner from the back of the house as Toby reined up and dismounted.

The man, who was wearing work clothes and heavy boots, looked at Toby suspiciously. "Can I do something for you?" he asked, his voice curt and wary.

"I'm looking for Mr. Alexander Woodling," Toby replied. "My name is Toby Holt."

"Toby!" the man exclaimed, smiling and hurrying forward. "I'm your cousin Alex. Eulalia wrote and said you'd be visiting, but I had no idea when."

"I've been looking forward to meeting you, sir," Toby said as they shook hands. "You certainly have a nice place here."

Alex took off his battered hat and pushed his unruly shock of hair back as he glanced at the house. "It's a nice farm, but it's seen better days. And call me Alex, please. I'm sorry I was so cold at first, but I've got to where I'm leery of strangers. Some men have been trying to buy my farm, and they won't take no for an answer."

"You mean they're trying to make you sell it?" Toby asked, frowning. "Who are these men?"

"Oh, just some riffraff. Come on and bring your horse back to the barns. I was working in my smithy when I saw you riding up the lane."

They started walking around the house. "Well, don't let me interrupt your work," Toby said. "In fact, I'd be glad to help. I'm pretty good with a hammer."

"No, no, I'm not about to put a guest to work," Alex said firmly. "Just let me finish up while the forge is hot, and then we can talk. Now, let me see, Cindy just got married, didn't she? And I believe you have two children—isn't that right?"

The clanging of a hammer on metal issued from the small smithy beside one of the barns as Toby and Alex approached. The noise stopped, and a small, wiry older man stepped outside. "Jonah, this is my cousin, Toby Holt," Alex said. "Toby, this is Jonah Venable. He's supposed to be a hired hand, but he's more like family. All of my other employees left over the years, but I can't even run him off."

The thin, leathery man moved a chew of tobacco to the other side of his mouth as he nodded to Toby. "Pleased to meet you," he said. He wiped a grimy hand on his apron before holding it out to Toby.

Again Toby offered to help with the work, but having no success, he led his horse into the barn, where he unsaddled it, put it in a stall, and forked hay into the feed bin. Back outside, he looked around.

Even more than paint and repairs, what the place needed was a woman's touch. The rose garden at one side of the house was overgrown, and the curtainless rear windows had the same blank, dingy look as those in front. A clothesline tied between a post on the back porch and a tree had garments carelessly tossed over it instead of pinned neatly.

The forge bellows puffed and a hammer rang on metal as Toby sat down on the stool outside the smithy door. Over the noise, he thought he heard hoofbeats approaching the rear of the barn, bringing to mind his earlier encounter on the road. It occurred to him that he could ask Alex about the identity of the young woman; a tomboy who wore riding breeches was certain to be the topic of gossip throughout the surrounding area. Surely Alex would know her name and where she lived.

A moment later, however, as the hoofbeats ceased,

Toby realized that such an inquiry would not be necessary. And all at once it was clear to him why the young woman had failed to tell him her name.

It was because she had recognized *his* name, knew who he was, and knew he was coming to the farm. Her smile admitted as much as she came around the barn and walked toward him, slapping her riding crop against a boot. Her hazel eyes also revealed what they had before, an eager, responsive echo of his reaction to her.

Standing up as she approached, Toby now also knew why her features had seemed so familiar. Like his mother, she was a Woodling, with family characteristics that had been passed down through generations.

Alex, also seeing her approach, stepped out of the smithy. "Toby, this is my daughter, Alexandra," he said proudly. "Alexandra, this is our cousin, Toby Holt."

"We've met," Toby said, lifting his hat and smiling. "We almost ran into each other on the road, as a matter of fact."

"Yes, we certainly did," Alexandra agreed cheerfully, then turned to her father. "I jumped Turco over the hedge onto the road and almost landed on top of Toby and his horse. It startled Turco, and he flung me into the ditch."

"Well, no harm done, apparently," Alex said, patting her hat fondly. "But it's no wonder that stallion needs new shoes every month or two, the way you ride him."

Despite the mild reproof, the deep affection between father and daughter was apparent to Toby. Clearly the old man doted on the child, who doubtless was the joy of the autumn of his life. In the absence of a mother's guiding and restraining hand, it seemed he had raised his daughter much like a boy, allowing her to do whatever she wished.

Alexandra glanced between Toby and her father. "Dad,

Toby said that you should take me in hand. What do you think about that?"

"I think he's absolutely right," Alex replied. "But that would be about as hard as holding on to a greased catfish."

"Harder," Alexandra said, giving Toby a disarming smile. Then she disappeared behind the barn, apparently to take care of her horse. Toby sat back down on the stool, looking at her as she emerged from the barn a little later and walked toward the house. Considering the way she was dressed, he knew that he was staring rather than looking, but he was unable to shift his gaze elsewhere. Her slender, shapely thighs and hips in the tight riding breeches were more than fascinating. . . .

Suddenly she glanced back at him. When she saw him staring at her, she gave him a radiant, pleased smile. As Toby smiled back, he could feel his face becoming uncomfortably warm, and for the first time in many years he felt ill at ease and awkward. He forced himself to look away from her, both exhilarated and troubled by this new, unexpected power in his life.

A short time later, Alex and Jonah finished their work. While Jonah cleaned up, Alex gave Toby a tour. After commenting on the poor condition of the buildings and the farm in general, he candidly admitted that when his wife had died he had lost interest in everything and begun drinking too much.

"All of my hired hands and the household staff left," he said. "Not that I blamed them, because I had gone into debt and they weren't getting paid. Jonah was the only one who stayed on. Then, a few years ago, I came to my senses and started building the place up again."

"Well, no lasting harm has been done," Toby offered. "You have good breeding stock, and all the place needs is some paint and repairs."

"Yes, I didn't ruin anything," Alex agreed ruefully. "Most important, I didn't damage my daughter's love for

me. Of course, she was in a good boarding school during
most of my bad time. I kept enough money at hand to pay
for that."

"I find it hard to picture her in a boarding school,"
Toby said.

Alex laughed. "Yes, I know what you're thinking.
Without a doubt, she changed that school more than it
changed her. Her mother was ailing for years, and I
suppose I let Alexandra run wild. But she put that school
in first place in every equestrian event in this region, and
the trustees wouldn't let the headmaster throw her out.
And even if I could, Toby, I wouldn't change anything
about her."

"I know how you feel," Toby said. "My daughter has
a mind of her own, and I feel the same about her. I've
been around horses all my life, but I've never seen anyone
who can ride like Alexandra."

"I haven't either, and that's not just pride speaking,"
Alex said. "The girl took to horses like a duck to water,
and she was riding not long after she could walk. But she
also got a good education out of that school—better one
than I ever did." He sighed, looking around at the run-
down buildings. "But just about the time when I was
about to get this farm back on its feet, this depression
came along and smacked it flat again."

"Well, you couldn't get anything like the value of
your horses by selling them to the cavalry," Toby said.
"They're paying very little for what horses they're buying,
and it would be a shame to sell thoroughbred hunters as
cavalry mounts. But my mother and stepfather would be
pleased to make you a loan, and I would as well."

"No," Alex replied quickly. "I'm most grateful for the
offer, Toby, but I can't accept—"

"We're family, Alex," Toby said, interrupting him. "It
isn't right for you to turn me down out of hand."

The old man frowned and shook his head stubbornly.

"If I can't sell some horses, I can at least cut some corners and get by without being a burden to others."

"It won't be a burden, believe me. My mother and stepfather wouldn't make the offer if they couldn't afford it. The same goes for me. Now, the least you can do is think about it."

Alex was silent for a long moment. At last he grudgingly agreed to think about the offer; but then, as if apologizing for his uncooperativeness, he began talking about other options he had for raising money.

A final solution, he said, was to sell the farm. It was one of the most valuable properties within many miles of Lexington, and for years numerous people had been trying to buy it. Toby, reminded of his own initial reception, asked once again about the men who had been attempting to force Alex to sell. Again, however, Alex shrugged off the matter as unimportant.

The sun was setting, and Jonah had gone to the house. The appetizing aroma of food cooking carried from the kitchen as Toby and Alex crossed the back porch and went inside. The kitchen, built and equipped to provide food for large social events, was enormous, and its windows were open to the evening breeze.

It was immediately obvious to Toby that meals and housekeeping chores were shared responsibilities. Jonah was at the stove, his sleeves rolled up as he tended the pots and pans. Alexandra, wearing a pretty gingham dress, was setting the table. She looked somewhat older in a dress, as well as more feminine.

Alex went to the sink to wash his hands. As he worked the pump, he glanced over his shoulder at his daughter. "Are you going to church, or to the city or something, honey?"

Her expression abruptly changing to a dark frown, Alexandra turned on her father. "Is it Sunday?" she demanded crossly. "And do you think I'd be setting out for the city at this time of day?"

"Well, why are you wearing a· dress, then?" Alex asked, perplexed.

"Because I feel like it!" she snapped angrily. "Why are you going on about it, Dad? I often wear a dress at home."

Alex's surprised expression cast some doubt on the accuracy of her last statement. Jonah chuckled as he glanced between Toby and Alexandra, eliciting a glare from her. Alex then looked at Toby in sudden understanding.

To break the tension, Toby helped Alexandra finish setting the table. Dinner, dished up by Alex and Jonah, did not reflect the straitened finances of the farm. Thick slabs of sugar-cured ham were accompanied by fresh vegetables from the garden and well-seasoned rice. Steaming cornbread with fruit preserves and coffee completed the meal.

Toby complimented Alexandra on how delicious the food was. "I've been eating in hotels for the past few weeks, and I almost forgot how good a home-cooked meal is," he said.

"That may be," Jonah interrupted dryly, "but you're talking to the wrong one, young man. *I* cooked this dinner. Miss Alexandra trying to cook is about like a mule trying to preach a sermon."

"That's not true," Alexandra protested. "I can cook some, even if you can cook better. But I can make good bourbon."

Both her father and Jonah nodded in agreement. "You make better bourbon than anyone else in Kentucky, honey," Alex said, "and people here know how to make bourbon. My own daddy taught me how, Toby. I used to make a few gallons a year, but I don't touch the stuff now. Not enough time. I taught Alexandra how to make it, though, and she took to it so fast she's been making it for us these past two years."

"Where do you make it?" Toby asked.

"We have a still out in one of the barns," Alexandra replied. "I'll show it to you tomorrow, and I'll show you the cellar where we keep the kegs and age it. Incidentally, your room is ready for you, Toby."

There was a momentary silence. "Well, I do have a hotel room," Toby said. "And I might need to attend to some things in the city."

"You can attend to them from here," Alex said firmly. "You're not going to come here and offer to lend me money, Toby, and then refuse hospitality. I'll ride to the city with you tomorrow so we can return your horse to the stable and bring your things back."

"No, he'll have too much baggage to carry on a horse," Alexandra said. "I'll take him in the buggy."

Toby, feeling somewhat caught up in the flow of events, agreed, to everyone's approval. Alex asked about Toby's business in the city, and he explained that he was performing a mission for the government. "I can't say much about it," he continued, "but right now things are at a standstill. So I'll probably be in Lexington for a few days."

"Then you can spend that few days here," Alex said, getting up and ending the discussion.

Everyone helped wash the dishes and clean up. Later, Jonah went to his room, and Toby went out on the back porch with Alex. Alexandra joined them a little later, with glasses of mint julep for Toby and herself, and cider for her father. She sat down on the porch swing with her glass.

The tall mint julep was frosty cold, and the evening breeze felt refreshing. Fireflies twinkled over the pastures in the darkness, and the croaking of frogs along the creek and the chirping of crickets made a pleasing harmony. It was a peaceful, enjoyable time for Toby.

It was also disquieting. He had wanted to stay at the hotel in order to put distance between himself and Alexandra—distance and time to think logically. Despite the powerful attraction between them, the difference in their ages was simply too great.

Everything had happened too quickly, and Toby mistrusted his own feelings. Yet when he was near her, nothing else seemed to matter. He listened to Alex as the man reminisced about his younger years, but Toby's eyes were on Alexandra. She touched a toe against the floor and moved the swing back and forth, gazing reflectively back at him in the moonlight.

XII

Only three days had passed since Toby had arrived at Fair Oaks, but already he felt perfectly at home. Alex and Jonah let him help out with the morning chores, and in the afternoon he was able to relax and enjoy Alexandra's companionship.

They had their love of horses in common, but there was something more between them, which they both recognized. Toby had not talked with Alexandra about it, because he was reluctant even to consider the subject when there was such a difference in their ages; yet that didn't prevent them from getting along as friends, and in the meantime, being near her was a new and entirely different experience for Toby.

As they toured the far pastures on their third afternoon together, Alexandra playfully poked fun at the saddle Toby was using. He was mounted on a hunter gelding almost as large as Alexandra's stallion, and Jonah had found him an old western saddle in the tack room. "If you had a riding saddle," she said, "we could take some fences. But your horse has so much weight on him that he wouldn't be able to jump a matchstick."

"That suits me fine," Toby said. "I don't intend to risk my neck trying to keep up with you. I like a western saddle, and I don't see how you manage to stay on that little leather postage stamp you use."

"I don't always stay on it," she quipped, "as I thought you'd noticed. I'm accustomed to a competition saddle, and it's the only kind I find comfortable. I don't even like an ordinary riding saddle, much less a western saddle. I know they're for working, but it still seems to me that they're much larger and heavier than necessary."

"Not really," Toby said. "When a rope snubbed around a saddle horn has a half-wild longhorn on the other end, a smaller saddle would tilt up or pull off the horse. Believe me, no cowboy wants that to happen."

They had been approaching the western boundary of the farm, and as they breasted a hill they came in sight of crop fields and a group of small, well-kept buildings. Toby recalled that Alex had mentioned an orphanage owned by a minister named Ezekiel Quint, where some forty boys lived, and that Quint had free use of a large tract of Fair Oaks land on which to grow crops.

Alexandra told him a little about the orphanage, saying she liked and admired the Quints, then turned her stallion to the south, with Toby following. A little while later, an idyllic wooded area came into view ahead. There were just trees and grass and no underbrush, and as they approached, Alexandra reined up.

"Now, there's a fair race," she said. "That woods is about a furlong deep, and there's pasture on the other side. I'll bet I can get there before you can."

It was a fair contest, Toby acknowledged. Racing through the trees would be strictly a test of skill in avoiding obstacles, eliminating her advantage of lighter weight and a more powerful horse. However, it was also dangerous. "What will Alex say when I take you back to the house with your head cut open from hitting a tree limb?"

"The same thing he's said when I've been hurt before," Alexandra retorted, gathering her reins. "Are you ready? Get set! One, two, three, go!"

As she shouted and leaned forward in the saddle, Toby loosened his reins and jabbed his horse with his heels. The gelding lunged into a run toward the trees. Alexandra's stallion immediately followed and quickly pulled ahead. She veered away to the right, toward an open area in the trees.

Urging his horse to full speed and letting it choose its path, Toby bent low in the saddle. A horse would not run into an obstacle, he knew, but even when running at full speed it could come close enough to brush a rider off the saddle. As he entered the woods, Toby swung from one side of the saddle to the other to avoid the trees, sometimes lifting one foot from a stirrup and over the seat while holding on to the wide horn of his saddle.

The gelding, a hunter, was accustomed only to a rider who stayed on top of the saddle. At first the animal was confused, thinking that Toby was about to fall, but it resumed its full running pace when Toby snapped the ends of the reins across its shoulder. As he ducked limbs and slid from side to side, he heard Alexandra's stallion pounding through the woods off to his right, keeping abreast of the gelding.

The trees thinned ahead, and the pasture came into view. A large oak was to his right, and as the gelding skirted it, Toby slid down on the left side of the saddle in a crouch, the ground rushing past below him. As the horse ran out of the trees, he heard the stallion dash out in the same instant, the powerful, agile horse having zigzagged so rapidly that it had kept up with the gelding.

He started to pull himself back into the saddle. Then, deciding to tease Alexandra, he ducked his head back down and, holding on to the saddle horn, clung to the opposite side of the saddle from her.

The trick worked. Thinking that he had been un-horsed, Alexandra rode back into the trees. "Toby!" she shouted. "Where are you? Are you hurt?"

Chuckling to himself, Toby pulled himself back up, tugged on a rein to turn the gelding, then slid over to the other side of the saddle. The horse obediently walked behind and to the side of the stallion as Toby kept hidden. Alexandra continued shouting for him, her voice becoming more alarmed.

"Where are you, Toby?" she called. "Can you hear me? If you're hurt, try to answer me! Try to tell me where you are!"

The gelding caught up with the stallion, walking be-side it, and Toby was only a few feet from Alexandra as she called out again and again. After going all the way back through the woods, she reined up at the edge of the trees, intending to double back.

Toby lifted his head and looked across his saddle at her. "Are you looking for me?" he asked.

Alexandra turned, startled. She was red-faced for a moment; then she found her tongue. "What on earth are you doing there?"

"Just following you around," he said innocently, stand-ing up in the stirrups. "And showing you what a rider can do with a western saddle. Being able to hide behind a horse is handy at times."

"But I was worried to death about you! I thought you had fallen and were hurt!"

"Well, now you have an idea of how your father feels about you at times, don't you?" Toby couldn't keep from grinning.

Alexandra stiffened and her eyes became wide. In an instant, to Toby's astonishment, she had jumped out of her saddle and was pulling him off his horse, flailing at him with her fists. Taken completely by surprise, Toby fell to the ground with her in a tangle.

The deep grass cushioned the impact, and Alexandra threw herself on top of him, pummeling his chest and laughing. Toby began laughing, too, then gripped her wrists and rolled over on top of her, pinning her arms at her sides.

Then their laughter and their smiles faded. Alexandra moved slightly, adjusting to a comfortable position under him, and then she was still. Her auburn hair had fallen from her cap, and her hazel eyes gazed up at him. Their lips were only inches apart, and she was the most desirable woman Toby had ever seen.

The breeze stirred the grass around them, and they were motionless for long seconds. Finally Toby sat up. Lifting himself off her without even kissing her was one of the most difficult things he had ever done, but somehow he did it.

Toby had made mistakes before, but he valued Alexandra too highly to give in to a moment's passion. He stood and helped her up. "I'll have to watch you," he said. "You can jump around like a monkey."

"No, I'll have to watch you," she replied. "You fooled me completely, hiding like that. I wouldn't have believed such a tall man could do that."

Toby chuckled as he brushed grass off himself and helped her brush the back of her jacket. The moment of temptation was not completely over. He still longed to take her in his arms, and he was sure Alexandra would not stop him. But they remounted, and as they rode slowly back toward the house, their conversation was more subdued than before.

The sun was low in the west when the farm buildings came into view ahead. As they neared the stock pens at the rear of the barns, Alexandra tugged her cap down, leaned forward in the saddle, and gave the stallion its head.

Toby watched in admiration. She seemed to be part

of the animal as it effortlessly leaped the fences and ran across the pens to leap another fence. Alexandra reined up behind the barns and waved to him.

After they took care of their horses they went to the house, joining Alex and Jonah, who had ended their work for the day and were in the kitchen, putting the finishing touches on dinner. Apologizing for their tardiness, Toby and Alexandra washed up and helped.

Later, when dinner was finished and the dishes were washed, Toby and Alex sat on the back porch as darkness fell. Alexandra joined them, bringing out the customary drinks. Toby, not knowing how much longer he would be in Lexington, wanted to resolve Alex's indecision about accepting the loan. He was waiting for the right moment to broach the subject when Alex suddenly brought it up himself.

"I've decided to take that loan, Toby," he said, "and I'm more than grateful to you and your parents. It occurred to me that I was being foolish to risk this farm because of pride."

"Not at all, Alex," he replied. "And I'm sure I speak for my parents as well as myself when I say I'm pleased by your decision. I'll go to the city tomorrow and attend to the details. I need to go anyway to check for mail."

"I'll go with you," Alexandra put in quickly. "I need to shop for a few things."

Realizing he would have been greatly disappointed if she didn't come, Toby smiled at her in the dim light. Still, his happy anticipation of her companionship was clouded by the knowledge that a hard decision awaited him. The emotional bonds between them were growing stronger every day, yet the fact remained that Alexandra was so very young. Toby was reluctant to ever leave her, yet he knew that each day he remained with her his decision would only become harder.

*   *   *

For the drive to Lexington the next day, Alexandra wore a colorful summer dress and matching bonnet, and she chatted gaily all the way to the city, every so often asking Toby a question about his family.

While she was doing her shopping, Toby went to the bank, where he wrote out a draft for his share of the loan and deposited it in Alex's account. Then he went to the telegraph office and sent a telegram to his mother, informing her of Alex's decision and the address of the bank so she could have the money transferred to his account.

Next he stopped at the police department and talked with the chief of police, who said he had received the bulletins from Frankfort on the men involved in the demonstration, but that there had been no other developments and no messages for Toby.

At the post office, however, two letters awaited him. One, from Claude Leggett, was barely legible. It began with an apology for the poor handwriting, explaining that several weeks before, when Claude had returned to his studio at night, he had surprised a burglar. The man had shot him in the shoulder and got away, taking with him, for some strange reason, a set of glass plates from which Marjorie's stereopticon slides were made.

The wound had been more painful than serious, the letter continued, although Claude still had a little trouble using his arm. The reason he had written, however, was to notify Toby that his recent telegram had been forwarded to Marjorie in Arkansas, where she was photographing plantations along the Mississippi River.

Glancing over the letter again, Toby frowned in puzzlement, wondering what a burglar would want with photographic plates. He opened the other letter, which was from Dieter Schumann. It was brief, written hurriedly to keep Toby informed of developments at the lumber company.

The financial outlook, the letter stated, was confused

at present, which made it impossible to determine if the
company was yet making a profit. There was a sentence
about the steam launch, which was now making daily trips
once more, towing full loads of twelve to fifteen logs down
the lake from the logging camp in Wisconsin.

The letter was as troubling to Toby as were the note
and the mortgage he had received before. He could not
understand why Dieter was unable to determine if the
company was making a profit, unless he was awaiting
payment for large amounts of lumber, which seemed unlikely. Just as puzzling was the enormous amount of timber being brought from the logging camp. Unless sales
had mushroomed, which was inconceivable, the yard was
not large enough to hold the stacks of lumber that would
be milled from the logs.

Dismissing the matter from his mind, Toby left the
post office and returned to the store where Alexandra was
shopping. He was looking forward to the highlight of the
day—taking her to a restaurant for lunch. He insisted on
paying for the selection of notions she had picked out, and
then they walked down the street to a restaurant.

As they went inside, something happened that served
as a painful reminder to Toby of their difference in age. A
young man who was leaving the restaurant bowed to Alexandra, and she returned his greeting, then introduced him
to Toby. The man, whose name was Brooks, was stiffly
formal as he acknowledged the introduction.

Going to a table with Alexandra, Toby commented on
the man's unfriendly attitude.

"Pay no attention to him," Alexandra said lightly.
"He's been trying to court me for the past couple of years,
but I have no interest in him. His nose is out of joint,
that's all."

Toby had guessed that the young man was a year or
two older than Alexandra. At the same time, he seemed

hardly more than a youth. Feeling glum, Toby took a seat and tried to forget the incident.

Then, as they were finishing their meal, there was an incident of the exact opposite nature. It highlighted an aspect of Alexandra's personality that spanned generations, a quality she possessed that made a difference in age between her and others inconsequential. A man who looked to be in his sixties, wearing an expensive suit tailored in the style of the previous generation, approached the table. Beaming with pleasure, he bowed over Alexandra's hand. "It's been ages, Miss Alexandra!" he exclaimed. "It's so good to see you again."

"It's always good to see you, Colonel," she replied with equal charm. "Please allow me to introduce my companion—this is Mr. Toby Holt, my cousin three times removed. Toby, this is Colonel Basil Claibourne, hunt master of the Fairfield Hunt of Lexington."

The title explained the evident close friendship between Alexandra and him. The man was courteous and smiling as he exchanged greetings with Toby, but it was obvious he was eager to return to his conversation with Alexandra.

"We've certainly missed you this year," he said to her. "The chases have been much slower without your Turco pushing the hounds."

"It was for want of three hundred dollars to pay hunt dues," she said without embarrassment. "Fairfield isn't a hunt for the thrifty, is it?"

"No, and more's the shame," Claibourne replied, sighing. "I believe we could do with fewer than sixty hounds and economize in other ways, and we may have to. I understand that Stone Ridge has lower dues now. Have you thought about riding with them?"

"Those yard dogs they have for hounds can't put game to earth. In any event, their dues are still a hundred dollars, and I wouldn't want to ask my dad for it. We're on hard times, Colonel."

The man lifted his eyebrows. "Everyone is, Miss Alexandra. You know, I'd like to have your Turco, ah, keep company with one of my mares, but I might have trouble finding the fee. I have several good colts, though, and I could offer one of them as fee."

"I'd have to talk to my dad about wintering another head of stock. And it would depend on the breeding and the show of the colt, of course."

Claibourne nodded and briefly described the colts that he had. He and Alexandra made tentative plans to get together and look at the colts, then began exchanging news about area horses and hunts.

It was obvious that the man enjoyed talking with Alexandra. However, not wishing to intrude, he reluctantly ended the conversation, shook hands with Toby again, and left.

During the drive back to the farm, Toby offered to pay Alexandra's dues to join one of the hunts. She thanked him but refused.

"Belonging to a hunt is a luxury," she said. "Anyone who must count the cost of luxuries should do without them."

Toby persisted, trying to persuade her, but she continued to decline his offer. When they reached the farm, however, the subject was suddenly forgotten. A carriage was parked in the front drive, and two men were talking in heated tones with Alex. Jonah was looking on from the porch.

"The short man," Alexandra said quietly, "is a real estate dealer named Johnson. He's been here several times, trying to talk Dad into selling the farm, and they've argued every time. I've never seen the tall man before."

Toby did not need to know who the tall man was in order to know *what* he was. His flashy suit and hard, sardonic features identified him as a type Toby knew well from when he had clashed with criminals in New Orleans, Memphis, and other places.

The men fell silent as the buggy drew up in front of the house and Toby stepped down. Alex introduced him in curt tones. "This is Mr. Toby Holt, a relative. Toby, this is Tom Johnson, a real estate agent from Lexington, and that's Elmer Sewell, his client."

No one offered to shake hands, and Toby had noticed that Sewell's eyes had changed when the name Holt was mentioned. The man apparently knew him by reputation, and the dark, penetrating eyes were wary. Jonah helped Alexandra down from the buggy, and Toby stood beside Alex.

Johnson resumed talking, insisting that Woodling would never get a better offer for the place. With a hefty commission in prospect, Johnson was impatiently aggressive and far less cautious than the watchful, cunning Sewell, who said hardly a word. Toby immediately saw that Johnson was all bluster, whereas Sewell would be genuinely dangerous.

Johnson referred to the number of times he had visited the farm and talked with Alex. "But either I ain't using the right words, or you ain't listening," he continued. "Now, we want a fair bargain all around, but we'll go the extra piece on our side. And like I said, we're willing to put down hard cash."

"You're the one who's not listening," Alex said. "I've told you my farm's not for sale, and that's the end of it."

Johnson scowled and shook his head. "Then the circumstances just ain't been made right. We're willing to do whatever we have to, and that includes making the circumstances right."

For the first time, Toby spoke up. "Exactly what do you mean by that, Mr. Johnson?"

Johnson hesitated. He wouldn't meet Toby's gaze.

"Well, I mean that my client wants to buy this farm under any circumstances," he said. "Mr. Sewell has traveled a long way to see to this."

"Yes, I thought so," Toby said, turning to Sewell. "You don't appear to be a horse breeder, Mr. Sewell, so it seems strange that you would want a horse farm. I'm curious about that, about where you're from, and about what sort of business you're involved in."

"None of that makes any difference," Sewell replied woodenly. "All that makes any difference is that I want to buy this farm."

Johnson grunted in agreement. "We've made an offer that's more than fair. It would be mighty wise to accept it."

"You've also just made a threat," Toby said quietly, "and by doing that, you've made a serious mistake. You've been told that this farm isn't for sale, so neither of you has any more business here. Now both of you get in that carriage and leave, and don't come back."

Johnson blinked, his assurance crumbling, and turned to Sewell. The tall man was glaring at Toby, who stared back. It was a contest of wills that lasted for several long, dragging seconds.

Flushing with anger, Sewell finally looked away. He snapped his fingers at Johnson and turned to the carriage. The two men climbed in and drove off without another word.

"Well, you got rid of them," Alex chuckled. Laughing and commenting in agreement, Alexandra and Jonah joined them.

Toby kept his eyes on the carriage until it disappeared at the end of the drive. "Are there any criminal organizations around here, Alex?"

"Criminal organizations?" Alex echoed, surprised, then shook his head firmly. "No, not here, Toby. We have some gambling at the racetracks, of course, but it's only individuals making bets. It's nothing like what goes on at the big tracks in the East. I hear they drug horses there, bribe jockeys, even steal horses from one track and run them at another under a different name."

"Yes, I know," Toby said. "But that's only one aspect of what they do. The bigger organizations are involved in all types of criminal activities. It appears to me that someone is trying to get a toehold here, Alex, because that Sewell looks and acts like one of their front runners."

"Maybe so," Alex said. "But you nipped their plot in the bud, Toby. I reckon that pair won't be back."

His voice was confident, and Alexandra and Jonah commented in agreement. Toby, however, was not so sure.

Indeed, early the following afternoon it appeared that another confrontation was at hand. Toby was helping Alex and Jonah repair a fence beside the barn, and Alexandra was putting a young horse through its paces on the training course when a covered carriage rolled up the drive. Toby walked rapidly toward the house, with Alex and Jonah following.

He reached the front drive as the carriage drew to a halt. To his astonishment, however, Marjorie White stepped out of it. "Marjorie!" he exclaimed. "I expected to hear from you, but not in person!"

"I decided to stop and see you on my way back from Arkansas," she said. "I got your telegram, and the chief of police in town told me where to find you. How are you, Toby?"

"I'm fine, and I can see you are," he replied, taking her hand. "Marjorie, I'd like you to meet my friend and relative, Alexander Woodling. And this is his friend and employee, Jonah Venable."

Just then Alexandra came around the corner of the house and saw Toby holding Marjorie's hand. The younger woman slid to a stop, frowning. Only when her quick glance picked out the wedding ring on Marjorie's left hand did her composure return.

Marjorie was taken aback for just an instant by the young woman's riding costume. Toby introduced them, explaining to Alexandra that Marjorie was a professional photographist, and soon the two women were talking like old friends.

"Marjorie," Toby interrupted when he got a chance, "did you bring your baggage with you?"

"Yes, and I have that note you want in my cases," she replied. "I'd hoped I could impose for the night."

"You'll stay as long as you wish," Alexandra said, taking Marjorie's hand. "And it certainly won't be imposing. Come, we'll prepare your room while the men are bringing in your things."

Later, on the back porch, Marjorie handed Toby the note and sat down with him. He thanked her but shook his head when she asked if he could tell her why he wanted the note. "I'm sorry, but I can't, Marjorie," he said. "It concerns the work I'm doing for the government."

"Yes, I thought it might, even though I fail to see how. Well, I do hope it's of some help to you, Toby." She smiled as Alexandra appeared with tall glasses of mint julep. "Thank you, dear. That looks very refreshing."

"I hope you like it," Alexandra said, then tactfully left them alone to talk.

As Toby studied the note, Marjorie took a sip of her drink. "That's absolutely delicious!" she exclaimed. "I've never tasted a better drink."

"You've never tasted one more potent, either," Toby said wryly. "Drink that slowly, Marjorie. Alexandra has a talent for hiding enough bourbon under mint and sugar to knock a mule flat."

Marjorie took a smaller sip. "Toby, if I may be so bold," she said quietly, "it appears to me that that girl loves you to distraction. Those big eyes of hers melt every time she looks at you."

Toby sighed in resignation. "The trouble is, I feel the same about her." He was eager to dismiss the subject. "But we'll have to see how things work out."

"What do you mean?" Marjorie prodded. "She's young, but she's an adult. As long as you love each other, what else matters?"

"My children, for one. I also have to think about Alexandra, and if she would be happy. Timmy and Janessa aren't easy to deal with, and I'm gone from home for months at a time. There are many things to consider, Marjorie."

"Yes, I can see that," Marjorie agreed. "Well, I do hope that things work out for the best, and I'll leave it at that. I suppose you heard what happened to Claude."

"Yes, I received a letter from him. I was shocked, of course, and I hope he recovers completely. Why do you think the burglar took those photographic plates?"

Marjorie shook her head. "I have no idea. The plates of the Great Chicago Fire would have been much more valuable, but they weren't touched. The only ones he took were a series I made in Connecticut."

"Connecticut?" Toby looked again at the note. "This man, Howard Cummings, said he met you in Connecticut. Maybe he was trying to find out where you live because for some reason or other he wanted those plates. Maybe he was the burglar."

Marjorie shook her head. "I thought of that possibility, Toby. But then we get back to why he would want the plates. It simply doesn't make any sense."

"Precisely what did you photograph with them?"

Marjorie started to reply, then stopped and rose from her chair. "Those are the plates I developed in Portland," she said. "I made a set of proofs of them, and they may still be in one of my cases. I'll be right back."

Toby sipped his mint julep until Marjorie returned. Smiling triumphantly, she was carrying oblong sheets of photographic paper and a magnifying glass. "Here they are, Toby," she said. "You'll need this glass to see them properly."

Toby began inspecting the proofs, which Marjorie explained were contact prints of the plates that had been stolen. The third one he looked at showed a man standing in front of a statue. Stifling an oath, Toby peered at the man's face through the magnifying glass. He was certain it was the same face he had seen on the tintype on Howard Cummings's arrest record.

The man who had been a bystander at the demonstration in Frankfort was the same man who had followed Marjorie from Connecticut to Boston and tried to get her address. He was also undoubtedly the burglar who had taken the photographic plates, one of which had been a photograph of him. Apparently he had wanted to get the plate of himself, so that no one else would see it and know he had been in Connecticut. But why?

"Do you know this man?" Toby asked, pushing the proof across the table and handing Marjorie the magnifying glass.

Marjorie looked through the glass and shook her head. "No, definitely not. I didn't even notice his face when I took the picture. As far as I know, he's simply someone who lives in Talcott."

Toby sat up in his chair, speechless for a moment. "What did you say?" he demanded, finding his voice.

"I said that as far as I know, this man is simply someone who lives in Talcott," Marjorie replied, surprised. "That's where I made these photographs. Talcott, Connecticut."

Ursula Guthrie, working in the garden with the others, turned to look as Paddy Rafferty commented that someone was coming to the house. Her hope that it was a customer wanting to buy beer faded when she recognized the expensive buggy. It belonged to John Kirchner, the Milwaukee businessman who supplied the ingredients Maida used in making beer.

"Sure and it's only Kirchner," Paddy confirmed, gesturing for his wife and children to return to their labors.

Fred, who had been working next to Ursula, scowled as he leaned on his hoe. "It's always Kirchner," he grumbled. "Coming here again to tell us how much money he has to buy us out. I'll go show him the road."

"No, certainly not," Ursula replied, putting down her hoe. "We must be courteous, as he always is. I will go and talk with him."

The others resumed working as Ursula walked toward the house. Her feelings toward Kirchner were mixed. To the man's credit, he had a deep reverence for the long line of Oberg master brewers. But at the same time, he was a wealthy businessman who viewed the brewery as a good investment. With virtually no beer being sold, and Maida still brewing tun after tun, the brewery was near bankruptcy. Kirchner was eager to take advantage of that, and Ursula knew that sooner or later she would have to accept his offer.

A heavyset, florid-faced man, Kirchner smiled expansively and bowed as she approached. A younger man was with him. "Good afternoon, Ursula," Kirchner said cheerfully. "And how are you today?"

"I am well, John, thank you. And you?"

"Oh, I've seen better days," he said, grinning. "Times are rough, you know." His grin abruptly disappeared. "This is my son Frederick."

Ursula recalled that Kirchner had mentioned having two sons. He had said that one of them was in business, like himself, while the other showed little promise of doing anything useful. From the old man's tone, Frederick was the disappointment. Ursula shook hands.

The youth looked nervous and awkward, and Ursula felt sorry for him, knowing that Kirchner would be a demanding father. In his early twenties, Frederick was slim and handsome enough, with a quick, shy smile. He appeared to be the quiet, studious type, the complete opposite of his aggressive, outgoing father.

Ursula nodded toward the lawn table in the shade of the house. "If you and Frederick would like to sit down, I'll fetch some beer."

"Thank you, I've been looking forward to a glass of delicious Oberg beer," Kirchner replied effusively. "But first, Frederick has something to show you." He turned to his son. "Well, why are you just standing there?" he snapped.

The young man fairly jumped, then quickly retrieved a small box from the buggy. Stuttering, and clearly flustered by his father's glare, he tried to tell Ursula about the contents of the box, but Kirchner sighed impatiently, silenced him with a gesture, and said that the box contained hops.

"Frederick has been attending college in Massachusetts," Kirchner said. "He met a man there named Burbank, who shares his interest in plants, and he helped Frederick develop a new variety of hops."

Ursula smiled and lifted a hand as Frederick started to open the box. "I know very little about hops, Frederick," she apologized, "but I'm certain Maida will want to see what you have. John, if you will sit down, I'll take Frederick and introduce him to Maida. Then I'll fetch beer, and we can talk."

Ursula beckoned Frederick after her to the brewery. Inside the converted barn, the air was thick with fumes from beer fermenting in the massive tuns. At a workbench at the rear of the building, Maida was occupied with one of the obscure tasks that filled her waking hours.

Characteristically, she made no acknowledgment as Frederick was introduced to her, but when Ursula explained in German that Frederick had developed a new variety of hops, her gaze moved at once toward the box the young man was holding.

Ursula turned to Frederick and spoke in English. "Maida can readily understand what Paddy and his family say to her," she said, "but everyone else using English must speak slowly and distinctly."

Frederick, who was staring transfixed at Maida, nodded in reply, because a nod was the only response he was capable of making. Actually, conversation with Maida was far from his thoughts, for he was more than content merely to look at her. When Ursula left, he opened the box and handed it to Maida.

He had chosen hops as a plant to experiment with because he had thought it might please his father— something he had long tried to do, but without much success. But the hops, too, had failed to make any impression, serving only as a pretext for his father to come to the brewery and renew his attempts to buy it.

Now, however, his father was the last thing on Frederick's mind, for he was in the presence of the loveliest creature he had ever seen.

Small and slender, with delicately modeled features and thick black hair, she had not yet made a sound. Yet her lack of greeting when they had been introduced and her silence as she took the box were not discourtesy, he was certain. Her thoughts were simply elsewhere.

Silence fitted her completely, Frederick reflected, because she looked like an angel, a being who lived in another world. Her huge, dark eyes, dreamy and unfocused, gazed at things only she could perceive. Her smooth skin, as white as a lily, looked as if it had never been touched by the sun. Her small, delicate hands moved gracefully as she took one of the hops cones from the box. Her lips parted, and she closed her eyes, wafting the cone back and forth near her nose.

Most remarkable of all, Frederick reflected, she seemed to have some kind of tranquilizing effect on him. He was almost always ill at ease around others, yet while looking at Maida he felt completely relaxed, and she seemed perfectly willing to allow him to gaze at her.

In actuality, Maida was scarcely aware of the young man near her, for her full attention was on the cone of hops she was holding. A different type from any she had ever seen, it was also superior to any she had ever seen, even though it had been plucked before being fully mature.

Other immature hops had a weak, sour odor, because the petals lacked a full infusion of the oils of the plant. Yet this cone had a stronger, more pungently bitter scent than even many mature hops, and the petals felt greasy with oil. When mature, it would be superb.

Explaining that to the young man would be a problem, however, because of her poor English. She put the cone back into the box and looked up at Frederick. He was staring at her fixedly. Unlike most people, he was quiet and unobtrusive, his presence not in the least annoying to her, and his gaze gave her a pleasant feeling.

This novel, warm sensation grew within her as they looked at each other. He smiled tentatively, and she smiled. His smile became unreserved. She reached up to straighten his tie. He suddenly seized her hand and pressed it to his lips, kissing it ardently.

Surprised, Maida almost pulled away, but a keenly enjoyable reaction sprang to life within her. Frederick flushed as he came to his senses, and he looked at her to see if she was angry. She was not, and she even smiled as she pointed to a stool near the workbench. "Have a sit-down, boyo," she said.

For a moment Frederick failed to understand her. Then he realized she was speaking in a bizarre combination of a thick German accent and the Irish brogue she had picked up from the Raffertys. It was almost unintelligible, but the melodious inflection of her voice was the most beautiful sound he had ever heard.

"Are you daft, or are you only deaf?" she said. "Sit down straightaway, boyo."

Frederick sat down on the stool. On the bench was a calendar Maida used in scheduling her tuns. She picked it up, pulled up another stool, and sat down beside Frederick.

The days of the week meant nothing to her, and the rest of the world had moved ahead by a few days during the years she had been using the same calendar. When she pointed to it, there was the inevitable moment of confusion, but Frederick was far readier than others to adjust to her unique framework in time.

Once she determined the day he had plucked the hops cones, she turned the calendar forward to show him that he should have waited another month to five weeks. She took a cone from the box again, then put the tips of her fingers together to illustrate that the petals should be formed together at the point of the cone, which they were not.

"He's no more than a babe, and all and all," she said.

Understanding her completely, Frederick suddenly had a wonderful idea. The plants were growing in the garden behind his father's house in Milwaukee, and he began slowly explaining that he could transplant them. "I can plant them here," he said, pointing to the side of the brewery. "Then you can watch them grow and pick them when they are ready."

Having her own hops garden appealed to Maida, and she nodded in agreement. "It'll be me that's thanking you," she said.

Frederick was delighted, for now he had an excuse to

come and see Maida again. He knew that his father, too, would be pleased that he was already on cordial terms with the Oberg master brewer. It would be, he reflected, one of the rare times that his father was pleased by something he had done.

But it hardly mattered now. For years Frederick had yearned for his father's approval, but from today onward someone else's approval had become more important to him. With the change in his loyalties complete, Frederick wondered if Maida knew about his father's schemes to buy her brewery.

The moment he began talking about the poor sales of beer, however, Maida waved the subject aside. "Sure and that has naught t' do wi' me," she said. She pointed at the tuns, then at herself, making the connection clear. Then she pantomimed counting out bills and shook her head vigorously. Her meaning was obvious to Frederick: She had nothing to do with the financial side of the business.

Taking a different approach, Frederick, using short, simple sentences, referred to when she had worked at a brewery in Germany. Then he explained that she would once again be only an employee if his father bought the brewery. "Would you like that?" he asked.

Maida shook her head again. There was no comparison between her present freedom and the restrictions she had endured in Germany. She would never forget the times when men from the brewery office had tried to make her father use inferior ingredients, or how they had ranted and raved at him constantly about his calendar. "No, I want none of that," she said. "But how can we belay it?"

Frederick frowned and shook his head. That was a point, he reflected ruefully, on which both his father and his older brother would have many ideas. In fact, he suspected that they already had some plan in mind for making the brewery profitable. For the first time in his life, he envied them their practical, dogged minds, because in business or financial matters he was hopelessly inept.

Desperately wanting to help Maida, he began biting his fingernails, as was his habit. Maida leaned closer and looked at his fingertips, then smacked his hand sharply and pulled it away from his lips. Smiling to show him there were no hard feelings, she pinched his cheek. "Have done wi' that, boyo," she said.

Frederick gazed at her as she took his hand and laced her fingers through his. Looking into her deep, dark eyes, he became determined to find a way to help her. He stood up, lifting her hand to his lips. "I will think about it," he said slowly. "I will be back with the plants within a few days, and then we will talk again."

Maida nodded. Frederick released her hand and started to leave. Then he turned back, leaned over her, and touched his lips to hers. When they parted, Maida smiled radiantly. Frederick walked toward the door, his steps light with joy and with a new purpose in life.

XIII

Thomas Haines was among the passengers filing off the train at the Lexington depot as Toby Holt walked along the platform toward him. Haines looked weary and rumpled after his hurried journey from Washington, but his square, strong face reflected barely contained excitement.

The two men greeted each other, and Haines shook his head when Toby said that he could have come to Washington instead. "No, until this business is settled, I don't want anyone else to know you're handling it," the Secret Service director said. "I made certain very few people knew I'd left Washington, and I'd like to be on the next train heading back east. That gives us about an hour to talk."

"That's plenty of time for what I have to say," Toby replied. "We can go to a restaurant down the street."

As they walked out of the station, Haines glanced around to make sure no one else was within earshot. "I have something to tell you as well, Toby," he said. "But first, who is Talcott?"

"It's not a person, it's a place. It's a small city not far from Hartford, Connecticut."

Looking at Toby in shock and dismay, Haines stopped in his tracks. Toby waited for him to speak, but he merely nodded grimly as they continued along the street. They

224

went into the restaurant, where they sat at a corner table and ordered coffee.

"While I was waiting for a reply to the telegram I sent you," Toby said, finishing his explanation, "I made a trip up to Frankfort. The police there have found two of the men who were involved in the protest against demonetization. They were paid to stage the demonstration, and they identified the man who paid them." He took out a photograph and handed it to Haines. "That's a copy of the tintype on Howard Cummings's police record."

Haines studied the tintype, then handed it back. "That's undoubtedly an assumed name," he said.

"I agree," Toby replied. "Now, will you tell me why it bothers you so much that Talcott is a city in Connecticut?"

Haines took a drink of coffee, then began explaining. The President, he said, had recently become increasingly annoyed over the restrictions imposed on his movements during the past months. Forced to remain close to Washington, he had been deferring many matters of importance to him.

One such matter, Haines continued, was the reelection of Representative John Stevens of Connecticut. Many members of Congress were facing tough reelection fights because of the economic depression, and Stevens was one of them. He was a close friend of the President's and one of the administration's most reliable allies in Congress, and Grant wanted to help him.

"In short," Haines said, "the President has given us an ultimatum. He intends to go to Connecticut to campaign for Stevens unless we give him concrete reasons why he can't. I'm not sure precisely where Stevens's district is, but I know it's near Hartford."

"It must include Talcott," Toby said. "Which doesn't leave us much time. The city is having a centennial observance that will end next week—I'm not sure exactly which day—in a big celebration, which would be the best possi-

ble setting for campaign speeches. The man who calls
himself Cummings figured all this out months ago. He's
very cunning."

Haines frowned. "You're right—that doesn't leave us
much time. The problem is, we don't have enough conclu-
sive evidence to offer the President."

"You think he'll definitely go to Connecticut?"

"I'm almost sure of it. The man still thinks like an
army general, and once he sets his mind to something,
he's very difficult to sway. He's also a very courageous
man."

"Yes, we all know that," Toby said. "Well, if that's
the situation, then we'll have to deal with it. I'll have to go
to Connecticut right away, find out the details of the plot,
and stop those involved."

"That's the only way I see to handle it," Haines
agreed. "Needless to say, I'll give you all the help I can.
You've done a great job so far." He went on to tell Toby
that if the President overruled his advisers and left the
capital, Haines himself would be in command of the Secret Service escort. So he might well meet Toby again in
Connecticut.

"Meanwhile," Haines said, "I'll make sure you have
the full cooperation of the authorities. As soon as I return
to Washington, I'll send a telegram to the police chief in
Talcott and let him know you're working with us on the
protection of the President. I'll leave it up to you to tell
him about the plot."

"Good, Tom. And keep me posted on the President's
schedule. It may be that I'll need some help."

His expression somber, Haines walked with Toby
back to the station. While waiting for his train to pull in,
he and Toby checked the rail connections to Connecticut
and decided that Toby should leave on a train that evening.

Later, as he rode back toward the farm, Toby thought
about his heavy responsibility for protecting the Presi-

dent. He thought, too, about Alexandra, yet he remained torn with indecision about their future. While his heart tugged him strongly in one direction, his mind pulled him with equal force in the opposite direction.

At the farm, Alex and Jonah were repairing a gate on one of the stock pens, while Alexandra was putting a horse through its paces on the training course. She rode over as Toby dismounted and talked to the men, informing them that he would be leaving in a few hours.

"In that case, I'll go to the house and get started on supper," Jonah said. "You'll want a good meal before you set out."

"You certainly will," Alex agreed. "I'll give you a hand, Jonah. We'll see you at the house directly, Toby."

Toby nodded, suddenly feeling downcast at having to leave. As he led his horse toward the barn, Alexandra walked beside him, leading her own mount. The two of them were silent, but Toby's mind was filled with conflicting thoughts. All of the reasons for and against his involvement with the young woman beside him suddenly seemed clearer than ever. In her riding breeches, boots, and shirt, Alexandra looked so very young, far too young to be a mother to a rambunctious boy and a strong-willed girl only a few years her junior.

But even if she was young, she was a woman, and a captivatingly beautiful one. As the two of them unsaddled their horses, Toby kept glancing at her. Her riding breeches left very little to the imagination as she knelt to examine her horse's feet, and Toby's powerful attraction to her was stimulated by their being alone in the barn.

"You should have brought your friend here," she commented, carrying her saddle into the tack room. "He could have had supper with us and rested from his journey."

"He had to get right back to Washington," Toby replied. "I'm sure he's accustomed to traveling, working for the government as he does."

"Yes, I can see that," Alexandra said. "You travel, too, but I suppose it isn't too much of a hardship if your children and your ranch are being attended properly."

"Not too much. I'm fortunate in that I have a good foreman and an experienced mother to look after my children."

"It takes more than experience to attend to children properly, from what I've seen. Anyone can become experienced by doing the same thing wrong a thousand times. Doing it right the first time takes common sense."

"Yes, well, Mrs. Hemmings has common sense, too."

Alexandra fell silent, having made her point. Toby felt like a heel, for he knew that he had merely to hold out his arms for her to rush to him. Falling silent again, they turned their horses loose in the pasture, then walked to the house.

Toby went to his room and packed his bags. By the time he had finished and joined the others in the kitchen, dinner was almost ready, and Alexandra had changed her riding clothes for a pretty blue dress.

During the meal, the atmosphere was subdued because of Toby's imminent departure, but Alexandra tried to keep up the conversation. The hunting clubs in the area were organizing a horse show, which she intended to enter. She was certain of winning a share of the prize money but was undecided on how to use it.

"Use it to pay your dues to join a club next year," Alex suggested. "And you don't have to worry about wintering that colt Colonel Claibourne is giving you as stud fee for Turco."

"I do if it's my colt," Alexandra objected. "If wintering it is a farm expense, then it'll have to be a farm colt."

Her father shook his head, disagreeing.

Jonah spoke up. "Both of you are counting your chickens before they hatch, it seems to me. How do you know Alexandra's going to win enough money to pay anyone's dues in one of them fancy hunting clubs?" He grinned in anticipation of the scoffing replies that he knew were coming.

"Nonsense," Alex retorted. "She always wins."

"How much would you like to bet," Alexandra challenged, "that I take no less than a second in any event?"

"Nothing," Jonah replied, "because I got nothing to bet."

The three of them laughed, and Toby smiled as they continued talking, the friendly banter demonstrating their close bonds of affection. He had heard many such conversations during the past days, which would provide him with fond memories of the farm. But Alexandra, he knew, would always be far more than a memory.

After dinner, Jonah left to hitch a horse to the buggy, and Alexandra went to her room to fetch a hat and shawl, intending to accompany Toby to the station. Alex expressed deep gratitude for the loan Toby had arranged. "But I'm just as grateful for your company," the old man continued, "and I'm sure you know that our door is always open to you."

"I know, and I appreciate that, Alex," Toby said. "You can be sure I'll be back whenever I find an opportunity."

"I'll look forward to it."

Outside, Toby shook hands with Alex, then stepped into the buggy beside Alexandra. Since it was already dark, Jonah would escort Alexandra back, and he sat in the rear of the buggy with Toby's bags.

The moon cast its pale light between the tall hedges bordering the road as the buggy turned off the drive. After a time, Alexandra spoke quietly to Toby. "There's the place where we first met," she murmured. "I'll never forget that place or that day."

"Neither will I," Toby replied, and fell glumly silent.

"I know that you can't talk about what you're doing,"

Alexandra said, "but I wonder if I could at least know where you're going and whether or not you'll be in any danger. I promise that I won't repeat it to anyone else."

"I know you won't," he replied. "And I know I can trust you. As it happens, I'm going to Talcott, Connecticut. I don't believe I'll be in any danger, because I'll be working with the chief of police there."

The lights of Lexington drew steadily closer. An hour later, when they arrived at the depot, Toby checked his baggage and walked out to the platform with Alexandra while Jonah took his time parking the buggy.

On the platform, both Alexandra and Toby found it difficult to keep up the pointless, falsely cheerful conversation of those who were close and were about to part. The long silences between them were strained and awkward.

At last the train pulled in, and passengers filed down the steps. As the conductor called out and people began boarding, Alexandra asked the question that both of them had been contemplating during the past hours.

"When will you come back to Kentucky, Toby?" She could not meet his gaze. "Or do you intend ever to come back?"

Toby had to be honest with her. "I don't know, Alexandra," he said. "I'm just not sure what would be best for everyone involved."

Her hazel eyes filled with tears, and her lips and chin began trembling. Toby, although he was not conscious of having moved, was suddenly holding her, and the two of them were kissing.

All the kisses they had not exchanged during the past days, all the words of love they had not spoken, were in that one kiss. They clung to each other hungrily, not letting go even as the whistle hooted and the conductor shouted a last warning for passengers to board. The train began moving along the platform, picking up speed, and Toby finally released Alexandra and jumped onto the steps of the last car.

In the lantern light of the platform, Alexandra was a picture of despair as Toby waved to her. Tears streamed down her face, and her wave was more a reaching out to him than a farewell. Then her hands went to her face, her shoulders shaking with sobs. Jonah suddenly appeared beside her to comfort her. He waved forlornly at the disappearing train.

Toby went into the car and looked for an empty seat. Finding one, he slumped into it, sighing heavily. He had known disappointment and grief before, but he had never known a more despondent moment. With the taste of Alexandra's lips still on his, he looked out the window, the night seeming very dark and lonely.

Toby changed trains in Cincinnati, and the next morning, during a layover in Columbus, he used the time to write a letter to Dieter Schumann. When he reached Connecticut, he planned to devote himself fully to what he had to do, but perhaps later, if things turned out well, he could visit Henry Blake. In the letter, he informed Dieter that he would be out of contact for the next few days and asked that all of his mail be held at the lumberyard until further notice.

After mailing the letter, Toby bought a newspaper, and a half-page advertisement on the back page immediately caught his eye. All at once, what Dieter Schumann had been doing in Chicago became clear to him.

The advertisement showed sketches and floor plans of a three-room and a four-room house and stated in bold print that a North Chicago Lumber Company house package, consisting of all necessary materials, would be sent via rail anywhere in the nation for sixty-five dollars for a three-room house and eighty dollars for a four-room house, plus shipping.*

The house package, the advertisement said, included assembly instructions "prepared by master carpenters and tested by people who were not carpenters." The packages also included "sheet-metal roofing, miscellaneous hardware, and nails," which explained why Dieter had wanted the ironworks. The large amount of timber being brought from the logging camp also made sense now.

While the entire idea was novel and ingenious, Toby wondered if it would also be successful. Later in the day, when his train stopped in Pittsburgh, Toby saw a larger version of the same advertisement on a billboard in the station. People had gathered around it and were discussing the unusual idea and commenting on the reasonable prices. The advertisement was also in the Pittsburgh newspapers, and Toby even overheard a young couple discussing buying one of the packages.

And that was not all. As the train passed through the Philadelphia yards late that evening, Toby's attention was caught by a flatcar on a sidetracked freight. The car was stacked with lumber, metal roofing, and large wooden crates, and attached to the lumber was a sign proclaiming ANOTHER CARLOAD OF NORTH CHICAGO LUMBER COMPANY HOUSE PACKAGES EN ROUTE TO THEIR DESTINATION. Toby smiled as he looked at it, confident now that Dieter had hit upon a successful idea.

The following morning, Toby was in Connecticut. His last stop was at Hartford, where he had an unexpected five-hour layover before the next train left for Talcott. Deciding to take the opportunity to visit Henry, Toby asked the stationmaster about the weapons procurement detachment. The man nodded knowingly, and after explaining that soldiers from the detachment were constantly coming and going by train, he gave Toby directions to the headquarters building.

It was only a few blocks away, and Toby enjoyed the walk. The city was large enough to bustle with life, yet small enough to retain a rural atmosphere, and Toby received friendly nods from the passersby along the wide, tree-lined streets.

Near the center of the city, he found his destination, a brick office building with an American flag flying over the entrance. Inside, he was approached by a young second lieutenant who was walking down the hall with a folder of papers in hand. "May I help you, sir?" the man asked in a southern accent.

Toby, having spotted the sign that identified the commanding officer's office, shook his head. "No, thank you, Lieutenant," he replied. "I've found the right place." He knocked on the door, then stepped into the office. Henry looked up from his desk.

"I'm looking for the man in charge," Toby announced. "I want to know how he always ends up with soft city jobs instead of being stuck on some army post."

"Toby, I can't tell you how pleased I am to see you!" Henry said, springing up and shaking hands. "I was hoping you'd be able to come here before I had to return to Germany."

"So was I," Toby replied. "Luckily, I had the opportunity, so I took advantage of it."

Henry grinned and shook his head, clearly shocked by his old friend's sudden appearance. The lieutenant Toby had seen in the hall stuck his head into the office, and Henry, after introducing him as his second-in-command, turned back to Toby.

"Well, where's your baggage? You'll stay at my apartment, of course, and we can flip a coin to see who gets the bed and who sleeps on the couch."

"You know better than to gamble with me, Henry," Toby said with a chuckle. "I'd put you on that couch eight nights a week. But I'm sorry to say I can't stay—I have to catch a train in a little less than five hours."

Henry looked disappointed. "Five weeks wouldn't be long enough, Toby, but five hours is that much more than I expected. Let's go to my apartment, then, where we can talk, and I'll see you to the train station. Walter, I'll be back this afternoon."

As the two of them left the building and walked along the street, Toby explained that the mission he was performing for the government had brought him through Hartford.

"Your timing was good," Henry commented, "because I'll be returning to Europe within a few weeks. By the way, I've seen the advertisements for the house packages being sold by your lumber company. That's one of the most original ideas I've ever heard of."

"I wish I could claim credit for it," Toby said, "but in fact my manager came up with that one. I've been away from Chicago for quite some time."

As the two friends talked, Toby marveled at how much Henry had changed during a span of only a few years. He looked older and seemed far more mature than most men his age, and he had an unmistakable air of authority about him. At the same time, Toby observed less obvious changes in his old friend, mannerisms that were so slight that they would normally escape notice. Any man who seemed to be loitering drew Henry's attention, as did any sudden noise. He scanned the street ahead, occasionally looked behind him, and even veered a few feet away from blind corners, casting a quick glance to the side as he passed.

Knowing that Henry had been assigned to intelligence duties during the past years, Toby realized that anyone occupied with such work would become more watchful and suspicious of his surroundings. However, the sense of caution that he detected in Henry was too keen for that to be the only explanation.

At the apartment, Henry took Toby's hat, poured him a drink, and offered him a comfortable chair. Toby did not fail to notice the expensive furniture, but a framed photograph of a woman was what caught and held his attention. She was strikingly beautiful, but Toby thought it a cold, hard beauty. The haughty uplift of her chin and the unsmiling stare into the camera revealed a domineering personality. Toby recalled what Andrew Brentwood had told him about the woman Henry was involved with in Germany.

Henry saw Toby looking at the picture and answered the unspoken question. "No, Gisela and I aren't married yet," he admitted. "The situation is difficult to explain, but somehow marriage doesn't seem right for us."

Toby shrugged. "It isn't up to me to tell you how to conduct your affairs, Henry. You mentioned before that she was ill. How is she now?"

"She has a very serious, recurring condition called a perityphlitic abscess. In some cases it lingers on for years, coming and going, but any onset of it can result in death. It's been some time since Gisela has experienced an attack of it, though, and I hope it has abated entirely."

Toby, wanting to clear up past misunderstandings, briefly related what Andy Brentwood had told him about Henry and Gisela. "It was a revelation for me, as it was for the general when I told him about it. I'm afraid, though, that Mama will never understand."

Henry nodded regretfully. "I gathered as much from the general's letter. And I'm grateful for Colonel Brentwood's intervention. Ending the misunderstanding between us was very important to me, Toby."

They talked for a while about Toby's children and the incident involving the glider, which set both of them to laughing. Henry brought out a tray of food, then port and cigars, and he and Toby filled each other in on the events in their lives since the years they had been together. Henry even offered Toby some advice on Alexandra Woodling.

"You're using logic to reach a decision, Toby, but logic doesn't always apply when dealing with people. I can tell by the way you talk about her that you love her, and that's more important than anything else."

Toby had to agree, but further discussion was cut

short when he took out his watch and grimaced. "It's time for me to leave, Henry. These past hours have flown."

As they walked to the train station, Toby again noticed how alert and watchful Henry was. When Toby brought up the subject, Henry hesitated before he answered. "When I left Europe this last time," he finally said, "there were two attempts to kill me. The consensus of my colleagues was that the attempts might have been related to my work. But there wasn't enough evidence to conclude who was involved, or why."

"Then you don't know what you're up against," Toby commented grimly. "That's a very bad situation, and I'm glad to see you're being cautious. What happened to the men who tried to kill you?"

"Neither of them will ever try to kill anyone else."

Toby was slightly taken aback by the toneless, matter-of-fact reply. Although Henry had always been capable of taking care of himself, he had never seemed so remorseless, so hardened. Still, Toby reflected, his attitude was understandable.

When they were at the station, however, and Toby's train was pulling in, Henry broached the one subject that Toby had expected him to avoid, and for an instant the young officer's professional façade seemed to slip. Toby was facing the old, slightly awkward Hank Blake he had once known.

"I certainly hope that Cindy and Reed Kerr have a happy marriage," Henry said, with an uncharacteristic catch to his voice. "There's every reason why they should, of course. Both of them deserve the very best."

Toby took Henry's offered hand. "I'm sure they will, Henry. And they would appreciate the sentiment. I can't tell you how good it's been to see you again."

"And you, too, Toby. Good luck to you."

The train had stopped, and Toby climbed the steps at the end of a car. A few minutes later, he was crossing the wide Connecticut River, on his way to Talcott.

*   *   *

The marriage was not a happy one for Cindy. As she sat on the back porch of her mother's house and talked with Eulalia, pride kept her from mentioning that her marriage had fallen far short of her expectations. Even if she did admit the truth, she knew that her mother's sympathy would be strongly mixed with an admonition that life was not always pleasant and had to be faced with resolve. Cindy was already doing that, and she had found a kind of contentment, but not the happiness she had anticipated.

Uncannily, Eulalia seemed to read her thoughts. "If you're having to adjust to marriage, dear," she said, "it's very normal. I had to when I first married your father, then again when Lee and I were married. A team can pull a plow much easier than a single horse, but only after they become accustomed to each other."

"No, I'm not having to adjust to marriage with Reed," Cindy replied truthfully. "In fact, it would be impossible to find a man who's more considerate and obliging."

"My word," Eulalia commented wryly. "You are fortunate."

"In that respect, I certainly am, Mama. Still, I don't have nearly as much to occupy my time as I did when I was at the ranch. And I miss Janessa. She and I used to sit and talk or read to each other almost every evening."

"She wouldn't have as much time for you now," Eulalia said with some bitterness. "Her working at that charity hospital is a disgrace! I expect that doddering old Robert Martin to come up with such ideas, but I can't imagine what possessed Toby to allow that child to work there."

"Toby knows that in time Janessa will be one of the finest physicians in the country," Cindy defended. "And no one's forcing her to do anything."

"She's a child!" Eulalia snapped, annoyed. "And her working at that charity hospital is a disgrace!"

"Maybe so, Mama," Cindy said, not willing to argue the point. She rose from her chair and gave her mother a kiss. "I'd better be getting back home now."

Cindy walked the short distance to the quarters for married junior officers, a line of small houses on the other side of Fort Vancouver. Although she and Reed could have rented a house in town, Cindy was determined to make ends meet on Reed's salary, rather than dip into the money his parents had left him. And even though the tiny cottage was cramped and uncomfortable, Cindy knew she would have been perfectly happy with her present circumstances, save for one, unavoidable fact: She did not love her husband.

A hasty marriage with another man after a broken romance was pitifully trite, she reflected, but that was exactly the trap she had stepped into. Her love for Henry Blake had been the foundation for all her hopes and ambitions. When that had been taken away, her future had crumbled before her. With a terrified feeling that life was passing her by, she had acted too quickly and blundered.

To make matters worse, Reed was so kind and loving to her that she felt guilty for not loving him. She was fond of him, because he was easy to like. His companionship was enjoyable, and she respected him. She even had a measure of contentment in her marriage. But she did not love him, and therefore she was not happy.

Exchanging a wave with a woman who was hanging out washing next door, Cindy went into her house. In the small bedroom was a cupboard—a wedding present that was too large for the kitchen—and most of it was filled with Meissen china, a constant reminder of Henry. Cindy opened a drawer and took out a notebook and pencil, then sat down in a chair by the window. With the book spread open on her knees, she leafed slowly through the sketches she had made in the past days.

She had always had an ability to draw, but it had

never been more than a rudimentary skill at best, one that she had never had the time or the desire to develop. The most use she had ever made of it was when, as a girl, she had drawn caricatures of friends to amuse them.

Since her marriage, with too little to occupy her time, she had returned to it. She had found that her despair over her future must have fueled some subtle impulse within her, awakening a depth of talent she had never realized she possessed. Even with the plain pencil and notebook paper, the poorest of materials, her drawings were good. Proportion and perspective came effortlessly, and the scenes and figures were imbued with feeling and life.

After turning to a fresh page, she began sketching the scene outside the bedroom window. As the pencil moved rapidly over the page, her unhappiness faded and she escaped the confines of her surroundings into another world that she could shape and alter at will. Then, seemingly only moments later, she suddenly sat up, becoming aware that it was now late afternoon.

After putting the notebook and pencil away, she went into the kitchen and began preparing dinner. It was a simple task, because Reed was easy to please, and her own appetite for food had been poor during the past weeks. Presently she heard his footsteps approaching the door, creating within her the usual mixture of pleasure for his cheerful company and guilt for not being able to return his love, for having entangled his life with her own confusion.

The tall, handsome man was smiling broadly, as he always did when greeting her. And as he did every other evening, he was carrying a few wildflowers he had found somewhere. He kissed her, and she took the flowers and put them in a vase, shaking her head to his offer to help her with dinner. "No, take off your tunic and relax, dear," she said. "Have you heard anything about the transfer?"

Reed hesitated in the bedroom doorway. "No, not yet," he replied. "It still isn't too late for me to ask to stay here, you know. Some cavalry posts are miserable places."

"If we get one of them, then that's what we'll have," Cindy said. "You're a soldier, and I'm a soldier's wife. Your prospects for promotion will be much better in the cavalry, and that's where you want to be."

"I do, but most of all I want you to be happy, Cindy."

"It's inevitable that you'll be transferred somewhere, and I'd as soon be on a cavalry post as in Washington. I'll have my drawing and other things to occupy me."

Reed's expression reflected some doubt, but Cindy turned away and busied herself with dinner. Later, as they ate, they talked of the day's events. Conversation with Reed was never difficult, because he was easygoing and capable of filling silences. After they finished the meal, Cindy cleaned off the table, refusing his offer of help.

While she washed the dishes, Reed sat at the table and glanced through the newspaper, keeping up a flow of comments. He folded the newspaper when she finished. "Would you like to walk to the river and sketch a scene?" he asked. "There's still enough light."

"No, not this evening, Reed."

"We can stay at home, then, just you and me?"

Fully realizing the implications of his happy grin, Cindy acted as though she did not. "If you wish, you could go to the officers' mess for a drink." The sudden disappointment on his face, however, created such intense guilt within her that it was like a physical pain. She quickly smiled and added, "But you don't have to rush off this very moment, do you?"

His wide, happy smile returned, and he put an arm around her as they went into the bedroom. From a tentative sense of pleasure and exploration during their honeymoon, Cindy's lovemaking with Reed had changed to where it was more of a duty to her than a pleasure. They undressed and lay down on the bed, and Reed took her in his arms.

Afterward, Reed got up and dressed. He leaned over her and kissed her, then left to go to the officers' mess. When he was gone, Cindy began weeping. She felt desperately unhappy, imprisoned by her mistake. After a while she wiped away her tears, got up and put on a robe, and lit a lamp.

In the cupboard drawer where she kept her notebooks were a few hidden pages on which she had tried to sketch the face of the man she loved, a man who was lost somewhere in the past. She took out the pages once again and studied them. The face of the new Henry Blake had kept surfacing in her memory, blotting out the vision of the Hank Blake she had loved. She had finally given up and drawn the face she had seen the day he had come to Portland to end their engagement.

But she had been unable to draw the eyes. Unlike the cheerful, smiling eyes of the young man she had known, they were strangely hard and penetrating—the eyes of a man who had seen too much of the world. And they had been frightening.

Looking at the sketch in the lamplight, she once again began trying to draw the eyes of the man whom she had loved.

XIV

When Toby Holt stepped off the train in Talcott, a boy was selling newspapers on the platform and shouting the headline: President Grant was coming to the city for its centennial celebration.

Toby bought a newspaper, and during the carriage ride to the hotel he read the story on the front page. The news about the President's visit to Talcott had been released by the White House the previous evening. The President, Representative John Stevens, and others would make speeches.

The hotel was near the center of town, and while Toby was signing the registration book, a man stopped at the desk and asked for his room key.

"Yes, sir, Mr. Beasley," the clerk said, taking a key from the slot.

Toby glanced at the man in disbelief, then forced himself to look back at the registration book. The face he had caught a glimpse of was thin and angular, with the same sharp features and glaring eyes that Toby had seen on the tintype in the Frankfort police station. The key the clerk handed Beasley was to room 209.

The man walked away as Toby finished signing the book. "I'd like a room on the second floor, if one is available," he said, firmly controlling his excitement.

"Yes, sir, Mr. . . . Holt," the clerk said, glancing at the registration book. He turned to the key slots, took down the key to room 214, and handed it to the bellboy. "I hope you enjoy your stay with us, sir."

Toby followed the bellboy upstairs. When his bags had been placed in his room, which was across and a few doors down the hall from Beasley's room, Toby sat a while in deep thought before unpacking. Spotting Beasley—the same man as Howard Cummings, surely—had been an extraordinary stroke of luck. Toby had originally intended to show a copy of the tintype of Cummings to the local police and have them keep an eye out for the man, but that would have risked warning him off. Now that risk would not be necessary.

After forming a tentative plan of action in his mind, Toby unpacked, went back downstairs, and left the hotel. A short walk brought him to a grassy park in the center of the city. A courthouse with a wide expanse of steps stood facing one end of the park, and businesses lined the streets on the other three sides. Flags and bunting hung from the buildings, and among the people on the street there was an atmosphere of anticipation of the coming celebration. Toby crossed the park to the police station, which was adjacent to the courthouse.

The chief of police was John Pennington, a tall, beefy man of about fifty, with white hair and a mustache. He was obviously eager to cooperate with Toby, but he also seemed troubled. "I received a telegram telling me you'd be here, Marshal Holt," he said, escorting Toby into his office, "but this is a little unusual, isn't it? It was my understanding that the local police and the Secret Service took care of protecting the President."

Toby closed the door, then replied quietly. "I've been working with Thomas Haines, the deputy director of the Secret Service. We have evidence that an attempt will be made against the life of the President while he's here in Talcott."

Pennington, who had started to sit down behind his desk, froze and looked at Toby in consternation, the color draining from his face. He stood back up. "Then his visit here will have to be canceled!" he exclaimed. "We can't take a chance on his life!"

"As far as I know, canceling his trip has been eliminated as a possibility, Chief Pennington. The President is aware of the danger of traveling, but he's coming here for a purpose that's important to him, and as yet we don't have enough evidence to persuade him otherwise. We'll simply have to deal with the plot."

The police chief shook his head and sat down heavily. "Well, if that's how it must be, then you can depend on me to do everything humanly possible to help. Just how much do you know about this plot?"

"The ringleader, a man named Beasley—although he also uses the name Howard Cummings—is here now, but he might not be acting alone. If we arrested him today, we probably wouldn't have enough evidence to convict him. And his henchmen would still be on the loose, and another plot could be hatched up. So I'll have to find out the extent of the plot, and then we can put an end to it once and for all."

"That makes sense," Pennington said. "How many men do you want me to assign to help you?"

"None, because Beasley or some of his friends might recognize them. In fact, I'd rather not take a chance on being seen coming here myself. Is there somewhere else we can meet?"

"How about my house at night?" Pennington suggested. "I live down at the end of Drake Street, just beyond the water tower. There are brick posts on each side of my carriage drive, so you can't miss it."

"Good. I'll come there tonight. Haines will be sending me an itinerary, but in the meantime, can you tell me anything yet about the plans for the President while he's here?"

The police chief shook his head. "No, but I'm expecting a telegram myself from Washington at any time. As soon as I get it, I'll be working out with the county sheriff exactly where and when we'll post our men. Of course I'll make you a copy of any information we receive." He described the tentative plans for the other dignitaries, explaining that a podium would be set up on the courthouse steps for official speeches and ceremonies, as was the city's custom.

When Toby rose to depart, he asked a favor. "Chief, if you have a set of skeleton keys, I'd like to borrow them."

"That's no trouble," Pennington said, standing up. "We have about a dozen sets we've taken from thieves over the years. I'll get them."

Toby followed Pennington into another room, where the chief opened a safe and handed him a set of keys. They shook hands again, and Toby was shown out the back door.

Beasley's room key was still gone from its slot when Toby returned to the hotel, indicating that the man had not gone out. Toby sat down in a chair in the lobby with a newspaper. An hour passed, while he surreptitiously watched the stairs. Finally Beasley appeared.

Holding up his newspaper, Toby waited as Beasley crossed the lobby and went into the dining room; then he moved to a chair that gave him a partial view of Beasley's table. As soon as the man had ordered his meal, Toby put down the newspaper and went upstairs. The hall was deserted as he walked along it to room 209. He took out the skeleton keys, and the second key he tried unlocked the door.

He stepped quietly into the room and locked the door behind him. In the light of sunset coming through the window, Toby began methodically searching the room, putting everything back the way he had found it. The contents of a satchel in the closet answered many of his questions.

Among other things, the satchel contained a charter for a silver mining company in Nevada. Along with it was a letter from the San Francisco Stock Exchange to Orville Beasley, the owner of the company. The letter stated that trading in the company's stock had been suspended, the value of the shares having fallen from forty to less than two dollars each. Toby put the papers back and took a notebook out of the satchel.

As he peered at the pages in the fading light, it became obvious that Beasley was a very methodical man. He made lists of things to do, then checked them off. On one page was a list of names with dollar amounts beside them; the names were those of the demonstrators who had been arrested in Frankfort.

A key question in Toby's mind was how many were involved in the Talcott plot, and he thumbed rapidly through the notebook. He stopped at a page that had the name Ira Farley written on it, with amounts totaling several hundred dollars beside the name. Two other names were below it, with smaller amounts written beside each one.

Amounts paid for horses, a rifle, ammunition, and various other purchases were listed on other pages. Another page listed amounts paid for rent, but there was no indication of the location or type of property being rented. Toby put the notebook back into the satchel, which he replaced in the closet. He noticed a rifle case leaning in a corner of the closet, and boxes of ammunition on the shelf above.

Toby took the case out and opened it. It was a .40 caliber Sharps, a good rifle. He opened a box of ammunition and started to close it, then paused. A hole had been bored in the tip of each bullet. Well aware of the deadly effect of the holes, Toby looked at the bullets for a long moment before closing the box and replacing it.

Stepping to the door, he glanced around the room to make certain he was leaving behind no sign of his presence. He unlocked the door and opened it a crack, peering out, then stepped into the hall and closed and locked the door behind him.

When Toby returned to the lobby, Beasley was still in the dining room, finishing his meal. Toby went outside and walked across the street, where he stationed himself in the shadows of a building and watched the hotel entrance.

A short time later, Beasley came out of the hotel, and Toby followed him along the street to a tavern. Walking slowly past the tavern doors, Toby glanced inside. Beasley was sitting at a table with a short, ferretlike man, the two of them talking quietly. Crossing the street and finding a place in the shadows to wait, Toby concluded that the other man must be Ira Farley.

An hour passed before Beasley came out of the tavern and walked back in the direction of the hotel. Toby waited until Farley came out, then followed him along the dark streets to a boardinghouse. The man went inside, and Toby waited until a lamp was lighted in a room upstairs, then walked back across the city to the street where the police chief lived.

Pennington himself answered the door. He was in his suspenders, with his shirtsleeves rolled up. "Come on in, Marshal Holt," he said. "We can talk in the parlor. My wife is keeping the children in the kitchen."

They sat down, and Toby related what he had learned. "Nothing is sufficient reason for what Beasley is doing," he said as he finished, "but now we know what started his plotting to kill the President."

"Plenty of people are upset because silver coinage was stopped," Pennington agreed. "I don't like it myself; but being upset is one thing, and plotting to kill the President is another. And you believe that the other man you saw is the one named Farley?"

"Yes, I'm fairly certain. That leaves two men unaccounted for, but they must be either here in Talcott or close by. Tomorrow I'll keep an eye on Farley, and perhaps I can find them through him. Did you receive the telegram about the details of the President's visit?"

The police chief nodded, took a folded paper from his pocket, and handed it to Toby. "Here's a copy, which includes the itinerary you were expecting. It arrived shortly after you left. Mr. Haines himself will be in charge of the Secret Service escort, and the President will arrive in a private railcar. Instead of going to a hotel, he'll stay in the car, which will be parked on a sidetrack behind the station. That'll make it considerably easier to guard him, won't it?"

"Yes, it will," Toby agreed. "Tom Haines must have talked him into that. The only time he'll be vulnerable, then, is during his speech and while traveling to and from the railcar. I'll take a look at the route between the train station and the courthouse to see if there are any places along it where someone might wait in ambush."

Pennington nodded. "You've certainly found out plenty since I saw you this afternoon. It's easy to see why Mr. Haines got you to do this."

"It isn't over yet," Toby said, standing up. "I'll talk with you again tomorrow night, Chief. There are still a few things to find out before we put a stop to this plot."

The streets of Washington were teeming with people going to work when Henry Blake arrived in response to a telegram from his project officer, John Simpson. As he left the train station and walked toward the War Department, Henry felt more than a little worried. Unlike the cordial notes he usually received from Simpson, the telegram had been a peremptory order, summoning him to Washington.

When Henry reached Simpson's office, his suspense was not immediately dispelled. Unsmiling, Simpson nodded curtly and briefly shook his hand in greeting. "Well, you got here quickly enough," he said.

"What did you expect, John?" Henry replied. "When I receive a telegram as brusque as the one you sent, I want to know what's behind it, so I took the first train out of Hartford. What's wrong?"

"Undersecretary Rollins wants to see you immediately," Simpson said. "I'll have to let him tell you."

Walking down the hall with Simpson, Henry became more concerned with each step. Simpson did nothing to alleviate his worry, and when they were ushered into the undersecretary's office, the usually mild-mannered Charles Rollins merely nodded coolly to Henry, then pointed to the door. "John, please close the door," he said.

Henry glanced between the two men. "Mr. Rollins," he said, his patience wearing thin, "may I ask why I was summoned to Washington?"

"Because," Rollins replied sternly, "I find that I have the unpleasant duty of giving you a reprimand."

Henry stiffened. "A reprimand for what, sir?"

Rollins opened a drawer and placed an envelope and a small box on his desk. "I must give you a reprimand because I find that you are not in proper uniform, Captain Blake," he said.

It took a few seconds for Henry to catch his meaning, but then he saw the stern expressions on the two men's faces dissolve into wide smiles. They burst into laughter, and Henry felt slightly embarrassed. "Well, that's one promotion that I sweated over," he said with relief. "I couldn't imagine what was wrong."

"We thought we should make you sweat a little," Rollins said as he opened the small box and took out a set of captain's bars. "Although there is no one more deserving, you do happen to be the youngest captain in the United States Army by several years."

"Yes, by quite a few years," Simpson added, taking

one of the sets of bars. "In fact, all of the officers in the class ahead of yours at West Point are still second lieutenants. Step over here, if you would, Henry, and give us the pleasure of pinning these on."

Henry moved closer to the desk, and Rollins and Simpson replaced his insignia of rank with the new double bars. They shook his hand in turn, and then Rollins gave him the envelope containing his promotion orders.

When they sat down to talk, Simpson brought up the subject of the new Winchester rifle, which had been approved for purchase by the army as a result of Henry's report. "The present plan is to completely equip the cavalry with that rifle within the next two years," he said.

"As far as I'm concerned, we can't buy them fast enough," Henry said. "It'll give me great pleasure to send out teams to inspect shipments of them."

"Well, I don't want to deny you that pleasure," Rollins put in, "but I hope you'll be back in Germany before any of them are shipped. When the secretary called me to his office yesterday to give me your promotion orders, he reminded me that you've been away from Mauser Arms Works some five months now. When do you think you can finish up here?"

Henry did not hesitate. "Walter Stafford is a good man, sir, and I believe he'll be able to handle anything that comes up. The detachment is running smoothly now, and I could turn it over to him and leave within the next few days."

"Excellent!" Rollins exclaimed. "Then by all means wrap up your work here. The one thing we don't want to do is to jeopardize your position at Mauser."

They talked a while longer, and later, back in Simpson's office, Henry went over the details of turning the detachment over to Stafford.

It was still before noon when he was on a train pulling out of the station and heading northward. Weary from the morning's excitement and traveling through the night, Henry found a seat at the rear of a car and made himself comfortable.

His promotion to captain, a significant step in his army career, gave him a deep sense of satisfaction. But he was even more gratified by the fact that he could begin turning over the detachment to Stafford and making preparations to leave. The months that he had been separated from Gisela felt like a lifetime, but now he could be back at Grevenhof within a matter of weeks.

The journey back north seemed endless to Henry. In the still hours of early morning, the train finally reached Hartford, and Henry walked along the quiet streets to his apartment.

When he lit the lamp in his sitting room, he saw a telegram propped on the desk. Feeling suddenly uneasy, he tore it open to find it was from Germany, in German. Most of it was a meaningless jumble of letters from poor transmission on the transatlantic cable, but the last two sentences and the name at the end of the telegram were legible.

It was from Emil Koehler, Gisela's father. The first legible sentence stated that Dr. MacAlister had been summoned to Grevenhof to attend to Gisela. The other sentence was an urgent request for Henry to return to Germany as soon as possible.

Crumpling the telegram in his hand, Henry thought about his conversation with MacAlister the previous year. The Scotsman was staff physician at the British embassy in Berlin, and it was he who had diagnosed Gisela's illness. He had said there was no cure for it and had warned that death could strike at any time.

Fighting his mounting panic, Henry went to the liquor cabinet and poured himself some whiskey. He drank it, then collected his thoughts. There were legal records to be signed over to Stafford and many other details that had to be attended to before he could leave. He began reviewing them in his mind, estimating how quickly they could be done.

Then a completely unrelated matter forced its way to the forefront of his thoughts. For years he had thought that what bound him to Gisela was a combination of circumstances and some compelling physical desire that only she could satisfy. But he had never believed he loved her. He had thought that Cindy was the only love in his life.

Perhaps, he reflected, that had been true at one time, but it had changed. He still loved Cindy, and he knew that he always would. But now he also loved Gisela.

The shock of reading the telegram had opened Henry's mind to a moment of truth. The threat of losing Gisela had forced him to realize that he not only needed her, but loved her from the depths of his being. Yet at the very moment that he finally recognized the truth, she could be dying in agony.

Toby Holt was watching the boardinghouse when Farley came out the door into the morning sunshine. As soon as the little man turned toward the stable behind the building, Toby hurried back down the street to a livery stable where he had a horse already saddled and waiting.

His haste proved unnecessary, however. Farley rode only a block before he reined in his pinto in front of a general store and disappeared inside. Toby waited and watched from in front of the livery stable.

Ten minutes later Farley reappeared with a full gunnysack, which he tied onto his saddle before remounting. He rode a short distance down the street to a tavern, where he again dismounted and went inside. He came back out a minute later with two bottles of whiskey, which he put into his saddlebags. When he began riding purposefully in the opposite direction, away from the city, Toby mounted his horse and followed.

Near the edge of town, where the houses gave way to gently rolling farmland, Toby slowed his horse to let Farley widen the distance between them. A few other riders and vehicles were on the road, and Toby dropped about a quarter mile behind his quarry. Several miles from the city, where the farms became interspersed with wooded areas, Farley turned off onto a footpath along a creek and disappeared from sight.

When Toby reached the creek, he reined up and looked at the pinto's hoof marks. The same horse had gone back and forth along the creek a number of times, and the hoofprints had been made over the space of several days. It appeared likely that Farley had been carrying provisions to the other two men listed in Beasley's notebook.

Toby rode along the footpath at a canter. After a few minutes he came to where the pinto had turned off the path and gone up a slope away from the creek. Toby followed the trail, and from the top of the rise he saw Farley in the distance, crossing a meadow toward a dense woods.

Toby halted behind some trees. With no other riders about, it would be obvious to Farley that he was being followed if he looked back now and saw a rider. But after the man returned to the city, it would be easy enough for Toby to follow the pinto's trail and see where it led. Deciding to do that, Toby turned back.

When he reached town, he returned the horse to the livery stable and walked to the train station. The rifle Beasley had chosen indicated that he intended to shoot at the President from a medium distance, probably no more than a hundred yards. Toby looked at the siding where the private car would be parked, but he saw no good vantage point where Beasley could hide and wait with the rifle.

From the train station, Toby walked along the street that led to the courthouse. Both sides were lined with well-kept homes, all of them occupied, and Toby saw no place, other than the houses themselves, that would offer both concealment and a clear shot at the street. At the park in front of the courthouse, Toby sat on a bench and studied each of the buildings around the square. Then he saw that Beasley had made a mistake.

All the windows in the office buildings were open on the warm afternoon to catch the breeze, with only one exception. A single window on the top floor of a building across the corner from the courthouse was closed, and Toby recalled that Beasley's notebook had listed rental payments over a period of months. He crossed the park to the building, went inside, and climbed the stairs to the top floor.

Every office door and transom in the hallway was open for ventilation, except for one door with the name of an investment firm on it. Toby tapped twice, waited a few seconds, and tried the knob. Then, glancing around to make certain no one else was in the hall, he took out the skeleton keys and unlocked the door. He stepped inside the office and relocked the door.

Stuffy and stifling hot, the office was empty of furniture. Toby stepped to the closet at one side of the room and opened the door. It was also empty. He went to the window and looked out. There was a full view of the courthouse steps, less than sixty yards away, where the President would stand to make his speech. Having seen enough, Toby left the office, locking the door behind him, then walked back down the stairs and went to the basement.

The janitor, a grizzled old man with an empty corncob pipe in one side of his mouth, was washing his mops in a sink. He nodded and grunted in reply to Toby's greeting.

"I knocked on the door of that investment company on the top floor," Toby said, "and there was no one inside. Do you know what their office hours are?"

"Investment company?" The old man chortled, taking

the pipe out of his mouth. "Mister, if you've got money to throw away, why don't you just give it to me. I could put it to good use."

Toby smiled. "Don't worry, they're not going to get into my wallet. Do you know who works in that office?"

"Nope," the old man replied. "Mister, I've never seen anybody come or go in that office. Not that I'm complaining, because they don't create no trash for me to carry out. It's rented, though, to a man by the name of Farmer, or something like that."

"Farley?"

"That's him," the old man said. "Yes, he's had it for a few months now, but I've never seen him personally. I wouldn't know him from Adam."

Toby thanked the old man and left. It was midafternoon, several hours after he had turned back from following Farley. He walked along the streets to the boardinghouse where Farley was staying, then went around to the stable behind it. The pinto was in a stall.

A boy who was cleaning the stable shook his head when Toby asked if the horses were for rent. "No, sir," he said. "We just stable horses for the lodgers in the boardinghouse here, and for a few people who work around the neighborhood. There's a livery stable down the street."

"That's a fine-looking pinto," Toby commented. "Who owns it?"

"Mr. Farley, who lives in the boardinghouse," the boy replied. "The roan in the next stall is his too, but he don't ever ride it."

Toby was deep in thought as he walked back toward the center of the city. In the distance he heard a steam calliope playing, its lively blare carrying along the streets. People passed him, hurrying toward the music, and when he reached the park he found it teeming with excitement.

Along with the calliope, several large, colorful circus wagons had arrived to put up exhibits, amusement booths, and refreshment stands for the centennial celebration. The name on the side of the calliope and circus wagons was Phineas T. Barnum, Connecticut's celebrated showman and circus owner. A large crowd of onlookers had gathered as workers unloaded the wagons.

At sunset Toby went to a restaurant for dinner, and afterward he returned to the park, which was now ablaze with light. People were milling around the stands, and boys were shooting off firecrackers while the calliope played. Toby walked toward Pennington's house.

He was greeted as on the previous night. In the parlor the chief listened as Toby again related what he had found out during the day. The man was amazed when Toby told him that the office in the building adjacent to the park had been rented months before. No one else had had any indication that the President would be coming to Talcott, Pennington insisted, and he agreed that they were indeed up against a cunning adversary.

"Do you intend to follow Farley's trail tomorrow?" he asked Toby.

"Yes, I don't see any alternate course open to us. We can't wait to find out the others' exact role in the plot. Beasley has a good horse, and it appears he intends to assassinate the President and then flee to a hideout to wait until the search dies down. Farley looks like his errand boy, and those other two may be simply guarding the hideout, or they may have another purpose."

"For example?"

"Beasley may intend for them to be in the crowd with pistols in case he misses, or somewhere along the route from the train station. I don't think that's likely, because they would be at great risk, and it's hard to hire someone to take a chance on being killed. But where the President's safety is concerned, we can't overlook any possibility, however remote."

Pennington nodded agreement.

"I'll pick up Farley's trail first thing tomorrow. If those men are there, I'll arrest them and bring them back. If they aren't, then we'll know that we're going to have to find them fast."

Pennington frowned. "I can't think of anything more dangerous than going into a place where two armed assassins may be hiding out. And if they're the kind of men we think they are, I don't believe they'll be taken alive. Why don't you let me and some of my men come along?"

Toby shook his head. "More than one rider would make too much noise, and we can't take the chance of scaring them off. Since the celebration is the day after tomorrow, Farley's probably made his last trip. If I arrest them, I'll bring them to the rear of the jail. We can keep them in an isolated cell, and Beasley will be none the wiser."

Pennington looked skeptical, but he agreed to Toby's plan. "When the President's train arrives tomorrow afternoon, I'll talk with Mr. Haines and tell him everything you've done. And I'll be expecting you here, same time."

Toby rose to leave. "Of course, if I don't show up, then arrest Beasley and Farley. You might be able to get Farley to confess enough to convict them, and at least they'll be locked up while the President is here."

In the dim, lavishly furnished master bedroom of a mansion in Berlin, a sense of relief passed over Adela Ronsard as a movement in the huge bulk under her signaled that she had finally completed her task. Damp with perspiration and trembling from exhaustion, she moved off the enormously fat man and lay beside him on the oversize bed.

That, she thought as she panted and caught her breath, had been more of a job for an acrobat than for a courtesan. The man had lain supine throughout and expected her to do everything, which had been like performing on a mountaintop. And the exotic techniques that it had been necessary for her to employ would have been much less unpleasant if he were not so disgustingly fat.

However, she reflected, he was a wealthy man. A plush private carriage had brought her to this palatial mansion, and the pay promised to be at least ample. Adela wiped the perspiration off her face with the sheet and waited to see if he would want her again. But the man heaved himself up to a sitting position and began sliding off the bed.

He was a shapeless mass of flesh, his thighs as thick as her waist, and his flabby arms almost as large. Looking at the quivering rolls of fat and his wide, pendulous buttocks, Adela felt a sense of revulsion. But along with the skills she had developed to perfection, she had a business-like attitude toward her profession, and she never allowed personal feelings to interfere with her work.

Sitting up, she tossed her hair back and looked at him poutingly. "Are you leaving me so soon?" she asked. "I've enjoyed it, and I'd hoped I could spend the night." She nodded toward the valise she had brought, which contained her costumes and implements. "If you'll allow me to stay, I promise you an evening you'll remember."

Hermann Bluecher shook his head as he picked up his robe from a chair and put it on. His moment of entertainment was finished, and he had serious matters to attend to. "The butler will pay you," he said, pushing his feet into slippers. He shuffled out of the room.

As he walked ponderously down the staircase, the butler stepped silently from a doorway at the foot of the steps and waited for instructions. "Pay her well," Bluecher said. "Twice the usual amount, and write down her name so you can send for her again. But first bring me an evening repast in the library."

The butler silently bowed as Bluecher passed him. In the library, Bluecher turned up the lamp on his desk, lowered his bulk into his chair, and picked up a telegram he had put aside earlier, unopened. From an informant at the German embassy in Washington, it was a report on Henry Blake.

A short while later the butler came in with a tray laid out with a platter of pastries, a large bowl of chocolate pudding, and a mug of hot, sweetened milk. He waited until Bluecher tasted the milk to make certain there was enough sugar in it, then left. Bluecher put the telegram aside and began with the pudding.

Eating slowly at first, the fat man sighed and murmured in satisfaction as he swallowed the rich, sweet confection. His enjoyment increasing, he began plying the spoon more rapidly, gulping the pudding. It oozed down his face and double chins as he spooned it into his mouth faster than he could swallow.

When the bowl was scraped empty, Bluecher looked at it in regret. After licking the last traces off the spoon, he tossed it into the bowl and pushed them aside, then took a deep drink of the hot, sugared milk. Belching, he picked up the telegram, and as he began to read, he reached for a pastry and pushed it into his mouth.

With cheeks bulging and crumbs spilling from his lips while he chewed, Bluecher read the report. His murmur of satisfaction over the taste of the pastry changed into a heavy sigh as he shook his head. The telegram said that Henry Blake had been promoted to captain and would soon be returning to Germany. Pushing another pastry into his mouth, Bluecher pondered what to do next.

Disposing of the American had proved to be far more troublesome than he had expected. For one thing, while he had anticipated some reaction from the Baroness von Kirchberg over the Bremerhaven incident, he had not foreseen her frenzy of outrage and the powerful influence she could bring to bear.

Her protests and threats had been so vehement that

the Ministry of Justice had been thrown into a panic and actually sent two full deputy ministers to investigate the matter. No connection could ever be made between him and the attack, of course, but Bluecher found all the high-level attention unsettling.

Even more unsettling was what had happened to Schneider. The man, one of the most skilled, reliable agents Bluecher had ever employed, had simply disappeared. He had boarded the ship in Bremerhaven, intending to assassinate the American, but had vanished without a trace before the next port of call. The facts indicated that the American, who should have been no match for the wily agent, had simply swatted Schneider like a fly, then gone quietly about his business. To Bluecher that was extremely unnerving.

Underestimating an opponent, Bluecher knew, was a serious error, but it was obvious that he had made that error. Together, the American and the baroness were formidable, and he would have to watch his step in dealing with them. Reaching for another pastry, he found that the tray was empty.

Bluecher impatiently rang the bell on his desk and sat back in his chair, waiting for a servant. The next time, he decided, the circumstances would have to be exactly right and the plan foolproof. It would take time, patience, and careful preparation, but in one way or another he would dispose of the American.

XV

The morning sun warmed the chill air as Toby rode out of town. With the President due to arrive late in the afternoon for the following day's celebration, the road was much busier than before, with buggies and farm wagons filled with people coming to the city. At the footpath beside the creek, Toby turned off the road.

The bustle of passing vehicles was soon left behind, and the quiet of the countryside settled around Toby as he rode along the footpath. Following the pinto's trail, he turned his horse up the slope opposite the creek. At the top of the bank was the broad meadow he had seen Farley riding across the day before.

Toby reined up and looked and listened for a time. Detecting no sign of life, he urged his horse forward. The woods in the distance ahead were dense, with thick shadows under the trees. Conscious of his exposed position, Toby knew he would be an easy target for a hidden rifleman, and the minutes seemed long as he crossed the meadow.

At last he reached the edge of the trees. The pinto's hoofprints in the blanket of fallen leaves made an easy trail to follow, and Toby rode along at a slow walk to make as little noise as possible, all the while listening to the forest sounds. The birdcalls and the scurrying of small animals seemed normal as he rode deeper into the woods.

After a few minutes, the breeze·carried a faint scent of woodsmoke, a warning of danger. As Toby smelled it, he heard a jay's raucous call ahead. The sentinels of the forest, jays became excited over any disturbance, and the sound made Toby uneasy. He heard a twig crack.

Kicking his feet out of the stirrups, Toby leaped from the saddle toward a large clump of brush. At the same instant, the roar of a rifle shattered the forest quiet. Tumbling through the air, Toby felt the menacing breath of wind as the bullet passed within an inch of his head and slammed into a nearby tree.

He landed heavily in the brush and instantly pulled his pistol from its holster. His horse reared in fright and began racing away, and Toby took advantage of the noise to scramble through the brush away from the man with the rifle. A second and a third shot rang out, the bullets clipping through the leaves, and then Toby reached a large tree and took refuge behind it.

Birds scattered through the forest canopy, and a steely silence settled. Toby peered around the trunk. The shots had come from some fifty feet away, but he could see nothing. He turned and began darting at a crouch through trees and brush to circle around to where the man was hiding.

Like an Indian, Toby moved swiftly and silently through the forest. A minute or two later, back near the area from which the shot had come, he heard a stir in the underbrush, then spotted his quarry: A tall, bearded man wearing a dark coat had lifted himself to his knees to peer toward the place where Toby had jumped from his horse.

Toby carefully aimed his pistol and thumbed back the hammer, intending to call to the man to surrender. But the metallic click of the cock was too loud, and the man heard it. Turning toward Toby, he started swinging his rifle around. Toby squeezed the trigger and the man jerked back, the roar of the falling rifle blending with the pistol shot.

Quiet settled again, and Toby moved silently to the man's body. He was dead, with a bullet through the heart. Toby walked a short distance away and crouched next to a tree. He waited patiently, his pistol cocked and ready. A few minutes later, he heard a nervous whisper—another man calling the first man's name. Twigs cracked and footsteps approached.

The second man, heavyset and also bearded, came into view. Carrying a double-barreled shotgun, he walked in a half crouch as he looked around cautiously. When he saw the body, he stiffened and began glancing in fright in all directions. Toby, well aware that the shotgun was a deadly weapon at close range, put a hand beside his mouth to cast his voice to one side.

"Drop your gun and put up your hands!"

As the man wheeled toward the sound, Toby took aim. The man saw him at the last instant, but it was too late. Toby pulled the trigger, and a red spot appeared on the man's forehead, both barrels of the shotgun belching smoke and discharging harmlessly into the ground.

Toby rose to his feet and let out a deep breath. He reloaded his pistol as he inspected the bodies, then went to find his horse. Walking back in the direction of the road, he spotted the animal at the edge of the meadow, where it had stopped to graze. Toby mounted it and rode back into the woods.

It took him almost two hours to find the hideout. Reasoning that it would be near where the two men had camped, he began at their campfire and rode slowly in expanding circles. Footprints were everywhere, indicating that the men had scrounged the forest floor for firewood. When he reached an area where he could find no more tracks, Toby returned to the campfire and began over, riding in circles.

Finally, about a hundred yards from the campfire, he found a cave, its mouth almost completely hidden behind thick clumps of brush. Toby went inside and struck a match. Food, water, and other supplies filled several gunnysacks—enough provisions, Toby estimated, to last until the search for the assassin died down.

Toby rode back to the bodies, lifted them across the saddle, and took them to the hideout. As he pulled them from the horse and dragged them inside, he reflected that the cave had probably been destined to be their final resting place in any event, since Beasley would not have wanted to leave witnesses behind.

It was afternoon by the time Toby got back to Talcott, where a full holiday atmosphere now prevailed. Many businesses had closed for the day, and the park teemed with activity. Toby took his horse back to the livery stable and went to a restaurant to have lunch.

An hour before the President's train was due to arrive, Toby went to check on Farley and Beasley. In contrast to earlier, the streets were almost deserted, the people having gone to the train station. Even the stable behind the boardinghouse was unattended.

Finding the pinto still in its stall, Toby set off down the street to the tavern where he had seen Farley the previous day. Sure enough, the little man was there, virtually the only customer. Toby returned to the hotel and scanned the key slots. The key to room 209 was gone, Beasley evidently in his room. Toby went outside to sit on the porch, satisfied that for the time being the President was safe.

Later that evening, Toby returned to the police chief's house. Thomas Haines was behind Pennington as the man opened the door.

"Toby!" Haines exclaimed happily. "It's mighty good to see you again. We've been waiting here for you, nervous as a couple of hens."

"I would have come sooner," Toby said, "but I wanted to make certain Beasley was in his hotel room for the night."

It was obvious that Pennington had updated Haines on Toby's plans, for the Secret Service man could hardly wait for Toby to sit down. "Well, did you find them?" he asked. "Did you figure out what Beasley intended them to do?"

"Yes, I found them," Toby replied. "And I believe they were only going to guard the hideout—but we'll probably never know for sure. Whatever they were going to do, they won't do it now."

Haines looked pale but relieved.

"Good, and good riddance," Pennington pronounced. "So where was the hideout?"

Toby took a cup of coffee that the chief poured for him, then reviewed the events of the day. Haines shook his head in disbelief several times.

"Well, thanks to you," Haines said when Toby had finished, "this plot is ended, except that Beasley doesn't know it yet. In fact, we could go and arrest him and Farley right now and finish this thing up within the hour."

Toby shook his head. "Tom, I'm not a lawyer, but I know we don't have enough evidence to convict Beasley. And convicting him for a lesser crime just isn't good enough. He plotted to kill the President, and he should be punished for that."

"Well, you've handled it this far," Haines said, "so I'm going to leave it up to you. As long as there'll be no risk for the President."

"There won't," Toby assured him. "Tomorrow morning, Beasley will come to that office with his rifle, and I'll be waiting for him with this." He pulled his coat back, revealing the Colt in his shoulder holster. "I'll arrest him if I can, but if I can't—" Toby left the sentence unfinished, but both men nodded in understanding.

A little later, Toby walked back to the center of the city. The calliope music had stopped, and the exhibits and stands in the park had closed for the night. Most of the people had gone home, but a few merrymakers were still about, and Toby turned onto a side street to approach the office building through the back alley. The building was dark and quiet, closed up for the night. Toby took out his skeleton keys and let himself in.

As the sun rose in Wisconsin, Ursula Guthrie emerged from her kitchen door. The tranquil beauty of the garden, pasture, and surrounding forest at dawn always gave her pleasure, and she wondered, as she often did these days, how much longer all she surveyed would be hers. The money she had saved over the past years had been dwindling steadily, and there was not enough left to last through the coming winter.

As she was looking around, Ursula noticed that Frederick Kirchner's buggy was gone from where it had been parked the previous night. In many ways the young man was as impulsive and impractical as Maida. Always coming and going at odd hours, and often staying overnight and sleeping in the brewery, he was hard to keep track of. He must have left during the night, Ursula decided.

During the past weeks, Frederick had spent much of his time at the brewery. After planting the hop vines, he had begun helping Maida with various other chores, and at first Ursula had been surprised, because Maida was anything but tolerant of outsiders in her brewery. But eventually it had become evident to everyone that a romance was budding.

That had surprised Ursula even more, for Maida had never before shown interest in a young man. But the qualities that made Maida and Frederick different from others apparently also drew them together. It had occurred to Ursula that the romance also undoubtedly pleased John Kirchner, for now his son was on the best of terms with the Oberg brewery's indispensable master brewer.

Hearing the others stirring, Ursula went back inside and started breakfast. Soon coffee was perking on the stove, and the appetizing scent of bacon spread through the house. Colleen Rafferty appeared and, bidding Ursula good morning, busied herself setting the table.

A little while later, Paddy came in, filling the room with his cheerful chatter, and Fred and the Rafferty children followed.

As they sipped their coffee, Fred and Paddy discussed the work they had planned for the day. For the past week the two men had been digging and building a root cellar, and although Fred was in a hurry to finish the job, Paddy said he had some urgent work to do for Maida.

"The flume between the pond and the brewery is leaking, and I'll have to be repairing it straightaway," he said. "Maida's had it running full force for the past two days, and the ground out there's like to become a swamp."

"Running full force?" Fred echoed, sounding annoyed. "How many tuns is she going to start now?" He turned to Ursula. "Has she been ordering more supplies?"

Ursula, who was breaking eggs into a skillet, shook her head. "No, she had sufficient for several weeks. Perhaps she's been cleaning out some tuns."

"Aye, that's probably it," Paddy said. "She must a' been at it until late last night, for she's not stirring hide nor hair yet."

Ursula wiped her hands on her apron. "Colleen, take over the eggs, if you would. I'll go upstairs and see if Maida wants to get up now."

While Fred and Paddy began talking about the flume, Ursula climbed the stairs and stuck her head into Maida's room. When she saw that the bed had not been slept in, she was not overly concerned, for Maida often stayed in the brewery all night. Indeed, it occurred to her that it had been several days since a tun of beer had been drawn down, and one must be almost ready. At such times Maida worked herself into a frenzy of anxiety over the beer and spent the night hovering around it. Ursula went back downstairs.

"Don't make plans for the entire day," she announced to the others. "Maida is not in her room, so we'll be drawing down a tun before sunset. Do we have ample casks, Paddy?"

"Aye, more than ample," the Irishman replied cheerfully.

"Far more than we have customers," Fred grumbled.

Ursula helped Colleen serve the food, and while the others ate, she went out to the brewery to check on her daughter.

Entering the huge, dim building, Ursula expected to see Maida on a stool beside one of the tuns, weary and perhaps in tears. Not seeing her, she started to call out softly and soothingly—then abruptly stopped herself. Everything looked normal, as orderly and spotlessly clean as always, but Ursula could smell the difference. No beer was brewing.

Quickly Ursula walked back and forth among the massive tuns, her footsteps echoing. The brewery was deserted. Fear began to race through her. Maida followed a routine of activities like a machine, becoming furious if anything interfered. Like her father before her, she was the most predictable of human beings, and anything different was not good.

Ursula hurried back outside. "Fred!" she shouted toward the house. "Fred!"

Her husband, still chewing his food, appeared at the

door. "Fred, Maida is not in the brewery!" she gasped. "You must help me find her!"

Paddy came out, followed by his wife and children. "Sure and she may be up at the head of the spring," the Irishman suggested optimistically. "She thinks a lot about that water, she does."

The remark was an understatement, for Maida's reverence toward the pure artesian water was just short of religious.

Fred nodded in agreement. "You children scoot up there and take a look," he directed. "Colleen, you search through the house, and let's me and you go look around the barn and pasture, Paddy. Ursula, you go and look down by the road. She can't have gone far—I'm sure we'll find her."

Ten minutes later, however, they were all back together behind the house. There was no sign of Maida anywhere.

As they tried to think of where to look next, Ursula was suddenly gripped by paralyzing terror as a hideous possibility occurred to her. The color left her face, and she gasped and swayed on her feet.

Fred grabbed her arm. "What is it, Ursula?" he asked anxiously. "What's wrong?"

Ursula could hardly force herself to speak, the thought was so horrible. "Years ago in Germany," she whispered in a trembling voice, "I heard of a brewer who fell into a tun of beer and was drowned."

The others exchanged glances, motionless for a moment. Then they all began racing toward the brewery. Paddy was the fastest, and he stumbled in a rush through the doorway, skidded to a halt by the nearest tun, and pulled himself up the ladder leaning against it.

Silence fell as everyone else pressed beneath the ladder. Paddy's mouth dropped open in surprise.

"Well, what is it?" Fred barked. "What do you see?"

"Water," Paddy replied numbly. "It's full o' plain water."

As the others exclaimed in amazement, Ursula pushed forward and pulled Paddy down by his belt, then climbed the ladder herself. Sure enough, the huge oak vat was filled to the brim with water. She stepped down, lifted the ladder and carried it to the next tun, then climbed it again. More water.

"*That's* why she's been running so much water in here lately," Fred said. "But why would she fill all the tuns with water? Does it make any sense to you, Ursula?"

Ursula was thinking. "Yes, she has put them in storage," she said distractedly, her mind racing. "They will dry out and crack when they aren't being used, so she filled them with water to keep them moist."

Fred exchanged a perplexed look with Paddy. "Then she's been getting ready for days to leave. But where would she want to go? She hates to leave the brewery."

Ursula had already dismissed the one obvious answer— that her daughter had left with Frederick Kirchner. In any case, Maida's safety, rather than the reason why she had left, was her immediate concern. On her own in public, Maida was almost helpless. In town Ursula had to hold on to her arm at all times, because the young woman would walk into a street in front of a wagon. Most people could not understand her English, and she could not even eat the same food as others. And, of course, she had no money.

The others followed as Ursula walked slowly out of the brewery. Back outside, Fred pointed to where Frederick's buggy had been parked. "That boy has been courting her," he said. "Maybe they've eloped."

"No, never," Ursula replied firmly. "If Maida wanted to marry, she would tell me to send for a minister, and that would be that."

The Raffertys nodded in agreement, and even the

children did not dispute her opinion. They all knew that Maida never did things in a roundabout way. If she wanted something, she simply demanded it.

Ursula tried to think of where Maida might have gone. Some unknown purpose had apparently taken root in her childish mind, and if she had set out on foot in the middle of the night, there was no telling how far she could have gotten. She would be tired, hungry, and terrified by her strange surroundings, and no one would be able to understand her.

Bursting into tears, Ursula turned to Fred. "Find my Maida for me!" she sobbed. "Please find my Maida for me."

With cases of bottled beer rattling in the rear of the buggy, Frederick Kirchner tugged on a rein to guide the horse around a deep rut in the road, then glanced adoringly at Maida on the seat beside him. Having traveled at a steady pace since well before dawn, they were now on the road south of Milwaukee, en route to Chicago.

Wearing gloves, a wide hat, and a scarf around her face to protect her pale skin from the sun, Maida was barely visible. And as usual when she was not working, she appeared to be almost asleep. Asleep or awake, however, to Frederick she was rapturously lovely.

His happiness was tinged with only a shadow of regret that he himself had not found a means for Maida and her mother to keep their brewery. Instead, he had overheard his father and brother discussing how they would immediately make the brewery profitable.

With good wine in short supply because of the economic situation, many restaurants were serving beer with meals. His father and brother had intended to take bottles of Maida's beer to large restaurants in Chicago and simply ask the owners to sample it. It was so superior to any other beer that orders would unquestionably be forthcoming. His father had commented that the penalty for locating a brewery miles from any market was that no one knew about it, regardless of the quality of the beer.

Frederick had intended to enlist the assistance of Fred Guthrie or Paddy Rafferty in taking the beer to Chicago, but when he had mentioned the idea to Maida, she had demanded to go herself. Maida, it seemed, was either completely indifferent to an undertaking or else intensely involved—never anything in between—and their conversations on the subject had caused her to become frantically worried that the brewery would be sold.

Eager, of course, to take Maida with him, and knowing that Ursula and the others would prevent her from going, Frederick had left with her during the night. He felt unsure about negotiating with the restaurant owners, for business matters were a mystery to him, but he was certain that Maida could answer any questions about the beer itself. As far as the price went, though, he would just have to feel his way along.

The only remaining problem he had been able to envision was one that he found fascinating rather than forbidding. He had deferred bringing it up to Maida, wanting to wait for the right moment, but now he decided that the moment had come. "You know we will be gone for several days," he said. "We will have to stay in hotels."

Maida nodded sleepily. "Aye," she replied, "hotels. I catch yer drift."

Heartened, Frederick went on. "Of course, a man and a woman cannot stay in a hotel unless they are married," he explained.

A total pragmatist on such matters, Maida shrugged. "Then tell them we are married."

Expecting some such reply, Frederick took a ring from his waistcoat pocket. "I will—and you will have to wear this, Maida," he said happily.

Maida took the ring. For days, since he had bought

it, Frederick had been anticipating the moment when she would put on the ring. Her attitude, however, conveyed nonchalance rather than the momentous significance he felt. She even yawned as she took off a glove and slipped the band onto her finger.

Pulling her glove back on, Maida glanced behind her. The cases of tall bottles, as well as the picnic Frederick had packed, were covered with straw and a tarpaulin to protect them from direct sunlight, but the day was unusually warm. "Our beer," she observed, "is getting hot, and all and all."

Frederick nodded. "When we reach Chicago, we'll get ice from an icehouse to cool it before we start taking it around to the restaurants."

"Aye—ice." Maida yawned again, then leaned against him and settled herself comfortably. Putting an arm around her, Frederick gazed at her devotedly.

A few minutes later, a horseman came along the road in the opposite direction. The man was riding bareback and staying on his horse only with great difficulty, for he was carrying a broken carriage wheel, apparently taking it to Milwaukee to have it repaired. He lifted his hat to Maida as he passed, but his expression was grim.

A mile farther down the road, Frederick saw the disabled carriage parked in a shady glade beside the creek, its rear axle propped up on rocks and a wheel missing. The shade looked inviting, and many hours had passed since he and Maida had set out from the brewery. After waking her gently, he asked Maida if she would like to stop and eat. She nodded sleepily.

A portly, middle-aged man in an expensive business suit was sitting on the step of the carriage, scowling impatiently. Frederick turned off the road and drove toward the other end of the glade. As he neared the carriage, he reined up. "Can we help you, sir?" he asked.

"How do you propose to do that?" the man replied

sourly. "You attend to your affairs, young man, and I'll attend to mine."

Her drowsiness abruptly disappearing, Maida glared angrily at the rude stranger. Frederick, however, was accustomed to such behavior and simply snapped the reins and drove on, dismissing the matter.

At a pleasant spot, Frederick stopped the buggy and helped Maida down, then put a bottle of beer and a bottle of Maida's artesian water into the creek to cool. He spread a cloth on the grass for Maida to sit down on and took the picnic basket out of the buggy.

Sensing the man watching him, Frederick felt compelled to offer a share of food and drink, since the fellow was obviously stranded far from where he could buy anything. "Would you like to join us, sir?" he called. "It may be hours before your driver returns with the wheel."

The only reply was a silent, morose shake of the head, and once more Frederick dismissed the man's rudeness. Maida's anger, however, boiled over. "Stay dry and empty then!" she barked. "Or you can go and sup wi' yer brother, Auld Nick!"

Eugene Franklin was unable to understand what the young woman shouted at him, and he was even unsure of what language she was using. Her tone and withering glare, however, made her meaning clear. While he seldom took pains to be courteous to anyone, Franklin knew that he had been churlish toward the young couple. But the twinge of guilt that he experienced was completely lost in his seething frustration.

Knowing that he had smoked his last cigar hours before, he nevertheless felt his coat pockets hopefully. Finding them empty, he sighed in disgust, sat back on the carriage step, and looked at the young couple. They were an unusual pair, the man as bland as the woman was quick-tempered. She seemed healthy enough, yet she was as pale as an invalid as she sat in the shade and took off her scarf and gloves.

Curiously enough, the man was waiting on the woman, instead of the other way around. Yet on his plate he put plump sausages, bread, and cheese, while on hers he put only two boiled eggs and lettuce leaves. Then he stepped to the creek for the tall, unusual-looking bottles, which had wire frames holding the ceramic stoppers in place. After pouring a glass of water for the woman, he poured beer for himself.

The unequal fare was obviously satisfactory to the woman, normal for them. The man lifted his glass of beer to the woman, and she lifted her water. "Health and happiness, boyo," she said. "Drink up."

That time Franklin understood her, realizing that she was speaking English with an outlandish combination of an Irish brogue and strong German accent. The young man, grinning in anticipation, took a deep drink. He sighed in satisfaction, then began eating.

Beer had become the bane of Franklin's existence during the past months. Because of the recession, even poor wine was expensive and difficult to obtain, so he had been forced into buying beer, which anyone could get at the cheapest waterfront tavern. As a result, each week fewer customers had been coming to his restaurants in Madison, Milwaukee, and Springfield, as well as to his flagship restaurant in Chicago.

While even the thought of beer was distasteful to Franklin, the brew the young man was drinking had a much better head of foam than any he had ever seen, and it was a golden color, darker than other beers. The man was drinking it with such evident enjoyment that watching him made Franklin feel thirsty. A glass of it, he reflected, would cost him only some pride and a coin, and would satisfy his thirst better than the water from the creek.

Franklin walked over to the couple. "I'd like to apologize for how I acted," he said, lifting his hat. "Business problems have been plaguing me, and my carriage broke down at the worst time. If the offer is still open, I would appreciate a glass of beer. However, I insist on paying for it."

The young man smiled readily, but the woman, who for some reason was removing the large center vein from a leaf of her lettuce, still glared at Franklin.

"I do apologize, madam," Franklin said, bowing. "The reason I acted as I did was my problems, not a desire to offend."

"Sure and yer blarney will get you naught from me," she replied.

The young man, however, was already reaching for the bottle and taking another glass from the basket. "That's very good of you," Franklin said, starting to fish in his pocket for money.

"No, no, you won't need to pay, sir," the young man said, filling the glass. "We have plenty of beer."

For some reason the remark was a private joke between him and the woman, for the two of them exchanged a smile. Franklin wondered if his thirst was making him imagine things, because the beer smelled good even as the glass was handed to him, and he didn't even particularly like beer. He lifted the glass in a silent toast, then took a drink.

Suddenly he almost choked. Instead of the weak, sour taste he had anticipated, a rich, full-bodied flavor livened with a tangy overtone of hops exploded in his mouth. It was delicious, but so entirely unexpected that the sensation was almost like a physical blow. Franklin took another drink. The brew was so flavorful that it should have been heavy, but it was light and delicate, alive with effervescence.

The young man, smiling at Franklin's bemusement, nodded toward the woman. "Maida makes it," he said.

"What do you mean she makes it?" Franklin exclaimed.

"This is the best beer I've ever tasted! It couldn't be home brew!"

The young man still looked amused. "Maida has a brewery up north of Colmer," he explained. "She comes from a long line of Oberg master brewers in Germany, and she was trained by her father."

It was the most unlikely story Franklin had ever heard, but the beer spoke for itself. Then he recalled a conversation with a customer in his Chicago restaurant. The man, a lumber camp owner who had since gone out of business, had talked about a brewery far out in the Wisconsin woods that made exceptionally delicious beer, which he had bought for his lumberjacks. Apparently, Franklin reflected, that was the same brewery, because Colmer was very remote.

As he savored the taste of the beer, the unremitting melancholy that had burdened Franklin for months began lifting from his shoulders. The misfortune of his carriage breaking down had changed into priceless good fortune. He had found a delicious beverage to serve with meals in his restaurant, one that would bring his customers back, as well as draw customers from other restaurants.

It seemed strange to him, however, that he had not heard more about the brewery near Colmer. It must be very small, he decided, and his satisfaction quickly began fading as he wondered if the brewery could supply a sufficient quantity of beer for his restaurants. "You must not have been selling very much beer, or I would have heard of it," he commented. "Or do you have only a limited quantity?"

"We're on our way to Chicago to begin selling it now," the young man said. "Maida has been making it right along, and we have a good supply." He turned to her. "How much is in the cellar, Maida?"

"One thousand four hundred eighty-six casks," Maida

replied promptly. She took a bite of her lettuce. "Eight hundred thirty-four casks fully lagered, ready to drink."

Franklin was speechless, astonished both by the immense quantity of beer and by the woman's precise knowledge of her inventory. Turning back to the young man, he cleared his throat and offered his hand. "Excuse me for not introducing myself," he said. "My name is Eugene Franklin."

"Pleased to meet you, sir," the young man replied as they shook hands. "I'm Frederick Kirchner."

Again Franklin was surprised, for he immediately recognized the young man's family name. "Are you related to John Kirchner?" he asked.

"Yes, he's my father," Frederick replied.

Draining his glass, Franklin reflected that the way the brewery had remained in operation without widespread publicity was now explained: The Kirchner fortune was behind it. John Kirchner was one of the most astute businessmen in Milwaukee, and people had told Franklin that Kirchner's son was almost as sharp as his father. They had been wrong, Franklin decided.

The elder Kirchner, he knew, looked and acted like a capable businessman, but the son was deceptive. Behind those bland eyes and that imperturbable, naive manner was undoubtedly a mind so cunning that it would have the gold fillings out of a mouth that smiled too widely.

Franklin held out his glass when the young man offered him more beer. "I may be interested in buying some beer from you," he said cautiously. "You've heard of Franklin's Chicago House, haven't you? I own it and several other restaurants."

Pouring the beer, Frederick reacted with unconcern that was not a pose. He had been looking forward with eager anticipation to the trip with Maida, and the last thing he wanted to do was immediately conclude a deal and return to the brewery. "Yes, everyone has heard of the Chicago House," he said. "We'll come by there and talk with you when we get to Chicago. Maida, would it be all right if I cooled another bottle of beer?"

"Aye, more beer," she replied. She was peeling a boiled egg. "Drink up, boyos."

Forcing a smile as the young man and woman laughed, Franklin concluded that he had been absolutely correct; the man was as cold and hard as steel. Franklin waited until Frederick had put another bottle of beer in the creek, then sat down and broached the subject once more. "Mr. Kirchner, what have you set as the asking price for your beer?"

It was precisely the question Frederick was least prepared to answer. "Well," he replied hesitantly, "it would depend upon how much the customer buys."

"Yes, of course," Franklin said. "But I have restaurants in Madison, Milwaukee, and Springfield, as well as my restaurant in Chicago. Now, we're talking more than a dozen casks a week, aren't we?" He paused, then lowered his voice confidentially. "I'll be very straightforward with you, Mr. Kirchner. If I could be your only customer in the restaurant business, it would give me an edge over my competition. I would expect to pay a premium price, and as soon as we get to Chicago, I would give you a thousand dollars against deliveries to show good faith. You see, I want to make a bargain with you, sir."

Knowing that a thousand dollars would be a fortune to Ursula, Frederick was torn with indecision. He started to lift a hand to bite his fingernails, then lowered it again as Maida leaned forward and raised a hand to slap his. "Well," he said, "your restaurants can't sell all of the beer Maida makes."

Nodding in acknowledgment of the point, Franklin thought about the movements of the couple's hands. They were, he concluded, communicating by means of secret hand signals. He reflected that he had never met two

more extraordinary people. Behind their pose as an innocent young couple, the woman knew every detail of brewery operations and the man was a business wizard.

Franklin thought furiously for a moment, and then a
solution to the problem occurred to him. "I know a man in
Chicago named Dieter Schumann," he said. "Among other
interests, he has a large produce store, and you could sell
your excess beer through him. While you're discussing
arrangements with him, I would be pleased to host you at
the best hotel in Chicago." Noting the interest in Frederick's eyes at the mention of the hotel, Franklin pursued
the point. "The best accommodations at the very best
hotel, Mr. Kirchner. I can see that your good wife re-
quires special food, and I'll have it prepared in my restaurant and delivered to the hotel."

The offer was indeed appealing, and Frederick wished
he knew how much to ask for the beer. "Well, I'll think
about it," he said, temporizing as he tried to recall what
he had heard Ursula mention about the price of the beer.

"Mr. Kirchner," Franklin said desperately, leaning
over and putting a hand on Frederick's arm, "I want that
beer. If you'll agree to sell to no other restaurants except
mine for six months, I'll advance two thousand dollars as
good faith money against deliveries as soon as we get to
Chicago. Now name your price and shake my hand."

His mind a blur, Frederick thought that he remembered Ursula wistfully talking about the time she had been
able to sell beer for fifty cents a gallon. "Sixty cents a
gallon, and the casks must be returned," he said.

Franklin winced. The price was almost four times
what he presently paid for beer. But it was incomparably
better beer, he reflected, and if he could get it for a few
cents less, he could break even on the beer and make his
profit on food. "Fifty cents a gallon, and I'll pay the
freight," he said, putting out his hand.

"Very well," Frederick said, shaking hands. "We should

be able to reach the hotel in Chicago this evening, shouldn't we? That beer will be cool by now, so I'll pour us another glass."

Franklin nodded and sighed in relief as Frederick went to the creek for the bottle of beer. Satisfaction swelled within him as he thought about the bargain he had just made. The decline in business that had hurt his restaurants over the past months would soon end. When word spread about the beer, he would be turning customers away.

But most of all, Franklin thought with a spreading grin, he felt an immense sense of accomplishment at having concluded a reasonable deal with two of the shrewdest business people he had ever met. It was, he decided as Frederick poured him another beer, his lucky day.

XVI

Near dawn, Toby had stationed himself in the closet in the rented office, with the door opened a crack so he could see into the room. Hours had passed, the noise from the street becoming louder, sunshine flooding through the office window. A firecracker popped on the street outside, and then their crackling became frequent, punctuated by the booms of larger fireworks.

Taking out his watch and holding it to the light, Toby saw that it was almost time for the President's party to arrive. A few minutes later, the noise outside grew to a roar of cheers and whistles.

As the crowd greeted the President, the office window vibrated from the volume of sound. Toby could barely make out the clatter of the cavalcade as it pulled up near the courthouse steps. Then he heard a key rattle in the office door.

Over the roar of noise from the crowd outside, the office door squeaked open and closed with a thud. Then there were softer sounds, footsteps and movements. The rifle case was laid on the floor, and Toby heard the metallic clatter of the weapon being loaded.

Footsteps crossed toward the window, and Beasley finally came into view through the narrow crack in the closet door. Standing to one side of the window to avoid being seen, Beasley opened it with one hand. Then he stepped back from the window and looked out.

Toby could visualize the scene outside from the changes in the noise. The roar of the crowd became deafening, indicating the President had dismounted from his carriage and was climbing the steps toward the podium. Beasley's plan, Toby reflected, had been almost perfect; the noise would have masked the direction from which the shots came.

Beasley took a sheet of paper from his pocket and unfolded it on the floor, then placed a single silver dollar on it. With his face twisted in a sardonic smile, he straightened up and watched the scene outside. As the crowd cheered, Toby cocked his pistol.

He had waited long enough. Before Beasley could lift his weapon, Toby pushed the closet door open. "Drop the rifle and put up your hands!" he ordered.

Beasley's head snapped around, his eyes wide with consternation. He fumbled to cock the rifle and swing it toward Toby, but Toby's sights were already on the man's left lapel, and he squeezed the trigger. The rifle fired an instant later, splinters and plaster exploding from the wall not far from Toby's head.

Beasley dropped the rifle and collapsed to the floor, his face reflecting shock and pain. By the time Toby came to his side, the man was dead.

Toby walked to the window and looked out. The crowd was still cheering wildly, the gunfire in the office having been drowned by the noise. The mayor was at the podium, raising his hands for silence. Representative John Stevens and President Grant were seated behind him.

Toby glanced at Beasley, then at the paper the man had put on the floor. Printed in block letters, it was a demand to reinstate silver coinage, and a warning that others would be killed if that was not done. Toby reloaded his pistol and left the office, locking the door behind him.

The cheering continued, echoing through the building as Toby went down the stairs to the ground floor and the back door. He opened the door and stepped outside, his pistol ready.

Two horses were in the alley, the roan and the pinto. Farley, his face pale and drawn with tension, was standing on the far side of them as he tried to look in all directions at once. Seeing Toby, he lifted a pistol. Toby didn't have a clear shot, and he leaped back inside the door.

Splinters flew from the doorjamb, and then Toby glimpsed Farley jumping onto the pinto and riding away. Toby stepped back outside and aimed his pistol, then lowered it and eased the hammer back down, for the chance of hitting the horse was too great.

Holstering his pistol, Toby stepped toward the roan. Frightened by the pistol shot and the noise from the crowd, the horse kept moving away from him, and at least a minute passed before Toby could get close enough to catch it. He immediately mounted and set off after Farley, knowing where the man would go.

The road leading out of town was deserted as Toby galloped his horse along it. At the edge of the city, he spotted Farley in the distance, riding toward the hideout and beating his pinto mercilessly. The roan was a young, powerful animal, and Toby let it run at its own pace, knowing that Farley would quickly exhaust his horse.

Inevitably Toby began closing the distance between them, and Farley glanced back in fright. It was evident that the man did not know that the hideout had been discovered, for he was frantically trying to reach it, thinking he would be safe there. As they crossed the meadow toward the woods, Farley began shooting at Toby, no doubt hoping to alert his comrades with the sound of the shots.

The man's aim was wild, but Toby saw no reason to take needless risks. With the roan running at a good pace, he veered off to circle around to the cave. His horse could still reach the hideout before the pinto, which was nearly exhausted.

Farley fired two more shots, then reined up to reload as Toby rode into the woods a hundred yards to one side. Ducking to avoid branches, Toby guided his horse through the trees. Not long afterward, he reined to a halt near the cave, where all was quiet. He dismounted and tethered his horse, then waited behind a clump of brush.

In a few minutes Toby heard the pinto crashing through the forest. When it drew near, he took out his Colt and stepped from behind the brush. Farley jerked the panting, lathered animal to a sliding stop and gaped in astonishment. Toby was standing near the entrance to the cave, his pistol pointed toward the ground and his thumb on the hammer. Farley's own pistol was in his hand, but he hesitated.

"That's right, I know where the hideout is," Toby said. "I found it and your friends yesterday. Now drop the pistol and put up your hands."

The man's flushed face went pale, and his eyes were glazed with fear. "Where's Beasley?" he asked hoarsely.

"He's dead," Toby answered. "Now drop the pistol, and let's go back to the city."

Tense seconds passed, the only sound the deep breathing of the winded pinto. A frantic gleam came into Farley's eyes, and his hand tightened on his pistol.

"Don't try it, Farley," Toby warned softly, pulling the hammer back on his own pistol. "Believe me, you'll never make it."

"If I give up and you take me in," Farley blurted in a quaking voice, "what'll happen to me?"

"What do you think? You'll stand trial for conspiring to murder the President of the United States."

Sweat began breaking out on Farley's deathly white face, and he swallowed audibly. "But they'll hang me!" he cried out, his voice trembling.

"That's up to the judge and jury," Toby said grimly.

Farley was breathing rapidly, clearly on the verge of hysteria. Toby saw his eyes change, becoming wide with panicky determination. A bare instant later, the pistol moved.

Toby was faster. Farley's arm was only halfway up when the hammer on Toby's pistol fell and the weapon bounced in his hand. Farley reeled back as the pinto reared and plunged, tossing him from the saddle. He lay crumpled on the ground.

When all was silent again, Toby walked up to look at the body, shook his head sadly, then holstered his pistol and took the frightened pinto's reins. After fashioning a lead, he mounted the roan and started back through the woods.

With the plot against the President ended, a heavy weight had been lifted from Toby's shoulders. As he rode back to town at a leisurely pace, for the first time he was able to enjoy the verdant beauty of the countryside.

When Toby reached the center of the city, President Grant was speaking, and the crowd was respectfully silent. Toby tethered the horses in the alley behind the office building, then walked around to the park. The carriages in which the President and his party had come from the train station were drawn into a line at the foot of the courthouse steps. Haines and Pennington were among the policemen and Secret Service agents on the steps around the podium.

Toby moved slowly and quietly through the crowd to avoid making a disturbance while the President was speaking. He noticed that both Pennington and Haines were occasionally glancing toward the top floor of the office building, their faces revealing tension. Haines saw Toby first and smiled in relief. He pointed to the last carriage in the row, then beckoned Pennington to follow. Toby edged his way through the crowd to join them.

"Well, it's finished," Toby said, after the three of

them had stepped into the carriage and sat down. "Neither Beasley nor Farley would surrender, and both of them are dead."

The two men sighed in relief, and Pennington seized Toby's hand and shook it. "That's the best news I've heard in a long time, Marshal," he said. "This town won't be able to thank you enough for what you've done."

"It certainly is good news," Haines said. "When I called upon you to do this, Toby, I knew I was asking the right man. Now, you stay right here in the carriage, and as soon as this gathering is over, we'll follow the President back to the private car. I want him to shake hands with the man who did more than his duty for his country."

"What I did *was* my duty, Tom, and no more," Toby said. "The man who did more than his duty, and the one who deserves the real credit, is James Gifford. He used his dying strength to give us the clue that revealed the plot, which otherwise might have succeeded."

"Jim did more than his duty, no doubt about that," Haines agreed. "But I don't know of anyone else who could have accomplished what you did, and that's what I'm going to tell the President."

Haines and Pennington climbed back out of the carriage to return to their places on the steps. Toby, weary from the events of the past twenty-four hours, relaxed on the soft seat and listened to the President. It sounded as though he was nearing the end of his speech, and his next words confirmed as much.

"My friends and fellow citizens," the President said, "I have finished what I came here to tell you. But before I leave, I would like to use this opportunity to make an announcement."

There was a stir of interest in the crowd, and Toby saw the newspaper reporters at the foot of the steps become more alert. "Silver coinage was stopped," the President continued, "to prevent foreign speculators from manipulating the price of silver here in ways that were detrimental to the nation and its citizens. However, that has caused hardships among our citizens, so we will find other ways to thwart the designs of the speculators. Upon my return to Washington, I intend to submit a bill to Congress, for speedy enactment into law, to reinstate silver coinage."

Cheering began breaking out among the crowd, but the President's voice rang out over it. "However," he called, "I need you to return Representative Stevens to Congress to vote for that and other bills!"

A roar of applause and shouts erupted, and the President waved and walked down the steps toward the carriages. Thinking about the paper Beasley had put on the floor of the office, Toby shook his head at the irony of the situation.

When she heard the report of a rifle from the direction of the road, Alexandra turned Turco and rode to the top of a rise in the pasture. The rifle cracked again, and she saw a puff of gunpowder smoke in the hedge bordering the road. The horses in the pasture near the road were racing about wildly. All the evidence was there, but for a long moment she was unable to believe what she was seeing. It was too savage, too brutal.

Someone was shooting at the horses.

She saw her father and Jonah run out of the house with rifles. Using the trees at the sides of the lane for shelter, they ran from one tree to another to get closer to the hedge as they shot at it. Then she saw her father fall and Jonah pull him behind a tree. The stallion lunged into a pounding, headlong run as Alexandra snapped the reins and leaned forward in the saddle.

Her first, panicked thought was to go to her father, but over the sound of Turco's hoofbeats and the wind rushing past her ears she heard both her father and Jonah still shooting at the hedge. Swiftly deciding on another course of action, she turned Turco toward the house.

The water in the creek erupted into sheets of spray under the stallion's churning hooves. A fence loomed up ahead, and the stallion vaulted lightly over it. Then the barns and pens were before them. Turco soared over another fence, sprinted across the pens and vaulted again, then Alexandra guided him toward the side of the house. Reaching the house, she reined up and jumped off the horse.

The door banging behind her, she ran along the hall to the parlor. The gun case was standing open, and the ammunition drawer at the bottom was ajar, her father and Jonah having snatched out rifles and ammunition. Only shotguns were left, and Alexandra hesitated a second or two before choosing the largest one, which also had a leather sling.

She broke open the long, heavy gun and looked in the drawer for shells. After loading both barrels and pocketing a handful of extra shells, she ran back through the house. Outside, she slung the weapon over her shoulder, leaped onto the stallion, and gathered up the reins.

The hedge stretched from her left to her right directly ahead in the distance, and the men shooting through it were to her left. Alexandra veered Turco toward the right, intending to reach the hedge, then cut back and ride the men down, keeping the length of the hedge between them. As her horse vaulted a fence, her father and Jonah saw her. They shouted and motioned her back, then began shooting rapidly at the hedge to keep the men on the other side of it from shooting at her.

Over the pounding of her horse's hooves, Alexandra heard bullets whine past. Then, as she neared the tall hedge, she was at too sharp an angle for the men on the other side to see her. Turning the stallion, she rode along the hedge toward where the gunpowder smoke marked the men's position, some fifty yards away.

As the stallion rapidly closed the distance, Alexandra unslung and balanced the long, heavy shotgun, cocking the hammers. When she was only ten yards away from the gunpowder smoke eddying in the hedge, she reined up and turned Turco to get his head out of the line of fire. Quickly she lifted the shotgun and pulled back both triggers.

A huge cloud of smoke belched from the barrels, and the thunderous roar made Turco rear in fright. In the same instant, the gunstock slammed back against her shoulder with a jarring impact. Feeling herself falling, she kicked free of the stirrups and tumbled off the horse.

As she fell she saw a wide circle in the hedge exploding into fragments of leaves and twigs. Hitting the ground heavily on her back, she was stunned for a moment, the world reeling around her. Dimly, over the ringing in her ears, she heard someone on the other side of the hedge screaming in agony.

A heavy fall was nothing new to her, and Alexandra shrugged off the numb feeling, realizing that Turco was close enough to the men for them to shoot him easily. She sat up and scrambled for the shotgun as she took out more shells. Then she heard the men on the other side of the hedge mounting horses. Before she could reload, she heard the sound of hoofbeats racing away along the road.

Jonah was running toward her, his rifle raised, but he lowered it as he, too, heard the retreating hoofbeats. "You gave us a scare for a minute there, Miss Alexandra," he panted, joining her. "But you sure lit a fire under their tails, didn't you? It sounded like you got at least one of them."

Alexandra nodded, but she felt no sense of victory. Three horses lay dead in the pasture—an act of senseless, brutal savagery. "They even shot my colt," she said.

Jonah shook his head sorrowfully. "Hanging is too good for snakes that would do something like that. I'd bet anything that man Sewell was behind this."

"You're probably right." Alexandra looked across the pasture toward her father, who was sitting against a tree. "How bad off is Dad?"

"It ain't good, but I've seen people get over worser," Jonah replied. "He could use a doctor pretty soon."

Alexandra whistled at Turco, and the stallion trotted up to her. She took the reins and led him as she walked quickly with Jonah toward her father. Fear struck deep within her as she saw his condition.

He had been shot in the left shoulder, and his shirt was soaked with blood. She had never before thought of him as old, but now he looked his age, his face pale and drawn. He smiled wanly as she approached. "You shouldn't have done that, honey," he said. "But no one could have done it better." His smile faded as he nodded toward the pasture. "I'm sorry about the horses."

Fighting back tears of rage and grief, she handed the shotgun to Jonah. "I'll go fetch the doctor," she said. "And I'll stop and ask Mr. and Mrs. Quint to look after you till I get back."

"All right, honey. And ask the good reverend to send a boy for the sheriff as well. We don't want something like this happening again."

Alexandra had already mounted her horse. "I'll send for the sheriff," she said, "but he won't be able to deal with the ones who did this. Only one man can, and that's Toby Holt."

"That may be," her father said, "but we don't know where he went, honey."

"*I* know where he is," Alexandra replied, turning her horse. She nudged Turco with her heels and set off at a headlong gallop down the lane.